CHOOSERS OF THE SLAIN

Choosers
of the
Slain

The Valkyries
BOOK I

Ann Chamberlin

EPIGRAPH BOOKS
RHINEBECK, NEW YORK

Paperback ISBN 978-1-948796-93-4
Hardcover ISBN 978-1-948796-94-1
eBook ISBN 978-1-948796-95-8

Library of Congress Control Number 2019916105

Book and cover design by Colin Rolfe
Cover image: "The Ride of the Valkyries" by Arthur Rackham

Epigraph Books
22 East Market Street, Suite 304
Rhinebeck, New York 12572
(845) 876-4861
epigraphps.com

For my brother

author acknowledgment

This book is dedicated to my wonderful brother Ralph. I remember hurrying through the fields of Willershausen Kreis Marburg with him, wet feet, late for school because we'd been playing 'car cards.' I also remember being blown off our feet by the Icelandic wind on an August day.

Thanks to his wife Ute, too, and their three sons. They've been welcoming, patient, and helpful in my shop, willing to store more books in their garage than anybody ought to.

As usual, scores of teachers, family members, friends, librarians, and publishing people have helped. Here is a list of the most outstanding: Linda Cook, Jeri Smith, Francesca Koomen, all the women of the Wasatch Mountain Fiction Writers; Teddi Kachi, Karen Porcher, Curt Setzer, Ernö Steinmetz, my mother, my sons (the one who helps with the computer and the one who speaks German and attends operas with me), Marian Florence, Rod Daynes, Giles Florence, John Keahey, Connie Disney, and members of Xenobia writers' group – Natalia Aponte, Christine Cohen, Vaughne Hansen, Virginia Kidd of blessed memory. Paul Cohen and the folks at Epigraph. The Salt Lake Folkdancers, especially Ann Wright. Miguel, Don Juan, and all my friends at the Arizona Renaissance Festival. Reinhard Hermann who assured me when I asked what a German would have for breakfast before they had potatoes, "No. First the potato was invented, then the

German." I hope his memory is not offended that I gave my characters no potatoes. All of the wonderful people I've met over many years in Germany. *Viel Spaß beim Lesen.*

Those people I may have overlooked know who they are and know that I couldn't have done it without them. Thanks to one and all.

In case anyone is marveling that this sex should have sweated in warfare, let me digress briefly to explain the character and behavior of such females. There were once women in Denmark who dressed themselves to look like men and spent almost every minute cultivating soldiers' skills; they did not want the sinews of their valor to lose tautness and be infected by self-indulgence. Loathing a dainty style of living, they would harden body and mind with toil and endurance, spirits to act with a virile ruthlessness. They courted military celebrity so earnestly that you would have guessed they had unsexed themselves. Those especially who had forceful personalities or were tall and elegant embarked on this way of life. And if they were forgetful of their true selves, they put toughness before allure, aimed at conflicts instead of kisses, tasted blood, not lips, sought the clash of arms rather than the arm's embrace, fitted to weapons hands which should have been weaving, desired not the couch but the kill, and those they could have appeased with looks they attacked with lances.

—Saxo Grammaticus,
Danish historian
(1150?–1220?)

pαrt 1

Brynhild's Beginning

chapter 1

 AM BRYNHILD OF THE peoples of the North, of the followers of the Aesir of the Sky and the Vanir of the Earth. I have been a daughter of Odin, a Valkyrie, a Chooser of the Slain. Chooser of many things, not every one of them the best.

It is the custom for tellers of tales to begin their words with a proverb, some saw of common wisdom on which everyone can agree. In my experience, however, that 'common wisdom' contains so great a part of platitude that it may be called forgetfulness. Indeed there exists in the mid-earth the very elixir of forgetfulness. I have known those who were blessed to drink of it and know its peace. But alas, I have a resistance to its effects. And, as this must be my own unquiet story, platitude would be out of place.

I remember the valley where I was born to the kindred of the Angles. The land, shaped like a hook, slowly undulated with green crops, gold-brown plains, and dark heather slopes. It extended from the northern low hills we called the Big Bears to the even lower southern hills called the Little Bears. The Bears were the edge of sight on a clear day; more often than not, they were invisible in the mist.

And then there was the Bog.

The Bog was the center of the valley, towards which everything yearned. In my memory, the Bog was the only place where full-grown trees stood: wild cherry, blackthorn and crabapple with bloom like the white breath of Elfin folk in the spring, willow with the yellowy catkins. The Navel of the Earth we called the Bog. Because we thought of the valley as a woman, that 'navel' was clearly kenning for another part, conforming more with the growth of rushes and soft bog cotton over that low-lying land. The Bog was sacred, sacred in the only true way of sacredness, that which comes with a tug of dread and fear at the vitals.

I could clearly recall the old folks saying, "We have always lived in this valley. We do such and such because it is a time-honored tradition with us. It has always been done so, and this way of life has always sustained us."

On the other hand, that wasn't quite true, because they also said, "My great grandfather cleared this field with his axe and his firebrand and his bare hands.' And, 'When we first came here, there was fall wood to be had just by bending for it.'

Was that a fairytale, a land like that where the wood was to be had for the bending? Some fable to while away the dark winter hours with dreams of a better world? It certainly wasn't life in the valley when I knew it. As a girl not quite ten years old, I could spend the whole day looking for something to burn, and by nightfall I'd still have only as much as I could carry.

Never one to suppress any thought that occurred to me, I had to say, "I'll wager we could find some fall wood in the Bog."

"Bite your tongue for saying so," some adult would answer. "And be sucked down into the waters so we'd never see you again, child? The Bog is sanctuary."

I'd sulk and speak quieter, though I never could quite bite my tongue. "I'll wager we could, for all that."

Then some folks began to say, "A person can burn peat. If he has it." And they'd look toward the Bog, making signs to avert evil, for peat was the very flesh of the valley.

I recall that winter in particular was bitter cold, and, before it, the fall came with a warning chill. I'd asked, "What's that you're making, Uncle Erik?"

"A shovel. You've never seen a shovel before, a strapping girl like you?"

"Never one that shape, big and square at the bottom."

"It's a shovel, that's all."

"But, Uncle—"

And then someone else pulled me aside and whispered, "It's a peat-cutting shovel your uncle's making, so be quiet about it."

I was as quiet as I could be. But I had to tell Uddrun. She and I told each other everything. I got my chance at the barley harvest.

"Don't worry about your uncle's shovel," Uddrun whispered back to me over a bundled sheaf. "My father's already gone and cut some peat."

"He hasn't!"

"He has. He's stacked it to dry out of sight behind the hummock near our back wall. I'll show you if you like."

"I don't think I want to see."

"I know how you feel."

"Your father's not dead for this?"

"No."

"Not sick in any way?"

"The gods forbid. He did offer my grandfather's beautiful old goblet to the Bog before he cut."

"I should mention that to my uncle. I mean, if he really intends to use that shovel."

"I'm sure your uncle knows to make offerings."

Uddrun was my second cousin. But then, everyone in the valley was related. More than blood, Uddrun was my best friend. For all that, she was five years older than I. Her hair was blond, nearly white, like a bunch of tow, and she wore its two thick braids under a scarf woven with a pattern of rust and blue.

"How can my uncle know how to cut peat?"

"He knows how to make a peat shovel, doesn't he?"

Any job that was to be done, Uddrun and I contrived to do it together, chatting all the while. But a shadow fell between us that bright, blue day at the barley harvest. We dropped what we knew was a forbidden subject and straightened our bodies to face an older kinswoman. We prepared ourselves to be rebuked for our topic of conversation, but she had something else in mind.

"Cut more to the edge of the field than that, girls," she said, not harshly.

"But, Aunt," Uddrun defended us, "there's no barley there at all."

"There is. See, a stalk. There, another."

"Well, one or two. But the rest is all weeds."

"Yes, the weeds too easily overcame the grain we planted this year," our kinswoman said sadly, almost fearfully.

"We hardly thought it worthwhile to cut further," I added in Uddrun's defense.

"Well, you'll think it worthwhile before spring comes again."

"You want it cut and bound with all the—?"

"With all the weeds, yes."

"We can't eat—"

"You can. If you get hungry enough." The woman moved on, muttering under her breath, "Oh, Great Ones of Aesgard. Are we to lose this field as well?"

"You see how it is," Uddrun said, sinking into our whispers again. "The old people know. The women know the famine foods, the men know how to cut peat. We'll be hungry and cold this winter."

I glanced at my friend over our sheaves. She shivered and looked pinched as if we had already reached that pass.

"But just look at this sheaf," I protested, holding it out to her. "You can't eat this."

"That dried tassel is yarrow," Uddrun pointed out. "You've never eaten tiny yarrow shoots in the spring?"

"All right, yarrow. That's fine. But this? And this? Clover, white and red? Black nightshade?"

"Goosefoot. Corn spurrey."

For a while we made a game of naming the plants that almost drowned out our barley.

"Field cow-white."

"Sheep's sorrel. Sheep's bit."

"For sheep, not people."

"Hair grass."

"Trefoil."

"Heather."

"Of course."

"Those stubby, dagged leaves are buttercup."

"The little feathery leaves are chamomile."

"I hate the smell."

"It does smell like there's sickness in the house, doesn't it?"

"Well, at least we know it's edible."

"If you're already sick to begin with."

"What on earth is this?"

"I think I heard Aunt Lise call it hawksbeard."

"Something with a name like that doesn't sound like you should eat it at all, does it?" I commented. "Hawksbeard?"

"Look. See how much shorter the stalks are this year, how much lower we have to bend over."

We stopped to stretch our backs together. I noticed that, for all the years between us, our eyes were almost on the same level. "Perhaps we've just grown."

"You, perhaps. Brynhild is the girl who never stops growing," she teased. "But I reached my full height last year. It is as our aunt said. The soil is losing its vigor."

"How can that be?"

"Just look at the grain," Uddrun said wisely, stopping to hull a bearded stalk and hold the kernels in her hand. "Have you ever seen them so coarse and small?"

"It'll be hard going at the grinding quern," I had to admit.

Uddrun touched her pretty tongue to the grain in her hands and sucked on that small mouthful for a long, long time as we worked.

Was it merely that I had grown up, or did the work indeed go much faster than it ever had before? Soon, all too soon, the men ahead of us called out, "Last sheaf! Last sheaf!" and we stood and straightened our backs and tried to make the celebration as festive as ever.

The last sheaf we stood in the center of the field for Odin's horse, should the one-eyed god happen to ride by. It was a good sheaf, cut from a center patch where the grain had been strong enough to hold its own against the weeds. Even the fiber with which we twisted it was good grain. But all I ever saw come to feed on it were sparrows and the greedy starlings, not even an Odin raven. "Why do we give him the good sheaf?"

"Brynhild!" Uddrun was shocked. "He is a god."

"But if we set one of these weedy sheaves out, he might get the message that we're suffering here. He might deign to help us."

"I see your point. But Odin is a god of Aesgard, lord of the young sky deities, not one of the ancient Vanir, who are more quiet and careful and who look to earth's fertility."

"Then why do we give Odin anything?"

There was a gentle smile in my friend's concerned eyes. "You, Brynhild? You think such things? You, they always say, must be spawn of the powerful Aesir?"

"Because I am big and strong and lack patience."

She laughed. "Exactly." Then she grew more serious again. "The best is always left for All-Father. That's the tradition, and our traditions have sustained us on this land–"

"That's not true!" I cried, loud enough that Uddrun had to hush me and look around cautiously to see if others had heard. She did not want us to be forbidden each other's company for sacrilegious talk sooner than the winter mud and weather would ground us in our separate hamlets. And I didn't want it either. I resolved to speak more quietly. "It's not true," I whispered, but with no less passion. "Our traditions have *not* sustained us."

"Brynhild, how can you say such a thing?"

A shout went up as the second-last sheaf was lifted into the cart. It would now be brought home in triumph, with the traditional songs and merrymaking. At least, everyone was making a brave attempt to be merry.

Uddrun and I fell into step behind the throng, and I hissed at her, "They say, 'We have always lived in this valley,' but they know it's not true. They know the names of the men whose axes first cleared this valley. They say the names, and they are no more than our three great grandfathers. They know that what is now heath, useful only for sheep, if that, was once forest. The valley was once forest, and everybody knows it. Forest thick with beech and fir – fir, even, Uddrun. Have you ever had the happy chance to gather fir wood?"

"No," she admitted. "Only heard of it in the old tales. What you say is true. We do have all these traditions."

"And how do they know how to cut and stack peat if our people haven't done this before, come to the last tree, with only the Bog in the middle? How do the women know the names of these famine foods if there wasn't another valley where famine came once before?"

"A valley our forefathers left? Perhaps you're right, Brynhild. When our forefathers came, yes, there was forest. All the old folk agree."

"They slashed and burned enough for their first fields, and the soil was strong. Slowly the heath encroached on the grain, and then it was good only for sheep."

"So they had to cut and burn more of the forest."

"Yes, but by that time, there wasn't just the one farmstead. There were children's children in many hamlets, and they all had to slash and burn a field–"

"Until there was nothing left," Uddrun said. There was a great hollow terror in her voice. "Nothing but the Bog."

"But that's my point. There *is* something left, Uddrun. The world is wide."

"Not my world. My world starts and stops with the Big and Little Bears, Brynhild."

"It doesn't."

"Yours, perhaps, Brynhild. You were never afraid to climb to the top of the ridge pole. Perhaps what you saw there–"

"You can only see to the Bears from there, too," I confessed.

"You are never afraid to wrestle with the boys. I am afraid to get hurt."

"Won't we be hurt even more if we just sit here and starve? No, Uddrun. I am convinced. Our life here and all its ways does no sustaining, or not for very long. The life of our people is a tumbling thing."

"It shouldn't be." She shuddered.

"It doesn't matter what it should or shouldn't be. It *is*. A tumbling thing, like a stone, once set into motion..."

"Downhill. A stone stops when it reaches the lowest point. When it reaches the Bog."

"No, Uddrun. I know that beyond the Bears, although I have not seen them, there are other valleys. Valleys still thick with forest."

"But not valleys for us."

"Yes, valleys with living room for our people. Have you never heard of the tradition, how in a bad year, come spring, young men will be chosen by lot to go out and find new land for our people to fill?"

"There is land, there are valleys, yes, but they are valleys already possessed by others."

"So, we must take them from them."

She smiled indulgently. "You do sound like one from Aesgard."

"That is why the strong young men go first."

"Brynhild, our neighbors are people with women and hungry children, too."

"They are not real people, they are not *our* people."

"Perhaps that is so. But they are fierce people – the Cimbri, the Lombards, the Goths. These people hang their war captives on trees for the gods. They rape the captive women," Uddrun said.

"So, we – I mean, our men – do the same."

Uddrun's knowledge of the neighbor tribes came from the talk of the menfolk, men who had gone beyond the valley and knew. But I knew my side of the argument from the talk of menfolk, too. "The fact that our men go off every spring to do battle," I said, "is proof again that we are meant to surge forward."

"We, as women, cannot do that."

"But as women, we can urge our men to do so," I insisted. "If he has a good woman behind him, one of our men can be as brave as any two Lombards any day. Far to the south, they say, is a very rich land. Richer than Lombardy. None of our men has been, but they've spoken to those who have. It's a land glittering with silver and gold, that sits on its hoard like a dragon on its brood. Fáfnir, some call this beast. Others call it Rome. There are men who have served in the sunny south, who come home carrying booty in great sacks, so much gold that they must have pack animals..."

"You can't eat gold," Uddrun said practically. "What good is gold if there is no food in the neighborhood to buy with it?"

"They have golden fruits, too, as sweet as honey and full of juice, these dragon-Romans. And wheat that comes in great ships—"

"These are fairytales, Brynhild."

"They aren't."

"Have you ever seen such fruit? What fruits are there more than crabapples, plums and the small, tart bog berries?"

"Well, maybe it's not all true, what we hear. But I'm sure it's out there for the taking, for the strong and fearless. Something. If we only break the bonds of this valley."

"Break the bonds? And, like the Fenrir wolf, go ravaging from one corner of the world to the other, devouring both people and gods? The jaws of the Fenrir wolf reach from Earth to Heaven. When the Fenrir wolf breaks his bonds, Brynhild, it means the end of the world."

What she said was prophecy-myth, and so I had to agree that it made sense, at least enough that I fell silent, then joined the singing celebration for a while. The second-last sheaf rode before us like a god in his carriage. But that sheaf – which would hang from the rafters to preside over the long, hungry months of winter – that sheaf was disconcertingly full of weeds. The Thaw Gruel, which would be made from it, would be coarse and bitter, nearly inedible.

Uddrun's thoughts must have paralleled mine and then run ahead to the fear that could be seen on every adult face about us. She stopped mid-song to whisper, "There will be a stone in the Thaw Gruel."

A stone. For Death.

"You see," I said. "If we do not break the bonds, we shall die."

"Some of us, surely. But not all. Life will be sustained, not snapped out completely within the jaws of the Fenrir wolf."

I followed everyone's eyes to the Thaw Gruel sheaf and then echoed the prophecy it took no great gift to see. "There will be a stone in the Gruel this year. And She of the Bog will not be content with mere goblets and bangles in exchange for Her sacred peat."

chapter 2

INTER CAME, AND IT SEEMED as if the dark and the cold and the hunger would never end. But at last there were signs. And then came the thaw.

We all knew the story, how Balder, the young god of spring and green growing things, was killed – like some tall oak – by a sprig of mistletoe tossed by his blind brother. And how, to win Balder's ransom from Hel, Divine Lady of the Underworld, every creature on earth had to weep.

So, as happened every year, they were all weeping with the thaw. I could see it on the south face of a bank of snow, tears dropping one by one as from a thousand eyes. A great labor of crying, streams of tears, torrents carving up the paths and wagon roads. Those few scrawny sows who'd been suffered to live through the winter sank up to their sagging teats in the tear-mud of their pens.

And then came the cart, carved and inlaid until the wood seemed to breathe with life. Within the cart sat concealed the Goddess at whom no human eye could peek and not die. It was the Goddess Nerthus coming on her spring progression, sticking up to her hubs in the tears of the world, calling us all from our hamlets to flow like rivulets of tears ourselves down to the Bog on the appointed day, weeping.

Uddrun and I could hardly contain our joy with ritual sorrow, for we hadn't seen each other since the snows set in.

"Brynhild, you've grown," she said. "You're taller than I am."

"Uddrun, you've grown ... grown, too." *Grown gaunt,* I thought, but didn't say. *Grown pale and old.* But so had we all on that winter's diet.

"I was so sorry to hear of the death of your little brother," she said, and wept without ritual urging. "He was – he was such a sweet little lad."

We all had real reasons to weep at that thaw. No fewer than ten of the youngest and weakest children besides my brother had died when their mothers' milk gave out and their little stomachs couldn't tolerate the heavy doses of roughage the rest of us consumed to still the pangs. Nearly as many of the older folks had gone, too, long-time illnesses catching up with them, their stubs of teeth balking at what they were asked to chew.

"And I was sorry to hear of your granny," I said, comforting Uddrun. "Did you have to keep her out in the smoke shed like they did my brother – like some ham – until there was thaw enough to bury him? Father said there wasn't enough fuel for a proper cremation." I shivered in horror at the memory, and that was enough to bring on the tears.

"My father had anticipated something like this," Uddrun said. "He had a plot dug and filled with straw before the snow."

"I hear your granny just refused to get out of bed one morning."

"'Give my food to the little ones,' she said." Uddrun didn't bother to wipe the tears, her white face running like any south-facing snow bank. "'I've lived my life.' Just like that. 'Give my food to others.' I wonder if I could do such a brave thing? All winter I've been wondering–"

"Oh, look!" I must confess I was anxious to change the subject. "There's Olaf."

"Where?" Uddrun went pale and then blushed to the pale roots of her hair.

"To the left. Come with his family from over by the Big Bears."

"Yes." Uddrun looked down and blushed so, I thought her tears would sizzle.

At Yule, the very last time we had come together, while the men had caroled and toasted the fruit trees, we had undertaken the custom together of tossing our shoes into the old crab tree. This was to see if we would gain our hearts' desire in the coming year. My shoe had failed to catch, even after three throws, which is all one is allowed.

"You throw too hard," Uddrun had said, gentling my disappointment. "Maybe next year."

"Am I likely to throw any less hard with a year of growth behind this arm?" I'd countered.

Uddrun's shoe, of course, had caught on the first try. I had thought then, with only the merest twinge of envy, for Uddrun always got her wishes, that this meant Olaf, of course. Now I pursued the subject of Olaf unfittingly but relentlessly. "I hear his family has sent presents. A shield? A spear and sword?"

"Yes."

"And a pair of oxen?"

"My father is delighted. He will use them in the spring plowing, since we were obliged to eat our old Boss this winter, and Clover won't plow without him."

"Certainly sounds like dower gifts to me."

"Yes."

Olaf was winking and nodding in our direction as frantically as the solemnity of our downward march behind the cart would allow. Uddrun ignored him. He was a rough man of two and twenty who had already killed an enemy, as a man must before he marries. But he was not unkind, I thought. And able to produce a yoke of oxen for his intended's family in a year like this! But Uddrun was a beauty whose skin, nearly as pale and soft as her hair, was a byword throughout the valley.

"So you'll be married, Uddrun!" I said. "Perhaps by Midsummer's Eve."

She continued to ignore Olaf, almost ignored me. That didn't seem usual for a bride to act exhausted, almost disgusted by the little bits of joy the gods offered us.

"By this time next year, you could be a mother." I used this bait because I knew Uddrun, unlike me, had a soft spot for children. And they for her. All of them flocked to her instinctively, loved her store of songs and stories, even the movements of her hands over their heads and their snotty little faces, as if she were born to that job.

But she is so thin this spring, I thought as I struggled to see motherhood in her. *I wonder if she, like her grandmother, gave up a good deal of food this winter for the little ones. That would be just like her.*

Uddrun looked at me with grey in her blue eyes, as if to say, "There you go again, Brynhild, breaking out of bounds. This is the solemn, dangerous time of thaw, when the world weeps the death of Balder, who may not return. You have already escaped in your thoughts to the garlands and dancing of Midsummer, to the carefree meeting of couples, as if there were no tomorrow, no dark winter nine months hence, when another mouth to feed would be such a burden."

All she said aloud was, "My parents have accepted the gifts, but they must respond with an armed corselet before it is certain."

We both stole a glance over to her father who, like everyone, wore his best. He wore the corselet, chain links hanging loose down to his thighs, as if to make up for the flesh he had lost, as if to protect himself from what Fate planned for this day.

He is afraid, I thought. *That once-big man is afraid. They are all afraid.* Fear rose from our procession like mist.

I looked again at the corselet Uddrun's father wore, thinking with envy, *I will never wear such a thing because I am a girl, even though my parents made the first half of my name 'brynie,' which means 'corselet.' That is the armor they gave me, a name.*

Uddrun continued. "I don't know how we are to come by such a thing in a year like this – unless Father can bear to part with his own, which would never fit Olaf." She shook her head.

Watching her father, I thought it unlikely he would give up his own corselet. The cares of the winter required murder – for which he would require a corselet.

We reached the sacred site now, and once within the wicker-work fence, chatting ceased. The aged priestesses, three of them in their long loose white linen and long loose grey hair, had already sanctified the interior with the clan's war banners – boars' heads and eagles' wings. Now they sanctified it further with their low, tuneless chanting and splashes of brew made from mistletoe they shook here and there with branches of heather. The brew splashed everyone as they arrived.

The priestesses had removed the god images from their secret abode in the Bog where they'd slept all winter and set them in their appropriate places to receive the cart and the people's offerings. The stick image with two knobs on top and heavy rounded hips received the thanks of the women, especially those who'd been safely delivered. Balls of finely-spun wool and broken crockery stood in this poor year for whole pots. And the stick that branched three ways, two legs to stand on and the third rising proudly, manfully, from the crotch, received the prayers, the broken knives or war booty of men, or offerings of women who had yet to conceive.

And there, where the cart was brought front and center, just at the edge of the Bog, the new-struck fire was burning so hot, it was almost invisible in the damp air.

A wood fire, I thought. *Oak. Oak stings the eyes, makes them tear. Where have they got the oak, when all winter we have known only the smell of peat? Peat smells nice enough when it burns, once you're used to it. Still, I cannot help but wonder, every time it enters my lungs, am I also breathing in a curse of the gods with this smoke?*

"Well, anyway, with this marriage ahead, no one will expect you to eat the Thaw Gruel," I whispered to Uddrun.

"I intend to eat the Gruel," she said.

I looked at her in wonder and a little confusion. Grown men were expected to eat the Gruel, of course. As they were expected to charge head-long into a rain of enemy spears. And old folks always ate, for they'd seen their days anyway. But young mothers, once they'd paid their devotions and been blessed by the mistletoe water, always departed from the solemnities. With them they took as many of their children as they could still command out of the wicker enclosure and out of sight over the hill. So, from infancy until she no longer had children to bid, no one expected a female to partake. I certainly had not expected to do it, though I prided myself that I was as brave as any boy I knew. I'd always thought I would have an easier time with spears than with the Gruel. If I were as brave as any boy, then I must surely be as brave as pale, soft Uddrun.

"Well, then I must partake, too," I said.

I ignored my mother's entreaties as she scurried my brother and sister away. That was easy enough, considering I was notorious for disobedience. I watched them disappear over the hill where I could have run and skipped and pretended it was already Midsummer's Eve. My heart, bidden by fear and longing, urged me to turn and leave, but I stayed. That part was not so easy.

"Brynhild, you mustn't," Uddrun said kindly. "Not for my sake."

But I wouldn't do her bidding any more than my mother's, once the challenge had been laid. Uddrun smiled at me as she smiled at any child. She took my hand, and we stood side by side in the circle of the people of the valley that formed against the wicker perimeter. Perhaps two hundred in all elected to stay. Most, like Uddrun, understood the seriousness of the rite this year. I think more attended than usual.

"All those not desirous of facing the will of the Great Mother," moaned out the fearful voice of the priestess, "depart, depart!"

That voice we knew from other years, heard from the safety beyond the hill. It had no more reality even now when I could actually see the old woman who made the sound. The rest of the ritual was new to us, although we were somewhat aware of what was to happen from hushed recitals among those who had been there other years. We sang for a while, solemn hymns, weeping songs for Balder, and then the mead, the oath-mead, was ready. A priestess with a gold-encrusted wild auroch's horn filled with the bitter-sweet drink approached each person in the ring. The old woman hooked each one by her wild blue eyes and asked, "Do you willfully submit to the Great One?"

"I do," said Uddrun, and she drank.

"Do you, Brynhild?" The priestess knew my name.

I still had time to escape over the hill. Until one had taken the cup, there was still time. But the priestess knew my name. Uddrun may have drunk because, like her dear granny who taught her to be a woman, she wanted to improve the odds for others. But I – I could never back down from a challenge.

"I do," I said. I drank the sweet, bitter, heady brew.

The cup proceeded around the circle.

Perhaps there will be no stone in the Gruel as everyone assumes. There hasn't been one since I was born. I think since my mother was born, or she would have told me.

And these old women, these priestesses, they surely knew how to grind grain and cook a gruel without getting stones in it. After all these years, surely, they did not make the mistakes of little girls taking their first aggressive, careless whacks at the quern. Thusly I gave myself courage.

In the great bronze cauldron, all embossed inside and out with scenes of the gods, the Gruel was ready. The priestesses dipped in their ladles, then moved about the circle, plopping a serving into each person's held-out bowl.

Then I remembered. "I haven't a bowl," I hissed to Uddrun. "I wasn't planning – I mean, I forgot–"

"Never mind," she whispered back kindly again, as if to a child. "You shall share mine."

"Another ladleful, please," she said without flinching to the priestess whose dollop landed in her wooden bowl. "I'm sharing with my friend."

Uddrun did not begin to eat until the second helping had come. Then we ate together, dipping from her single bowl by turns, taking the clots slowly with the two fingers of our right hands. It was not a remarkable gruel, neither better nor worse than what we'd all been eating since midwinter, bitter with unaccustomed weed seeds and unpleasantly coarse on the tongue. I found it much more difficult to eat, however. Uddrun matched her pace to mine. Others around us were finishing, sighing with either satisfaction or relief. Over by the fire, I could hear the priestesses scraping out the cauldron for their own portions.

And then I bit down on something hard.

What seed is this? I thought. Then my tongue found it again from the mess of gruel. A smooth, small, but definite – stone.

Swallow it! was the first panic of my thoughts. *No one will know.*

But I had seen the eyes of those priestesses and knew they were not to be fooled.

My gorge rose at the gruel I'd already forced it to take. I slowly brought my hand to my mouth and removed the stone. It lay there in my palm, so little, so white, so innocuous – so deadly. It seemed light, as if it would float away. Or was it only my head that was light, on the verge of fainting?

It is the stone, I thought. *It is I. I am the Devoted One, the one the Gods have chosen. Chosen to die.*

The stone was so light, it suddenly wasn't there at all. Astonishment made me hesitate longer. And then, beside me, I heard a thing that froze the thaw in me. Uddrun's voice, half in triumph, half a wail, "A stone! I've found a stone!" All the winter's grief from every hearth, there in her voice.

She had palmed the stone from me while I stood there too frozen to move. I couldn't believe it, couldn't get my mind around what she'd done. At the same time, I found I couldn't do anything to counter her claim. She was the adult. I, the child.

Her wail became a common wail, "A stone in the Gruel!"

And then, "The Devoted One. The Devoted One!" rose like a dark thunder from our kinsfolk. It was like all the fiends of Hel broke upon us – but no. They fell upon her alone as my hand was firmly jostled out of my friend's.

I would never have thought it, never would have believed our usually kind and gentle kinsfolk had such fury in them. How could they do it, and do it to one of our own, yes, one of our most gentle and innocent ones? Uddrun, Uddrun, who had run their errands without complaint and laughed with such a light and merry tone at everyone's jokes. Uddrun, Uddrun, who had loved their children, taken them from their hands when the work was too much and played with them with endless patience. Uddrun, who had loved me.

I alone did not raise a hand against her, but neither did I raise a hand for her. This hard world, I learned with every blow that fell, was no place for those who loved children. Or for those who loved me.

I even saw Olaf first among the fiendish faces, Olaf for whom

Uddrun had been worth a pair of oxen, a sword, and a spear to marry. But they did it – her father, with all the violence he thought he deserved for cutting his peat; her mother, turning outward and away the helpless anger she felt for being grateful when her mother-in-law said she'd eat no more. Everyone had done things they could be cursed for. The Gods knew I had. But if one died, all could live with themselves another day.

The one with the stone instantly became as hated as the ice-hearted ogress, the only creature on earth who had refused to weep and bring Balder back from the dead. Blame for all the anger and sorrow my kinsfolk felt now found its place. The pain of mothers whose infants had died as their milk dried up. The frustration of battle-hardened fathers who were powerless to wrestle a man's living from the very soil on which their fathers had raised them. The grief at a parent's passing. The nameless dread when the cattle sickened and died. The long, dull anger at always being hungry, at having to stomach, once again, food that hardly deserved the name. All of this suddenly exploded out of them, for at last they knew where to fling their torment. It fell upon Uddrun, my friend.

"Uddrun, Uddrun!" I wanted to cry out. But she was Uddrun no longer. She had become nameless, the Devoted One.

They fell upon her with staves, with clods of mud and with stones, with the nails of their bare hands. They tore her clothes from her as from a beast on whom clothes and modesty were ridiculous. The hair, the pretty fair hair, was ripped from her head with bits of skin and blood in clumps, trampled in the mud like straw in a barnyard. I heard when a particularly brutal blow broke the hand I'd been holding for security, the hand which she'd raised to her face on impulse to fend off other blows.

I stood frozen.

The Devoted One never screamed, never made a sound. She knew from the first that this was the fate of the stone. She could have escaped it earlier. She could have gone behind the hill and escaped it altogether, but she did not then, and now she did not cry out. But she did flinch – she couldn't help but flinch – and she did begin instinctively to look for refuge, as even a man under such an onslaught would do. She began to try to make her way through the crowd down toward the Bog.

Then, dazed by a blow, she fell to her knees and had to crawl, holding her broken hand tenderly to her breast as if it were a wounded child. Somehow she managed at last to make it to the refuge of the skirts of the high priestess.

I stood frozen.

The priestess drew out from her bosom a short length of twisted rawhide, and the crowd fell back, their part done, their fury spent in the awe of Heaven. With the hand of mercy, the priestess wound the cord about the Devoted One's neck like a royal jeweled heirloom. Then the priestess slipped a smooth little twig between the pale skin and the cord at the back of the neck and gave one good, brief twist. The head of the Devoted One fell sideways most unnaturally, then her whole body slumped onto the broken hand. But she could no longer feel it.

Quickly, the three priestesses scooped up the naked body, one of them casually tossing over it a cloak that had not been totally trampled and torn by the crowd. Swiftly they made their way into the Bog along solid paths known only to the priesthood and the Gods, to a point where we could just see them. Two men followed out, carrying between them a great smooth slab of rock. They dropped it where the priestesses had dropped the body. Then forked branches were hammered over each end of the Devoted One, to make certain she could not rise and come to haunt us in our habitations.

I looked up and away and saw the bloom on thorn and crab like the breath of some supernatural being that could swallow all the Bog in a single gulp. So, the people comforted themselves. The Gruel was eaten, the deed was done, the evil averted, and the year's sowing could begin with the confidence that its harvest would be better this year than last.

But what confidence was there for me? I was a fraud. I couldn't even reveal the depths of my grief, for what deed of courage in time to come could cover it? A pale and fragile girl had died for me.

But the female in me died that day, so I often thought, sacrificed to the Gods. From that day I became determined to leave the valley, to break the bounds of the Bog and fight for my place in the world. Not to accept what Fate dictated for me, but to fight for mine. My place was not – by my life, I had to prove it! – a small hollow, ankle-deep in bog water. I had to escape before it was discovered, before the Gods let it be known that they'd been tricked, that a serious mistake had been made.

chapter 3

O DISTILL THE ELIXIR OF forgetfulness is a great skill. I have this skill. But it is of no use for me. I have never been able to forget my childhood friend. Or her death.

Nor can I forget how, not long after the Thaw Gruel, my brother was due to depart for our maternal uncle's house where he would finish becoming a man and fulfill whatever Fate spelled for him. In order to read that Fate which had hung over everything in Angle-Land since the events in the Bog, Mother had called for a *seiðr*, a scrying invoking the time-spinning Norns and the Vanir Earth Gods.

Mother's own Fate was as pale and pudgy as her face, as shapeless as pudding, with only two permanent spots of feverish color to pick out the cheeks one might otherwise miss. Her body, too, was pudding-like from much childbearing, and she still knew the grief of my younger brother's death that winter. A Fate that removed one of her children from the pudding texture of her life might be a curse as surely as if she'd read death in the scrying bowl. And so she had sent for the old women as she had done when each of us was born and when my little brother's death had overpowered her attempts to fight it off.

The voice of *seiðr* was the voice of the gods. Even more anciently, it was the word of the timeless Norns, and they couldn't lie. I imagined that those three old crones spinning the Fate of the world between their wrinkled fingers were as tired as everybody else was of calling me down from the ridge pole. And on that day we had the three old crones in our very house, impersonated by the three priestesses of the Bog.

They came, toiling up the hill from the Bog, leaning on their knotted sticks with hands swathed in white cat fur. Their blue eyes darted about and fixed a little too often on me, even though I tried my best to avoid them. They had known my name at the ceremony of the Thaw Gruel, in spite of the fact that such women usually kept their distance from mundane things, such as the names of this season's little girls. What else did they know? Well, that was what they'd come to tell us.

Now, our farmstead was not large. We shared the roof with our grain, out of reach of the rotting weather, letting it ripen on the broad dirt floor where we would thresh it. We shared it with our stock, too, their stalls separated from the single room where we ate, worked, and slept, by a wicker wall that missed a few more canes every year. In winter, the smell of chaff and the warm breath of our cows, the sound of their great bodies shifting and their cud-chewing drifted cozily through the missing canes as our fire drifted back to them.

For this day of *seiðr*, the house and yard about it were packed with folk, for no one in our hamlet or the next two would miss it. I wished I could. Uddrun's absence among the usual faces was to me like an amputated hand, but nobody else gave any sign that they even remembered her. Of course, acknowledging her would be courting her return to haunt us all, if any reference to a Devoted One passed our lips. Some even thought all it took was to let her image shadow one's mind.

I did not want to face the old crones – I, who'd been afraid of nothing in my life before. I tried to hide in the crowds, but I was much in demand to fulfill our house's guest-due for the priestesses. I was glad my sister, as eldest daughter, had to serve them their special dish. I could not meet their eyes as she did. Their special food was the roasted hearts of every animal we could find. We all knew a dragon's heart lent to anyone who partook of it the ears to understand the speech of birds and to know the future and the past. People said these crones had once eaten dragon heart. Having no access to a dragon ourselves, we had to kill a dog, a cat, a sparrow, a pigeon, a frog, a rabbit, and a mouse, as well as the more commonly eaten hearts of chicken, pig, sheep, horse, and cow for our sacrifice. Beyond that, we hoped that the high priestess had enough power to make up for a lack of it on our part.

When they had pecked at their meal – all our efforts appreciated only by the appetites of three withered, birdlike old women – the priestesses took up their positions.

Two great alder trees supported the high point of our roof. In my great grandfather's time, the trees were alive, and the house had been built around them. Being trees, they outlived my great grandfather. But being mere trees, no divine Yggdrasill, they had in the meantime died, an evil omen for the fortunes of our family, an omen which had certainly come true in the last few years.

Still, the whitening trunks held up the roof, and between them stood the room's high seat, a substantial bench with arms and a back, where my father sat and presided when he was home, and Uncle Erik in his absence. Some crude carvings had been made in the trunks over the years, commemorating special events in our family's history – a slash for the birth of a son, nothing for that of a daughter. Other signs called down special favor for the Gods when that was needed. Uncle Erik had nicked a sun wheel with six quick strokes of his knife before he went to dig peat from the Bog.

While we'd been cooking hearts, Uncle Erik had knocked together the wooden platform between the two skeletal trees, over the high seat. Here, the high priestess sat, mediator between Heaven and earth, on a cushion stuffed with only the feathers of hens. Her two associates flanked her on stools, lower to the ground. And I, after a box on the ear for trying to get out of it, was plumped down on a bench next to my brother, facing her directly across the fire pit, which the press of people did not require to be lit that day. The assistant priestesses sang and drummed the ancient chant that mesmerized the entire gathered room, heating it as if there had been a fire. It didn't take the high priestess long to enter her trance. She told what she saw, and this was what she said. "There is a tall old linden tree outside the door of his boyhood home. The fallen warrior can see it against his burning lids, as if he were even now walking under it to the close meadow to see a new colt – Greyfell, that little colt. Greyfell, who'd only that day been cut from under him…"

"No," I whispered, wanting to speak up and tell the priestesses they had it all wrong. "Greyfell is still but a frisking colt–" My brother gave me a kick to keep me from interrupting their scrying of his vision. And a vision it became for everyone in the room, including me…

It was Midsummer, the linden a mass of yellow flowers and yellow bees dusty with pollen until one couldn't tell the pollen from the bee. Mead made from the honey of those bees would have the same wild, sweet flavor on a winter's night. The smell of linden, so sweet he thought he'd swoon with it, did not fill his nose. Rather, it was the scent of blood – his own blood from the wound in his neck that smelled strange and sweet. And the loss of that blood and the agony made him light-headed, made him keep his eyes closed. Suddenly, a wild, high-pitched cry slashed the hum of bees in his head. His eyes, which he'd thought never to see with again, wrenched open of their own will at the sound. There it was, the battlefield…

Across the room, my mother stifled a cry. So, now she knew. My brother would die in battle. Others would tell her it was an honor, but she could never see it that way, nor know whether it would be on his first ride out, or much later in life, after his sons stood at her knee to replace him. Women near her told her to be quiet and listen to the Gods…

At dawn, the field had spread an even carpet of summer flowers, still and empty. Now it was roughly strewn with boulders, boulders of horse and human flesh, still and empty again. With his final morsel of will, he did not want this to be his last view of the earth. Much better the linden–

But the hoarse, wild cry came again. He had to look and, as he looked, he saw. First, a flitting of shadow crossed the field. Other shadows. Then, with a stiff ruffle of feathers, the shadow dropped to one of the nearby boulders. That boulder was Greyfell. The shadow was a blue-black raven, messenger of Odin and of death.

He watched with frozen fascination as the bird side-stepped along that dear grey backbone, cocking its bright-eyed head this way and that in a grim appraisal of the many wounds along that back. At last it began to peck. It found a stringy, bloody morsel and seemed satisfied, for it gave its wild call of triumph to the sky. Other shadows dropped. Eight, ten, a dozen at least. One landed very close, on the boulder he knew was Arne, his boyhood companion.

A shift in the room let me know where Arne stood, but I'd become so enthralled by the seeress's sight and her high-pitched drone that I didn't care, even should he be dying now.

Arne's helmet had fallen askew so the deer horn emblems by which he had always known his friend in a fray could not be seen. Still, he knew Arne's blue eyes, open to the sky, but dull and lifeless. And the fallen warrior knew that tawny hair, even spiked with sweat and grime. Amongst those spikes the grey talons landed. This bird did not hesitate a moment, but went at once for the tidbit of the eyes.

Another shadow, another cry, and this one was upon the warrior himself.

"Wait but a moment, All-Father, Odin," the warrior wanted to shout. "I am not dead yet, not yet." But he found the wound in his throat left him no voice. Then he saw that the bird coming at him had landed on — or came with — a great golden breastwork. He remembered the breast of his mother's grey woolen dress when she'd been gathering linden blossom among the bees to dry and later steep against winter sore throats. If only it were his mother with such a brew now, for the pain in his throat...

Now he saw that the bird meant for him was not alive. Instead it was a black featherwork upon a golden helmet, cunningly fashioned so the dead wings seemed about to alight and still flapped stiffly in the wind.

And then, between helmet and breastplate, his focus found the face. No dark and crowishly angled face such as had been coming at him all day with merciless eyes. It was a fair face framed with braids of gold, with blue eyes, icy, but not unkind. Such a bloom of life tinted the cheeks as the dark elves of the South could never muster. And on the lips, bloom and a little half smile.

"Here is one, one for me!" the lips called to unseen companions in a wild, birdlike crow. Then those lips dropped to his in a kiss with the power of dark mead; it quite took his breath away.

His heart leapt with joy and unearthly passion. More than a minute had to pass before it came to his mind, slowly, that it was to be his last heartbeat. But now, lanced as he was on that golden breast, it no longer mattered. For he knew one of Odin's fair battlemaids had chosen him. Eternity waited ... in Valhalla.

The company turned with whispered awe to gaze on my brother Bjorn. Bjorn stirred next to me on the bench under their scrutiny. Clearly he was trying to take on that hero's agony and death with all the courage a twelve-year-old could muster.

Our older sister sitting on Bjorn's left, and I, younger, sitting on his right, looked at him with awe due to one the Gods had chosen. At least in my sister's eyes, the awe was total. Jealousy dragged claws through my own awe. I would never be chosen thus for eternal glory, even though I would undertake any physical challenge presented to my brother more readily than he. I had been born a girl. The three Norns had given a linen thread at my birth rather than a boy's woolen one.

Presently the high priestess wiped the *seiðr* sight from her eyes. Her assistants helped her back down to the ground. She met my brother's eyes first and smiled at him encouragingly. No doubt the idea of death from a cut throat as seen in the vision, for all its glory, was something for which he'd have to muster courage.

But she did not stop before Bjorn and did not speak to him. Nor to my sister, although the old rheumy blue eyes did wander to that side for a moment, disoriented by the scene to which the magic had called her. Another quick smile. I did my best to shrink behind my brother's shoulder.

The stone. I hadn't claimed the stone.

Her darting gaze finally settled on my face. And now, though perhaps she attempted it, no quick and easy reassuring smile came to her lips.

The priestess reached hesitatingly through space until she caught my face between her hands. The hands were old, frail, swathed in cat fur, skin side out. But these were also hands that had dispatched a Devoted One with a single quick twist. I felt claws hidden in those paws. They dug into my cheeks and drew me toward her.

"Brynhild," she said, pouncing on my name like a cat on a mouse. "Brynhild," again, as if it were strange to her, as if she herself had not given me that name, which means "battle armor," when she'd attended Mother's lying in. "Brynhild," she said. "*This* is the face I saw."

"What? On the fallen warrior?" I spoke as well as I could with my face caught in such a vise. "But we don't even have a linden tree in our yard. Our family trees are alders..."

On the next bench, Mother frantically tried to teach me proper reverence with shushing sounds.

"Not on the warrior," the priestess hissed. "Beneath the feathered helm."

There was a silence. Even the two subordinates stopped their low chanting and drumming to listen. After a long moment, and in a hush, only I dared to break the spell. "Me? A Valkyrie?"

The priestess let my face go as if it were a pan so hot, she could not hold any longer. She plunged her hands into her sacred cauldron of steeping herbs to cool them.

A Valkyrie! A Valkyrie! I had such questions to ask, such things to wonder. But the priestess was clearly not going to answer them for me. She might have pronounced a curse. After all, the Valkyries were daughters of Odin, battle lord of the Aesir Air Gods, and she, the priestess, a mouthpiece for the Vanir Earth Gods.

Before she had a chance to dry her hands, she fell back from the cauldron. Then, with froth on her lips, came a great tirade. "Odin, by guile, sleeps with the daughters of men. Beware, oh daughters of men. And on them he gets beings to join his host. Takes them from our ranks, from the ranks of Vanir, to exact his untempered revenge. Odin, Odin, this one you have won, snatched from us what was ours. But in the end, old one-eyed man, you will know the bounds of the earth – Vanir. And she, she like an old worn battle corselet tossed in the Bog, she will return to us where she belongs."

Mother wept in the same frenzy as the priestess; so did many of the women who hadn't fainted dead away. On our bench, my brother and sister clung to one another in terror, and the men were grave, ashen-faced, and silent. Give them a fear to fight with the sword or the axe any day – not this, not this wild, writhing thing of another world.

But I sat silent, unmoving and alone – inhuman, one might say – and listened as if I had known these words all my life. My face, after all, which I had never seen but which truly represented me to the world, was doing all the prompting.

The high priestess croaked with exhaustion and thirst. She brushed the floor rushes out of her skirt, took a deep draught from the magic in her cauldron, then remounted her platform without another word. The chanting and drumming began again. Quickly the trance was reached, this time answering for Bjorn, next time for my sister, and then the priestesses departed as they had come.

Later in life, the truth would come out, but not that day of prophecy, and not for some time to come. That day was full of magical dread and sadness for knowing the fated future. Bjorn was to die in battle from a slit throat, and dear Greyfell nearby, fallen also. My sister would live and die as most of her sex lived and died, toiling at the hearth and in the fields, bearing children and burying some of them.

For me, the unknown of my own Fate fled with heightened excitement. I was to be a Valkyrie! But my future... Well, they hardly knew how to mark it on the trunks of the great alders when the platform was taken down, and lives – some of them – went back to normal. What the Norns meant for me might indeed happen. No mistake had been made in the sanctuary before the Bog. I would indeed manage to escape from the confines of the Bears and win myself a glorious future.

But ... a Valkyrie? What did that mean? A daughter of the god Odin? How did that happen?

I noticed the change already, the morning we packed up my brother to set off for his manhood. As they folded up the new clothes they'd woven for him and packed them in a sack, Mother, my sister, and the maid did not chat about Bjorn's future. And Father, he too grew grave and solemn and neglectful of his oldest son on this very important day of a boy's life. I doubt Bjorn ever forgave me for cheating him of that morning.

Although no one mentioned it again to me, my life became

instantly unlike any other's who'd ever lived in that house before, or I'm sure, who would ever live after. The daily and yearly rounds of work continued to circle about me. I don't remember too much of them, for they, I realize now, had never had reality for me. What did change was that my elders ceased their futile attempts to bring my mind into that reality with sharp words and an occasional sting of their hands. No one dared to cross a Valkyrie, even if she was but a child and Valkyrie in scrying alone. If I climbed on the ridge pole now, that was an expected thing. My boy cousins who had come to us to find manhood would hand me their practice swords and shields if I but looked in their direction. They let me practice with them, but they also let me win, which spoiled it for me.

Ever since the *seiðr,* everyone tiptoed around me. Giving me my every desire was the easiest way to separate from me. I had become like an enemy from a far land, a Dedicated One never to be stoned. *Valkyrie, Chooser of the Slain.* Might not a Chooser of the Slain, unlike an ordinary child, hold a grudge for some act of discipline and come for the punisher too early? Certainly the battlemaids were known to be dependent on the will of All-Father and the Norns, never their own wills. But to everyday mortals, they seemed capable of some influence at least. *Cross her,* I read in everyone's eyes, *and no, the Valkyrie might not come too soon. She might whisper in the Sky-god's ear some word, and he might not send her at all. Then death would be in truth what it seemed ... the end, a cold mound of earth and worms.*

Mother suffered frequently from stitches in her side, and the only thing that seemed to help was the recitation of a little verse:

> Loud were they, lo, loud, riding over the hill.
> They were of one mind, riding over the land;
> Shield thyself now, to escape from this ill.
> Out, little spear, if herein thou be.
> Under shield of light linden, I took up my stand,
> When the mighty women made ready their power
> And sent out their screaming spears...

The gist of the verse was that the spears of the Valkyrie were responsible for the pain, and one must praise them so they would go away and leave all in peace. Obviously, Mother found it difficult to recite this verse with any effect if I happened to be in the room.

And Father, when a fine swarm of bees did their ritual dance in the branches of a crab tree, set after them with bundled straw and smoking rags in a pot. It was just after Walpurgis, early May. A hive begun so early would have surely provided us with a massive amount of honey for baking and for mead by wintertime. But he failed to get them, where he'd never failed before. He always said he'd called the swarm *sigewif*, "victory-women," a euphemism both for bees and for Valkyries, and one of us, either I or the queen bee, must have taken offense and caused his failure.

So, everyday life detached itself from me as much as ever I detached myself from it. And if my life, by rights, should have ended in the Bog that spring when I was ten years old, I had somehow cheated – changed – my Fate. It would only be much later that I would learn how Fate has a way of turning out not always as expected, even when cheated.

Bjorn would become a warrior like his father and father's father before him, but he wouldn't distinguish himself either in cowardice or with enough bravery to win the honor of a heroic death to be immortalized in Valhalla. For all my later dealings with battlefields, I never saw him again. Mostly he was a farmer, farming the land of our fathers' valley into deeper and deeper exhaustion, until he himself was exhausted and died, not as he had feared from a cut throat, but in the bed where he'd been born.

My older sister's life would not go the way of the unexpected either. I suppose she brought her plentiful sons and daughters to a similar *seiðr* and read similar Fates for them when the time came.

But for me, I can say for certain that my life, my future, began anew that spring at the Thaw Gruel, when Uddrun gave her life for me.

All-Father? Me – a Valkyrie? The Norns had decreed I would ride with the Daughters of Odin. But how did that happen? And when?

I knew no one who knew the answers to my questions; no one had even seen such a being, except the priestess in her vision. And how much of that was because she suspected I'd let Uddrun die in my place at the Thaw Gruel?

My father went every year to his small desperate fields of war where men fought and died with never a visitation from a battlemaid to let them know their sacrifices were to some greater purpose. All I knew were the myths. Valkyries rode. I did not ride. No girl did. My family owned only one horse, my father's. He and it were often away from home, seeking to become Valhalla heroes. When he did return, the horse was needed on the farm, the work falling on it as a famished man on food.

Had I spoken the word, of course, the horse would have been instantly bequeathed to me, work or no. But the work horse was not a really striking example of horse flesh, not material for Valhalla, for all my father's imagination. So I never did speak for it, being content to hoist myself up on bareback at widely separated times when I thought no one was looking, to spare my dignity. I was loath to appear the fool, which I might have without lessons, had the horse not been so stupefied with labor.

What else was I to do? I awaited the word of an entranced priestess, and nothing came. The world, I knew, was full of myths. This world where battlemaids selected the dead might well be another. How else to get men to fall on enemy spears when sense would say, "Run!" But what other choice did I have? Only that, or to await another Thaw Gruel. Without belief, that seemed an acceptable fate. Unless the myth were true. Unless the God came.

And then, come fall...

The God came.

chapter 4

 DON'T REMEMBER WHAT MUNDANE errand I was about when he came, what basket of new wool I was carrying to my aunt in the next hamlet, or what herbs I had just gleaned from the heath for winter drying. But I do remember where I was – on the path of dust that ran along the lower field my ancestors' ancestors had cut from native woods, where we'd grown, or tried to grow, oats that year.

And I do remember that I had a premonition of his presence before he even appeared. Something in the field made me look up from the path and in that direction. A sudden stillness, perhaps as the birds forgot their usual carefree chatter while gleaning the new-cut field. I stopped to see what this presence might mean and saw only dusty heat waves rising from the denuded field. In the next plot, still uncut, the grain became possessed by the shadow of a single cloud blowing by and shivered the way a dog's coat does when you scratch his spine – nothing more.

They used to tell us, when we were children, that an old woman in the wheat might steal you away if you ran off in the grain to play. I was old enough to realize that this ruse kept children from trampling and ruining the crop. So might all the Vanir Gods be, simply boggles. So might Odin be.

I turned back to the path. I had learned that keeping my hands full made the time pass quicker, and my time was always spent in waiting. Three more steps ... waiting for what, I knew not. Until he came.

Something made me scan the field again that afternoon and there, feeding at the last sheaf, the sheaf left for Odin, stood a horse. My first thought was, *Who dares such sacrilege to eat from Odin's sheaf?* Then I saw it was no ordinary horse, but a monstrosity, a horse with eight legs. Then it became clear this was no monstrosity, but divine – Sleipnir, the magic fleet-footed horse of Odin, the horse for whom the sheaf was left.

And then, there was the God, leaning on his staff before the horse and watching me. He was tall with solid width in proportion, and not the slightest stoop to his shoulders, although his beard lent him age. It hung like a massive clump of grey-blue icicles spun from the house eaves on a day fit only for whittling wood by the fire. His cloak was a blue that matched the sky. I later learned that it always matched the sky, whether lowering grey or smiling like forget-me-nots, as it did this day with one of the last bright skies of autumn. The wide brim of his hat he wore sloping over the right side of his face, but from where I stood I could still see the eye. Or rather, the eye that wasn't, for the right lid hung slack over an empty socket.

As soon as his one eye – blue, like his cloak, changeable like the sky – met mine, he gave me the closest thing to a smile I ever would see come out of that glacier of a beard.

Would he speak? What would a God sound like? How could I know? He said:

> "Do you begin to behold my beckoning,
> O tree of the Traveler's trappings?"

I laughed out loud, then quickly stifled myself. I saw from the look he gave me that he meant his words in earnest. The God always spoke thus; often the verses were riddles as well, full of dark kennings. It was part of his power, his magic. It took some getting used to for mortals to understand him – and for me to understand that no pomp sat here that didn't belong.

Very well. "Traveler" was another name for the God himself, like "All-Father." And "tree" was a term for a mortal, a woman in this case. He spoke to me. He called me his own, as if indeed I were. I did feel proud to unravel the gist of his speech on the first pass. I knew I was destined for higher things. What would have happened if I'd failed to figure out the puzzle? I would not find out.

"Yes," I replied.

I dropped whatever I was carrying and walked toward him over the field's stubble without a backward glance. When I arrived a comfortable distance from him – not too close – I stood there for a moment before I realized he wanted me to kneel. I did, every new-cut straw like a needle beneath my knees. Then he drew from the bosom of his cloak a twisted noose. My heart raced, my innards churned with panic. Here I was in the same attitude Uddrun had taken in front of the high priestess in the mud before the Bog. Here he was, reaching around my throat with his cord. I must confess I struggled a bit and made a little squawk of protest. A sharp kink of pain caught the flesh of my throat as in a vise and twisted to accommodate the noose. I struggled again, trying to regain my feet, but the strength of his hand on me was too great.

Then I relaxed, realizing at last that the cord was of gold alloy, not rawhide. Warm from having ridden inside his cloak, the hard metal had been forged in the shape of a sacrificial garrote. Inflexible, it could not be made to constrict any more.

"Repeat," he commanded.

> "I am prepared to plight
> All liberty, limb and even life.
> By this torc, my troth,
> And by Traveler God."

"I am prepared..." Swallowing hard over metal, I repeated the oath he gave me.

If I acted according to rite, it was because I had been taught the myth from childhood. I would wear this torc as a sign of my dedication to the God, dedication to death, if need be, yes, as the sacrificial garrote Dedicated One. But dedicated to life and work as well. The gold had the benefit of serving as a sort of gorget: a blow to the throat by an enemy would be deflected.

Wearing the torc of Odin was an honor. But my momentary flash of misunderstanding set it in my mind that the honor was not untainted. Until that moment, I had looked to the arrival of Odin as my escape. I was free, yes, from the constraints most other girls must live and die under. I was free to carry weapons, free from skirts and grinding stones. I was free from marriage, free from childbearing. I was free, most importantly, from the bounds of our valley and the Bog. But I was also marked now as Odin's slave. I hadn't considered before what that might mean.

Odin said:

> "Brynie and breastplate of battle.
> It's Brynhild your by-name might be?"

He was asking if my name was in fact Brynhild. "Yes." I was somewhat relieved to find I could still speak with the weight of the torc around my neck.

He nodded his head and confirmed that I was what he was looking for.

> "The well-grown rowan
> Is the rune for right."

I breathed with relief around the tight torc.

Then he threw back his head and gave a long, wild cry. In answer, two great black ravens descended from the sky and perched, one on each shoulder. Having done that, he waved his staff. Before my eyes, the horse Sleipnir divided itself and became two normal horses. Perhaps that is why he is called Sleipnir, "Slippery," because he has that ability.

As I think back to that day, I reason that perhaps the horse had always been two, one standing behind the other, and my eyes were fooled into believing magic. But I have become older and more doubting – not always the best way to be.

"The bridle-burden can you break
And sway the saddled scion of Sleipnir?"

he asked. *Could I ride?* he was asking. In truth, I did not ride well. *Could I "sway the saddled scion of Sleipnir?"* Everyone knows Valkyries ride. I answered according to the myth, a simple, "Yes."

The God pointed to the younger, smaller chestnut mare that had divided herself from the great white stallion any child would have recognized as his. This other horse was mine.

I was pleased to find that a fine leather battle saddle helped the mounting and maintenance of the seat over bareback. This compensated greatly for the start of suddenly finding some intelligence and spunk snorting there beneath me. The trick of hitching up my skirt I'd already mastered.

My companion nodded with approval.

"More relevant riding array
They'll give the gold-tree at our goal."

Tree. Woman again. *Gold-tree*, some honor attached. He promised me better riding clothes when we arrived wherever we were going. I nodded, my neck pinching in the torc.

The ease with which he climbed into his own saddle was like magic. "Then, daughter," he said, turning the reins, "let's drive and no more dally." Fortunately, my mount followed his without any instruction from me.

As he knew my name, I knew his. And so would anyone from the hamlet who might happen to see us ride out. But even if they didn't see, they would find my abandoned basket of wool and herbs by the nibbled-on Odin sheaf, and they would know. We'd all been waiting for this for so long.

Without a backward glance at what had always been my home, I rode after Odin. My kerchief blew off almost at once, and the wind through my hair was freedom.

On horseback we rode up and over the hills of the Little Bears in no time. It wasn't until then that I dared to speak to my Aesir companion, probing for what of the myth might be true of my fate. "Are you taking me to Valhalla, All-Father?"

He didn't answer. We dropped over the rise and found another valley beyond, just denuded heath and bog like that place I'd called home. The blue cloak rode silent as the sky above me.

My heart beating faster with the mere thought, I pressed, "Will we go across the rainbow bridge to Aesgard?"

The single flint-sharp eye turned on me, cutting as if it would slash the very heart from my chest. He thought my chatter the idle gossip of women. Either that, or if I were truly the girl he'd come for, I'd already know the answers to such questions. However the matter, I knew I must keep my tongue behind my teeth.

In rare glimpses from a distance I spied arms of water. I wanted to ask if that was the sea, for I had never seen it. But I kept that question and all the others to myself.

We crossed another valley. And another. I couldn't tell which rang louder in my head, the silence or my hunger. Then I recalled that Odin never ate with mortals, no matter how long the gift of his presence on earth might last. He only took swigs from the skin strapped to his shoulder that left his breath smelling of mead, but I supposed it must be more than ordinary drinking mead. In later days, when he would be gone from Valhalla, we understood he had scooped up Godhood again. Consorting with his peers in Aesgard, he was eating the food that made them divine.

Like the horses, I began to help myself to the hard dry kernels of Odin sheaves in each valley as we progressed. Again, Odin didn't comment, but I surmised from a raised brow that a girl who couldn't forage for her own food would perish on this first journey, and that would be the end of her calling. That night I slept saddle-crippled on the needles of a new-cut field.

By the end of the second day, a few more trees dotted the land, standing sentinel before the whitewashed farmsteads we tried to avoid. The next morning, I saw what I took to be the dark front of a storm rising from the south in front of us.

All-Father explained.

> "View the vested villeinage
> Of Vidar, the averred Vanir."

That took some puzzling until I understood that before us lay a forest, and the god named it for his son Vidar, Lord of Forests. All-Father hadn't said much before that, and he said even less now, all his attention focused on attaining that dark cover of trees.

My previous life, Bog and Bears and all, blurred in unreality, but I can recall the minutest details of that first entrance into the woods. The entrance was sudden, for men had clear-cut their own edge to the marvel for their fields. The cool, almost frightening dark at midday, dappled and moving in the breeze, felt like something alive. And the smell, the deep living humus scent of dirt and mushrooms and moldering leaves blended with sticky-sweet pine sap odor, was like incense that nearly stifled me in later years on entering the few Christian churches to which old age brought me. Alongside pines stood oaks, sacred to the gods, and hazel and hawthorn, even a few beeches. Not only were these upright and growing, their leaves just beginning to turn, but many fallen trunks and limbs formed a network like fine tatting across the forest floor. Such fall wood wouldn't have lasted a day in our valley before someone would have snatched it up and carried it home to her fire. It was all I could do to avoid the long-taught reflex to drop down and help myself before somebody else took a claim. But here, always more grew ... more and more, beyond every rise, more wood.

That first night in the woods, I found the leaf bed softer, but I was cold and afraid, for the place seemed more alive at night with the hunting calls of wild animals than it did during the day. In a desperate attempt for human companionship, I tried once again to get All-Father to talk. I hoped he would tell me about Vidar the forest god who was, after all, his own son. A human father would at least smile at the mention of a strong and powerful son. And by what means would I know how to be a daughter if I couldn't learn how All-Father treated a son?

Here indeed is Vidar, I thought, *the silent God. His head is crowned with sere and yellow leaves, long white moss hangs from his brows and cheeks, and his garments are rusted with age. On his feet are iron shoes, with soles made with scraps of leather gathered through centuries past.* I could easily see why only great Vidar would be able to kill the Fenrir wolf at the end of time when the Gods and the world were doomed. Was this how myth worked?

But my attempt to engage All-Father in conversation about his son went unacknowledged. The ice-cold beard didn't even twitch. I sighed. "Can you tell me then how you lost your eye?"

The single good eye winked at my impertinence.

"Wrested at the well of wisdom,
For a sip of the sacred spring.
In that burrow between the Bears,
Daughter, do they dampen you in darkness?"

I wasn't sure what he meant, but I wouldn't let him know that. He was silent again, teaching me that silence was part of the divine wisdom he had gained with "a sip of the sacred spring." I fell asleep in the midst of the God's silence, shivering with fear and cold, but biting my tongue ferociously at both.

We traveled for four more days on no trail that I could see. I knew my companion was leading us in ways far from human habitation. His ravens came and went from his shoulders, telling him in the tongue of birds which directions to avoid. I could not have found my way back to the valley if I'd wanted to. I knew we had traveled south all the way when we crossed open heath, and I had a sense we kept to that general direction. I almost supposed we might go so far south, we would enter the dragon land of Rome. But I knew one had to cross a great river first, and as we never crossed anything the horses couldn't splash over with ease, I learned that the world was even greater than I had imagined.

chapter 5

N THE EVENING OF THE seventh day, we reached our destination. I knew it was our destination the moment it broke upon our view through the trees – trees that, together, were dubbed Odin's Wood and had a reputation for being sacred or haunted, which kept the folk in the neighborhood at a respectful distance. Holy mistletoe heavily draped every oak in the place. Guarded by the loop of a narrow but loudly roaring river appeared the largest throng of buildings I had ever seen. Of course, I'd only ever seen our little hamlet and others like it in the valley. Imposing as the rookery was, and set up on a hill, its site was so well-concealed in the forest that very few mortals would come upon it by mistake. Those who did would be turned away by watchful sentinels in the name of Odin, or slain as they tried to cross the one narrow bridge.

Four great low buildings set at right angles formed a square. It would not be misleading to call the assemblage they enclosed a fortress, for although that was not its main function – the religious awe of the place would be enough to turn away all unwelcome comers – it would nonetheless be very easy to defend. A single entrance pierced the walls that only raven-sight could peer over. A wooden gate three times the height of a man formed the entrance. It was studded with metal and wide enough to allow the warriormaids to ride out together four abreast.

This entrance opened at sight of us as if by magic, and through it All-Father led me. A tall young woman was waiting for us there, to whom he turned over both me and the horses. Then, without a word of parting, Odin strode across the courtyard and entered the great building at the center of the complex.

"That's it. That's Valhalla," the tall woman told me with appropriate awe in her voice.

Valhalla, of course. The Great Hall of the Slain.

She smiled down at me, as I couldn't take my eyes off it. "You will not enter that hall unless and until it is Odin's will that you are initiated," she warned.

She would not satisfy my curiosity about this, but she let me stand and look my fill of the outside.

Like the home I'd left and like the four buildings that formed the outer walls of the stronghold, Valhalla was built of wood, long and narrow. The roof extended over an all-encircling porch where fuel and such things were stored. Except at the single doorway, the overhang dipped lower than my ten-year-old height, but the roof leapt up from these eaves to the highest ridgepole I'd ever seen.

In the Valley of the Bears, no one dreamed there could be single beams big enough to make the span. But there they were. The roof's cross ribs at front and back were rough-hewn logs carved with patterns and magic symbols. Each ended in the head of a dragon with chunks of coral forming the eyes, and they crossed their necks at the roof's peak.

Thatch or sometimes wooden shingles were the only roofing material I'd ever known, and doubtless Valhalla was this underneath. But the visible shingles were the overlapping shields of the hundreds upon hundreds of slain heroes who had entered the glory of the hall. Some of the shields were very old, the ensigns weathered off, exposing the wooden core from which bosses and rims were curling away. But these bits of metal, along with the gold-encased ridgepole itself, caught the last of the sun with blinding force and lent an air of hallowed age to the building.

Upon their master's entering the hall, his two feathered companions had flown up to this ridgepole where they joined scores of their kind in a constant coming and going. My guardian pointed out an old woman who stood at the foot of the hall, watching the ravens. "She can read the language of the birds," she said. "They bring us messages from all over the world."

I stood and watched the envoys arrive and depart, but reading the whirl of their formations in the sky, while fascinating, was a rare and difficult skill to master. "Is she a Valkyrie?" I asked my companion of the bird watcher.

"She was, but she has now grown too old to fight. She watches the birds instead."

"Are you a Valkyrie?" was my next question.

"Yes, I am. My name is Thora. I will be your guardian. And teacher."

So now my attention turned to her with fascination no less than awe. She was tall with hair the color of rust on an heirloom sword. Her features, under a liberal sprinkling of freckles, were fine and delicate, almost pinched and at odds with the big bones of her body. She had small breasts but broad, womanly hips. Fine linen – gathered at the shoulders with gold brooches formed in the shape of dragons with ruby eyes – draped her full length, leaving her arms completely bare. Around each powerfully muscled bicep she wore a heavy bracelet of brass. I would learn that these served as something of armor as well as lending any blow given by that arm the extra force of the metal.

Thora's right wrist also sported a cuff of fox fur, a personal badge. I didn't have a clue about its significance at the time, but planned to find out later. Over the linen gown, the Valkyrie wore a thigh-length brynie of leather sewn with metal disks as armor. As a hero was claimed for the hall by that maiden, his ensign would be embossed on a disk. My guardian already had ensigns on half the disks on the front of her brynie. Lastly I noticed around her neck she wore the golden torc of Odin.

"Are there other Valkyries here?" I asked.

"Of course. We all live here in Valhalla. We have the complete sisterhood at the moment, twelve of us. You will meet the others. Hilda will be your riding mistress, Thruðr is in charge of archery, Hlokk is our ironsmith. She will teach you how to mend your own weapons in case of emergency on the field. But let's get you settled tonight. First we must stable the horses."

And so Thora began to show the working details of what it meant to be a "nun of Odin." Odin himself I did not personally see again that day and for some time after. I assumed he had ridden off again on some godlike mission not of my concern. One of the great out-buildings was totally devoted to horses, stabling nearly a hundred of the finest war mounts in the world, all sired by divine Sleipnir. The Valkyries took the white ones, and the more mundane colors remained for those of us in training. But all were strong and swift with eyes that, even when they munched hay, spoke their wisdom.

In another outbuilding Thora showed me my space in the dormi-tory. Each girl was allotted less room than her horse in the stable. I would sleep on a narrow wooden bench with few blankets, even in winter. Thora gave me the clothes I was to wear. My girl's clothes were not thrown out, but hung in a cupboard at the end of the hall.

"In case," Thora said.

"In case what?"

"In case you do not pass muster, and you must be returned to the world."

It had never occurred to me that I might fail. I wasn't going to *become* a Valkyrie, I *was* a Valkyrie, as surely as I was female.

"I will not fail," I wanted to assure my guide. But the sight of my kirtle hanging there just before the closet door swung shut humbled me into silence.

The clothes Thora gave me in exchange were two pairs of trousers, one cool linen, one of doeskin, waterproofed for winter wear. Thora explained that one or the other pair would be worn most of the time and exclusively, and we girls would go bare-chested like boys. Like boys, we had to learn to endure cold and callous all parts of our bod-ies. We wore the doeskin until it was stiff with sweat and dirt and could stand on its own in the corner at night.

But I was also issued a knee-length linen shirt. Over this went a padded leather jerkin worked on the back in blue-black threads with the emblem of the nuns of Odin – the raven, with her wings outspread as she settles down to her business on the battlefield. This, Thora indicated, would be worn in the early days of any practice until I had perfected my maneuvers. The precaution was to ensure the girls in training wouldn't hurt themselves unduly. But everyday nicks and scratches were to be expected and endured, so mostly the jerkin was just for show. The trousers came with a belt and a small dagger in a smooth wooden sheath. In time, if I earned it when I was a Valkyrie, I would have a sword.

And finally, also mostly for show, were soft leather buskins in place of my clattering wooden pattens, which had joined the kirtle in the closet. They were new and well-oiled and tallowed to be waterproof – and stank abominably. The smell would lessen once I'd broken them in.

Thora smiled and nodded at my altered appearance. I was ready now. I was ready to go out and tour the realm of my new life.

Within the compound and on the training fields without, we saw many youths engaged in various activities. But they only appeared to be youths wearing trousers identical to mine. Young spring swelling on their breasts betrayed a few, and when they took off their protective helmets to greet me, out tumbled every tint of blond and red from the color of new-planed oak to the shade of fresh-polished chestnuts. All wore their hair long in two even braids, but over the left ear, a thin strand of hair was left out and braided separately. Should ever a maid's bow string snap in the heat of battle and she be without a spare, she was to rip this strand out of her head and use it as a replacement.

The tongues with which they greeted me all spoke the same language, but ranged in accent from the flat vowels of the west to those of the north and east. Those speakers' lips seeming constantly puckered in sultry trills and umlauts. There were girls from Suebia and Cimbia. There were Saxons, Burgundians, Franks, Danes, Allemani, and Goths. Girls from the lowlands where the great river Rhine emptied and earth life was a constant battle against the realm of Aegir, god of the sea. Even the far, far north where darkness reigned for months each winter and deep fjords riddled the coast was represented. So I would share my life with these girls, seventy-five of them between my age and womanhood.

All of us came to Valhalla, calling our master Oðinn, Woden, or Wotan, as dictated by our many dialects. Within a week, each girl gravitated to the common Odin. It was an early and constant part of our training to curb our various accents into one common speech, one not exactly like what any of us had spoken at home, but one that would mark us wherever we went as Valkyries. Any hero on any battlefield could understand and take courage from this accent, even if faint or delirious from loss of blood.

Even more important, more basic, and more quickly learned, however, was the communication by calls. The calls we learned copied birds, mostly raven calls that could penetrate a forest without disturbing silent old Vidar, but at the same time could pierce through the roar of a battlefield with unmistakable effect. There was a call for aid, for attack, for withdrawal, a call to others to come and share the spoil, and the pure warble of joy and triumph. Because I would take my turn standing watch like all the others from the very first day, I had to master the call of alarm at once.

My progress in other fields was not so immediate but constant. We learned all the skills of the battlefield as well as any warrior, some better. We learned to wrestle, both by the rules and the nasty tricks for when only winning mattered. We learned both to attack and defend with daggers, swords, hammers, axes, and pikes. Archery, in particular, a skill not dependent on body mass alone, was where we were expected to excel any male hero. We learned endurance. Not only the endurance of hunger and cold, the endurance of an all-day run over rough forest terrain with armor and a pack, but also the endurance, in some ways more difficult, of sitting perfectly still for three days, vigilant, winning the struggle against sleep.

As Thora had promised, the wide-shouldered Hlokk taught us the basics of smithing; those discovered to have special gifts in that area learned to master the craft. We learned to climb. Climbing to the ridgepole was child's play. We climbed trees; we climbed cliffs.

Not all our study was physical. We learned the lay of the country about us. Here, girls from distant places were helpful because they told us of the lands where they had been born, what plants could be useful there, what to avoid. We memorized how the land spread from the Rhine and the Alps to the North Sea, and over the sea to islands. We learned of climates of snow and the midnight sun, from the Rhine to the Elbe, Oder, and Danube to the endless steppe beyond. Every river, every mountain chain, and every kindred therein became ours to know.

Each girl told us something of the heroes in her native land, those dead, who had entered Valhalla and myth, and those still living, whom we might meet on some future battlefield. In particular, the tale of Volsung and his sons stuck in my memory, a family living on the Rhine, the very rich heart of our north lands. The gods had blessed the man and his wife, a giantess, with ten strapping sons and one daughter. Then, I found it strange that I remembered none of the sons' names, only the daughter's ... Signy. Why should I remember the girl when she was bound to be overshadowed her whole life by brothers – and I would someday likely have to deal with them on the battlefield?

In Valhalla, we even learned something of runecraft, writing and fate-telling, but more to fear it than its use: this skill Odin kept for himself, having won it so dear, either by defeating Mimir the Vanir, as some said, or by hanging himself from the World Tree. It justified his lordship and our obedience.

And of course we learned to ride. Girl and horse had to move and think as one. We had to be excellent jumpers, tireless riders. All attacks and feints learned on foot were then mastered in the saddle. We taught our mounts to jump and kick at a signal – and learned to keep our seats as they did so, to keep foot soldiers at a respectful distance.

And finally, perhaps the most difficult but important skill of all, we had to ride at full tilt across an uneven field while parrying attacks. Although our teachers assured us that the mere sight of a Valkyrie was enough to bind most warriors with terror, they also warned us that a battle berserk was not the easiest thing to shake, even from the most pious heart. Riding thus, we had to lean down out of the saddle and pick up an object. We started with a handkerchief, but then sacks of greater and greater weight. At last, we had to learn to pick up a companion sprawled upon the ground.

"Wriggle, Herfjoturr! Come on, girl, fight and kick!" our riding mistress yelled to the girl whose turn it was to play fallen hero. "Nothing I can teach you here can prepare you for the shock of picking up your first warrior in full battle gear. My own arms ached for a week. But Herfjoturr, you tiny little thing, if you don't wriggle and fight more, you'll only be doing your sisters a disservice."

All of us suffered our share of cracked ribs, slashed arms, and twisted ankles. We learned to bind our own hurts so they left little if any scar, and we learned to recover from them – if not stronger, then certainly wiser.

We did have one girl fall and break her neck at riding. Another girl, a big-boned Dane, had freckles on every inch of her strong, young body, similar to the color of scalded honey milk. Her sleeping bench was next to mine, so I often enjoyed the sight of her naked. She suffered a compound fracture of the leg. She didn't scream or cry out as we carried her on our shields back to the enclosure. She only begged us through clenched teeth to use our daggers at once to put her out of her misery. The Valkyries took her from us at the gate, and we never saw her again. I learned only later that she immediately did have her throat cut as a sacrifice to Thor. A wound like that, out of which we could see little bits of bone seeping, would never heal well enough to make her the warrior of prowess she had to be. It was better to go directly to Hel instead.

My instruction taught me that a Valkyrie remained in active service until her fertility was past. We had no retirements, and only one battlemaid failed to return during my third year. Hers had been an errand to Roman lands. Romans did not acknowledge the Gods of Aesgard; a dangerous mission honored her death.

Having lost only two of our number after several years – and having them replaced by new recruits – it became a puzzlement to me why there should be seventy-five of us in leather trousers and only twelve of the Valkyries themselves. Because a Valkyrie remained in active service until her fertility was past, I wondered how we should all fit into such a narrow space.

As they swelled into womanhood, the older girls seemed to vanish one by one without a trace. My peasant's dress, I remembered, was still hanging in the closet. It was far too small for me now, but immodesty would be the least of my worries if I ever had to put it on again.

Something loomed out there, something at the edge of woman-hood, dark and deadly. One day, when I had been at the compound for seven years, I found out what it was.

"I became a woman last night," I whispered to Thora one day at the end of summer when at last I'd managed to get her alone.

She looked down at me – she was still taller – without her usual smile when I showed her the bloody rags sticking to my fingers. Her normally dancing blue eyes were hard and avoided emotion. She nodded. "I thought your time was coming. See that you tell no one of this."

"All right."

She looked at me sharply. My compliance had been too careless. "On your holy oath to All-Father, swear it." I swore until she was satisfied. She nodded again but still seemed displeased. "In a few months, I will let you know what must be done."

Two, then three months passed. Three times I had a woman's period in secret. Snow dusted, then larded the earth in white mourning. It was a time of little hope, yet I hoped, waited – and feared.

"Brynhild." Thora's voice woke me at its first whisper. Her breath formed an eerie aura about her face in the single rush light she shielded heavily with her hand. "Get dressed. Quietly. Yes, now. Yes, every-thing. Everything."

The emphasis in her last word made me stop and stuff some of the rags I'd gathered for my menses into my boots for extra warmth. She said nothing at this but nodded slightly, indicating that I had the right idea. So I took off everything and started again, layering my changes of clothes until I had on all the community considered mine: linen trousers under doeskin, linen shirt under jerkin.

"Dagger. Flint. Tinder bag."

I strapped these on my belt.

She nodded that I'd done well and that I should follow her. We made our way to the little porch that leaned beside the compound gate. Together we looked out through a crack in the doors. We could use our normal voices now, but the awe of a new falling of snow in its last dusting urged against it.

"You know that a nun of Odin is more man than woman. This is our calling, this is our pride. So when she becomes a woman, a nun of Odin must demonstrate that she turns her back on womanhood and embraces the male. This deep and awful struggle few, very few, succeed in, turning one sex into the other. If you succeed, you win a hero's victory. The door to Valhalla stands open to you. You earn the right to a sword and the right to fill the vacancy and become one of the twelve. She who succeeds becomes Valkyrie. She rides with us throughout the battlefields of the world, with power to choose, under All-Father's wisdom, who will live and who will die. She chooses who of the slain will enter the glory of life ever after among the heroes. This power turns wars."

"What must I do?"

"Leave this place."

"Leave?" The word was an icicle in my mouth.

"For two weeks, now, in the dead of winter. Each nun of Odin, upon attaining womanhood, must face the world alone, as a man does. Without warning, without time for preparation, without friend or instruction, she must prove herself victorious over death and Hoder, the winter god and his giants of the hoar frost."

"You did this?" I asked in awe.

"Yes," said Thora. She rubbed the fox cuff on her wrist and shuddered as if chilled by the memory.

"How?"

She was silent for a time, looking at me. "I may not tell you, even if I knew, which I am not certain I do. Why me, and not ... not another?"

This speech, I could tell, was her first departure from what had, until then, been rote. She fell into rote again. "Some girls find that the trial, the physical demands and the hunger, makes them men indeed, that they never bleed again, or not for several years. After the next two weeks, you are free to return to us at any time – provided you remember the way."

That last phrase rang of another departure from rote. I gave myself silent but desperate instruction to always know where I was.

"But do not return before the two weeks – exactly two weeks, not an hour too soon–"

Another hint – keep track of the time. It must be easy to forget in some snow-blind, lonely madness.

"If you do return before the two weeks, well and good. You shall live. But you shall don the dress you came in, go home to your valley between the Bears, and never sit among us again. If you do not return to Valhalla – well, then, you do not return. You were never one of us. Let me also warn you against seeking solace among common mortals. Yes, there are mortals. Three summer days' trek from here. But be warned, All-Father and his ravens will know, and if you enter their homes, you must stay there. If you try to return, having spent time with mortals, you will not get your dress back. You will be killed."

The speech she had to deliver was over.

"Have ... have other girls gone out already this year?" I asked, although there was really nothing left to say. I was playing for time.

"Yes," she said.

"But none have returned."

She didn't answer. I remembered the few benches, suddenly and mysteriously emptied, and I knew.

"I tried to help," she said finally. "I managed to get you a night with a full moon, but as you see–" She shrugged toward the overcast world that was all the color of old grey ice until it vanished into blackness. "The Gods know best."

Something in her voice was strong enough to turn me from my own abyss to her. *The Valkyrie is not a woman*, her face told me in silence. *It is not all glory we gain with this renunciation – if we gain it.*

Girls like you are the closest thing we come to having children. And this is how we lose you, at least one of our particular wards a year, thus...

"The Gods know best," I echoed her.

Impulsively, she embraced me. "Now go," she said. "You must be gone before the watch comes back."

I took two steps beyond the threshold into snow up to my knees and heard the gate shut and lock solidly behind me.

Other girls had come this way? The new-fallen snow betrayed no trace of their passing.

I felt shut in on myself like a twig frozen in a block of ice. The silence and snow were like wool stuffed in my ears. My hands in their mittens and my feet in their boots, swaddled by the tokens of my femininity in a male world, felt their loneliness, too. As if they would never feel anything else, ever again.

I must go somewhere, I thought for the twentieth time. *But where?* Finally I formed something of an answer: it would never do to be found standing here in the morning. That was the most definite answer I could muster, but it was enough to set me off across the empty expanse of grey-white of our training yard.

The journey was much greater than it looked, certainly a greater journey than it was when soil lay underfoot and the shouts and laughter of companions urged one on her way. With every step, the effort of pulling myself up and over a bank of powdery, almost substanceless snow exhausted me. It snowed so much more in this part of the world than ever in my homeland, Anglia. But that was not my home now. Nor was Valhalla. I had no home. Or perhaps the whole world was now my home.

I shook off those circular thoughts as I finally reached the edge of the woods, but there I had to stop and rest. My heartbeat and panting echoed with a deafening sound off the walls of my icy isolation. Water drenched my body, but not from the outside. Tallow waterproofed our winter trousers and buskins, but it would only be a matter of time before that gave out. I was wet from the inside from my own sweat. Myself, trapped within myself. Is that what it meant to be a man? Or only a woman pretending to be a man?

The unspoken regret on Thora's face as she talked of leaving womanhood behind sent a shiver through the slick of sweat between my shoulder blades. I looked back to the compound, half hoping I might catch another glimpse of her, or at least find myself still dreaming on my little bench where I would soon wake...

Looking back confirmed several things to me. First, I had not gone nearly far enough before dawn. Not nearly far enough before Odin's ravens began to fly. Second, the clouds were clearing off. The full moon Thora had hoped for sat low in the sky over the compound. I sent silent thanks back to my guardian. But if I didn't hasten, no thank-you would ever reach her.

A man. Think now like a man, not a woman, I instructed myself. And then for some reason I remembered one man in particular, my uncle Erik, cutting out a peat shovel against all tradition. Was I already losing touch with reality? No, for then I remembered Uncle Erik making snowshoes from bent willow wands. I could hear his voice reciting the story of the god Ull, how he crossed the seas on a magic bone, and the goddess Skaði, she who is called Snowshoe Goddess or the Goddess on Skis. The path of the story told Uncle Erik how to twist the wands and fasten them to make the shoes. The Valkyries would not know this trick. Since battlefields closed down in winter, so did most of their activities.

Willow, that would be by a stream. I had also not garnered this knowledge in the compound where harder woods, yew for bows and hickory for shields, were of more concern.

I knew the stream where we fetched our water flowed a quarter of the way around the training field to the right. I would need water to drink, even if I did not immediately find willow. It also occurred to me that heading straight out the gate and to one's fate was the obvious way to go. Most of the girls would have taken the obvious path – and had failed. Any way was better than the obvious, well-traveled way.

And it occurred to me as I set off, struggling one foot after the other, up and down, up and down, that if I stuck to the stream, I wouldn't lose track of the compound when, in two weeks' time...

Two weeks. Yes, I could survive two weeks.

chapter 6

ERHAPS I COULD NOT SURVIVE, but it did seem possible for five or six steps. After that, two weeks seemed impossible again. The immediacy and isolation of my situation caught me, with only my feet and my lungs to speak encouragement.

I reached the stream but realized how much snow covered every sign of life when I found the slope I'd used as a younger girl to fetch the compound's water. I used that slope to go down and get a drink for myself and found the bank at shoulder level. This angle gave me a glimpse of an interesting tree that the stream seemed to be swallowing just at its bend. I climbed back up on the bank and found that it was indeed a willow.

I took out my dagger and cut likely whips of twig, two big solid ones as divine Ull did at the beginning of the myth, and ten smaller, more flexible wands. By sunup, I had a pair of shoes, not as elegant as Uncle Erik's, but I could lash them to my feet with a bit of bow string left in my pouch from my last practice.

No, say not last. Most recent. There would be others. Soon. In two weeks...

But I had been standing a long time at the work, and it had taken its toll on my physical well-being. I ate a few handfuls of snow for my thirst; hunger could be put off by sheer will. The need to urinate, however, could not.

If I were a man, I thought bitterly, *I would not have to bare my whole backside to this inhuman cold.* But I had no choice and dropped every layer from my waist.

When I finished, a strange sorrow filled me. What a shame to leave that melted stain on the pristine snow. Sorrow was but a faint reflection of deeper, all-consuming horror. I had had to take off my gloves for all of this, and I was now chilled to the bone. Yes, I still had my flint and kindling, but where would I put them to use? No dry wood could be seen.

I strapped on my snowshoes with a quick word of thanks to Ull – a Vanir Earth God, whose name was never mentioned in Odin's compound – and walked. That and the rising sun took care of the chill within an hour.

I failed to keep strictly to the stream as I had hoped. The tall banks of snow were unsteady in spots, and I couldn't risk a tumble down them into the stream. In other spots, trees hindered my advance. So I worked my way in the general direction of the stream's flow, its sound sharp and clear in the dead world.

But the world was not quite dead. I began to notice the tracks of other creatures that had passed before me. Some were too small to be anything but those of a mouse. And here, long oar-like feet doubtless indicated a rabbit. One could eat rabbits, but how to catch them? Valkyries hunted men, not other species. This was not a test of skills we had learned, I realized. If we had been trained as hunters and woodsmen, it would make sense as a test. But this was not a test. We were trained for the battlefield and this ... this was ritual sacrifice.

I shook my head at the memory this word conjured. *The Bog...*

The prints of birds cross-hatched the snow, not big enough to be those of ravens. I studied the sky. A raven hung there, flying too high for me to hear his call. I was being watched – not with sympathy, but a dispassionate, patient circling, just waiting for me to–

I had the feeling that the snow-capped and whispering pines formed a kindred of gnomes grown huge, frozen under an evil spell, watching me too, like the raven. The trees that lost their foliage were a kindred reduced to whitened bones that would utter no surprise at all to have another soul join their ranks.

Another mouse track. One could eat mice as well as rabbits, if one got hungry enough. I told myself this with detachment, as if for future reference. I'd stopped feeling hungry. Too much fear crammed my chest to leave room for hunger. At the moment I was just ... just looking. Sort of like the raven above me. But I didn't know what I was looking for, only to keep the blood circulating and the heart pumping.

All these creatures, these creatures who left their prints but no other trace as they came to the stream and returned to their homes, they belonged here. I didn't.

In Uncle Erik's great shoes, though, walking was now, in moments of forgetfulness, a pleasure as the sun rose and glanced brilliantly off the world of snow.

I am learning to survive in a place where I don't belong. The battlefield, the man's world.

How could I capture these little things that left their tracks, if I couldn't even see them? How could I command on the battlefield if I didn't make myself belong?

By midafternoon, I had come so far and was so tired that I could not go another step. I cut a few branches from a pine to rest on, set another few into a south-facing bank as a roof of sorts, then lay down in the pleasant but thin winter sun to rest – just for a moment.

When I awoke, it was pitch-dark. Fortunately, the moon had begun to rise, but the clear sky honed the night air so it cut like knives. I was colder than I had ever been in my life, and I doubted that I could move. Some of the snow of the bank had melted onto my roof, and my roof onto me. I found the branches clung to me when I stood up, attached by water turned to ice. As soon as I began to move, I was taken by a chill that shook me violently and uncontrollably in waves a second or two apart. It chattered my teeth so that I had to stumble dangerously close to the stream in the darkness before I could hear it over the noise in my own head. I had to force myself to walk, and walking was all I could think of to do, walking and sobbing with chill-choked sobs. *Like a woman.*

To walk at night, another whole night, was madness. Progress was at its worst, and my fears grew to overwhelming size. The pine gnomes seemed more capable of breaking their icy spell at night, especially when a breeze blew. But I knew no other way to keep warm; I had made no other plan.

At first light I will build a shelter, I promised myself.

You should have done it yesterday, myself objected.

I will find a shelter.

You had all day yesterday. At first light—

It's doubtful you'll make it to first light.

Somehow I did. First light came as a warning red. Red at this time of year, my mother always used to say, meant the Goddesses in Heaven's hall were busy about their ovens with their Yuletide baking. At home, Mother and Yule—

I must not think of such things, I told myself firmly. A Valkyrie did not think of such things. In my present case, such things were death.

By that first light, I made a more pragmatic discovery, an easy slope down to the stream. But here the stream had grown much narrower. I had to crack a thin sheet of ice to reach the sluggish water.

The light also revealed a set of very different prints than those of rabbits and mice I'd seen before. I counted the claws. I could not hope to match the prints, they were so much larger than mine. *An ogre. A wood giant.* I had come so far from humanity.

My first few attempts to get back up the bank collapsed in brittle heaps of chill and exhaustion. I didn't know whether I should bother to rise from such failures. I did, at last. But then, when I reached the top, I discovered what my predawn stumbling had been suggesting for some time: the terrain was rising, becoming steeper and more treacherous. Indeed, not fifty paces more, I saw a cliff. I could not climb that today. I'd hardly been able to climb the river bank. I could go no farther.

Then, the rays of the sun pressed higher and struck one section of the cliff.

Only that was needed to send a large clump of snow tumbling to bash itself to pieces and powder nearly at my feet. My eyes did not follow it, however. The sudden change in light and cliff shape caused by the fall revealed a darkness in the unrelieved white world.

A cave.

I was crying like a woman again. I slipped and shook and chattered my way up with the help of the branches of two nearly buried trees that grew over the face of the cliff. I reached the ledge at last and half crawled, half stumbled into the dark. Wondrously, I felt warmer instead of colder as night seemed to return. *Warmth!* It was so inviting, I moved instinctively towards it at the back of the cave. The rich scent of autumn leaves lingered here instead of the sterility of winter. The dark smelled like hunters returned in their wet furs with laughter and welcoming.

Then I touched fur and heard a low growl.

My reflexes were the result of long training, but how they managed to fling off my exhaustion, I'll never know. I leaped back, grabbed an exposed root that hung over the cave mouth, and swung myself up onto a stone ledge above the opening. The next instant, the great brown head and back of a bear emerged a hand's breath below me. Winter sleep dulled its wits, but being so rudely awakened did not improve its temper.

Again, my battle reflexes responded instantly, and I found my dagger sunk to the hilt in the bruin's back. The blade had gone true between the shoulder bones, and the gore that it released on the brown fur was like dawn rising in front of me. But the bear was fattened for the winter, and my knife seemed to have no other immediate effect besides the blood and making the creature angrier than ever. It whirled around and stood to face me. Its jaws, ribbed with saliva-laced yellow- ing teeth and reeking of a meat diet, gaped just where my feet would have been on the ledge above the mouth of the cave, had I not moved them instinctively just the moment before.

Then, as the beast swung around, I discovered that my dagger did not readily slip out of its back. I was not going to let go of my dagger, not for the world, and so I followed it down off the ledge to a point where it loosed. I finally dropped at the mouth of the cave. Behind me yawned the unknown blackness of cave and, in front, the bear's belly close enough to touch, blocking off any other escape.

I could touch the bear, and its long arms had no trouble finding me. I felt my face pressed into the fur like a mother's embrace, but the jerkin at my back was being razored through all layers of padding. Claws found my bare skin.

My dagger, however, had loosed itself. It caught the bruin under the chin in a second stab. I felt the instant the tip of the blade stopped fighting the toughness inside the skull and reached the softness of brain. And suddenly I was falling backwards into the cave under a monstrous but truly dead weight.

I lay with the bear on top of me. Its blood seeped into every seam of my clothes, into my hair, about my numb ears and fingers, into my eyes. It felt deliciously warm. I doubted whether I could move the corpse off me. If I'd been exhausted before, the fight had truly taken the last from me. But I had little difficulty in drawing my blade further down the belly, letting out more of the wonderful liquid, slipping my frigid body into those folds of warmth. I was asleep before another thought passed my mind.

I awoke with a rapidly chilling bear carcass on top of me. But when I did awake, I had strength enough to shove off that part of the carcass on me with no trouble. Next came a quick trip out into the fading light to strip the lowest branches off the two pine trees that guarded the entrance of the cave. I also took the exposed roots from my earthen roof and another couple of logs that were only half buried on the southern face of the cliff. *My cliff,* I was already calling it.

I was willing to coax wet and green wood into a fire if I had a dry floor to begin with and lots of dry kindling, which I did. The bear had dragged a huge mound of sticks and leaves into its home for its winter bed.

I quickly learned the important lesson that a man takes what he needs from the labor of others.

By the time of full darkness, I had a fire roaring quite merrily. It filled the mouth of the cave with me, safe on the dry side of it. Then I set about skinning and butchering my kill.

I set to work on the skin at once as a replacement for my torn jerkin. It was a magnificent trophy. My hand sank deep into the creature's winter fur, yet it had not been in the den long enough to wear spots bald as spring-killed skins tend to show. My skinning skills weren't equal to the glory of what a bear grows naturally. I hadn't the patience to skin out the paws and all the little crevices around the head. But as I worked my way to the end of the creature's limbs, I found myself fascinated by its claws. In the terror of the moment, I had only barely felt them enter my back, but there they lay with my blood on them. I cut them off and threaded them on a sinew. Then with a wild laugh, I yanked off my Odin collar and tossed it from me. In its place, I tied the claws about my neck as a new necklace.

I am surely going mad, I thought.

Then I remembered that all the Valkyries wore some personal and unexplained talisman. Thora's was her fox-skin cuffs. I would have my claws. This set me to trying to find the torc again, but I discovered in my exhilaration I had tossed it out into the night beyond the fire. I would look for it in the morning.

Simply moving the bruin from side to side, though not complicated, was hard going as I worked up from the tail and hind quarters, even with the help of a sturdy branch as a lever. When the branch broke, I fed it to the fire and satisfied myself with three-quarters of a skin instead. That was heavy and warm enough.

Then I set to gutting the beast, running my dagger first from throat to anus, hoping there was still time to let it cool fast enough so the meat would not become too strongly flavored. I did it like the hog killings I remembered as a child. As wintertime approached, in good years, squeals would fill the village for a week or more as the victims protested first their foodless confinement, then the death blow to the throat. We'd work our way from yard to yard, everyone helping with each kill, the buckets of steaming water – and steaming entrails as the men brought the entire insides down in a cascade from the upside-down and spread-eagle carcasses. I had no one to help me get this kill into that position where the pull of the earth could ease the business. I did the best I could with the bear on its side.

Remembering with longing the carefully cured blends, rich with salt and sage and rosemary, that would stuff intestines at home, I took the plain liver first. It wobbled raw in my two hands. One tentative nibble was enough to begin. After that, I fell upon it and ate ravenously. The heart or liver of a fresh kill, they say, can give one an understanding of the tongue of birds and animals. But either it was the wrong time of day or I was too hungry to listen, because I gained no such skill.

I continued my work, discovering the bear was a she. I cut into the womb and found two perfectly formed little cubs, their bodies still warm as she had fought to keep them. They were as blind and naked as mice, no bigger than my feet, and caught in a white membrane. They would have been born within the month. My brother and sister they were, for had we not shared the body of one mother, gaining life from her? I found myself weeping over those two little bodies for a very long time. I swore to bury them in the morning, no matter how much snow I had to move with their mother's shoulder blade to accomplish it, no matter how frozen the ground.

Some time passed before I could bring myself to continue the butchering, hacking the body into manageable quarters to do so. Even longer passed before I could bring myself to take more of the nourishment I desperately needed. I filled the last corners of my hunger with bits of flesh that I had time to roast deliciously on the fire.

Meanwhile, I also heated some of the fat in the curve of a shoulder bone and spread it as a salve on my wounds. It came out a pure white and cooled very hard with a surprising pleasant odor. My mother used to say bear lard was the best for pastry, but I think she knew that only from hearsay. Having no flour myself to cut it into, I, too, would never know.

The rest of the beast I cut into ham-size pieces, tying some with bear sinews outside in the branches of my pine trees to freeze and keep better. The bear provided enough, so I figured I could risk losing some to predators. In the trees it was out of reach of wolves, and if ravens chanced to come – let them help themselves. They would send a report of my triumph back to Valhalla. Anyway, what I kept inside would not be too rotten at the end of two weeks.

Finally, I turned to the cubs again. I wept a little more, with relief at my success, with sorrow at its cost. Then I laid the two little bodies carefully next to their dismembered mother and, warm and full at last, I tried to sleep. I found I could not for the longest time.

Finally, I rolled over onto my dagger, still sticky with its day's chores, and worked the smooth wooden handle hard between my thighs to release the tension. We were all taught to do this. A nun of Odin, of course, never gets other satisfaction. With my knees spread, one pressed to the wall, the other almost to the fire, my head arched back, but my breast pressing against air, missing the embrace of the bear, I gave a long, lonely cry of having arrived. But was it the cry of triumph or of defeat?

Two weeks had come and gone. I had not consciously been keeping a record, no notches in a stick or such. But the unfailing time-keeper within me said it must be so. The two weeks had failed to take the woman out of me, and I came to my woman's time again while I was there, bleeding onto the floor of the cave, my blood joining that of the bear because I'd used most of the rags from my boots to salvage the fire the time or two I'd nearly let it go out.

I could return. I was a Valkyrie now. Except that, although I'd managed to bury the cubs under a stone on bare ground and although I'd marched most of the snow away from anywhere near the cave, I'd never found the torc I'd tossed away. I didn't suppose that would matter too awfully much, as long as I came back alive.

Still, I didn't leave. *Another day*, I told myself.

I had learned to mistrust inklings in battle training, and I remembered Thora warning that returning even one hour too early would mean failure. Then, too, for several days now, a deep fog had enveloped my cave. Going out into its moistness was like breathing water.

I found it difficult to tell when day ended and night began, and I also had to take into account that it was now the dark of the moon. What irony that would be, to have survived two weeks only to lose my way at the end and perish in fog and moon darkness.

There was something else about the fog. I woke from a daydream and was able to give it a name. The fog, half concealing, half revealing the tree world around me, reminded me of nothing so much as of the membrane that had surrounded the two bear cubs. By this foggy membrane of a great she-bear, I was protected in a womb of a cave. I touched my bear claw necklace, enjoying it better than the torc I'd worn for seven years until I'd tossed it away, not to be found again. I was loath to leave the protection of that membrane, loath to leave what I had become on my own. So I fed my fire for another night and waited.

The next morning dawned to reveal that the fog had risen only to the tops of the near mountains but at least enough to tell that it was dawn. Wisdom said I must not put off my departure any longer. Who knew when a blizzard might blow in or the fog return? My store of meat grew more decidedly off every day, making the first breath I took every time I returned to the cave nearly enough to bring back up what I had eaten. I could not say I would ever find anything else to kill.

So I slipped a last cooked bear steak into my jerkin and buried the rest of my cave companion right where she lay. Then I laced her skin to my back. Doing so, I noticed for the first time – now that I considered seeing other people again – how rank it smelled and how, for want of curing, the beautiful hair was falling off in patches. I strapped a new improved pair of Uncle Erik's snowshoes to my feet. The first had been shattered in the battle with the bear and had been unraveling seriously before that anyway. I filled my kindling pouch with the last of the bear's bed and kicked out my fire. With a final and unsuccessful look for the torc and a sigh, I began my descent from my cliff.

The lift in the weather only lasted the morning. By midafternoon, the rags of fog stuck to the tops of the trees again. In an hour, they had wound even lower as I descended all the while, too. Yet, by then, I had long reached the point where the stream was unmuffled by a crust of ice. I had been moving with such confidence and ease downwards that

I had become certain, by various landmarks I descried, that I could reach the compound not long after nightfall.

The question became, *Is this what I want to do?* The closer I came to Valhalla, the more I began to doubt my certainty to move forward. *Perhaps I am too early. How could my trial be over so soon, so easily?* It didn't seem fair, somehow, that I had succeeded where so many others had failed.

Then I stopped dead in my tracks. There, up ahead, I heard the caw of one of Odin's messengers. Was it a warning? Should I stop where I was and spend another night? I had to confess that the prospect, without my bear and her cave, was not welcoming. Even to stop moving for a moment brought the leaden cold curling into my limbs like the fog around the trees. To escape that cold, I took another step or two forward.

Out of the fog came another scream, then a sudden whipping of black. One of Odin's messengers materialized out of the world of spirits and landed some score of feet ahead of me. I took another step or two in the bird's direction. Then I saw what had attracted him. It was the body of one of the girls in training to be a nun of Odin. Friagabi. We were a good match at sword play. She had been asleep quietly on her bench when I left the hall.

Friagabi was dead, but only just barely. A light dusting of fog crystals had begun to drop, coating her with a white membrane that fell with a faint but definite sound. Through this, the raven and his mate were obliged to peck. I recalled the death of Uddrun. Friagabi was about the same age as Uddrun had been when she'd given her life in place of mine at the Thaw Gruel. The memory stung, although it seemed more like a dream – nightmare – that had happened long ago in another lifetime. If only to tear myself away from the sight, I followed Friagabi's footsteps for some distance, enough to discover that she had been walking in circles in the fog, without snow shoes. More I didn't follow, lest my own way become confused. And I would not be confused anymore.

The raven looked up from his grisly chore and cocked his head at me as I trudged past. The eye of Odin glinted in his black eye,

All-Father's cauldron of Fate. "Well, have your way then," he seemed to say. "Survive, cheat me, go back."

Was the bear's liver working on my ears in some belated fashion? Or was I only coming to a deeper understanding of the ways of these merciless birds? I tried not to listen, but I couldn't help it.

"You will not escape me forever," I was sure he'd said. "Someday everyone, even the Gods, become scavenger food."

As fast as I could, I escaped out of earshot.

Night fell, and I said to myself over and over, *I should have reached the clearing by now.* I couldn't see the hand in front of my face. I worked the icy way before me with an oaken walking stick. I could still hear the stream, but would I recognize where the footpath from the compound came down to the invisible bank? *Perhaps I should stop. Perhaps I was already overshooting my goal. No, if I stop, I will freeze to death.*

Just then, I saw a smear of light as if through a bit of greasy parchment. It vanished just as quickly, but when I stopped and strained in that direction, I knew I heard voices. Girls' voices, high and quick, laughing, half with excitement, half with near terror.

"Whatever can Thora have been thinking to send us out for water on a night like this?"

"Surely it could wait for morning."

"She did this last night, too, you know. With those Anglian girls, Bede and Fimmilene."

"Maybe Thora's going crazy."

"Here it is, girls. I think I've found the way down to the stream."

I can imagine what blinding horror went through their minds when I stumbled up to them out of the fog in bear skin and monstrous feet, two weeks steeped in a she-bear's gore. I should have called and given warning, but I was focused on moving my feet in their direction so I wouldn't lose them. I hastened to make good my oversight by giving the "Welcome, have no fear, I am one of you" call at once, for two of them were screaming and stumbling over one another in an attempt to flee. They put out their single light in the process. Only one had the Valkyrie courage to turn and face me with her dagger drawn, but she didn't seem at all happy about the prospect. *Ah, it is the very youngest recruits who are sent for water.* I certainly hoped they would learn much and quickly, or they would never survive to be on my side of a return.

"Have no fear," I said. "It is I, Brynhild."

"Brynhild? Brynhild? Brynhild's dead."

"Maybe Brynhild's ghost?"

I gave the call again and heard it repeated from the unseen watchtowers of the compound.

"Fill your leathern buckets, girls," I said. "Let's go home."

They skirted furtively around me, saying nothing, not even to each other. Suddenly we heard the swish of hoof beats through the snow and a high, long call. I answered it.

"Thora!"

"Brynhild?"

"Yes, it's I."

"You've returned. You made it!"

"Yes."

The hoof beats were upon me, and suddenly I felt myself swept up into Thora's saddle on the run, as a hero is from the field of battle. She drove her horse in a wide circuit of the field before the compound, we two making a chorus of our cries. Then, in triumph, was I carried into the Hall of the Slain.

chapter 7

CAUGHT A GLIMPSE OF a great wolf skin stretched above the doorway as we rode into the hall, and then all was pitch dark. And cold. In spite of Thora's body behind me and the horse's below, the sudden chill which caught hold of me was worse, or so I thought, than any I had endured until then.

Thora helped me dismount and, feeling my shivers, she kept an arm about me as she eased me deeper and deeper into the heart of the darkness. At length, we reached a point where she stopped and indicated by a squeeze of my shoulder that I must be still.

A strange whirring sound filled the air, increasing my panic. And then a smell. I couldn't place the smell, but it overwhelmed me and seemed to carry a panicky whirl of waiting all its own.

Was it only my imagination? Or was that a sudden spark of light? I strained toward it. Another spark appeared and caught on a nest of kindling, then to a small heap of logs and ash below. The flame leapt up and illuminated the one-eyed, icicle-bearded face of Odin. I hadn't been in the god's presence since I was a child. The curl of flame showed his cloak the blue-black of the winter night sky. And, like the flame, my heart leapt with the half terror, half thrill of awe.

I could see that I had grown since I'd last seen him. Or he had shrunk. I could look into his one eye – and the empty socket of the other – dead on. He did not otherwise seem perceptibly older, God that he was.

The God paid no notice to me at first. And then between his hands I saw the fire wheel drill, the sacred Yule from which each year New Fire is spun in the halls of the Aesir and their devotees on the most holy night, the darkest night of the year. All fires throughout the world had lain extinguished on this day. And now, at midnight, the wheel in the hands of high priests magicked new light into life on the heart and ashes of the previous year's Yule Log. The year would turn, and the days grow longer as life and light returned to the earth.

Then I knew that by no coincidence I had returned on New Fire Night, Mother Night as it is called, the first night of the Yule Watch, those Twelve Nights of Smoke necessary to keep evil at bay. And the knowledge that in this, Valhalla was no different than any other hall seemed somehow to confuse the value of my own acceptance there. I have often wondered if I had returned on any other night whether my future might have been different, more straight and single-minded.

I struggled to make myself realize that here I stood, where no mortal but the immortalized had ever been, that the dream of a lifetime was here and now.

No actual heroes sat with us. They had died on the battlefield like any other. Valkyries may have carried them away, but the maids simply buried the corpses out of the sight of men. Here in Valhalla, only the shields and arms of the fallen lined the walls.

Those men died for a lie.

I could not think like this. Men needed encouragement to live against horrible odds. Instead, I had to thicken my thoughts with the others, willing the Vanir to arc back into spring.

As soon as we were assured that the fire would take, we drew torchlight from it, enough to light the way for thirteen white horses to be driven in. Among them, the steeds pulled the new Log, a great oak lacking its branches but draped instead in sacred evergreens and holly. And when it had caught fire, Hlokk went out with light for the rest of the compound where the girls waited, huddled in darkness, hardly daring to whisper until the light came.

A great sigh of relief rose from the hollow of the hall. We would have fire for another year.

Hlokk returned, and now I could see that, besides All-Father, every Valkyrie sat there in her holiday best. There were eleven of them – twelve now, counting me.

"Now that the turning-time is past," said Thora, "we can set to work on you."

I noted the regret in her voice. Was it because of the detraction, as a mother might speak sorrow to her daughter whose wedding day had been spoiled, and she now promised to make it good? It could not be regret that I was to become a Valkyrie, could it?

"I'll take that," said Göll, at the forefront of the warmaids crowding around me.

She removed the bear skin from my shoulders, which made me realize again just how fiercely it had begun to stink.

Those who crowded at my back now couldn't help drawing in their breaths. By firelight, they examined the claw marks in my jerkin and the wounds slowly scarring.

"Well," Thora said, nodding in wonder, "I see now you'll want to keep the skin. Göll will tan it nicely for you."

Everything else came off then. The snowshoes – which called for comment of their own and were passed around the company – boots, trousers, jerkin, until I stood naked before the fire and the one-eyed gaze of Odin. I hugged my arms about my nakedness.

Is this what a bride feels, I wondered, *in the eyes of her bridegroom?* I knew there shouldn't have been any, but supreme male power aimed at me gave the spirituality a tinge of the sexual – all I would ever know of human love.

Then Thora reached for my necklace of bear claws, and I forgot all about my nakedness. With an animal noise, I shoved her hands away.

Thora took a quick glance up at Odin and then said, "Yes, you must keep your claws. They will give you a power. I can't explain it more than that. You will come to understand it. I have my fox fur, you see. But Brynhild," and her voice suddenly dropped, "what have you done with your torc?"

I felt through the claws to my bare neck defensively, but I dared not raise my eyes to All-Father's single one. I froze and said nothing.

"Never mind," Thora said quickly. Perhaps she'd received another message from that single all-seeing eye. "We have another for you."

The Log had warmed some water now, and Thora began to bathe me in it tenderly, like a mother bathes an infant, from the top of my head to my feet. The warmth and moisture brought to life the dried blood. The smell of dead bear permeated the air. And then that too washed away. My skin grew warm, whole and glowing. Thora toweled me dry with a linen cloth. Still, I saw no clothes forthcoming.

Then Odin rose to his great height. One of the Valkyries presented him with a cobalt vase. He pulled out the diamond-shaped stopper, and a strange odor filled the room, the honey smell of angelica, the bite of birch. He approached me with measured steps, chanting a string of strange runes under his breath.

> She with a sigh may shiver shackles,
> Or heat the Hel-bound's hauberk
> 'Til the chest be charred off the unchary,
> 'Til the willful have no wish but Woden's...

More of his words I either didn't hear or didn't comprehend. They resonated like words whispered into a cave.

"Odin's ointment," Thora murmured to me as the god proceeded to anoint every joint of my body with the thick yellow-green cream. Every joint had a rune of its own, but the words were ancient and unintelligible. He anointed my head as well, and the stuff trickled down behind my ears and onto my neck.

"The ointment is full of magic." I hardly needed Thora's word to tell me that. "It will make you invulnerable on the battlefield and will strengthen every joint. Let it firm your heart as iron to always do All-Father's will. Then you are a Valkyrie."

Odin carefully recapped the vase and set it down. Then he drew a new torc out of his cloak. I knelt and, with a sharp twist, he slipped it on over the ointment slithering down my neck. There the braided gold knocked among the bear claws and seemed to take a very long time to gain my body heat.

"Behold, a new heroine of Odin," the god announced without pomp or poetry, making it more real.

Now came the Valkyries' turn. They circled around me, and each presented me with a gift.

"Welcome, Brynhild. I, Valfreya, present you with this linen dress to wear in the Great Hall, with these heavy golden armbands."

"Welcome, dear battlemaid," said Raðgriðr, pinning the dress up at the shoulders with two golden brooches.

Some poor woman, condemned never to be among our holy band, had put her all into this linen and then offered it to the God. I wondered briefly, as I smoothed her handiwork down with pride, whether her prayers had been answered as fully as mine.

"And these riding boots and leather trousers for the field as well," said Skeggjöld.

"Welcome, Chooser of the Slain. I, Göll, present you with this tooled saddle." Göll, always so playful on the training field, winked.

"Welcome, sister," said Hilda as she led forth a white horse from among the thirteen that had earlier dragged in the Log. "Gotten from Sleipnir. His name is Faxi."

"The Maned One," I repeated, touching the silken hair that glowed in the firelight, thick and shaggy for winter protection.

I had long since learned that Valkyries rode geldings, as only such transformed beasts had the temperament to hold consistently steady in the presence of other horses, particularly mares, or in the heat of battle. He, like the rest of Sleipnir's children, but very few of common horsekind, could take not only the four regular paces, but also *tölt*, the magical running-walk where the rider's head remains level, much easier on both horse and rider for long distances at a brisk speed.

The horse breathed a greeting on my hand.

"Thank you," I told my sister. "We will be good friends."

"Welcome," said Thora, smiling as she slipped a leather knee-length jerkin sewn with metal disks – disks as yet unembossed with the arms of any fallen hero, over my head – and laced it up over the linen dress. "A brynie for Brynie."

Then came Thruðr with a good, strong, stiff yet flexible yew bow, a spare, and a quiver full of arrows. Thruðr was sometimes sharp and unkind as archery mistress; under her short-tempered eye, small failings could swell to hopeless clumsiness. Although it had never been popular to say so among the girls, archery had always been my favorite. With this bow, I felt confident I could hit objects even beyond my sight. And I could see from the melting in Thruðr's eyes that, for her, this was an offering of peace and sisterhood. She was thrilled at how I had rewarded her impatience.

Four Valkyries remained: Eir had the shield embossed with the raven design, Geirönul a sheaf of spears, Reginleif the feathered helm. Last but not least, Hlokk, the broad-shouldered smith, approached. Held straight out on her palms lay a sword, the sword of a Valkyrie. Like all of Hlokk's swords, the edges were hammered and honed until they could split a falling leaf. Each sword of her making entered the flame two hundred and forty times. Formed of bars of iron twisted round one another again and again, the blade held a pattern that seemed by the firelight to breathe life.

A touch from Thora told me to reach toward the splendid blade and take it in my hands. It was mine. I knew I had earned it, yet I hesitated at the wonder of it. Another touch, and I had the courage to take it by the hilt as my own possession and try it against the air. It was a masterful thing, perfectly weighted towards the tip for the slash and parry. And in the firelight, the patterning of the blade swam like a fish.

"What name will you give your sword?" asked Hlokk. "Every sword must have a name."

Where before I had been stupefied with wonder, now with a sword in my hand I found my tongue. "Fish-Scale is its name," I said.

"Fish-Scale," repeated the maids approvingly.

Now, once again, Odin left his place in the high seat. Valfreya brought him a bowl. In spite of the gold work and jeweled encrustation, I could see that the bowl was fashioned of a skull. It was the skull of Mimir the Vanir, whom Odin had defeated as he rose to power and from whom he had captured the secret runes of wisdom. Over this trophy the god waved his hand and swore a chant.

> Above this bowl, I bind my word
> To fight, to fend the fame
> Of this Hall to the hithermost
> Limit of my limbs and life.

He drank, and the bowl passed then from Valkyrie to Valkyrie. Each swore with similar words and drank the honeyed mead from the very teats of the divine goat Heiðrun.

I took the grizzly vessel into my hands and was surprised at its lightness despite all the attempts to weight it with goldsmith's work. Inadvertently I let my little finger slip off the cranium into an eye socket. My shoulders and the pit of my stomach felt cold fingers of both horror and awe at once. My throat tightened as I brought the bowl to my face. For all the feel of gold and the taste of sweet, strong, divine mead, I smelled the mold of death.

Finally, when I, too, had sworn, All-Father said, "Be welcome, brynie-wearer."

And there we stood, thirteen, a coven. "Welcome, Brynhild!" my sister Valkyries cried. And then, "Welcome, Yule!"

For Yule it was. The Yule Log blazed fiercely now, and the leaping flames drew my glance way up to the rafters. Shields of fallen heroes lined the inside of Valhalla like the outside, and bundles of their lances and spears formed the beams. For the holiday, the ancient beams and joists were twined with new greenery; the mistletoe with the power to make men throw down their arms and embrace as brothers, the pine boughs and holly holding green within while the rest of the world was frozen white.

Now I knew what scent had greeted me on my arrival. It was the scent of pine sap, and as it entered my nostrils anew, I felt a sudden pang for home. We had always welcomed Yule by forcing green from dead-seeming twigs set among red hawthorn berries. I drowned the thought quickly. I was at home in Valhalla now.

And as the fresh new garlands of Yule entwined the weapons of the ancient fallen heroes, so the rites of the feast entwined my entry into Valhalla, so the rites of the Vanir entwined those of the Aesir. A great boar had been sacrificed to honor the Vanir god Frey. When the flesh had finished roasting, it was served up with a crabapple between its tusks, and bay and rosemary about its trotters. We passed it around the benches, and each of us attacked it with our knife. Yule carp came as well, white with its own juice.

In the past two weeks, I'd had my fill of flesh, even though, as Valkyries, it is the staple of our diet. So much bear, such sweet, tough meat, had been enough. I filled up instead on the crullers, special egg breads, crisp honey cakes of the season, and the plum strudel. Even in Valhalla, such could not be missing from the Yuletide board. Little spiced man-shaped sacrifices loaded a sacrificial gallows tree decorated with nuts, apples, ferns and ribbons. All of it we washed down with great quantities of mead. A long life is gained, so they say, by eating and drinking quantities of honey, that gift of the gods, at Yule.

Soon the mead washed away the solemnity of the first rites, and entertainments began. Skeggjöld and Raðgriðr presented a little skit in which they portrayed Gods and heroes with such irreverence that even Odin had to chuckle – although he didn't smile. Hlokk juggled daggers. She could keep seven in the air at once, with the light of the fire leaping on them as if they, too, were flames.

Thruðr had a drum. It was made from a barrel with the ends removed and covered with pigs' bladders. Through the bladders ran a horse's tail which, when drawn back and forth over the bladders and through the echoing chamber of the barrel, made a weird humming sound that was said to frighten spirits. It certainly sent shivers down even the spines of Valkyries and caused us to sing to regather courage.

And so then the singing began, the old songs of the season we all knew from childhood, some accompanied by Thruðr's drum, the softer ones not. Strong feminine voices twisted under and over one another like the bars of a sword in the making until they, like the blade that hung now at my side, seemed to be a thing alive.

In that warm ambiance, I leaned my head against Thora's breast.

She combed out my drying hair with a hart-bone comb as we sang, releasing with every rhythmic stroke of the comb the strong magical smell of birch and angelica. I felt the deep source of her voice as it rose and fell. I had almost drifted to sleep thus when I felt a drop of water on my cheek. My hair had long been too dry to scatter drops. I reached up to brush the drop away and felt another.

"Thora?" I sat up. "Thora, you're crying?"

"It's nothing, child. Go back to sleep. Only I mustn't call you 'child' anymore," she murmured with a deep, gentle laugh. "You're all grown up now and one of us. My sister."

"But why are you crying?"

"This song they are singing now is a song we sang when I was a child."

"We sang it, too. That's no reason–"

"No, it's not," she agreed.

"I didn't think a Valkyrie could cry."

"They probably don't. Perhaps I'm not truly a Valkyrie."

"Not a Valkyrie!" We had been speaking lowly so as not to interrupt the singing. Now I nearly did interrupt with the force behind my cry.

"Hush. Of course I wear the golden torc of Odin. It's just ... just on a night like this when I remember ... home. And to have you returned to me! You, a child ... a child I thought dead like all the others."

She sighed and then said, "When I was a girl falling asleep before the Log, watching the magic of the new flames, and the house was hung with greenery, I always imagined someday I would share that same magic with a daughter of mine. 'Yule, the Wheel,' I told myself. 'It must keep turning, mother to daughter, daughter turning to mother...'"

I could tell she was reaching for something with her words, and I felt I must reach for it, too. But all I could say was, "Yule at home always meant thaw was not so far away. We must have thaw before the spring. Thaw is a dreadful time. How glad I am to be free of it." Even my mouth was becoming clumsy with sleep. I didn't try to make it say more.

"But thaw, too, is part of the wheel. I always ... I still, on a night like this ... hope to turn the wheel myself..." Her voice murmured, taking on the rocking rhythm of the carols. "To leave the sterility of the sword and the brynie and open my heart ... I suppose it's true we cannot have or be both. But there is the wheel that turns..."

She probably said more, but that was all I heard. My thoughts drifted as I gave in to my exhaustion. *Valhalla has no Thaw Gruel. I am free of that terror. I am a Valkyrie. The world must fear me now, as it fears my father Odin.* The constraints of the Earth Gods, the Vanir – the turning wheel of the year that must always come back to winter again – seemed nothing more than the memory of a childhood nightmare. *I am free of the call of the Bog!*

chapter 8

ITH THE THAW, WE VALKYRIES began to move out among the children of men. Being the youngest Valkyrie, my first few tasks were nothing more than to make the rounds of the shrines of Odin throughout the land, collecting the tribute on which Valhalla lived.

As the Norns determined – perhaps because these central lands were so rich and comfortable – my first stop was to the long house of Volsung beside the Rhine. I remembered the beloved of Odin and his ten sons. I even remembered the single daughter's name, Signy.

The Odin sheaves in Volsung's fields were weedless and fat. War booty lay within easy dredging in a shallow eddy of the great river. A wooden pillar that rose far above my head with a bearded face axed into its crown marked the spot. I came dripping from the water, having gathered fine spears and shields, a pair of greaves of Roman make, and a strong riveted helm Hlokk could easily refashion for a battle-maid's head.

When I did climb up, no armed warrior stood on the bank to challenge me, but a slight blond girl perhaps thirteen or fourteen with large gold brooches clasping up her apron-skirt. Something about her reminded me a little of Uddrun, dead in the Bog at least half the time this girl had been alive. She stood there on the bank of the Rhine in the shadow of a chestnut tree with its spearheads of white bloom, as if she'd grown there.

I knew letting myself be seen about my work was never a good idea. I'd come at dawn, with just enough light to see the glint of metal under wavelets. But I hadn't considered that women were up at dawn, about their chores, while their men slept off the night's feasting. Had I failed so completely at my very first, easiest charge?

I recovered from my start, hoping it didn't show, and laughed. "What have you to do with Battle Blinder's hoard? Shouldn't one like you sue the gentler Vanir?" Then I added what must be her name. "Signy."

She was surprised I knew her name and was a little fearful at my power, Odin power. Nonetheless, she spoke up after only a moment's pause. "I am my father's daughter, and he is beloved of Odin. Besides, the Vanir don't seem to have the strength to overcome All-Father's decision in the matter that–" she whispered, bowing her head, "–that is in my heart."

I stood holding the dripping helmet and shield, deciding I should at least listen to the prayers of people who had given such fine treasures to my master's cause. "Speak it."

Another deep breath steeled her courage. "My father is arranging a marriage for me with Ermenaric the Goth."

"Ermenaric is a name famous throughout the land," I said. "Such a treaty with the very strong lord of lands at the other end of All-Father's realm must serve your father well. The God has already answered your prayers."

"Indeed, he has not." She stepped back, frightened herself by the fury of her feelings. "Gothland is far away."

"As I said."

"Too far from the protection of my brothers. With a man known to be brutal, one I do not know except what I know I cannot like. Warmaid, tell dreaded Raven Riddler I would rather become Freya than wed this man."

Out in the world, I would also meet love-gifted Freya for the first time not as the cart-driving goddess, unique and blessed in all the world, but as numerous mortal women. These women were beautiful, but strangely cursed in their beauty. Because of their looks, All-Father had come and chosen them, as he had come and chosen me. But their talents were different: he had chosen them and lifted them above the mortal plane in order to wed and to bed them. Like good housewives, they garnered his goods into storerooms, kept the keys at their waists, and waited for his favor. It mattered not whether his will came in person, or in the person of a Valkyrie. At least it shouldn't have mattered. But sometimes I could tell it did.

As I observed the fate of the beautiful Freyas from under the feathers of my helm, I could only rejoice that my lot was not theirs, that I was young and strong and felt eternal. Ever after, whenever All-Father set his one eye on me, I could not help but rejoice that mine was a virginal calling. If I lost my nunhood, I would lose my power – but so, then, would he. Wouldn't he? Such things made me all the more anxious to be about a Valkyrie's true business – choosing the slain.

"Volsung's daughter," I told her then, "I don't think you want that Fate."

"But I do," Signy insisted.

She suddenly pulled both brooches from her, causing her apron-skirt to slide to her hips, exposing the under kirtle. "Take these, please, warmaid, and plead with fierce All-Father on behalf of Signy Volsungsdaughter."

The gold lay heavy in my hand. I slipped it within my own breast-plate. "I will," I told her. "But a daughter must obey her father, you and I both."

"I know," she said before flinging one more "please" at me and turning to run back towards her father's hall.

I found myself uneasy. Here I was, claiming the goods of mortals who had just come through trying times of hunger. This formed the basis of our life of ease, free from worry. The mortals gave these things because they trusted in my ability to help them in their need. The prayers of desperation I heard! But when I took the prayers back to Valhalla, I was told with sharp looks and roughly cleared throats that the choice of whom to help belonged to All-Father. How could I presume? Had two weeks in the winter woods taught me nothing?

A warrior, male or female, earned his keep in this manner: pillage of others' labor.

Soon enough, it happened. One fine spring morning when the sun seemed to work even on Valhalla's dark interior as on the hard hull of a seed about to sprout, I attended my first war council. All-Father, whom we hadn't seen since Yule, presided. Before other matters shrank my resolve, I did not wait on ceremony.

"Lord, sisters, I beg a boon on behalf of Signy Volsungsdaughter, whose father I know is beloved–"

My attempt at God-tongue probably hurt my cause. Thora seated on the bench at my side pressed my arm and tried to get me to stop. I wouldn't. All-Father raised a hand to my sisters. Very well, this once he would humor me. I pressed on.

When I fell silent, he asked, "Let's view the value of Volsung's delivery."

I showed him the sacrifices I'd gathered from the Rhine. All-Father held Signy's brooches, as I had done. "Less than last year; his love lowers."

"But Signy offers herself as Freya–" I protested.

A sudden cold swept in through the hall, originating in the swirl of All-Father's cloak. The Valkyries around me seemed turned to icicles. I hadn't felt this cold or this alone since that moonlit night before I found the bear.

All-Father's lips twisted, his one eye a spear at my throat. He opened his mouth and – laughed. "Fresh fighting female forgiven – first fall," he said.

The icicles thawed. My sisters let out their breaths together; warm spring returned. Who would have thought Valkyries could be so afraid of anything? I had clearly misunderstood the meaning of "council," and of the nature of Godhood. Part of a god's power, which he shared with us, would be to ignore the prayers of such as Signy Volsungsdaughter. My sisters' silence told me they had relearned the same message; they would redouble their efforts never to appear soft or silly. I folded my hands in the chain link across my lap and resolved to learn it, too.

Certain now of our attention and obedience, All-Father settled back in the hall's high seat and announced, "Hated of the hour is Helgi Halfdansson."

Across the circle of Valkyrie, I saw a broad smile cross Valfreya's face. *Again?* it seemed to say. In spite of the warning I'd just provided, she almost burst out laughing. *The time and energy All-Father had spent against one single mortal!* she seemed to be thinking. *Helgi Halfdansson, the Dane.*

All-Father scowled at his head daughter. She quickly sobered.

"Again and again, and yet once again," he snapped threateningly,

> "A virile and very old vendetta
> Hero-Lover holds against Halfdan's son.
> His ward shall the warriormaids wend.
> Let some speak, some stay silent."

The God could hate whomever he wished as often as he wished. He could, we were reminded, turn the same hatred against us with our divinity removed.

Now came the time for each Valkyrie to present her comments – as long as they didn't contradict the God too much. Having never been to Dane-mark, never dealt with Helgi Halfdansson in my brief Valkyrie travels, I remained silent. But the others had plenty to say about this year's target. I leaned forward on the bench and listened, working my hand on my sword's hilt at the prospect, swearing I would never question Odin's power again. Thora sat at my other side, leaning her arm on my shoulder in camaraderie.

"Every year at this time," said Skeggjöld as if she were beginning an old and well- known saga, "Helgi Halfdansson sets out in his long boats and tries to add something to his narrow-bounded kingdom of the Danes."

"If not land, then at least a little portable property," said Göll.

Thora leaned into my shoulder with her quick laugh. But with her, I could tell it was a laugh to steel her courage for an unpleasant job. They had foiled this Helgi's hopes before. Why did I also sense this nervousness, as if she feared to be caught out in something?

Something I would just speak outright. Were the others hiding similar discomfort? It seemed so to me.

Then I caught Thruðr's sharp, impatient eye on the wordless exchange we were holding. To care for one sister more than another was frowned upon. At that moment I felt as if I might have been a girl who had missed her target altogether out in the lists under Thruðr's archery teaching.

Outside Valhalla's door, open to the springtime air, birds sang, and the fragrance of moist soil and blossoms cushioned the sharp ash smell of the inside. I couldn't understand the birds' song, but I found it easier to fathom than the tension indoors, where before we sisters had been close comrades. The God merely spoke. He never bodily threatened us, not that I had seen.

"And every year, we repulse him," said Hlokk, firmly enough to repulse any mortal by voice alone.

"Who is Helgi going to attack this year?" asked Hilda.

> "His pursuit is southern Saxony,
> So tell my tufted intermediaries,"

replied our master.

The commentary rolled from shore to shore of our assemblage as breakers on the sea. "He is a rover, that Helgi."

"And flaunting of your authority, All-Father."

"He considers the sea his realm, not just his highway, and anything the sea washes is also his."

"A more aggressive, troll-like, fearless man does not exist."

I continued to fight down the feelings of unease I'd caught from my friend Thora as fiercely as I meant to fight down every enemy of my lord. Then, comforting as I found it to my untried heart, I shifted away from Thora's touch. A warrior would not probe the feelings of her battlemates quite as much as I was doing. But a warrior would also not hold her tongue when she might add something to the war plan. I shifted on the bench – and said nothing.

"What is our lord's decree concerning Helgi Halfdansson?" asked

Reginleif. Her usual tact hinted that enough glory had gone to Odin's hatred, and we should move on to acting upon it.

> "Hunding Syriksson and his Saxons
> Will send him into the sea,"

Odin announced. "Odin opens his mouth and ordains."

"Odin ordains," we all echoed, nodding around the circle in agreement. All twelve of us could not match the resonance of threat in the single male throat.

"But that doesn't give us a lot of time," exclaimed Geirönul. "Danemark is not far from Saxony."

"The warmaid has wisely worded," All-Father praised she who was so accomplished with spears in his cause.

> "And it is she who must saddle for Suebia,
> Put in knowing the nation of knotted ones,
> Put to field those who fear old Fire-Eye."

"I'll go to Suebia at once, my lord." Geirönul bowed her head in obedience.

Odin handed Geirönul a quiver of arrows with his magical runes on their shafts. No true worshipper of Odin in all of Suebia would fail to respond with all his retainers if he had one of these pressed into his hands by a tall, strong woman wearing the raven helmet.

"Thora?"

Thora stepped from my side and knelt before All-Father. "My lord?"

"Among the far-flung, Franks are friends."

So two whole other kindreds would be called by arrows to join us and the Saxons against the marauder Helgi.

"Yes, my lord." Was it almost a gasp that had passed my friend's lips the moment she heard the word "Franks"?

Odin pretended not to notice.

> "Maid, your mission is to muster them,
> A thing of Truth-Getter's every thrall.

Spur their spines against the south to Saxony."

For all my resolve not to try to read more than was required into any exchange after Thruðr's warning scowl, I could not escape the feeling that Odin was testing my friend. Was he teasing her as cruel boys might torment a bird they had caught after breaking its wing? Did he give the hope of escape, only to catch the bird again, over and over, until it died? Now I was heartily sorry to have moved from her. I wanted to shift my weight towards her, to lend her my support.

But something All-Father had said seemed to have put all thoughts of me from her mind. "Yes, All-Father. I leave at once." Thora lowered her head in a bow as she got to her feet. As she passed me for the door, she kept her head bowed over the quiver of summoning arrows our lord had given her for the Franks. I thought certainly she would at least smile a farewell in my direction. The smile on her lips remained a private one, however. She seemed to hope that the rapid setting of her feathered helmet on her rust-colored hair would hide the high color in her cheeks.

I wanted to ask her why she took an interest in the Franks. I did not know where her original home had been, but suspected it wasn't the Franks. What else could it be? I couldn't ask her. But I could ask something else. I broke into the steady beat of the god's unquestioned orders. "I wonder, All-Father..."

I ventured a sideways glance at the God. I felt rather than saw Thora freeze just in the doorway, half in sun, half in the shade of Valhalla. Nobody said a word; the Valkyries all looked away – all but Thora – as I continued. "Why is Helgi not one of your favorites, with all the merits my sisters spoke of? I'm struck that he comes south yet once again after so many clear signs of your displeasure. This is a man of courage, of defiance. A man after your own heart, All-Father. Why don't we ever ride on Helgi's side?"

All-Father turned a shoulder grown palpably cold, like a warm spring day at the first pass of a cloud. In spite of myself, I shivered at the blatant riddle – indeed wantonness – of the God's will. I had assumed that, as a Valkyrie, I would make sense of it. Even Valfreya was mystified, yet ready to shut her mouth and follow blindly – and that unnerved me. Undoubtedly this was how she had won her position of favor in the first place.

Then All-Father growled my name like storm clouds gathering. "Brynhild." The powerful hand with its golden braces pointed to the rushes at his feet. The eye caught my heart like a fish on an iron hook.

My guts roiled with fear. I could do nothing else but get to my feet. "I'm here, All- Father," I whispered, kneeling in my turn on the rushes before the divine feet. My heart beat with such confused emotions that I was grateful to be kneeling. Sable fur wrapped the top of black boots up to bare knees that looked as if cobbled of boulders. They seemed such mortal legs. That they wrapped godhood remained the unsettling part.

Quick as lightening, Odin reached out and caught my torc in a choking yank. In the silence that followed, disturbed only by my struggle for breath, came the terrible realization: the worst thing Odin could do to any of his daughters was not harm to the body, but to fling us back to that world of women we'd left, to remove us from the glint of knowing that we shared in his godhood. And I had questioned that godhood twice in one day.

Of all the Valkyries, only Thora stirred at my distress. She took a step or two in my direction, but then turned and fled. I could hardly spare notice. When next I was able look towards the doorway, she had gone. Only birds flitted through the spring sunlight. But it seemed like ages until that vision appeared. In the meantime, I struggled in the grip of Odin – that touch which controlled every blade swing and poet's word. Caught in the torc, making the twisting of my flesh twice as painful as Odin punished me for speaking out, were the claws of the bear I had slain, also around my neck. As he twisted, one of his hairy knuckles touched a claw, pushing it into my skin and making blood trickle onto my linen dress. But that touch stopped the twisting.

"Don't doubt me, daughter, or you're dead to deity," the god spat between clenched teeth.

I couldn't say a word. My next breath, I was certain, would be my last. My neck would snap. But then he threw me from him. I lay face down, trying to catch breath from the sodden rushes.

All-Father rubbed the finger that had touched the claw. He cracked his knuckles as if to rid them of further effect, then swept up his cloak and settled back in the high seat, the carved ravens perched on either shoulder. His cloak, I thought, went from thunderstorm to calm spring day. But that might have happened because my sight slowly cleared.

> "In Saxony are some on whom
> I'll set the surly shirt."

From the circle of Valkyries behind me, there arose a murmur of excitement. The shirt, the bear-shirt of overwhelming might in battle, had been promised to those who would fight against Helgi Halfdansson. The term bear-shirt – *berserk* – would bring fear into the heart of any German. I must confess, it brought tingles to my spine, just when I thought I had known as much fear as was possible to know and survive. And I had only ever seen the fearful results of the spell, not its working.

My sisters-in-arms' excitement came from more knowledge and promised this was going to be fun.

"Brynhild," All-Father said. The mere sound of my name in his rough voice sent my neck into spasms once more. But I pushed myself up onto my elbows, spat into the reeds, then knelt again on wobbly knees.

"Because the bear befriends you–" The God reached out as if to touch the claws at my throat, to claim them for himself, as if to prove to himself he could touch that power of my own and control it. But he did not touch me, and went on.

> "Because the bear befriends you,
> Here falls the favor to find amidst our friends
> Twelve men, twelve heroes true, tough, and tried,
> To have the honor, the hail of hardened holiness."

"Yes, All-Father." It was I – I who was to work this spell on mortal men! I – my first battle ride out! Not because of the power the god held over me, but because of the power I had summoned to myself over the bear – which he coveted. And this was a god?

"Don't worry..." The one eye softened. I had meant to betray none of the doubt I felt in my voice, but this softness told me I must have failed. Then I saw that he was mindful of my sisters watching. He didn't want them to know that I, the untried member of their group, had swayed this choice. He wanted it to appear as if he were gracious – and godlike. "I am with you all the way," he went on.

> "When potions are pertinent, I'll provide.
> And runes and rites and reason.
> Bear in mind, Brynhild, to bring your own bear skin."

My throat wanted me to rub it, to apply salve, but I refused. "Yes, All-Father," I said. But I thought, *What sort of god is this who can't even control his own temper?* And the look I exchanged with the one grey eye told me he guessed my thought.

Within the hour, all thirteen of us were on our way – Thora and Geirönul to their summoning, and Odin and we ten riding north at a pressed pace. This was more what I had hoped for when I became a Valkyrie – doing, not thinking, not trying to decide what was right and what was wrong. My will, one with the God's.

We covered much the same territory as All-Father and I had when I first came to Valhalla, for my home of Anglia was just north of Saxony, between it and the Danes. I wondered why none of my sisters had been handed a quiver and asked to round up men from my home to come to the Saxons' aid as Thora had gone to the Franks. I had been gone from Anglia for a long time, so long that it didn't really seem like home at all. Nonetheless, certainly men among my old heath and bogs would heed Odin's call. Did the God deny my menfolk this chance to improve their families' Fates for some random grudge, of which he held so many? I could think of no fault, nothing worse than Helgi's nameless crimes.

Missing Thora's horse at my side made me think like this, nothing more. A Valkyrie knows no home but Valhalla, after all. And certainly, choosing the berserks was calling enough. I definitely had plenty to occupy my mind all the way north. This was a great calling. I must do it well, to make up for the doubts I had voiced. And I wouldn't know how to begin – until it began.

We had four days' hard riding. I never saw a Valkyrie's horse fly, as parents sometimes told their children they could, but a good horse at *tölt* almost seemed capable of it. Everywhere the sweat of our horses fell like dew, the harvest would be good, so we did not hesitate to press our mounts.

On the fourth day, the Weser River, which we had been following much of the way, emptied into the sea. Land continued on the right hand in a parallel shore line northward, and we took our route there. But all to our left hand unfurled grey ocean, its rhythmic surf an overtone to the horses' hooves. The ground beneath our feet yearned towards the sea itself, being mostly marsh when it wasn't dune. On the dunes, tough tussocks of beach grass in texture like tightly-spun linen clung for dear life. The hand which worked this spinning belonged undoubtedly to the ocean, which likewise pounded the ground as flat as itself and provided the wildlife – the mourning gulls – with being.

Our horses' hooves slurped through the tidal pools and sand turned almost liquid, scraping on the sharp, chalky edges of razor-clam and oyster shells. Along this coast from the north, Helgi and his ships would sail. But they hadn't appeared yet. What did appear, like some great ship on the horizon, was a mound. We soon made out that what had looked like an island belonged to the more solid half of this grey, watery world that was Saxony.

"A wierde or terp," Eir called the mound. Eir herself originally hailed from Saxony, which explained her preference for the short single-edged sword, the *sax*. The Saxons' god-ancestor Saxsnot had lent his name both to weapon and descendants. Some claimed Saxsnot and Odin were one and the same.

"Wierdes are not a part of the world that owes its creation to the giants, but to the hand of men," Eir said, continuing her explanation. "My ancestors piled up these mounds, bringing basket after basket of clay and animal dung to the site. Terps provide a protection to houses, people, and beasts when the sea comes in."

"Is the sea likely to come in?" asked Göll, who was an Alemanni, an inland kindred, looking anxiously to our left.

"Yes, in a winter storm. But our people are quite safe on the wierde," Eir assured us. "With the normal ebb and flow of the tides, fish are caught in pools on this flat plain, making them easy enough for children to collect. You see, this land, though it looks forbidding, can be made to yield harvests as any acreland." Yet her voice carefully avoided all emotion, for a Valkyrie was not to revere her homeland with any favor among her sisters.

Such a great mound, even one of dung, made her ancestors seem something like giants to us. Because of the dung, the wierde was the most fertile spot around. It wore a crown of beeches just gaining the bright gauze of new-budded leaves. So large was the mound that nearly a score of long houses nestled there among the dark trunks with their attendant outbuildings, storerooms, kitchens, and workshops for weaving, iron, and leatherworking. All had crossbeams marked with the horsehead of Saxsnot or Odin, the symbol of the kindred. A fence enclosed the wierde, but it was not very solid, neither stone nor wood being something to squander in this land.

We often teased Eir about her liking for the *sax*, but soon would learn what an army of well-trained single-blades could do.

Odin's sky-colored cloak caught a gust of wind as he dismounted Sleipnir. When the folds of grey-blue wool settled again, they did so, patched and torn, over a form half the God's size. He had become a hunched old beggar. In this guise, he would break the news of our arrival and purpose to the king, Hunding Syriksson, living in the largest of the long houses on the wierde. Leaning heavily on his staff, Odin set off in this direction. And woe betide any man who turned such a beggar away, lest he be the God in disguise!

chapter 9

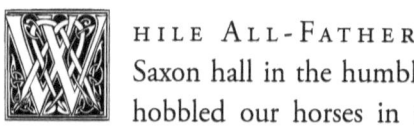HILE ALL-FATHER ODIN WENT off toward the
Saxon hall in the humble guise of a beggar, we Valkyries
hobbled our horses in a gully some distance from the
mound. The gully was rather shallow, but offered the landscape's best
shelter. We had to do what we could to avoid the attention eleven
divinely sired horses would attract. Everyone knew that any white
horse foaled in a common herd must be dedicated at once to the
Gods. Seeing eleven such beasts would no doubt expose us as Odin's
battlemaids. Mortal eyes should not set on Valkyries, certainly not a
group of them, until our time in the battle. My sisters and I took cover
not far off, where we could see the wierde and all approaches by land
and sea, yet remain hidden from the goose girls, sheepdogs, and water
bearers whose tasks brought them down off the wierde.

"Fall back a bit," Valfreya warned us presently. "Hunding Syriksson,
it seems, is the God-fearing man we always assumed he was. All-
Father's beggar guise has struck a responsive chord with him. Helgi
will not catch them unawares as he sweeps down from Dane-mark,
and we will be supporting these Saxons against him."

Indeed, some uncustomary activity on the mound soon spread
down toward us. All the warriors of the settlement, all Hunding's
retainers, fanned out over the plain, calling on goose girls and herd
boys and fisher boys with nets of woven sea grass to take their charges

and follow them to safety, to shelter on the mound. Then the men regathered and came as a group directly toward our gully.

The position to which Valfreya had called us proved to be perfect – a divine outlook site behind a scrubby copse of sea reed. We could see everything the men who had won our favor were doing. We even caught a word here and there of their speech and prewar rites.

First of all, those not blessed with natural red hair, the color of prowess, proceeded to dye theirs. A quantity of dock grew on the banks of the gully. The lance-shaped leaves were just beginning their launch to chest height, and some few had put out the first of their tiny yellow-green blooms. The men looked for those plants that were still low, in which the sap would be most concentrated. A few quick stabs with their daggers into the soft soil removed the ruddy tap-root, or at least part of it. These roots tended to break off before their full length was reached.

The warriors hacked off the leaves, rinsed the roots a little in the stream, then mashed all the roots, skin, and orange interior together on a flattish stone by the streamside. Centuries of warriors about the same business had stained the stone a dull orange, which even the sea's winter assaults had not washed out.

When the paste reached a good sappy consistency, each man took several handfuls and rubbed them into his hair, catching up the long ends with the rest and scrubbing it in. Then they sat to let it dry. While they waited, they exchanged stories of their previous exploits – or at least those of their fathers. They chanted the runes that would give the iron-red dock's strength to their limbs, the thrusting power of dock's lancet leaves to their weapons.

Some sharpened their weapons – in particular their famous *saxes*. These they tenderly brought from their sheaths like some wounded member of their bodies instead of things capable of wounding. Carefully they wiped the grease from the edge of the blades with handfuls of torn grass. Others had their shields with them and worked on smoothing them out so no enemy weapon could catch on a loose rivet and gain a foothold. Still others had their quivers full of arrows in want of new heads, their bows wanting to be restrung.

These little prewar tasks kept their hands busy while the magic took effect.

"Perhaps you should try to get a little sleep," Valfreya whispered to me, "instead of watching all this male preening. You'll see enough of that tonight."

I rolled out my bear skin and tried to follow her advice. Because of my night's duties, I was fasting and could not share the strips of dried meat the rest of my sisters were passing amongst themselves. Sleep would help me forget the hunger. But hunger wouldn't let sleep come.

Soon I heard the greeting call of the Valkyries. I left the futile exercise with my bear skin and peeked up over the top of the gully with the rest of my sisters. We saw a party of about twenty new horsemen arriving from the southeast.

Valfreya returned the call so that Geirönul would know where to find us. The appearance of this sister among them, and the tinkling amulets knotted in their horses' manes, told me that the new arrivals were the Suebians. The Suebians chose a site further down the stream in which to join in the men's rites.

The Suebians did not dye their hair like the Saxons. They did, however, believe that a man could bind vigor to himself by combing all his hair to the right side and knotting a bent birch twig in it over his right ear. This rune was the powerful symbol of fertility. In order for the knot to stay without pins, the hair had to be combed perfectly smooth first, which the Suebians proceeded to do as they sang the runes that called manhood to them.

While we watched this progress, Geirönul joined us in our hiding place. Using the Valkyries' quiet hand signals, she introduced her charges to us across the distance. They were blood brothers, the sons of famous heroes, most of whom were famous themselves. In the same way, the men of Suebia and Saxony introduced each other face to face. This would be important information for us to know when we came to fight amongst them. It would help us understand and lead the flow of battle.

"But you shouldn't be listening to this, Brynhild," Geirönul said. "You must choose the berserks, and nothing I say must prejudice you."

Again I tried to sleep, but by and by the Franks rode up and joined the war party. They numbered about twenty as well, and rode with their spears borne upright before them with honor – spears dedicated to Wotan, their name for spear-god Odin.

Valfreya called for Thora, whose arrows had summoned this cohort. No answer came.

I strained to see over the bear skin in the glare of a low-riding sun. I left my bed altogether, but it soon became clear that Thora did not escort the Franks. Valfreya looked at me, puzzled, a little worried, when I came up beside her. Thruðr gave me one of her scowls. I ignored them and attempted the greeting call again, but got no answer.

"Thora did get the Franks here," Valfreya said, putting an upswing in her voice.

None of us dared to speak more, lest giving voice to our worst fears might make them real. But I remembered how All-Father had seemed to be taunting my friend when he gave her charge of the Franks, and my heart sank. Now any attempt on my part to sleep was out of the question, but I also didn't bother to watch the Frankish war rites. No one introduced the character of the Franks to us, and we Valkyries remained only eleven.

The sun set, turning the North Sea molten, plunging the islands that leap-frogged parallel to the southern coast into stark profile until they appeared like a string of gold-inlaid lapis lazuli. The men finished their rites and got to their feet. The Saxons welcomed their new comrades to prebattle feasting and drinking on the mound: the womenfolk had been about preparations all afternoon.

So, in ranks five abreast, one half of the morrow's clash marched across the marshy plain. Enlivened by the beauty of the sunset, the men raised their shields and set them horizontal just above their mouths. Then, they began to sing, deep and low, the proud war chants of their kindreds. They threw their voices up to the concave shells of their shields as a sounding board. Then they paused, listening with care to the resonance.

A quick gesture from Valfreya, and we lifted up our shields too, giving echo to their song. So the men marched on with an even prouder stomp to their steps: they had heard the song of the Valkyries behind their own songs. They knew now that Odin favored them, that his voice was one with theirs, and his will had joined with them. Even if death should come tomorrow, it would be an exalted death, for they would be among the Chosen Slain.

The whole scene on an empty stomach brought an instant chill and loneliness to me. Without Thora's voice joining ours, my arms felt weak, as if the tendons had been cut. And what was this? I found myself weeping. I could not let the rest of my sisters see me weep, not even for pride or the emotions aroused by beauty, let alone for nervousness or fear.

"I'm going to see to the horses," I said.

Valfreya nodded. I think she avoided looking too closely at me. I went off on my own.

I cried alone into the rapidly descending darkness. I tried to count horses, just to say that I had checked on them, but I got thirteen, which couldn't be right. I wiped my eyes and tried to control myself, then counted again. Thirteen.

I went among them, letting each in turn breathe a deep night's breath into my hand. I got thirteen breaths and recognized Thora's mount among them, still saddled and quivering from the exercise of the journey.

Did fear or excitement or relief worsen my sobs? Whatever it was, several more came before my throat was clear enough to attempt a greeting call. The call only got half of the proper tremor behind it, for then I saw a figure step out of the dark towards me.

The figure was not Thora, however, but something perhaps twice her girth, an ogre with two heads and three or four legs. I tried to give the "Aid here!" call but found that my throat had instantly become too dry. I made the most threatening noise I could, pulling Fish-Scale out of its sheath, just in case this sound might scare off a rock-hurtling thing-of-the-night. Valkyrie though I was, I trembled to take on something like this alone.

Then the creature gave the Valkyrie greeting and, before I had a chance to wonder whether ogres had the wit to be so deceptive, the creature spoke in human tones. "Brynhild? Is that you? No need to get Fish-Scale riled up as yet. Save him for tomorrow. It's me, Thora." And Thora's broad-hipped figure did then extract itself from the beast.

"Oh, Thora!" I ran to embrace her. "We were so worried!"

The front of her brynie – where her own flesh could not touch the metal – seemed unusually warm. And then, over her shoulder, I saw the ogre's other half. It was a man. I stiffened.

"Brynhild, this is Geirðjof. He's a Frank who answered All-Father's call. He's come to win himself fame and fortune in tomorrow's battle." A smile lightened her voice, but the private joke seemed to be more for this Geirðjof than for me.

Thora didn't want to say any more, I could tell, but I held back from her and from this stranger, so she felt obliged. "He's a poor man, Brynie," she explained. "He can't afford a horse like the rest of them that set on this venture. Perhaps he may win one tomorrow. At any rate, I let him share my horse to get here."

"Thora!" I was so shocked, I could scarcely speak. "Thora, any man who shares a Valkyrie's saddle should be dead–"

She ignored me, or rather covered up my words with her voice. "That's why we're late."

"He's very dark," was all I could think of to say next, finding comfort in being able to make him an object like that. He was, too, perhaps the darkest man I'd ever seen, with straight black hair and eyes, even in that twilight, like obsidian. "And not very tall." His head only came up to Thora's chin. *Now, why did I link them together in this way?*

"Yes, but he's very brave." Thora cleared her throat and shifted a little to let me know she didn't approve of my speaking of him thus in his hearing. But we Valkyries always spoke in this manner when discussing warriors, as no more than a bit of horseflesh.

"His father was a Roman," she added.

Then I had a worse thought. *Is he – this little, dark man – is he what was so special about the Franks? Is he what brought the secret high color to Thora's cheeks when she left Valhalla and forgot me?*

Thora left me again quite abruptly and turned her full attention to her Frank. She pointed him off toward the mound and the rest of the warriors, and took him a step or two in that direction. "Until tomorrow," she told him.

"Until tomorrow," he replied, unusual liberty for any mortal to presume of a Valkyrie. And then, very quickly, so quickly it seemed sleight of hand and left me wondering whether my eyes had merely deceived me in this half-light, he reached up and stole a kiss of her cheek.

"So," Thora said with a deep breath – or was it a sigh? – coming to me quickly and forcibly turning me from my scrutiny of her Frank. "Take me to the others."

We walked in cold silence for a while until Thora felt she had to break it. "He's very brave. He means to win by that bravery what birth has denied him."

"Very well, you've told me already," I said, but wanted to warn instead that if a Valkyrie ever comes to know a man, she loses all her divine powers. But that, too, was unneeded. Hadn't Thora herself first taught me that law?

"Brynhild! Brynhild!" an excited Valfreya greeted. "Haven't you heard? All-Father's calling you. Three or four times now. Listen! There he is again."

The clear notes of my particular whistle came from the mound.

Looking over my shoulder, Valfreya said, "Oh, good. You've found Thora for us. But you'd better go answer Odin at once. It's time to choose the berserks, those bravest men who will lead the defense tomorrow."

I had no more leisure to wonder about Thora and the Frank. I scooped up my bearskin and ran off toward the mound and the sound of my call.

"Here," All-Father said, more impatient than glad to see me when I reached the wierde. Into my hands he thrust what felt, in the dark, like the smooth sides of an earthenware pot.

"Daughter, I will direct you to a door

Heading to Hunding's hall,
Where all the warriors wave
Drumsticks and down their drink.
I will proceed and prepare the path.
In the interval, you undress and anoint
The crucial contents contained
Within this jar over every joint.
Then fit up again, not forgetting your fur.
I'll announce when we've need of you."

They called Nanna Moon Goddess. In her quarter phase, when she had the appearance of a sharp clean blade hanging overhead, they called her the Brave One because she was not afraid to go out at night. *Why should she be?* I thought as I hastened to follow after All-Father.

A ditch and an oaken palisade surrounded the Saxon king's long-house, but the great gate stood open, despite the state of alert. We went right in. A wagon wheel marked the entrance, and horseshoes were nailed, prongs upward, over the doorway. This showed that, though the horse was sacred to the Saxons, when this house had been built, a horse had been such a luxury among them that they had had to dedicate it with the emblems of a horse sacrifice only.

All-Father left me by a woodshed, still almost empty from the winter, near the door of the longhouse. I entered it. Busy with their serving, women and children were going in and out of the hall through the opposite door, and no one would see me here. Nearby, some dogs yapped anxiously in the dark they found more penetrable than their masters. But because of the many strangers on the mound, they'd been tied up for the night. I ignored their yapping and stripped.

As I scooped the first handful of ointment out of the pot, I knew it was rendered bear grease. The distinctive odor brought my own battle with the she-bear flooding back to me. My back tingled with the memory of her claws. I had used bear grease before, to help heal those wounds. But the minute I smeared it on my skin, I knew more than fat filled the pot. Magic floated in this grease, perhaps some shoots of aconite, definitely nightshade, all infused with All-Father's powerful runes. The minute it touched my skin, I could feel my limbs tingle, then grow warm, then heavy. I thought I wouldn't be able to move in this condition, but it was a strange heaviness, full of life and a deadly power at the same time.

I scraped the last of the ointment out of the pot and rubbed it on my cheeks and neck. Then, when I tried to move my jaw in speech, only a low growl came out. The dogs nearby stopped yapping and growled back, low and fearful, almost a whine.

Quickly, before my hands grew incapable of it, I put on my jerkin and breeches and then, fitting the neck of it over my head, I worked my back up under the bear skin. I knew I was now possessed by the spirit of the bear I had slain, but that was my last lucid thought. After that, I thought like a bear.

With nature more than design, I pressed my shoulder against the dead trees that stood between me and the smell of roasted flesh that had suddenly become overwhelming to my empty stomach. The trees didn't give at once, so I pressed again. Then the wood splintered with a satisfying crack, and I found myself in a great high cave where fire was leaping. Here sat many of those creatures who walk upright like we do, but whose claws can fly through the air. The smaller ones and the females ran screaming from the cave, and even the big ones who remained reeked of fear. I knew I could have my way with them. They all fell back, giving me wide berth and a clear path to where half a carcass of one of their docile horned animals hung over the fire, the ribs showing most delectably. I swaggered toward the meat.

Suddenly, the figure of a small dark man blocked my way. I'd smelled him somewhere before and knew I didn't like him. The hair on my neck stood on end. I rose up on my hind legs to face him, taller than he was, even with my knees heavy and bent. I hung my claws forward and, bearing my fangs, I turned my muzzle this way and that to give more power to the message of my growl.

I could smell fear coming off him in waves, but instead of turning and crouching his rump to me as a clearly dominated bear would do, he paused only a moment before taking another step or two toward me.

Mankind! They are often too foolish to follow the good sense of nature.

Well, so be it. I lifted one great heavy paw and floored him with a single swipe. Then I lumbered over him as though he were nothing more than a half-rotted log on the forest floor.

After that, other men followed the small dark one's foolish example. None got the better of me.

Then suddenly, here came that small dark one again. Blood oozed from the side of his face where my claws had caught him. The fresh smell carved out a hollow in the pit of my stomach. He seemed none the wiser. I swung to swipe him again, but this time he jumped out of the way like a silly little grasshopper. I lunged at him, roaring. He jumped again. Another lunge, and I had him in the tight death hug. The man-blood smell overwhelmed me. I went for his throat with my fangs and did not let go until my tongue was warm and salty with a trickle of his vital fluid. Once again, he lay like a log before me, and I sauntered on.

A few more men presented themselves. Some proved to be my betters, and I had to confess with my rump, as I would have to any stronger bear in the wilds. Most, however, showed me theirs.

And then, there stood that little dark thing again, bleeding from face and throat, but with some other scent on him now, drowning out his fear. I was panting with exhaustion and it seemed harder for my knees to lift my weight this time, but his persistence made me angry. If I got hold of that throat again, I'd forget all about the cow. I'd have him instead.

We circled for a time, I swiping and he jumping. Then, as if at a common signal, we both lunged and held each other in a grasp neither could break. In a flurry of energy, fur and skin, we tumbled together around the cave, scattering the watching men like ants whose nest was opened by turning over a rock. We slammed and smashed into the tall tree trunks that grew here and there in the cave and sent their splinters raining down on us. At one point, we must have rolled so close to the fire that my fur was singed. I felt nothing – it only got the stiff guard hairs – but the stench filled my nostrils and beset me with renewed fury. This gave me strength enough to heave my opponent up and over. While he lay dazed from the fall, I turned to get a more brutal grip on him with teeth and claws.

And then a new scent permeated the air. I raised my head to shake it out of my nostrils, but could not. I saw the man I knew to be my master standing over us, waving a branch of that fetid, hairy plant that grows in damp meadow land. He had caught a bit of fire in its branches, where it smoldered thickly on account of the greenness.

Then, making those sounds that people make that are neither growls nor roars but something like the chattering of bothersome squirrels, the master approached. He caught me by the stone-hard vine he had once placed about my neck so long ago I couldn't remember. With that, he pulled me off the little dark man. I wanted to bite off that vine – I remembered I always had – but I knew I couldn't. More of that smoking plant thrust under my muzzle turned my angry energy into something like awe for my foe. Another of his species helped the little dark one to a seat on a tree trunk at the edge of the cave.

My master scratched me behind the ears, which was wonderfully calming. He made more squirrel noises at me. Then he slashed a chunk of the cow carcass with one of those great long claws men carry about them, not always at the end of their hands. He tossed the meat to me. I accepted it with a greedy growl as he led me to the mouth of the cave and set me out into the friendlier wild of the night.

I loped past the frenzied barking of the dogs, those silly creatures who let themselves be chained up by men, yet remain around to take more abuse even when given a chance to go free. I didn't stop my loping until I was off the men's mountain and into a place that smelled more of sea and grass. There I ate the meat, cracked and ate what I could of the ribs' marrow, then followed my nose to a stream to quench my thirst. As soon as I raised my muzzle from the stream, I found my face growing more mobile. I growled in surprise, but the growl was more like a word: "Bear."

Then I began to understand that I must roll in the water, rub myself off on the plants on the bank, then roll some more. I felt my nose becoming dull and insensitive, but my eyes and ears grew keener in compensation. And then I realized I was no longer a bear, but a woman, a woman and a Valkyrie, lying in a streambed, soaked to the bone on a dark, lonely night.

chapter 10

 AM PLEASED TO REPORT the pack is pre-
pared," All-Father announced when he found us
before dawn.

"A dozen drakes will don the drapery:
Eleven locals – and one lone Frank."

All-Father fixed his single eye on Thora as he said this, breaking the
alliteration to say "Frank" when "Lombard" would have scanned better. She turned from him to look at me. I looked away from everyone,
west to the sound of the sea.

All-Father continued, his words becoming a chant of magical challenge – a challenge I knew had been recited before, many times, save
for the change in name of partners in this grim dance of death.

"Past pattern persuaded people.
The sorcery sits solely with Saxons,
This being their thralldom to thrift.
Still, I spent the star-time sequestered,
And bestowed on each soul the sark
That possesses primal power.
And on tambour tegumented taut
With bear-skin, I beat and beat

A musical madness to their minds.
They stay solely for the song of swords,
Ere they drink the death-defying draft.
Blood-berried belladonna,
Maroon-marked mushroom,
Let that but linger on their lips and,
By the blood of my own body,
I'll boast such brave, strong brutes
As the whirl of the World-Spike may wonder at.
Let what tin-hat trees stride towards
This death-dealing delta now as dare!"

And so Helgi did dare. At that moment, just as if conjured by All-Father's words, seven grey shapes appeared on the sea out of the north, riding the waves like great dragons with their canvas wings at full span.

Helgi the Dane had come.

In a trice, so fast that I thought some God might be behind him too, Helgi's rakish ships braved the surf and slithered up on the sand. Fashioned of light clinkered larch timbers, the long, narrow vessels swept up to high horns at either end – horns embellished with dragon heads.

As soon as Helgi's men could walk without splashing, they realized the boon of surprise, which they had hoped to be their ally that morning, had deserted them. The Saxons on the mound had kept a careful watch posted.

Helgi did not turn back, even when he tested his war cry under his up-turned shield and heard no divine echo there. Undaunted by the lack of an echo, he had his men put their backs to the ocean and line up facing the Saxon host assembling into three wedge-shaped phalanxes at the foot of the wierde. The wedge shape, or boar's head as it was called, was a divine battle formation taught by All-Father only to those he loved. The best warriors stood at the fulcrum, the point of the arrow, as it were. The older heroes and those yet untried – their boyish faces quickened and flushed with anticipation – brought up the rear.

Again, the sight did not deter Helgi. A massive man under a helmet decked with wild boar tusks, his plaited beard woven with dirty red ribbons and bleached golden with lime, Helgi moved his forces closer. In numbers, the sides were almost equal. If anything, the Danes had the upper hand.

The sides drew close enough now that they could shout insults to one another. They proceeded to do so with energy, although my sisters and I were too far away to hear the colorful details. Helgi had a sorcerer with him who stood in the prow of one of their ships, chanting runes. But behind the Saxons, All-Father began to work the magic that would turn such air-poison aside and create some of his own.

> "I chant in the thick of battle.
> If my need be great enough,
> It will blunt the edges of enemy swords.
> Their weapons will make no wounds."

The sun rose at our backs, but we knew the moment it happened, for it struck the upheld *saxes* of the Saxons like lightning. Hunding and his men had taken the center phalanx, and they looked in that moment like a field of wheat, ripe for the harvest. But a like ripeness, almost a fire, ignited on Frank and Suebian, reflected on Helgi's boar helmet and on every nail in every shield and on every buckle.

Each side cast its first spear, the one dedicated to Odin, that sailed harmlessly over their opponents' heads. Although we couldn't hear them, we knew that the leader of each side had spoken the words, "May the sacrifice we make today please the One Who Loves Battle."

And then battle began. Rites ended; chaos descended. My heart raced in the echoing broil. The boar's head bit deeply into the Danish ranks like an iron wedge into wood. But then it stuck there, making no progress for all the warriors' flailing, as if the wood was still full of sap and tended to close in upon the wedge again.

My sisters and I took this opportunity to creep up the wierde to its seaside edge. We had to be careful not to be seen by the Saxon women and children who also claimed positions with a view. They meant to be at hand to spout their fearsome curses at the enemy, aid the wounded, or even rush down with a kitchen knife if they saw a chance.

The first pair of casualties came among the Saxons: Hunding took a staggering blow to the head, and the man just behind him got an arrow through the shin. Helgi and his men were not called Terrors of the Sea for vain flattery's sake. We Valkyries exchanged glances all around. Should we make our presence known now, so early in the battle?

But no. The next moment, the brew of the berserks took effect. From the top of the mound came a howling and roaring, as if all the hounds of Hel had been unleashed. Twelve new men, more beasts than men, rushed down the hill and through the ranks to the head of the fighting. There, nothing could stop them. They fought like bulls, like wildcats, like bears, biting and scratching and tearing flesh with their bare hands when weapons failed them, screaming with the madness that crawled under their bear skins.

It is said that if All-Father did not properly channel their madness, they would bite and tear themselves to pieces like so many rabid dogs. If wounded, they took no notice of it, or fought harder, like a beast will, cornered and mad with pain. I saw one berserk deflect a battle ax with his bare hands, then catch his attacker under the cuirass with the man's own spear. In the same moment, the berserk braced the spear against the ground and lifted his spitted opponent right in the air until his belly slipped down the shaft and met the berserk's hands. Such was the power All-Father's magic could give a man.

Among them, his cheek and neck bandaged but otherwise strong and whole, came the little dark Frank. He fought with strength and madness to match any of them, darting here and there on the battlefield, dealing with twenty Danes at once. A glance at Thora told me that, out of all the riot offering lures to notice on every side, she had eyes for only him. The Saxons and their allies quickly and clearly gained the upper hand.

"Look!" Valfreya cried suddenly, calling all of our attention to the center of the battlefield. "Helgi and about ten of his Danes are ganging up on King Hunding."

She spoke the truth. Hunding, who had somewhat recovered from his earlier blow, was sorely beset.

"That's a coward's tactic," one of my sisters said.

"Worse than a coward," said someone else. "Only a man totally without honor would do such a thing."

"Or a man about to desert the field."

"A man who wants to go with at least one hero's blood on his hands," said Thora, mounted at my side and nervously fingering her horses' reins.

"He knows that if their king is removed, the Saxons will be in disarray for months, if not years."

"They will make easy prey the next time he chooses to sail against them."

"Sisters, ride! We ride!" cried Valfreya.

But even as she gave the awaited signal, we saw Hunding die – Hunding, King of the Saxons, who had been fighting as valiantly as a mortal could. While Hunding caught one Danish blade on his shield and another on his single-edged sword, Helgi's battle ax bit him on the shoulder. That blade didn't stop until it reached his waist.

At the end, Hunding had received the support of as many of his allies as could beat their way to his side. This included that of the everywhere little Frankish berserk, who must have slain five large Danes at that peak of his frenzy.

"Ride, sisters! We ride now to claim a hero for the eternal Hall of the Slain!"

And we rode.

In all the countless times I'd felt a saddle spring forward beneath me before that day, I'd never felt so close to flying. As all the years, nay, a lifetime of eagerness turned to fact, the thrill of it grew to an agony in the pit of my stomach. *I, Brynhild, am riding with the Valkyries.*

And we rode. A split second suspended us at first as we gave the horses the idea with kicks to their sides. They responded quickly and perfectly, gaining energy as they hurtled us down off the mound and across the plain to the battlefield.

The driving thrust-lunge of horseflesh beneath me became the most passionate thing I'd ever felt. A dagger handle couldn't match it. The wind in my face teared my eyes and set the feathers in my helmet to a furious flapping.

We rode. We rode, pitching the pierce of our battle cries as high as we could so that none would mistake us for men. We screamed for the sheer joy of it.

In their poems, the skalds liken our ride to the ferment of clouds in the brew of a towering thunderstorm. That was just what it felt like, to ride over the little world of men and know that nothing in that world or in the sky above could stop us or our purpose.

I drew Fish-Scale from its sheath with a satisfying ring. I swung it above my head in perfect joy. I entered the din of battle, gritting my teeth as if I were diving into ice-cold water.

Like the rush of wind before a storm hit, I could hear the men on the field in the sudden silence that had fallen on them. They whispered to one another or only to themselves, panting, full of awe. "Valkyries! The Valkyries ride!" they cried. Few if any of them had ever been favored to see us before. They didn't need religion to tell them to drop their weapons to their sides, heavy with the weight of worship.

I swung Fish-Scale again and answered my sisters' calls. But I would need no weaponry. Valfreya had whipped Hunding's body up into the saddle with her, and others took up the six other dead or dying men from among his allies.

Helgi's Danes saw us. They knew at once their cause was lost. They began to shove their ships back into the waves. Only two of the ships were moving, for in this treeless plain, they'd had to beach without benefit of rollers. They would abandon the rest. Those two would not be so very overcrowded, for the attackers left behind them many comrades staining the waves red with their blood.

Then I saw that Helgi and those ten of his men who had assailed Hunding did not ride in the first two ships. They could have waded and then swum out to the boats already launched, but turned instead to a third ship, the flag ship. They set to that one, hauling at its gunwales and scarring the wet sand behind them with the hull.

And suddenly, that little Frank was right with them. He snarled, harrowed, bit with ax and teeth, like a dog who could not give up worrying its kill even when the life had left it.

Thora and I had wheeled up our horses together after the first charge. I could see only too well where her desire was yearning.

"He's to be forgiven his sacrilege," I shouted to her over what was now hardly more than the din of the waves. "He'll be forgiven for not laying down his arms when we appeared. Berserks are forgiven for that sort of thing while the spell is on them."

Thora shook her head in brief annoyance at me. "He'll be killed," she said and spurred her horse out toward the surf before I could say more.

Valfreya drew up next to me, pulling her reins over the hulk of her bloody burden. Hunding's gore stained her brynie, arms, and face, but that was the least of her worries. "What in the name of All-Father does Thora think she's doing?" our leader asked.

I couldn't explain it.

"She knows it's not our purpose to pursue an army in flight. It's beneath our dignity!"

As we watched, Thora drove her mount belly-deep into the grey surf alongside the ship. She began hacking away at the tangle of arms and weapons being drawn deeper and deeper out to sea.

From his place in the prow, Helgi watched this with wonder. No pious awe winked in his eye, only a sort of glee. In a moment, he had reached down into the hull of the boat and retrieved a length of rope from which he quickly fashioned a lasso. He swung it a few times over his head, then tossed it. It caught Thora neatly around the chest, pinning her arms to her sides and pulling her from her horse.

"Where do you think you're going?" Valfreya called after me in anger.

"To save Thora!" I replied into the wind over my shoulder.

"Fool! She has disobeyed command. We are better off riding home as eleven!"

But her words lost me in the roar of surf and the mayhem surrounding the side of the Danish boat.

The small, dark Frank had not waited for me to arrive before following his madness. Indeed, the sight of Thora in Helgi's noose acted as a new potion of his drug. He, as I did, must have heard Helgi chortle to his captive over the din, "A Valkyrie! I have always wanted a Valkyrie in my bed. To Hel with you, Odin! I have a battlemaid of my own now, see?"

Heaven could not remain aloof in the face of such blasphemy. Heaven sent a good-sized wave that hit the broad side of the boat at just the right angle. With the help of that wave as well as the weight of all the swarming Danes, the little Frank swung himself into Thora's empty saddle. He and I managed to capsize the boat. I did not have time to think that the bodies through which I ran Fish-Scale were not the straw-stuffed manikins of practice, but real flesh and blood. I hacked off limbs as they flailed upward for air with less thought than one gives to knocking the lug handles off a cooking pot.

Thora did plenty of fighting on her own account, wriggling herself free of the noose and then swimming clear of the ship. Helgi did not struggle to regain her. I heard him laugh, almost with glee, at the churlishness of Fate. Then we saw him set off swimming with powerful strokes towards his two fleeing ships.

In no time at all, Thora had swung up in the saddle behind her Frank, and here she quickly took charge. Berserker power is not like my bear transformation spell that washes off with water; it is taken internally. But the Frank, in his thin poor man's cuirass, had taken so many wounds in his torso that it looked like the straining cloth when making bloody headcheese. Besides, berserk that he was, he knew his place before one of Odin's maids.

So we trotted up onto the shore in time to see Odin waving his arms over the battlefield to end the carnage and signify that the sacrifice had pleased him well. His grey-blue cloak fluttered from his thin but powerful arms like a banner in the wind. He called down a great flock of his ravens to feed upon the dead Danes. Their fallen would remain nameless and would return to dust, to the cycle of growth and decay, without the blessing and glory of Valhalla.

For a moment, Odin's one eye turned from us – Thora, the Frank, and me – as if he rejected us, too, along with the ungodly Danes.

As his first rite after battle, All-Father walked withershins about the gathered mound of the dead, whistling and blowing in all directions. He raised the flies, mumbled ancient chants, and declared that these warriors must not rise again to do any harm to the living. In the meantime, we Valkyries felled a great old linden tree on the mound and, from its white heart, built a cone-shaped hut.

My sisters and I used the hut to change into our white linen robes. After we emerged in our divinity, which sank the Saxons to their knees before us, Valfreya returned within to lay out the body of Hunding and those who had fallen at his side. Some of their goods All-Father claimed for himself as payment for his aid in the matter, but most we laid beside them: their daggers and swords, their brooches and heavy armbands. The walls of the hut were hung with fine cloth and the fleeces of shaggy Saxon sheep.

Then my sisters and I served a funeral meal to all the mourners on the shore: boiled pork, mutton, beef, and plenty of mead. The best portions – the heroes' portion – we set inside the hut on the Saxons' finest crockery. Each of us Valkyries kissed the six pairs of cold lips in turn, promising warmer pleasures to come, although the smell of death made me draw back from the thought. I remembered myself and got through my part by assuming an air of divine coldness.

The bloodstains of the battlefield lost their starkness as the sun poured the day's last heat in a westward trail across the sea. All-Father took a hazel faggot and, murmuring the runes that only he could know, touched it in a ring all about the base of the funerary hut. A stiff landward breeze blew the flames clear at first, so some doubted whether the magic had taken hold. But then the fire curled its way past the linden and hungrily found fleece and cloth, mead, buckler, and human flesh. This turned the flames black, acrid, and red against the twilight. My eyes stung, and my stomach heaved with the smell. Without a strong force of will, what we had done and its result hardly seemed holy.

Then, just the moment before the hut fell in on itself, Hunding's queen cried aloud. She had been softly sobbing through the proceedings, supported by her children nearby. "Hunding, my lord, my lord!" we heard her cry. Before anyone could stop her, she dashed into the flaming hut. We heard one last scream like lungs made of fire. We saw her leap as the power of the flames hit her. Then she collapsed in a heap across the chest of her dead husband.

"The linden's red plague" was a poet's kenning for fire. Like plague, fire was catching. But nothing had more power than fire to immortalize the Chosen Slain. The victims of plague or fever, or any who died in their beds, were buried in flat, cold graves, and that was the end of them. They belonged to the underworld, to the realm of Hel, the dark Goddess, the Vanir. Odin's birds, the ravens, came and fed on them, sometimes wolves or dogs and worms, separating part from part until they were diffused over all creation from whence they came. They were not recognizable as individuals anymore. Some of their parts might be reassembled into a hero someday, a hero who will know eternity as himself, but they, the unblessed dead, would know nothing of it, nor would they care. Those whom All-Father and his battlemaids had chosen for the pyre, however, they and their goods were transported to another eternal realm on ethereal clouds of smoke.

We let our eyes follow the smoke upward to where it mingled in identical colors with the twilight. We could almost see the heroes as the beautiful maidens – our own counterparts who had gone on before us – greeted them in the great Hall, the heavenly reflection of our home Valhalla. In the boiling smoke, we glimpsed the faintest beginnings of their eternal pleasures on the battlefield. Any wounds got at this sport would be eternally healed. The heroes could rise from the field with youth and vigor to the endless nighttime pleasures of board and bed.

Come daylight, when the ash had formed a cool heap over the remains, the Saxons with their ever-diligent baskets of earth would form a great mound over the site. They wouldn't rest until the earth covering the place stood higher than a man, longer than four horses set nose to tail. From this place, Hunding would continue to benefit his people. Here his descendants could come with burdens on their hearts, heavy questions about the future, and he, from the sky, could counsel them. Rumors of a never-dowsed fire within the howe, or of supernatural warriors who might break out in a moment of greatest need, could keep future enemies at bay.

I looked across the flames now at the new King of the Saxons and thought he would need such aid. He was hardly more than a lad. He, like me, had seen his first fighting only today. Now he was orphaned of both mother and father in a single day and left with the care not only of many smaller brothers and sisters, but of an entire kingdom as well. Plucking up his courage, he approached All-Father, who stood watching the pyre, leaning thoughtfully on his staff.

"My lord," the lad said as he knelt in the sandy soil. "They bring me good news from the wierde. That dark little Frank – the berserker who fought so gallantly today – the healing women tell me that, although covered with many wounds, none is life-threatening."

Odin looked at the boy and grunted. All-Father, I could tell, was not happy with this news. Any man who has ridden in a Valkyrie's saddle should be on a funeral pyre before nightfall, whether dead or alive. Somehow the confused sorting of the dead and wounded had vanished from the God's hands there at the end. But All-Father said nothing, as if to do so would cost him godhood.

The young King Hundingsson took this as encouragement to continue. Once he got going, he had the gift of fine speech for one so young, and a clear head. "No doubt this is due to your all-mighty favor of him, Lord, for which we bless you."

All-Father grunted again, blinked his one eye, and said nothing.

"As this is the case, Lord, I beg to ask a boon of you. You know only too well how raw in your hallowed ways I am. Now here I am, thrust to this pinnacle from which Helgi Halfdansson will try to tear me, not to mention several of my father's retainers I could name. They think they are better suited to fill this spot. Besides all this, I now have the burden of avenging my father's blood on that sea king. If it is your will, then, Lord, considering all these strikes against the peace of my land, I would like to offer this Frank a position as my earl, to rule at my right hand and to counsel me. He is brave and faithful – we have had good proofs of that today. Such sure signs cannot go unrewarded. He is a poor man without conflicting fealty. In short, I can think of no better man to call to my aid at this juncture. I will even offer him my sister in marriage when she should come of age – with your blessing, Lord."

All-Father grunted a third time but kept his godhood and answered with a stiff nod.

"Bless you, my Lord," said the lad.

He kissed All-Father's feet, then got up to assume his duties with a heart so suddenly lightened that he ran and skipped along the way. He had forgotten with a child's depth of memory that he had been orphaned that day.

All-Father went his own divine way that night and left us to travel back to Valhalla on our own, there to await his next assignment. Away from the coast and the dissipating linden smoke, the sky cleared to a balmy, star-studded early summer's night full of peace. Stars shone across the night sky like jewels scattered over the dark loam of a great king's grave. We rode two by two as long as the trail allowed it. Thora, as usual, joined with me.

I could tell she had overheard All-Father's confirmation of her Frank's sudden good fortune. I could also tell she wanted to discuss this, but I would not oblige her. The less said on the subject, I thought, the better. "I suppose I'd do that, too," I said instead.

"Do what?" Thora asked.

"Throw myself on my husband's funeral pyre as we saw Hunding's queen do this evening. I mean, a woman – not a Valkyrie – can only gain glory in the eternal realm if she dies in childbirth. A woman suddenly finding herself a widow loses that chance in any case, doesn't she? Turning oneself into divine spirit along with the rest of a hero's possessions, I guess that's not such a bad choice, would you say?"

"She might have loved him."

"Oh, love!" I had only contempt for the notion. "There's not really any such thing, and you know it. What mortals call love is simply the fear of being so limited, the fear of being alone."

"The queen might have truly loved him," Thora insisted. "She might have been unable to imagine life without Hunding, and thus to die with him was the least painful way out."

We rode on in silence after that, careful not to let our dangling feet brush against each other.

I let a Valkyrie's day-to-day duties draw off the discomfort the death of the Saxon king had caused me. But within a month, All-Father returned to Valhalla from his wanderings and called the twelve of us to him once again. As usual, his rhymes had a reason that we soon discovered.

"I've nightwalked as a nomad among the Nibelungs," he said in the echoing Hall of the Slain.

> "The dark dwarves
> Cut beneath copious Erda's crust
> For all glittering rich goods of the Goddess,
> From which booty in bright birth
> Hails handiwork our Hlokk but halves."

Hlokk, our ironsmith, took no offense when the God called her handiwork half as fine as that of those small but cunning people, the Celts.

From beneath his cloak, All-Father withdrew a bundle of rare purplish fabric of the East with soft pile. From the folds of the bundle he pulled forth a silver sword.

> "Behold the blade of battle's blaze!
> When have you seen a similar corpse-serpent?"

He passed it around the circle, and each of us could tell at first touch that this was no ordinary sword. Comparing it to my own Fish Scale, it was a shark to my mackerel. A yellow jasper weighted its pummel, held tight in the intricate goldwork of the hilt, with a sheath of red-gold braid. More than that, along the center ridge shone engraved runes of magic, the symbol for "gift," the symbol for "need." Who could tell what deep things could be worked by those symbols and that blade in conjunction?

"This sword is divine," Hlokk confessed as she held it reverently. Since our own swordsmith had said it, all of us could agree without offending her. Hlokk didn't lie about ironware.

"It is so," confirmed All-Father.

> "In your mind's store, do you see the stones
> Gotland's sanctuary gave as sacrifice?
> Stones they said were a star
> Fallen in flame from firmament's fountainhead."

"That was just last year the comet fell in Gotland, was it not?" asked Valfreya.

All-Father nodded his agreement.

> "These stones I thrust upon Thjasse, whose thralls
> All the nightly Nibelungs are."

He dropped the name of the Celts' legendary smith and his people, as if any of us might meet these dwarves any day.

> "And in their nailery,
> The winter's wild windy while, they have worked,
> Twisting the eternal treasure
> With that sun found beneath the surface of Shout's
> Own mineral mistress. So these menials
> Cauterized the compound in their volcanoes,
> Then plunged it profoundly in winter's powder.
> Time upon time they took until
> This sword, set straight against a stream,

Can slice a silken string as it sails by.
On my soul, I've seen it."

"I have no doubt it can do this," said Hlokk.
"Does this blade have a name?" asked Reginleif.
"Yes," All-Father replied.

"Known as one knows the name
of a babe blessed ere he is born.
Gram is the glaive's given grace."

"Gram," we all said in unison, echoing the sword's given name with wonder.

"'Angry,'" said Valfreya. "How fitting."

"Master, to whom shall this sword be given?" asked Geirönul, her tone not invading.

Gram was not a sword for even a Valkyrie, and we knew it. We admired, but did not covet it. We knew All-Father had some great purpose in mind.

"I'll convey it as a vagrant to the Volsungs," All-Father replied.

On my bench by Thora, I shifted a little anxiously. I remembered the last council. I'd had the cheek to present Signy Volsungsdaughter's prayer asking to avoid her father's marriage plans for her. I thought my rashness had been forgiven and would be ignored. I began to doubt my belief.

"Ah, the Volsungs have been your favorites for generations," said Valfreya.

"Naturally," said Thora. "They are descended from Sigi, who is the son of All-Father himself."

The tale now moved around the circle as each warmaid added her part. I took it in, let myself be lured by the words, for I knew their magic would become part of my own.

"Rerir was the son of Sigi," said Hilda, first.

"But Rerir and his wife were unable to have children," said the next Valkyrie.

And the next, "Long days and nights sat Rerir on the burial mound of his father, begging Heaven not to leave him childless."

"Until you, All-Father, had one of your daughters here–"

"One long gone, but one of us–"

"Ride by Rerir as he sat, and toss a golden apple in his lap."

"He took the apple home to his wife."

"She ate it–"

"And thereafter found herself with child."

"For six summers she carried the child."

"For six winters."

"During which time Rerir died."

"At last she begged for the child to be cut from her."

"So he was."

"And his name is Volsung."

"Volsung has grown into a mighty warrior."

"And has won for himself a kingdom on the Rhine called Xanten."

"And you, All-Father, did him one better when it came to the begetting offspring."

"Not content to have one of us simply ride by–"

"You allowed one of your own daughters to be given to him in marriage."

"Ljod, once one of the Twelve."

"I remember her," said Valfreya, the eldest of our number. "She was among the Twelve when first I entered my training as a nun of Odin. She was our archery mistress."

"Since then," said our battle sister Göll, taking up the recitation again, "All-Father has blessed their union with ten sons and a daughter."

"It must be a powerful mother to bear such a family!"

"And all of us – except our newest sister, Brynhild – have fought at the side of the sons of Volsung on battlefields throughout the land, wherever their ambition carries them."

"Truly, All-Father, this is a worthy gift for your favored clan."

"Except–" said Valfreya, and she turned to study the single eye of our master with a new frown of dread. "Except that there are ten sons and only one sword. Even if you mean to give it to Volsung,

All-Father, he will not live forever. And, when he dies, leaving such a sword as this to ten sons, proud and fierce fighters..."

"You see beneath the skin of my skull," Odin said, and the one eye seemed to wink at the head Valkyrie. He turned to me and said,

> "It was bold Brynhild, if my mind's not blank,
> Who this year exhorted the extraction of Xanten?"

"I did collect Volsung's offerings, All-Father," I replied, growing cold with fear.

"Speak it now to your sisters: Of what did they consist?"

I told of the grain, the weapons sunk into the eddy of the great river.

"And further, as first feast-offering?" All-Father demanded.

"Not much, lord. Several large crockery vessels filled with joints of flesh, I believe."

> "Parts that had putrefied by the time you played
> Your juncture. Joints, not the whole jade."

"That is so," I admitted. I hadn't remembered that part. I'd thought so much of Signy's plight, of the brooches she'd torn from her apron-dress, the other details escaped my memory until renewed by All-Father.

"Can anyone comment," demanded All-Father,

> "How this compares
> With former years for our freshet here?"

None of my sisters said anything for a moment, but the answer was read in their faces. "Surely it is not the sort of offering one of the most favored of Odin should give All-Father," said Skeggjöld soberly.

"With so many mouths to feed–" Thora began, trying in her usual way for sympathy. "Just consider: some of his sons have already taken wives, and he has many retainers besides."

"Such is the same old sorry song." All-Father sighed with divine weariness.

> "When that ward of the weapon's way

Has little to lose, he loves the War Lord.
He fights fearlessly for my fame,
My glory, which I give back to him with gain.
But when herohood's at hand,
Here at home by his hearthstones,
He becomes cautious. His care
Veers off to the Vanir, the vegetators.
He prays to perpetuate his prosperity,
No longer to blind the beings here below with brief
But scalding ascendancy in my service."

All-Father took the sword Gram in his own hand now, let the runes catch the light and danced them on the dark back wall.

"A single sword should quite serve
To vent vengeance on Volsung.
The farrow of the once-favored, should they be fifty,
Shall not abide this brief bubble
Of a generation. Go, my girls.
Carry on your accustomed charge.
Know that no Volsung will need you
To pick him from the path of the pike.
Let them lie where the lance
Hits home, in the hill of their hearts."

"Your ways are cruel but just," murmured Valfreya, bowing her head and touching the torc at her throat.

All-Father had wrapped the sword out of our sight now, like an unclean thing, and rose to go. "But one lone deed lacks for their luck," he said.

"One hand to put Helway on their hub."

Then he was gone, riding faster than the wind on divine Sleipnir, northwest towards the Rhine and Xanten.

The doom to follow would be, in part, my doing. What I had thought good had turned to a thing of dread in the hands of the God.

PART II

SIGNY'S FATE

chapter 11

O MY MOTHER WRAPPED A cloak of bridal red about my shoulders in honor of Thor and fastened it with three great clasps that lay heavy on my breast bone like a sour stomach. On top of them went as many torcs and necklaces as could fit between them and my chin. Among these, my hair found a hundred hooks and encrusted gems to catch on. I couldn't lift my arms for the weight of armbands and bracelets. Each finger wore rings right to the nail. No matter that most of them didn't fit, that the gems slipped down to the palm side every time I moved a hand. I wasn't expected to do anything but hold them in my lap.

And finally came the crown, a golden wreath set with crystal that pressed down like a bad memory on my forehead and temples.

"You're beautiful," Mother said as she handed me an encrusted bronze mirror.

I found her face more fascinating. She was weeping, damp streaks on the cheeks, high cheeks they were, but slowly going soft with age.

Women weep, I've heard tell, when they put the crown on their daughter's head, because it is the crown they wore and their mother wore before them. So all these memories of lost youth and lost dear ones catch up in that gold. But this was not my mother's crown. She'd never worn a crown, having been given to my father not by her kin, but by All-Father himself, who needed no golden dowry to legitimize his daughters.

My bridal wreath was stolen, and all the rings and bracelets and necklaces too – even the mirror in which I was to admire myself. Well, not stolen exactly. Taken rightfully as spoils after battles won, my kinsmen would correct me. Won with the help of Odin. What could be more valid than that? Nothing, I supposed.

But one of those handmaids – busily hanging my bridal bed with furs, fine linen, and even a bolt or two of rifled silk – one of them, no doubt, had thought to place the crown on the head of her own daughter. I didn't dare look to see if any of them wept. They were the rightful plunder of war as well.

Mother's weeping gave me the courage to speak what I'd only dared to think until now. "Mama," I whispered. "I don't want to marry him."

"Don't want to get married, child?" Her face was suddenly cheerful, belying the tears. "Nonsense. Every girl gets married."

I wanted to say that wasn't true; nuns of Odin didn't marry. *You were a nun of Odin, Mama. Although, to look at you now, it's hard to imagine.*

My mother's belt rode high on her pouched belly, pressed up beneath her heavy breasts. I couldn't see the glories of the battlefield on her now through the scars won bearing eleven children – two of us, my brother Sigmund and me, at one lying-in. Perhaps a Valkyrie's creed was not to waste a lying-in to get a girl, but to have the girls only as a sidelight to the boys.

You, Mama, didn't have to get married, not until you were well ready and had won great honor in your own name. But what was the use of saying all that to her? It was clear by now that I could not be like my mother in this, if in anything. If I were to be a nun of Odin, he should have come to choose me seven or eight winters ago. And so, if I were not to be Odin's daughter, I must be simply Volsung's daughter, and be given in marriage as all other daughters were.

"I don't want to marry *him*," I whispered, this time trying for a bit more force.

"Not marry him? Not marry Ermenaric? But he is a king, Signy, the King of the Goths."

"I know, but–"

"Your father can't help but be honored by the proposal. You should be, too. What an alliance for your brothers! What glory for you, to be a queen!"

I guessed my mother, having been a Valkyrie, would always have difficulty feeling with a woman's heart. She thought like a man, and nothing else could be said, no other coinage evoked. I'd been lonely, the only woman in the family; I had often thought that. But certainly I would be lonelier still, queen or no queen, without any of my kinsmen, far away in the land of the Goths.

And now the time came to leave the bridal chamber. I had to go out into the loud brightness of my father's hall and embrace the Fate the Norns had spun for me, would I or no. Embrace Fate, as had the slave girl – whichever one she was – whose stolen crown I now balanced on my head. What could one expect from a bridegroom lured by plunder?

King Ermenaric of the Goths. I'd caught a glimpse of him at his arrival, huge and fearsome as he was, with an ax-scarred face and blond hair, dirty at the roots. I'd watched as he disembarked, stretched opulently, and took off his boar-crested helmet to rid himself of the effects of the voyage upriver.

Now that I sat beside him on the high seat, I couldn't bear to look more closely. No matter where I turned my eyes, I couldn't help but smell him. Male smell I'd lived with all my life: hard-ridden sweat and furs that had been through rain, mud, and salt spray. In Ermenaric's case, mixed with all of that came the gullet-rising smell of rancid butter.

The Goths put butter in their hair to make it gleam. It proved they had herds enough not just to keep butter for slathering on their pancakes. Of course, they didn't wash it out from one oiling to the next, for that would wash strength and prosperity from them. I understood that the smell of rancid butter must be a permanent part of the Gothic landscape, but I quickly became certain that I would never get used to it, never gain much of an appetite, never want to eat butter again, as the smell of it caught at my throat with every breath.

The word "Goth" in their ancient dialect simply meant "man." That is what entered their minds when they thought of man; that was all.

So my father toasted Ermenaric and said he gave me to him freely and with honor. And Ermenaric rose by my side. The grubby white fox fur of his cloak brushed my cheek as he returned the toast and said it was his honor to take me. Platters of food, mostly roasted meats of all kinds, kept going round and round, outstripped only by the frequency of drinking horns. I couldn't touch any of it. Even the mead had a smell of rancid butter.

My brothers took their turns to toast. At last came Sigmund's turn. Sigmund, my twin, strode to the center of the hall and crashed the flat of his sword against a shield that hung from the nether branches of Branstock. Branstock was our family's sacred tree, a great oak my father had selected for our protection, around which he had built his hall. It hurt me to think of leaving the shelter of its branches which still leafed in spring and dropped acorns onto our hearth in the fall.

All Branstock Hall stopped their festive chatter and laughter now to listen. For he was a feast for the eyes, my brother, strong ale for a deep thirst. He stood with his oak-thick legs in a powerful straddle, his sword in one hand, his drinking horn in the other. With a defiant gesture he tossed back the braids that caught his sun-blond hair at either temple and kept it out of his face. They say we are much alike, Sigmund and I, and how should we not be when we shared a narrow womb long before we shared daylight together.

He caught my eye prior to speaking and smiled encouragement. He knew my feelings on the matter – we shared everything – but he also had no fear. For the first time in days, I almost returned his smile.

"To my sister," he said into the quiet the hall left him. "By this cup and by this dagger, I swear, if she's not well-treated among the Goths, here's a blade that'll right her wrongs!"

The high seat beneath me rocked dangerously as Ermenaric leapt to his feet. I caught the fox fur in the face again. "Pup! Young scoundrel! Wolf-whelp! I'll teach that–" I heard my husband mutter this under his breath in the harsh gutturals of the Gothic dialect drowned out by the hall abuzz with wonder at my brother's nerve. Ermenaric gestured wildly for a horn, but by the time the maid handed it to him, he had bridled his passion somewhat and was able to toast. "Here's to the health and strength of my youngest new brother. I shall be happy of his vigor at my side on the battlefield someday."

The high seat rocked again as Ermenaric sat down, but at least he was down. Sigmund caught my eye across the hall again and gave me another smile, brave but grim.

Some stalwart soul tried to strike a harp then, but the company was not musical. Not a very musical harper, for that matter, although I suppose my father thought he did me a favor to hire one, any one. So the pots went round and round, and the harper drowned in the flood. The toasts flowed like the ale, and the tales of the braggarts grew in equal measure.

Overhead, oil lamps smoked on their chandeliers made of clustered stag antlers. The wedding guests launched into the game that made their proud words solid and began tossing their picked-off bones at one another as they tossed boasts. They started by throwing the smooth long bones first, then progressed to the hard, heavy knobbed ends. And then they hurled the sharp splinters left after cracking the bones for the marrow. Men have been maimed, even killed at this sport, and it seemed to me that an undue number of heavy, knobbed bone-clubs went flying. If men were hurt, they didn't say, but clearly they were growing angry.

While so much bone was flying, many of the men went in and out to relieve themselves. My husband himself had been out thrice. I tried not to think of that organ emptying which, come midnight, would empty into me.

With all the noise and commotion, nobody noticed when the stranger entered. How would they? Suddenly, there he was in our midst, standing beside sacred Branstock's roots. An old man, but large, in a sky-blue cloak and a floppy-brimmed hat drawn down over one eye. In his hand he held a sword and, with a single movement, as the company's breath swished in time with the blade, the stranger sank it deep into the heart of Branstock, burying the hilt up to the bark. Then said the stranger in a voice like doom:

> "Whosoever can slip this sword from this stock
> Shall gain the glaive as gift from me.
> And it will be that never was borne a better
> Sword than this by any soul, for sooth."

I didn't recognize the stranger, but I'm sure my father did, from the battlefield. "All-Father–" he began, but the old man had vanished with one last fierce gleam of a single eye.

At first it seemed a good thing that the men should lay off the toasting and throwing bones. They turned their attention to this tantalizing hilt catching the firelight on the otherwise dull and dark tree trunk. And so my hope continued for the first two or three attempts as men who, by mere virtue of being closest to the sword, took their chance to claim the prize.

But the sword defied them, winking its yellow jasper at them in the firelight, taunting like the single eye of a God. These were strong battle-tried men. One or two of them could be thought to be playing the weakling to flatter their betters, but not all of them.

All too soon, the stakes in honor became overwhelming. Bets were laid round the ring on this champion or that. And no man likes to lose, especially not the high wagers drinking encouraged. Anger and frustration seethed like a pot a-boil and let off steam in the form first of shouts of encouragement, then taunts, then battle cries.

Most of my brothers had tried and failed when, at length, Ermenaric rose to take his turn. I caught another face full of fox fur and ugly Gothic words about "this weakling spawn of Volsung."

Ermenaric met my father on either side of the shining golden hilt. They jostled for position a moment before it, but presently my father stepped back, half the gracious host and half because my husband had reminded him, "Everyone knows you are the beloved of Odin. Let others have a fair turn before you let the Gods cheat for you."

Odin's help he would claim, but not cheating, so my father stepped aside.

Ermenaric spat into both deep palms, took a firm stance, rubbed his hands together, and grasped the hilt. I didn't want to look at the way his hair hung – not strand by strand but coated with butter in thick strips like rags torn from old grey cloth. I prayed to all the Gods I knew, and I didn't open my eyes until groans and cat calls from every side of the hall assured me that he, too, had failed.

"It's magic," the King of the Goths exclaimed, stomping back to his place at my side. "Black magic. The sword is cursed. No man can pull it out." He caught my eye for the first time in our lives, and what I saw there made my blood chill. But he said nothing.

Then my father took his turn. Many present must have thought he failed on purpose, not to show up his honored guest and new son-in-law. But I knew that my father suffered from an old battle wound, a rupture in the groin. As he walked stiffly back to his bench, I saw that he had strained himself dangerously with the effort.

My eyes followed him with concern, and so I failed to see what happened next at the base of Branstock. My brother's voice drew my attention there again, as it drew the attention of everyone in the hall. "Father! Behold!"

And there stood Sigmund, wholesome meat to the belly, cool drink to the throat, holding aloft the magic sword. The hall stinted half in fear, half in amazement.

"Let us see this sword!" the cry rang out.

Sigmund proudly made the rounds and let all exclaim over the rare workmanship, the edge so keen it was invisible, the strange runes vining up the spine.

"I knew it was magic," exclaimed one.

"So did I. And these signs prove it," said another.

"The boy must have known a spell to say, to unlock it so like a key," said a third.

But no one denied Sigmund's right to the blade, magic or no. And my brother never denied that a power greater than flesh and blood had been in his hand that night. Still, as he took the blade on its round and received the compliments, unguarded envy and all, I saw how careful Sigmund was never to let the hilt out of his hand and to always keep the point between himself and any envier.

"A fine blade, fine," I heard my husband almost croon as it came his turn to pay his regard. For a moment I thought it might not be so bad to be wedded to this man after all. Then, "What would you say, lad? Can I buy it from you?"

Sigmund caught my eye and shook his head.

"Are you sure? I am a king. I can pay well for it."

"Kingdoms can be won with such a sword as this," Sigmund answered simply.

"As much gold as five stout horses can carry, I'll give you for that blade," said Ermenaric with a low rumble.

"There is not gold enough in all Gothland to make the price of this sword," returned my brother.

A possession envied carries evil with it. I tried to catch Sigmund's eye to warn him of that old word of wisdom, but he had already moved on with his treasure.

"By the Gods!" thundered Ermenaric, pounding the high seat until my bones jarred under the heavy burden of gold crushing me.

The sword consumed the hall until the moment someone announced that midnight had come and gone. It was time to bed the bride.

At first light the next morning, I found myself bobbing on the iron-grey waters of the Rhine in the hull of a Gothic warship. I was sick of heart and of body.

I had looked to dawn to deliver me from a nightmare, but here again I was betrayed – by none other than our old red cock, who would attack others but never me when I brought the poultry their scraps. No sooner had the bird given his first crow than the King of the Goths had stormed from the bridal room of my father's hall to rouse his men where they slept under his ships' awnings. The men had read their master's intent and quickly set themselves to this raid on a rich steading with speed and jolly good will.

I'd been led out to the moored ships in the pre-dawn chill with hardly time to throw a deer skin over the shoulders of my thin bridal dress. "Into the boat, lass," one of them had ordered me. I'd been unable to move, not so much out of defiance but from a numbing terror. The Goth had shrugged and hoisted me to his shoulder like a bundled rug.

Now I sat and watched all about me as the Goths in this ship and the two that flanked it loaded my dowry – I just one among many treasures. They hauled in the black awnings that served to make a temporary home of the ships on shore, then dragged the rest of their ships down on the beaching rollers with as little noise as rough logs on a hollow hull can be dragged. The Goths were doing all in their power to quickly satisfy the will of the vessel in which I sat, the vessel tugging at its moorings, anxious to be off downstream.

I'd been promised that should I be the first to break this silence, I wouldn't live long enough to make my rescue worthwhile. Still I couldn't help but pipe up, my teeth chattering with cold and fear. "Husband, two more nights of our marriage feast remain. We must stay."

"And I say we must not," he replied dangerously, reminding me all too clearly of what I'd already endured at his hands.

"We must stay," I repeated in a whisper. I had counted on those two more days, not for the feasting, but for the chance it would give me to do something – something to stop my departure to Gothland.

I must only tell Sigmund, had been my thought all night. *I need not even tell him; he will read it in my face. He will do something. He will kill this monster to whom they've married me.* I couldn't say I truly believed this was possible – at least, not without my brother's own death. The Goths too greatly outnumbered my father's retainers. But at least two days gave me hope.

"You will give my father deep offense if you do not accept his hospitality for this time." I tried to deflect those hateful eyes from my true thoughts. "It will be as if we are not truly married."

My husband laughed aloud, though his purpose 'til then had been for quiet. "You will begin to learn my ways, wife. After the insults of last night, I pillage Volsung in his lair and carry off his daughter to the bargain."

"It is – it is an offense he can only wipe away with blood," I whispered.

Ermenaric laughed again, and his men joined him. We were already on the riverside by then.

On the bank of the Rhine that had nurtured me, I hoped for help from our dogs. But those that had challenged the Goths' presence earlier had been taken off and chained up almost out of earshot before the wedding. The rest snuffled about at the Goths' ankles with the excited curiosity of such beasts. Whatever the plans of men, dogs never lose their faith that they are promised adventure and diversion, perhaps a little something to eat as well.

I prayed one of my father's men might need to relieve himself from the quantity of mead he'd taken the night before. Apparently such needs had been taken care of earlier. The men had taken wives or serving maids to bed with them and slept now as if they had three more days of bridal festivities in front of them.

As my hope dwindled, I realized how I ached all over. In particular, a crescent of pain across my lap made it a torture to sit down. But trying to balance on my legs in the waves hurt worse, so I stayed where I was. From time to time I could feel a trickle leave my body – I was still bleeding. I had enough aches elsewhere, however, to provide distraction.

My head throbbed, dizzy for lack of sleep. Who could sleep with that King of the Goths snarling about the bed all night, more like an ogre than a man? And the silks and furs of the bridal bed had been more a lure than a defense between us. My husband was not slow to take this lure – five times over – but never did slack his fury. He would leap up from me before his passion was quite spent, spilling seed on the way. He would throw only a bear skin over his shoulders and pace. He would pace until his fury over my brother and the divine sword was so roused that he could fling himself upon me again, as if Sigmund and not I lay cowering in that bed. What surely fed his fury against me was the truth of what people always said, that my brother and I looked as much alike as any male and female could.

Throughout the night, whenever Ermenaric's back was turned, I'd quietly removed the bridal jewels. It did not take more than one coupling to teach me what vicious welts and gouges fine jewels can make when an ogre is grinding them into one's flesh. I also learned the increased fury of such a beast when, trying as a mere reflex to defend myself, I scratched his face with a bracelet or caught his hair on the gem of a ring. By the second time, I had not yet managed to remove my earrings, however, and he had pulled the left one clean through the lobe. I would never wear earrings again. That wound still shot arrows of pain across my forehead and under my chin.

After that, having done everything in my power to remove myself from hurt, I still suffered. The fury in his fists was enough. The boar-bristles of his beard grew in unnatural directions out of the edges of his scar and scoured my face and breast like pumice stone. The stench of mead on his breath and rancid butter in his hair brought my stomach up to my chin.

Only moments from the sky being light enough for Ermenaric to cast off, the gander – the faithful old gander – flew to my defense. Once aroused, he was like one of Odin's berserks, oblivious to all danger and pain. One Gothic boot kicked him aside, producing a loud honk and flutter of stiff feathers. Undaunted, before he was even steady on his feet, the gander charged again with a great hissing.

To this noise, our men finally straggled out of the hall, rubbing their eyes in bewilderment. It took them a moment to call for their companions, and another to realize that, having taken their flesh swords to bed with them, most of them had only the foggiest notion where their metal swords were.

Only Sigmund ... Sigmund, I saw, had the divine sword strapped to his hip – the Odin-gift he had entitled Balmung. Sigmund had slept with his prize and virginity, as he'd promised to do in sympathy with me. The moment our eyes met, my eyes and throat flooded with the tears I'd been holding back all night. Balmung flashed instantly out of its sheath.

"Put it up, son," I heard my father say, his eyes counting Goths once again but finding none had vanished during the night. If anything, they'd gained in numbers. "Put it up, I tell you. We must try to find out what we have done to offend our guests. We must not give them cause to think they must pillage us. We must reason with them."

Reluctantly, Sigmund obeyed, but his fingers danced on the hilt as if the itch in them were unbearable. They say some magic swords are impossible to resheath until they have killed. Perhaps some form of this curse was true with this blade. Perhaps its owner could never rest easy again until he'd let it loose to do its work.

My father took hesitant steps down the grassy, dew-wet bank towards the boats bobbing eagerly. He did not cut such a figure as he might have, even with ten grown sons and twice again as many retainers at his back. He was sleep-disheveled and had only his short brown cloak to cover his nakedness.

"Now, King Ermenaric, my friend, my kinsman," he said, opening his hands wide in an innocent gesture. "What seems to be the trouble here? Have we not sworn alliance? Have our bridal gifts not been rich enough? If not, return the girl and we will make amends. Only do not, I pray you, go away so hastily and by stealth."

The King of the Goths stood his ground before the guy rope of his flag ship and faced my father. I could not see that hated face, but something in it must have sent a clear message to my father without a word.

"Ah, the sword..." My father turned to Sigmund. "Son, don't you think, for the sake of amity with these our kinsmen, you might–?"

In the rising light, Sigmund's face read clearly. Some might even say that a curse had hold on him. He would not put father-murder beyond the reach of his Balmung. Any man who offered compromise to such a blatant affront he'd deem a coward who deserved to be abandoned by Odin.

My father turned again to the ships and took a desperate breath. His eyes rose above the ships where, through the rising mist, the rough-hewn logs of the Roman palisade on the opposite bank had only just appeared. My father was federate with the Romans. By grace of their blind eye, he had been able to raid as he had and build up this rich holding here on the Rhine.

Though powerful allies, the Romans were no use when it came to disposing of a daughter. The Romans wanted German women as slaves only, not as wives. The Romans made treaties with arms, not bridal beds. So my father had turned to the Goths for this alliance. Too late he had learned, to his sorrow and mine, that he was too Romified to be an equal match in Germanic terms with the large tribe of Gothland.

Yes, he might signal the Romans for help. Guards on the Roman walls might even now be observing the doings on our side of the river with smirks of superior amusement. "And what are those barbarians up to now?" they might be saying. "What strange, wild rites!" And they would continue to watch in the bemusement with which one watched pigs in rut. In any case, by the time the garrison could be roused to the earnestness of the case and ferried over the river – assuming this feat could be accomplished – the Goths and I would be halfway to the sea.

So my father smiled at Ermenaric to put the best face on his situation. He opened his hands again in a wide, giving gesture. My husband snapped with distaste and temper, making a sign of his own, sharp and clean, for the commanders of his other boats to cast off. Then he turned to do the same for his flag ship.

At this moment, our gander, already bloody and with a broken wing, chose to make one final attack. He caught Ermenaric through the thick wool of his trousers right to the skin of his thigh and hung on for everything a waist-high grey bird is worth.

Ermenaric gave a roar of fury and pain and almost fell as he slipped on a rock ornamented with goose droppings that littered the rest of the beach as well. My father always remarked on the dung with pride as a sign of his wealth. In an instant, Ermenaric gained his footing, but the gander still clung. Then the King of the Goths raised his great battle axe and let it fall. The blade sliced the gander nearly in two. Ermenaric tossed him, still flapping convulsively, at my father's feet. Only the dogs might find the bloody heap worth sinking their teeth into.

Ermenaric grinned up at my father with that face that knew the bite of an ax and was still able to grin, but only in an ugly way. "Good father-in-law," he said, mockery in tone belying the sense of his words, "forgive our haste, but we must cross the high seas before the winter storms set in."

That line fooled no one. Even an early winter was more than a month away.

"But come, you," Ermenaric continued, "all of you Volsungs. Come to Gothland in the spring, and we shall be pleased to return your hospitality. Then we can discuss ownership of girl or sword or both at much more leisure. Come – if you dare!"

Balmung sang out of its sheath once more. It took three of my other brothers to keep it and Sigmund at bay. The blade quivered in his hand like a thing alive with fury, as if it could spring and strike like a serpent.

"Goth, I accept your pathetic dare!" I heard the dear voice whose wordless cry must have been the first thing I ever heard in this world. "By all the Gods, look for Sigmund Volsungsson in Gothland." But powerlessness honked in my twin's throat as if the gander spoke from the dead.

Beneath me, the ship, cut free at last, leaped eagerly downstream with a lurch that sent jabs of pain from my seat upwards. In spite of the stream's swiftness, Ermenaric had no trouble catching hold of the gunwale and swinging himself onboard, dripping Rhine water as he landed. This journey's plunder cut into his wonted space onboard and, in the wild joy of his movements, he knocked some of the treasures off their piles. From the planks of the hull he retrieved my bridal crown and set it none-too-gently on my head. Laughing, he said, "Well, your father's stolen goods will not become heirlooms in any kingdom on the Rhine, either."

I thought of the hidden sorrow of the slave girls who'd attended my maidenhood in my father's hall, the sorrow of every woman who'd ever hoped to pass her mother's treasures on to a daughter after her. My ears, certainly, would never wear rings again, and for the rest–

In our language, "wretch" and "one banished from his home" were the same word. Did they take the wretchedness of any female into account when they made their word-store? All of us, then, were wretches, for marriage banished us all.

Such thoughts as these brought the tears up now in a wild, helpless keening which, in conjunction with the crown, set Ermenaric to slapping his thighs with laughter. So deep was my grief that I took no opportunity to bid farewell forever, even with a glimpse, to the softly wooded, rolling hills of my childhood.

chapter 12

FTER THREE DAYS OF THE land growing taut-
er and tauter on its banks, the Rhine emptied through a
mouth as crumbly with dunes as an invalid's is with dried
rheum. Then we entered the open sea, the whale's roof top, as the poet
says, "The seething pot of Aegir, his never-empty horn of mead." With
such a thick and turbid drink, it was no wonder that Odin was such a
short-tempered, dangerous god.

To be on the sea with no land in sight was to me like falling through
thin air. My heart continually skipped beats in panic. Yes, we often
saw bits of land, islands or outcrops. We even set anchor on three of
them to pick up supplies. But since Ermenaric's manner of victual-
ing was the raid, I was not allowed to put my foot on solid ground.
Landfall meant a raid, meant leaving in a hurry with angry natives at
one's tail. It did occur to me on these occasions to try to slip away and
find refuge with some local cottager. But then I thought, when they
discovered whence I'd come – that I was no selkie or mermaid or other
daughter of Aegir – they would certainly want their losses made good
on my head. And since Ermenaric always came back with a bloody
sword, I did not take the chance.

Perhaps we were never so far from land that we couldn't see it, but
generally I saw fog banks instead of sand banks. This added to the
sense of falling through the sky. No one spoke to me to reassure me

of their seamanship. Did they know where they were going? Did they know the lands where we did see settlement were not the haunts of trolls or giants? I was their king's woman, and surely they should show some respect, even to a female, when their king was involved. As for Ermenaric, he obviously thought me too stupid to understand speech. So I was alone with my pain and my doubts until my throat felt dusty. Or misty, rather – as swathed with fog as any bank we sailed past.

We endured two weeks on the open sea, two weeks of falling through midair. Ermenaric had forecasted winter storms to keep my father from following us. We passed through a number of squalls with no roof or awning. Sea-god Aegir's watery mountains gained small snow caps, and I was uncomfortable enough, but the voyage passed uneventfully. We never had enough rough weather to make the sailors raise their voices.

Before the end of those two weeks, I knew Aegir's strong mead, as poets called the sea, was not what nauseated me. I was no longer alone – I was carrying Ermenaric's child. That knowledge made the nausea grow instead of fade as we entered a great harbor.

We first passed a bleak, sandy spit of land where Ermenaric went ashore to make thank-offerings appropriately enough to the Queen of the Netherworld, Hel, who gave her name to this peninsula. Beyond this point, westerly winds created currents that carried the ship directly to the safe arms of the mainland. A quick trip over smooth waters put solid land on either side of us as we entered the mouth of a river nearly on a scale with the Rhine. Its name is Vistula.

Gothic land spread on either side of us now. Gothiscandza, this area at the mouth was called, named for Scandza or Scandia, the bleak island far to the north where even the sun refused to shine for forty days a year. The Goths first set sail to come and settle on the mainland from that place. Gothiscandza or, as the word became on the chopping block of Gothic tongues, Gdansk. Others call it Bernsteinstatt, or Amber City, for the precious gemstone found in great quantities on those shores.

Ermenaric had not inherited this land by birth, for his branch of the tribe and the base of his power were centered much farther south.

These lands he had joined to his patrimony by conquest, these home-lands of the Aesti, the Veneti, the Antes, and the Sclaveni. Strange as their names sounded, his name was well known everywhere. We could draw ashore every night and be certain of hospitality, cramped with fear though it often was.

In this dark land, forest spilled at times right into the water. The soft reds and oranges of turning beech and oak padded as if for safety the needles of these virgin pines. An eternal drizzle of mist gave an air of dream-world to objects no farther away than one could toss a stone. It grew darker, colder, and wetter by the day.

For all its drawbacks, Gothland was solid land, and I was permitted to step on it. At first I doubted that my little-used and sea-tossed legs would stand up to the blessing, but they held, as did the misery of my fate.

I dreaded solid ground meant that Ermenaric would claim a hus-band's privileges with his original violence. A crowded ship deck with hardly room to lie elbow to elbow and foot to foot had not kept him from proving himself a man nightly to me as well as to his men. But it had turned his abusive fury into a certain rough humor. Our union onboard was in some respects communal, my husband making loud sounds to announce his satisfaction to the night, and the crew responding with longing sighs and smirking guffaws. I always kept as silent as I could, even if it meant biting my lip until it bled, to avoid being part of that dialogue. I feared that, once on land and my hus-band given the best, most private closet on any premises, the burden of dialogue would shift to me once more. Even if he had to beat me to get it.

But this proved not to be the case. Every settlement owed the King of Goths fealty, which included the provision of a virgin for his pleasure. Since he had made the trip downstream to wed me within the past two months, these girls were very young indeed – in most cases the younger sisters or cousins of girls who'd provided the service earlier. Nonetheless, most of them seemed determined to please and held their deepest grudges not against my husband but against me. I held the place of queen, something all of their efforts and good will brought none of them. So he left me mercifully on my own. Most of these people spoke no dialect that I could make head nor tail of, though I understood Ermenaric and his men's harsh gutturals well enough.

I proved of no use, even in the kitchen. The river banks we passed by day offered little sign of farming. I was hard pressed to imagine how the natives might feed themselves until, night by night, repeats of the same fare were brought up. Ermenaric feasted on boiled venison and wild boar, cakes of acorn meal, fresh-gathered, leached, and ground. No cheese or milk of any kind graced the boards. I liked milk, and the babe in my belly made me crave it even more. I couldn't help in cooking what we were served; I could hardly eat it.

Rowing our way upstream was slow going. Alone with my thoughts and relieved of the terror of the open sea as well as the nightly visitations from my husband, I thought long and hard about my physical condition. I was not alone, though perhaps worse than alone. I wished desperately for my mother, her sagging breasts and belly that spoke of nothing if not experience. I missed Sigmund, too, perhaps most of all. We had never slept under a different roof since we shared the roof of a womb. But he and his Balmung could do little to help in the present situation except – a quick prayer to Mother Frigga! – perhaps make my child an orphan before it was born.

While my mind swirled with such thoughts, slowly, almost imperceptibly, the land about us on either shore began to change. The forests thinned, then disappeared. The land, as far as weather allowed vision, stretched flat. The bows and quivers over the shoulders of the men who doffed their hats to us turned into sickles, then, with the season, to winnowing forks. These people were farmers with flocks and herds. They decorated their houses with loving detail – doves, hearts, spindles – carved on the gables and roofs of the porches. I fell upon the toasted cheese on crusty bread offered for supper before falling to sleep each night, exhausted from the double burden of mind and body. These folks' fields in stubble for the winter seemed, too, to be breathing the breaths of deep sleep.

A strange stillness cloaked the land, a close warmth almost. The sort of weather, my mother always used to say, when children grew unmanageable and had to be turned out of doors to run it off until the storm came. Then the first snow hit us, making the countryside even more uniform. Ermenaric pressed his men forward.

Then, one evening as darkness quickly closed in upon us over flat ground, we came upon a palisade of oaken logs bristling on the higher west bank. The logs had been rough-hewn to fierce points around the top.

"There she is," Ermenaric said. That "she" had more love in it than when he said it in reference to me. "Your new home."

I felt tears coming to my eyes. He'd never said anything nicer to me. But "home" conjured so many feelings – and this fort did not answer to any of them. Still, I fought the tears back and walked hopefully up through the gathering darkness and the thin crust of snow frozen to a stiff crunch, carrying such of my dowry that I could really call my own.

All at once, I screamed, dropped my bundle, and covered my eyes, shaking from head to toe and frozen to the spot with terror. Before me and on all sides I heard my escort shrieking, too, with laughter. I opened my eyes, but the nightmare still stood there. On a stake, at just man-height, sat a decapitated head. Who could blame me for thinking it a troll or ogre, the skin blackened by exposure, the brows sagging with rot, the cheeks bare to the bone, the hair standing up in bloody tufts as if in horror. Actually, a troll or an ogre might have been better.

"That, my good wife," said Ermenaric, still laughing and coming to set his hand in camaraderie upon the fellow's pate, "that is the former chief of the Antes, he who dared to oppose me in my march north. You see his comrades joining ranks beside him. A few Veneti over there. There, the dark Sclaveni."

And so they were: a good deal of the bristling effect of this lodge rested upon the stakes set less than three strides apart around its entire circumference, each with its troll-head trophy.

I recovered my composure enough to pick up my snow-covered bundle and carry myself into the hall. But I found little release from horror inside. Here my husband threw himself into the high seat like some kind of god, and was instantly served his home brew – in the bleached skull of the recalcitrant chief of the Veneti.

I felt someone pluck at my sleeve and turned with a start to find a solid, pink-cheeked woman who said in a kind undertone, "Lady, would you care to see your chamber?"

In spite of the fact that she'd crept up behind me silently as a cat out of the shadows behind, making me go blank with terror yet again, I gratefully took the opportunity to escape the presence of my husband. "Oh, yes," I said when I found breath again, "if you please!"

The room was a small converted armory from which the smell of honing grease had not been totally cleansed. This outpost had little use for home comforts. But a cheerful fire crackled in the hearth, furs hung on the walls to keep drafts out of the holes where spears had been tested, and simply the sound of another female voice made me feel better than I had for two months.

"I am Mathesuentha," the woman said.

Her smile revealed interestingly crooked teeth and tended to hide a blond but rather hairy upper lip. All in all, she looked nothing so much as like a cat, plump, well-fed, sitting by the fire and smoothing her yellow and cream tabby hair that strayed from her white linen headdress.

"I followed my husband here," she said, not meowed, as she puttered with egg batter and a skillet by the fire. "He came to fight under my lord your husband, but died battling the Alani. For his service, the king swore I should always have a roof over my head and his protection. I stay for that. And to tend my husband's bones."

Presently she set before me a platter of pancakes fried in butter and rolled up with a sweet, soft-curd cheese. Served to the side were crab apples stewed with a bit of honey and pork rind, and a big bowl of milk still warm and frothy from the evening milking.

"It's all so delicious!" I exclaimed and realized I had almost forgotten how to eat.

The crooked teeth exposed themselves with pride. "I like to make a house a home," she said, "although it isn't always prized – or easy in a land of trolls and berserks like this. Now, I'd better go see to his majesty and the rest of them," she said, wiping flour from her hands to her skirt on her way out. "But you make yourself right at home. If there's anything you need, you just let me know."

The platter was clean, and my shrunken stomach ached with satisfaction. I had almost forgotten I had been thinking of killing myself, and that refusing the king's boiled meat and strong mead had seemed the easiest way to go about it. "But I cannot go to the realm of Hel without another plate of Mathesuentha's stuffed pancakes," I vowed, sighing as I lay back on the bed.

Later that night, Ermenaric came, drunken, to me.

He was gone the next morning before I awoke.

"He and his men are traveling as far south as they can before the river freezes up," explained Mathesuentha. "A man like that, with such wide domains, he cannot rest for a moment, or something in his tail will crumble."

"But what of me?"

"This is your home. Didn't he tell you?"

"I suppose he did," I said, remembering what encircled the place. "In a way."

"He has other residences, to be sure. Many much grander than this. But they already have wives in them."

"Other wives. I see."

"He is a king, after all."

"After all," I mused. "And I suppose he doesn't mind that life?"

"The life of a king? What's to mind?"

"It is a life he's chosen for himself, after all."

"After all."

"For some, I guess, it is worthwhile moving all the time if you get to deflower virgins and take rebellious heads all the way."

At this, Mathesuentha laughed until the tears came.

Other queens, farther south. I learned my husband even had a firstborn son somewhere, named Gesimund – not named for him, but Goths do not always name the son to alliterate with the father. There were surely many other sons, but I never met any of them. As far as I was concerned, it was just Mathesuentha and I – and the little one growing inside me – safe in that cozy former armory.

Fifteen or so men remained of the garrison, and none of these had wives or children; few women in the world are like Mathesuentha. A handful of traders, a Vandal, and two assiduous Greeks had decided upon this place to claim winter hospitality as well. In warmer months, they bore pouches of amber and blue bundles of sable south, an assortment of pretty but fairly useless gauds from Rome north. Now I couldn't tell them apart from the garrison in drinking and carousing.

Even though we shared a roof with these men, we didn't share a fire. I was Ermenaric's queen, and Mathesuentha the widow of a fallen hero. Besides, she could take care of herself and wouldn't hesitate to strike a man who got out of line with whatever she happened to have in her hand – rolling pin, quern stone, or kitchen knife. They never dared to strike back and always remembered to keep a respectful distance from then on.

After Ermenaric had gone, Mathesuentha came and shared the bed with me. We had a ring of firelight and two rings of logs to protect us from the winter, the wolves, and whatever other evil Thor's mighty hammer could drive without hindrance over that bleak open plain. And the ring of staked heads around the stockade served as a warning to those outside of what happened to anyone who defied the honor of Ermenaric. Or was that warning meant for those of us within the compound?

chapter 13

ERE WE GO," SANG MATHESUENTHA
merrily. From her cloak and the bundle on her
shoulder, she shook the dusting of snow. It sput-
tered in the fire and freshened the air in the room which otherwise
smoked to toughness.

I looked up from my spinning, and she let the contents of the
bundle tumble to the bear rug on the floor. "Let's see what you can do
with this," she said.

There, catching on the stiff brown guard hairs as on the teeth of a
comb, was a great cloud of hackled flax. Mathesuentha knelt on the
rug and sorted it quickly with experienced hands into two bunches
of different textures: the shorter, irregular tow and the higher-quality
line. Some of the line, when stretched, would reach from the tip of my
nose past the end of my middle finger.

"Ah, yes, she said she'd already spun a skein or two of it herself."
Mathesuentha found the skeins and sorted them out into yet a third
pile. "Tsk, I would have spun it tighter, wouldn't you? But what's done
is done, I guess."

"She." I knew, when it referred to neither the cow nor one of the
hens, was a woman named Ababa. I'd never met her myself. She
reigned as mistress of the nearest croft. It took a morning's journey in
good weather to pay a visit and return.

Mathesuentha rocked back on her heels, still in her cloak, and smiled at her handiwork. Her face burned with the out of doors, exercise, and pride. "She's kept busy, you know, with her family, two boys, nearly grown, and a little girl who – never tell Ababa I said this – is less help than she ought to be at her age. Ababa was my only company before you came and, I must say, she was glad to see me today. She did wonder what had become of me, and on a nice day, as today started out to be. Who could have guessed it would be snowing by afternoon?"

Mathesuentha shook the rest of the snow off her cloak and hung it up to dry. "Anyway, I've told her all about you. She can't wait to meet you, come spring. And here we have it – her year's growth of flax. You know I don't grow it myself – too much work without a man to do the plowing for you. Oh, yes, there's men enough around here, big louts who can carry a shield and swagger about and think they've earned their keep. Otherwise, totally useless. But that's all right, I guess. My own man, rest him, was pretty much the same. And I never thought I needed more than a sheep's worth of wool, a goose or two of feathers, and a bit of leather to keep myself comfortable, so I never bothered. But today, with that last herringbone piece just ready to come off the loom, and the sun out for a moment and all, I just thought I should nip up to her house and see if she didn't have some flax to spare. She's given me everything she had, did I tell you? I've given her a pair of those golden brooches from your dowry in exchange. I knew you wouldn't mind. She probably would have given it anyway, just to be neighborly. But I thought, just to be neighborly, we ought to give her what it's worth."

Any girl, when she dreamed of her married future, must certainly count among her fondest imaginings the picture of herself with the keys at her waist. These symbolized her power, these keys to the household's treasure, not least of which was, one hoped, a splendid dowry. With these keys, she freed herself of paternal authority and a husband's authority as well. She was the mistress of her own fate, wealth, and happiness, as well as that of all those beneath her roof. The idea that someone had taken my keys, mere symbols though they were, without my knowledge, and bartered away a jewel, some emblem from my homeland and my family's care, should have given offense. And, for a moment it did. However, this was not just anyone. It was Mathesuentha. Truth to tell, I enjoyed having someone take care of me like this. Any surprise or hurt I'd shown should have been wiped from my face before her next sentence.

"Well, what else is a dowry," she asked, "but to be spent on swaddling for the babies of that marriage?"

And that sentence put the surprise right back on.

"You can't very well swaddle babies in wool, now, can you? Or leather. Don't be ridiculous. Linen is..."

"How did you know?" I felt my swelling belly gently, almost protectively. Mathesuentha couldn't tell, but I was trying to protect, not the baby, but myself from the betrayal of my own body.

"How did I know? My dear, haven't I swaddled enough babes in my time? Never one of my own, no, but plenty of others. And washed the swaddling out, too, every night in the bathwater after bathing them and popping them into bed. No, wool would never do. Of course, yours'll be spring, won't it? Late spring, I should think. Then the drying's not such a problem. You'll have all summer when you can even leave 'em bare-bottomed outside if you've a mind to. And that's good for them – if they don't get too much sun. Helps fight off the rash which, in the winter, as the gods are my witness, is–"

"Mathesuentha, how did you know?"

"What, child? That you're expecting? La, as if it weren't written all over your face!" She took my face in her hands and pinched my two cheeks.

I knew I was growing plump – but that could have just been Mathesuentha's stuffed pancakes. I had only just begun to tie my girdle a little looser. My dresses had not grown so tight that I couldn't wriggle into them. Women's wear, of course, presumed pregnancy.

"Now, don't you worry your head about anything. I've never had one of my own, that's true, but I've been at many a birthing, ready for anything. Birthed Ababa's youngest without anyone else. And she came buttocks first, that one did. I've made a study of useful herbs and magics. You needn't worry about a thing. It'll make this place a home, won't it, to have a young one creeping about? And swaddling to make from scratch when we've nothing but soldier's old bandages to use besides.

"So, let me see if I can't cut that herringbone down – oh, isn't that nice and wide! With a good stretch to it. It'll make you a nice new dress, love, which you'll be needing soon enough, soon enough. And you – you start to work on some more of that line. See if we can't get something done before those men start clanging their swords on their shields for their supper, eh?"

So Mathesuentha chatted on about what dear babies she had known in her life – and she had been the oldest of a family which, after two stepmothers, finally included sixteen children.

The men eventually clanged their swords, and she saw to them. "Just like a pack of children, aren't they?" she whispered when she returned and picked up the chatter from there.

Soon, however, she saw how tired I was and "for the baby's sake," told me to put up my spindle and get into bed. She brought me a bowl of warm milk and tucked me in.

"But I–" she said with a merry laugh, "–once I've gotten myself excited about something like this, I can't let it rest."

I watched her over the marten-fur coverlet in the shrinking lamp-light as she tied stones and clay weights to lengths of the linen line and hung them at minute intervals from the loom's crossbeam to make the warp. Her chatter faded to the tales she used to tell her many charges and then, in a soft, low tone, the lullabies.

I started suddenly awake. There before me stood Mathesuentha, not plump and pink-cheeked, but wizened and hollow grey. And, in her hand, instead of a warp weight, she was holding – holding out to me – one of the heads from the pikes outside.

I struggled to beg her to put it away, then to scream, but could do neither. Then, I felt the life within me stir. It took on a life of its own, horrible life, like its father, wrenching me apart from hip to hip, rip-ping my ear lobes, cutting my swollen breasts not with bits of jewelry but with greedy fangs. Its limbs were fat and childlike, but hairy with coarse black hair like an otter or marten instead of a human. Its face wore the hideous scar of its father, not healed, but open and freshly bleeding. Its coos and mews were the growls and snarls of trolls, and I saw at once that it meant to tear me to pieces. At last I managed to scream. And once started, I couldn't stop.

The next thing I saw was Mathesuentha again. She had regained her normal face, but her voice seemed as fierce as ever. "Begone, begone, vile night sending. In the name of Ermenaric the King, in the name of all the Gods, I conjure you, begone!"

She winked at me then and whispered in her own voice, "One must speak boldly to such spirits, show them that you are not afraid." She began again, very boldly, "In the name of Ermenaric..."

The shriek that came out of me convinced her never to say my husband's name again. When she had managed to bring my screams and my gasping for breath down to low sobs, she got up, throwing a fur about her nakedness. She blew the banked ashes to life and added wood enough that she could turn me over on my back and draw the covers down without fear of the chill.

What liberties is she taking now? was my thought, and I jumped from her first touches as from the evil spirit that wore her face. But she persisted with skilled hands I could not resist. She kneaded with such vigor, as if she wanted to reduce my whole body to its original elements. She rubbed my bared back with wads of hemp that scratched like brickbats. Her hands worked as they might on a skein a kitten had gotten to, finding out every knot, knots I didn't know I had, and teasing them out with firm patience. But still, like a wad of rags, lay the knot under my belly that wouldn't go away.

"Now, now, why don't you tell me all about it?"

I had not wished to spill my vision to the air, as if the very words might re-embody it. But my lips could no more resist her unraveling than could the knots hunching my shoulders. I gave her only snippets of the horrors of my "marriage," my abduction, and the journey here. My mind could retain only snippets of the horror, after all. But from such thread ends she had skill enough to extract the whole.

"I thought perhaps it was a nightmare," I said. "That if I ignored this permanent effect of ... of that man's attentions, it would go away.

But today you confirmed that it is real. It is real inside me. It will not go away."

"I am here to share your burden, child," Mathesuentha murmured, somewhere far away from the knots of my pain, just picking at them with the thinnest slip of a fingernail.

"That should make my burden lighter, shouldn't it? But it does not. It grows so heavy, I cannot bear it. I would give anything to make it unreal again. See what a haunting it already makes, although it must be no bigger yet than a mite. Such a haunting, in my dreams. It will consume me ... from the inside out..."

That's the last thing I remember saying, for though such a dread dragged through my words, once I spoke them, the terror vanished. I slept undisturbed until nausea forced me up and out of bed at broad daylight.

We worked at our spinning and weaving quite calmly that day, the nightmare unmentioned. As evening began to close in on us again, however, it brought a howling wind. I thought I could hear wolves in that wind. The haunting of my dream seemed to blow through the cracks, ruffling aside the furs. Then, once in the room, even though I was awake, the dream seemed to take on solid form and reach for me.

To spin swaddling linen was out of the question. Although Mathesuentha made her specially stuffed pancakes, I couldn't even sit to eat them. I could only pace from one short end of the room to the other, and that did not offer a broad enough walk to escape dark arms that would crush me with their embrace.

My hopeless flight soon exhausted me. I could hardly put one foot before the other, but still I didn't dare lie down upon the bed, where I would then be an easy target. I think perhaps I fell asleep on my pacing feet. Mathesuentha was then able to steer me to bed. I do remember her gentle crooning again, a bowl of warm milk, and more massage, the firm, bold kneading pushing out every pocket of evil vapor.

But sometime in the night it caught up with me again and rode me with spurs like a man with death itself behind him. For all Mathesuentha's clever hands and kind words, I could not sleep again until dawn.

I awoke still unrefreshed in late afternoon. Mathesuentha sat spinning beside me, and I could read by the concern in her face that more desperate measures were about to be taken.

"Come," she said, quickly packing up her work. "Throw this fur over your shoulders and put on your boots. We're going out."

"Out? With nothing on but a fur?"

"We're not going far."

We did have to pass out of the ring of spiked heads, muffled in caps of snow. They reached out dark hands of icicles towards me, and I clung closer to Mathesuentha. Once past them, however, the rays of the setting sun on the snow relaxed me.

Somewhat away from the stockade and down by the river stood the small wood-planked smokehouse. This location guarded against the spread of possible fire. I'd never ventured there myself, but the prints I matched my feet to, getting snow on my bare legs and down my boots as I did so, told me that Mathesuentha had already been down to the smokehouse at least twice that day.

As we drew nearer, I could see a great billow of smoke over Mathesuentha's shoulder. And as we drew nearer still, I got a full view. The door of the hut stood open and, through that door as well as through every crack and shingle, poured thick grey smoke. I stopped dead in my tracks. I had often heard that for a woman with child to look upon a house afire, even so small a house as a smokehouse, brought great misfortune to the unborn: birthmarks and such. Yet I couldn't tear my eyes away.

"There's nothing to be afraid of," Mathesuentha said, coming back for me when she failed to hear the crunch of my boots echoing hers. "It's quite contained." She urged me on. But then she actually wanted me to step within a burning building. I balked again.

"I know it only looks like a common smokehouse," she said. "And indeed, take a peek inside. We've a couple of hams and a handful of fish hanging from the ceiling. But magic also lurks here. Good magic I learned from a woman whose people came from the far north. She called it in her language a 'sauna.' You'll find it most healing, most renewing. But first you must remove all your jewelry, else it might burn you."

"Burn?" I stopped in the midst of taking my chains off, unable to believe what I heard.

"That's right. Now, come in." Mathesuentha took my hand and helped me up as if the step had been knee-high instead of barely off the ground. "We bend in humility as we enter – it is a holy place." Her voice dropped perceptibly. "It is like – it is like returning to the safe womb of a mother."

Of all madness, she shut the door behind us. The adzed logs of the smokehouse wall, caulked with moss, wore the soft patina of age. They pervaded the inside air with the smell of resin – and with heat.

"Take off your boots."

Then she stripped the fur off my back, and I stood there, absolutely naked, in a dry heat that crushed the breath in me. In another moment, Mathesuentha stood naked herself beside me.

"Now, sit down. Relax."

The heat oppressed so much, I had little choice but to do as she said. My bones seemed to melt in the fervent heat. In one corner of the house stood a mound of rocks, just piled there without mortar but in such a cunning way that a fire could be built in the hollow at their midst. The fire and its smoke were dying now, but the stones remained hot enough that when Mathesuentha dashed them with a scoop of water from a bucket, I could barely see her face for the steam. She scraped a spoonful of pine tar onto the smoking stones as well. Its scent made the steam even thicker, more ready to coat the passages of my nose and lungs. From such an unnatural mist, the nightmare would surely arise. My heartbeats, ready as they seemed to split my veins, fairly roared for it. But something in that steam seemed to gulp down the roars and calm them.

"Now," Mathesuentha said, "a quick roll in the snow."

I thought she must be truly mad. First to walk into a burning building, then to roll naked in the snow. But I found myself too weak to do anything other than oblige her.

How invigorating it was! We frolicked in the sting of snow like three-year-olds.

"Back to the house!" she shouted, just as I volleyed a snowball at her posterior and began to lose sensation in my feet.

In we went, and this time, as the snow and sweat began to curl off my body in milky ribbons of steam, she took up a bunch of birch twigs – she must have gathered them in the summer, for the leaves were still on them, though somewhat stiff and dry – and began to whisk me with it.

"Ow!" I exclaimed, but with surprise only, not pain.

"Here, you do it," she said, and took up a branch of her own.

I found myself whisking harder than she had done as every inch of my skin grew wet with perspiration. I might have just stepped up from total immersion in river water. A wonderful sweet spring smell of birch permeated the air and filled every pore. How beautifully pink my skin grew, how soft, how new.

When the magic bath was finished, we scurried back up to the stockade. Only when we'd regained the safety of our room did I remember we must have passed the bodiless sentries. In my delight, I hadn't even noticed them.

On our return, Mathesuentha regaled me with some delicious little pastries she'd made that afternoon, rye crusts stuffed with salty barley and baked to a turn, washed down with a thin, sweet cold mead in which she'd set dried currants to float. I could have been a newborn babe when she tucked me in that night, a babe with no life as yet to disturb her dreams. The magic lingered all the next day, and we got the woof started on the loom. But by early nightfall, the evil had inched back.

Repeated trips to the smokehouse kept the thing at bay for the better part of a week, but then it seemed to learn a counterspell. Mathesuentha hoisted her magic up another notch to meet it. She decided I must be cupped.

As I sat naked in the sauna, the sweat flowing and the blood pulsing just under my skin, my guardian took out her little paring knife. With this she made a number of quick cuts all over my shoulders and back. "Not too deep, so there's no danger of scarring." Then she brought out an equal number of cow's horns, whittled and smoothed out on the inside. Over the punctured point of each horn, she tied a small circle of clean, thin sow's bladder with a bit of thread. Over each cut she set a horn and, sucking on the bladder, caused the horns to stick to my flesh of their own accord. I must have looked like some warrior's battle mace, spiked all over with those horns.

Presently the horns began to slip from my skin, each one sated with blood. I began to feel light-headed.

"We must cup again," Mathesuentha said. "First comes the blood, then the clear fluid. It's in the clear fluid that the evil lies, and there is much dark blood. Your evil has set up quite a barrier."

She washed my wounds, scraped away the scabs beginning to form, set the cups and sucked again. I fainted.

Three nights later, the evil returned.

chapter 14

CANNOT CUP AGAIN," MATHESUENTHA said. "Your frail little body cannot take it, not to mention the baby. I must take an augury."

She set up a fortune table in the center of our room. Over a low bench she spread a cloth, then set a lamp burning at each corner. Into each lamp's oil she crushed a bit of dried herb. I think it was mugwort. The flakes sputtered and gave off some of their distinctive earthy scent when the tongues of flame lapped at them. Then she went down to the smokehouse alone, leaving me to watch.

Upon her return, Mathesuentha immediately sat down before the table again. She took up a cloth, bundled it and shook it. From the bundle she then tossed onto the table five pieces of smooth white pine, each carved with a magic rune. She studied closely how the sticks had fallen, nodding somberly to herself as she committed each piece to memory. With one final firm nod, she took a deep breath and popped a hard, dry morsel into her mouth, her first food of the day, as she had been fasting. Although in a dry state and hardly recognizable, I knew the morsel to be agaric mushroom, the red-capped kind with which you can kill a great number of flies if you put a little honey on the fungus and wait but a while.

We waited a while. Mathesuentha cast the lots again, then again. This final toss, she could not have had time to memorize the fall, for she was suddenly and soundly asleep, fallen herself over the lots on the table.

I watched in silence for a very long time. I didn't dare get up to touch her, to move her to a more comfortable position, or even to one where she was in less danger of catching fire from the low-sputtering lamplight. I didn't dare move myself to a less cramped position – and cramped positions came more and more frequently to me now as the baby grew.

Perhaps I nodded off, although I tried to keep watch. Leaving myself open to the evil when my guardian remained drugged and perhaps not strong enough herself to fend it off terrified me into wakefulness. But then I came suddenly and perfectly awake, and so did she.

She was so much herself, bustling about to clean her things up with only the slightest bit of tension in the normal prattle of her voice. Had she actually been to the other world to wrestle with spirits for me?

"I have dreamed. I have flown." Her first words of assurance might have said no more than, "I've fried us up some pancakes," with that same tone.

"You weren't a woman. You were a young man," she continued. "Very strong and handsome, with a wonderful sword."

"Oh, that would be my brother," I said. "I have a brother, a twin brother, Sigmund. They say we are very much alike."

"Ah, that'll be it, then."

"And the sword is a divine sword, a gift of the One-Eyed."

"Hmm." She did not seem to be so happy to hear this.

"Its name is Balmung," I said, to reassure her. "Is my brother all right?"

"Fine. Quite fine." Mathesuentha was brusque now. "He will come here to Gothland."

"Oh, I knew it!" I cried with joy. "Soon?"

"Come the spring. As soon as the ocean is passable once more. Braving Aegir's great calves that are born at that time, the icebergs."

"He – my husband – he invited my family all to come, and I know Sigmund will not fail me. I know he will come."

"It does not seem, however, that this young man comes to toast boon-fellow with his brother-in-law."

"Boon-fellow?" I laughed bitterly. "Would you? With Ermenaric?"

Mathesuentha sniffed in comprehension. "Your brother comes for war."

"He waits only for spring to come and for troops to be raised to aid him. Sigmund is going to rescue me, to avenge. I pray for no more. I pray for no less."

"Perhaps. For your sake, I hope it may be so."

"But he must."

"That part seemed dark."

"I live only for that."

"I saw your child."

"I am condemned to bear it, then."

"That part also seemed dark. Very dark. That seemed to be the source of your evil haunting."

"A child's the last thing I want if Sigmund is coming. I wish I could return to him a maid. To stay with him forever. Or at least to have it to do all over again, to be given to a man of Sigmund's choosing, someone close to him, and like him – caring. Someone picked with a kind brother's eyes, not with the ambition of my father's. That's what I ask, although I would really rather only stay with Sigmund, now that I've seen marriage."

"I fear the child you carry – and it is a son–"

"By the Gods, the more to be like his father."

"I fear he is destined not to live long. He will never be a man."

"Do not think to grieve me with such words. The shorter the better, as far as I'm concerned."

"Child, you should bite your tongue. I see much grief from this."

"Am I not nightly tormented by this evil? By the Gods, I would cut the thing from me if I could, if I did not fear my hand would fail me with the deed half done."

"Such is your resolve, then?"

"Indeed. Mathesuentha, how can you doubt it when you nightly must share my torment?"

"Ah, and I wished for this child, longed for it, as if it were my own, the child I've never had." She dashed tears from the corners of her eyes. "What matter if you didn't care for it – for him, I mean, the sweet little lad? I have care enough in me for twenty such. But now I see perhaps I have been selfish. It is not my body that must swell – alas, I shall never swell, I fear. Not my breasts that will become pendulous with nourishment. And I have no doubt that there is great evil here. If my dream had not told me so, then yours should have, long ago."

"I wish only to cut it from me, even if I must cut my own life in the process."

"There is a way," Mathesuentha said slowly. "I am mistress of yet another magic."

"By the Gods, I conjure you. You must use it, instantly. Why have you waited so long?"

"Yes, why? It is much more dangerous to attempt now than it would have been when first I guessed at your condition."

"Don't speak to me of danger. You know I am close enough to madness to presently kill myself with my own hand. You know."

"I know." She approached me closely now and put her hands on my belly. The full expanse she covered with caresses, as if trying to bring it to herself. Then her hands seemed to be taking measurements, as one might of a corpse for its shroud. "If such is your resolve..."

"Of course it is my resolve."

"The child isn't destined to live very long, in any case," she said, as if trying to convince herself, steel her own nerves. "There are no deeds of manhood in him. This I have seen." And suddenly dark smeared under her eyes, and the dream drug caught up with her.

"Mathesuentha, do not fail me," I pleaded to the terrible weakness I saw where I had only seen strength before.

"Lady Signy, I shall not ... shall not fail. Just give me ... just give me a few days to prepare. A week, no more. That's all that's necessary."

"I am at your mercy."

Mathesuentha nodded, blew out the lamps, and sank to the bed. No dreams bothered my sleep that night, nor any of the nights in the week that followed. Simply speaking of these things seemed to have set a protective circle about our bed.

chapter 15

WHEN, A WEEK LATER, MATHESUENTHA and I made our way one more time to the smokehouse, I noticed how late the sun remained with us. In patches, the snow had melted, revealing winter-crushed plants and mud over which the thaw ran. In one spot, the distinctive blade leaves and small rose blooms of a clump of hellebore thrust into view.

"I must mark that plant," Mathesuentha said. "When it finishes blooming, I'll come and dig more roots."

She needed to replenish her supply, for she'd used much of it in the brew she'd been pressing on me for two days. Other makings included hops, oil of the savin juniper, bitter chamomile, and a brownish-red powder made from a rock found, she said, only to the far east. Parsley, sage, rosemary, and thyme in equal measure also played a part, as I might have guessed from the chorus to many a maiden's song of betrayed love. If love were betrayed, such herbs might become necessary.

My guardian and guide tried to make the mess tasty with great spoonfuls of honey, but that only gave a bitter bite to the too-sweetness that caught at the back of my throat. Still, no pains came. I was now nauseated all the time, so nauseated I had trouble keeping down any of the other nourishment she allowed me: slabs of pancakes made from the rye at the bottom of her store, rye she hadn't had time to clean yet, rye which might be moldy.

As we made the trek down to the river that day, I was, in fact, so over-come by the effects of the herbs that I wondered how Mathesuentha could think of their gathering and preparation. Perhaps she only spoke of hellebore to distract me from the overwhelming, throbbing weight of my body.

"Should you later have a child you wish to keep," she prattled on, "as I pray to the gods you may, in happier times, be careful how you clean your rye. The mold – it usually gives a purplish color to the grain – is a very powerful thing. It is often wiser not to eat rye at all when one is with child."

Powerful perhaps, but either the season was wrong for moldy rye, or I was unable to keep enough of it down. In any case, neither brew nor mold had yet to work its effect. I noticed as we slid on the well-worn slush to the smokehouse that, among her other gear, Mathesuentha carried more pancakes and more brew. Although we were about to resort to the most drastic measures, she would not give up on the easier ones. She would keep plying me with all I could hold, as she had been doing for two days.

But by Freya's mercy, I cannot take any more, I thought as I stopped to retch. The warm contents of my stomach quickly melted through the last of the snow in that spot and settled on bare ground.

A feel of spring hovered in the air that day, though a firm north wind overnight could easily erase it all before morning. Mathesuentha already talked of planting peas. She had taken out her kerchief of hard, round pea seeds and looked at them longingly on more than one occasion between sessions with me. Misery made me impatient with thoughts of the future. The baby was due before summer came fully upon us, before we would eat of the fresh peas. How could I think or live beyond that?

Mathesuentha spoke to toughen me for what I must endure. I toughened. *This must work,* I determined, stopping to vomit once more. *I will eat anything, do anything, or kill myself.* And I called ahead to Mathesuentha that I would to try to keep another rye cake down, if only to take the taste of vomit out of my mouth.

Once inside the steaming sauna, Mathesuentha had me lie on my back – I couldn't lie on my stomach any more – and she began to massage. She centered her attention on the offending belly and went at it vigorously. In no time at all, she was sweating great drops into her work, mingling it with my own as her hand slipped over my tight skin. Pain jabbed where she pressed, but no other effect.

Panting now, Mathesuentha took up a smooth broom handle and whacked me as hard as she dared. I gritted my teeth and watched the bruises form, not really crying, but unable to keep the breath from escaping in little whimpers with each blow. I'd never been beaten as a child, for I'd been my brothers' and my parents' darling. This made up for it now.

Full darkness hung outside when she finally dropped the broomstick with exhaustion. "That's the most stubborn child I've ever heard of," she said grimly. "Let's give it a rest. I'll stoke up the fire again. It'll be cold in here in a heartbeat if I don't. Then I'll try a last resort. I've never done this before, and it's quite dangerous. But it's worth a try, isn't it?"

I nodded, but felt too exhausted, too sore, too numb to do more.

Mathesuentha tossed my marten robe over me. "So you won't get chilled," she said, then told me to eat or drink if I could. Unfortunately, what she left me to drink was only that too-sweet, too-bitter brew. I tried to eat another pancake instead, but my throat was too dry to accept much.

With my eyes null of feeling, I watched Mathesuentha herself go out into the night in only her fur. She stood with her back against the smokehouse wall, musing on the stars, sucking on bits of ice broken from the shadow side of the eaves and nibbling a mixture of dried berries and nuts to restore her strength and her resolve.

I think I dozed, for when Mathesuentha wakened me, the fire in the rock hearth was sweltering again.

"There seem to be an uncommon number of torches up at the stockade," she commented as she encircled herself and me with rush lamps that glowed like limp ribbons in the sauna's steam. "Well, we won't let that worry us, and they won't notice us here in any case. Let us get back to work, then, shall we? I'm going to have you bend your knees up like this – fine. Now, try to relax. It's going to hurt, I won't deny it. But I'll be as quick as I can. It'll go easier if you relax, but when you can't, you can grab on to the edge of the bench to steady yourself – and scream. Certainly, scream all you'd like. No one's going to hear you this far from the stockade."

I could see Mathesuentha quite well by the limp ribbons of light. I hoped she could see what she was doing, too, there beyond my knees encased in curls of steam. I saw her take a stiff goose quill in her hands, twirl it and bite that whiskery lip of hers with concentration. Why did the image of our goose at home suddenly flash across my mind's eye? The image of him a mass of bleeding feathers on the end of Ermenaric's ax–

Mathesuentha took a deep breath and I felt the feather enter me. Never was the King of the Goths so careful – or so hurtful. I screamed – and then felt a powerful pang.

"I think – I think it's coming..." I said. "I can feel–"

"Good..." Mathesuentha panted. "Good. Now what we need to do..."

I didn't hear more. Another crushing pain came, and I screamed again, totally consumed with riding it out. I trusted Mathesuentha to take care of whatever the outside world needed next. Every heartbeat pulled me deeper and deeper into a world like death, a world all mine behind fearfully clenched eyelids. No one else could share the burden of it, either for good or for bad.

But somebody did enter there. Cold night air blasted my naked skin. And then – an overrunning smell of rancid butter.

"By my sword, what is she trying to do?"

"Burn the queen alive."

"I saw all the smoke, but I couldn't believe it."

"The witch!"

"Good thing your wife has such a pair of lungs on her."

"Quick, men, haul the queen out of there."

"Give her air."

"By my sword, put something on her."

My husband's voice? *Lord One-Eye of my father, were the nightmares back?* Another pain came as I felt myself mauled and dragged in four directions at once. I hadn't the strength to fight off the one pain in order to comprehend the other.

"My lord, your wife the queen – she is with child!"

"By Odin, the witch was trying to rip it from her."

"To use the corpse for her hellish brew."

"I doubt it not."

"The witch!"

That word again. I shook my aching head against it.

"Don't let her get away."

"Don't let her shape-change on you, men."

"I always thought there was something unwholesome about that one."

"Witchcraft, Thor smite it."

"We should shut her in the smokehouse and burn it down, my lord."

"Just as she meant to do to your wife in her own childless envy."

"Since the time of my great ancestor Filimer, we kings of the Goths have known how to deal with witches."

I had no doubt now that my husband was talking again. I opened one eye and saw his large form, the image of my nightmare, waving to the cluster of men about him. Some of them had armed themselves with buckets of water which they used with such violence against the mortarless hearth inside the smokehouse that it collapsed in upon itself.

"We cannot leave witches in our midst."

Ermenaric agreed with this. "Witchcraft is a diversion from the single path of Odin we Goths must follow and never stumble from if we are to remain powerful. It brings the will of others than the war God into our midst and cannot be tolerated."

"Let's burn that Mathesuentha in the smokehouse!"

"We cannot leave witches in our midst!"

"Redbeard's right, men. Even a witch's ashes are dangerous near human dwellings. But my ancestor Filimer had a plan. Redbeard, Hulmul Battleax, you two know what to do. Take her away. Off to the swamp. Pin her down well. She will bother us no more from there."

The last glimpse I saw of Mathesuentha, she wore no more than her boots and her fur thrown over her shoulders. Two of Ermenaric's burliest retainers led her away into the night sharp with frost.

And my pains had ceased. Or they had just begun.

PART III

BRYNHILD'S BETRAYAL

chapter 16

 E VALKYRIES RODE, FOLLOWING A string of
mountains to the northeast. Like the bent backs of giants,
the mountains reared, wearing spruce furs on their shoulders and leafed trees in the green woolliness of mid-summer on their
loins. Here a giant flashed a metallic blade of iron-grey granite at his
flank, there thrust an outcrop of shale like a fist through the forest
green, and over yonder, a giantess preened with a necklace of gneiss
at her bosom.

"Ore sleeps in those mountains," Thora told me. "Silver, iron, lead.
People call them the Ore Mountains, Erzgebirge."

Spur by spur, we rode as usual, her posture spear-straight and ten-
drils of her red hair blowing about her face, rusting her helmet as
it were. I found it strange that, in spite of her words, her eyes kept
wandering north and westward to the scattered human dwellings and
the receding plain instead of towards the mountains. To my way of
thinking, the colossal figures practically shouted for attention. Like
the deep growls of giants, the granite did indeed echo our battle cries
when we tried them out just for fun. But I knew this little lesson in
the natural resources of the territory we patrolled did not really fill
Thora's mind.

Thora and I were the last of the battlemaids to cross a little mountain stream. Like so many rills in the valleys here, boulders thwarted

this one until swift rapids announced its vexation. We stopped on the bank to water our horses, smelling the dark leaf mold in the hollow.

With the noise of the water to cover our talk, Thora said, "You don't agree with this mission, do you?"

An instant's fear thumped in my throat. What had she seen, my friend who could read me like deep-cut runes? In shield-hung Valhalla, when All-Father had announced the mission, the things she had heard condemned me enough. Only I of all my sisters had had the cheek to speak up – once again. The words still made me hearthside-hot to remember. "But All-Father? Are we truly to ride against Agnar Geirrodsson? Help the Goths to gain the day over Agnar's Burgundians? After what Agnar did for you, after how faithful he has always been?"

At the time, I'd felt as if my words ran full force into a standing dolman of days ancient beyond the ken of mortals. All-Father Odin had stood silently, blinking his one eye at me, no more moveable than a stone. I thought he would strike me dead then and there. In fact, I had waited for the blow, thinking it would come down like the crash of mountain rock.

But All-Father's power had come in words instead. In his deepest, echoing tones, Odin had chanted at me the riddle song of his name magic, each name a blow at my nerve.

> "I am called Grim, I am called Traveler,
> Warrior and Helmet-Wearer...
> Truth, Change, and Truth-Getter,
> Battle-Glad, Abaser, Death-Worker, Hider,
> One-Eye, Fire-Eye, Lore-Master, Masked, Deceitful."

One by one, my sisters had joined him in the song, shaming me, warning me 'til the hall rang.

> "Masked I am called in the courts of Geirrod,
> Stirrer-of-Strife at Things,
> Equal-High, Shaker, Shout and Wish,
> Wand-Bearer, Grey-Beard among Gods,

Wakeful and Heavens-Roar,
Hanged and Skifling,
Goth and Jalk among gods,
Unraveler, Sleep-Bringer–
They are many names, but all really one for me."

Unlike Agnar's father in the ancient saga, I lived through the hearing of these words. But I could not forget that when his father had been killed on his own sword by All-Father's wrath, young Agnar had been the only one who had seen through the great God's disguise and quenched the divine thirst with a horn of mead. After this, Agnar Geirrodsson was now to die? Old One-Eye was a fearsome God indeed, as fickle as the natural forces he could command, smiling sunshine one moment, crashing tempests the next.

Even now, terror enough clung to the memory of his words that I turned my face from Thora, my friend. I stared at sun and shadow on nearby tree trunks. But my fear of the God did not justify in my heart the mission that had us skirting the Erzgebirge and heading to Burgundy.

I heard the creak of shifting leather and tack behind me. "I don't agree with it, either." Was it Thora's voice or only the stream?

Astonished, I turned to look at her and knew at once I could speak my mind here safe under cover of the water. I could always speak my mind with Thora. Still I proceeded with caution. "Agnar, from all I've heard of him, is the one we should support. The Goths are obviously the aggressors in this matter. When but a boy, Agnar saved our master, saved him from eight days' thirst when he hung on the World Tree, when no one else would. Isn't this so?"

"I have often thought such thoughts," Thora said quietly. "Not just of this mission. Many missions over the years. In fact, I've come to see that I usually think this. I get a sick feeling in my stomach before, during, after. Odin supports the treacherous because he himself is a betrayer. Or perhaps it is the other way around. Liars and betrayers usually win, and Odin supports their power by the same means they acquire it."

"But – but we must be obedient."

"Yes, we must be obedient." The mocking in Thora's voice was bitter.

"But we are Valkyries," I protested further. "There is no greater honor in the world for a woman than to follow Odin. What other women get to enter the ranks of heroes, take a hand in battle – and win?"

"What honor can there be if, deep in your heart, you have betrayed what you know to be right? If you have betrayed *yourself*?"

Her words certainly made me uncomfortable. "But what other choice is there, sister?"

"Yes? What choice?"

She wasn't looking at me, nor at our fast-disappearing comrades ahead. Across the meadows sloping down to our right through which the stream gurgled and sang, a lone horseman appeared.

"What mortal is this?" I asked, scowling in the interloper's direction.

Is he going the same way we are? I wondered. *His kind should avoid us. Perhaps he means to join Agnar's forces, and that brings him into our path.*

"It might be well if we kill him now," I said, "long before the battle starts."

"He is not to be killed," Thora said definitely.

The horseman seemed to have no doubt as to who we were. He stopped at a respectful distance and sat silently watching us. The sun had passed its zenith and hung nearly at his back. I found it difficult to look at him. I recognized neither face nor helmet. "Who is he?" I asked again.

Thora knew. "Geirðjof," she said.

"Who's Geirðjof?"

"You don't remember? You saved his life. And mine. In the battle against Helgi Hundingsbane. Geirðjof's now the Earl of Saxony, and heir presumptive to the high seat, although he was born to nothing."

"You don't mean that little dark Frank?"

"Exactly."

"What does he want here?"

"Brynhild, he's come for *me*."

I started to laugh, but something in her tone told me she did not joke.

"I am leaving the Valkyries, Brynhild."

"When?" Years from now was all I could imagine, at a time so far distant, it had no meaning in my young life.

"Now. As I said, he's come for me."

"But you don't have to do anything he says, Thora. He's a mere mortal."

"Brynhild, I *want* to go with him. I'm going to be his wife."

The scene of a two-headed ogre coming out of the darkness towards our hobbled horses came flooding back to me: I had caught Thora and this – this mortal – in an embrace, and it had seemed a monster to me.

"You can't," I said. "What will Odin say?"

"I've already had it out with Odin, and I've had enough of what he has to say."

"Blasphemy!"

"Odin may be a god, but he's not the only one in the world."

"You mean you would be content to follow the way of the Vanir for the rest of your life? The way of the Vanir is a way impeded by the seasons, by weather and harvests. By children, even?"

"Yes."

"You, who've known the onward rush of the battlemaids from its very center?"

"Perhaps for the very reason that I have known the ride. Because I've known the way of the Valkyries and the Aesir, I can better appreciate the freedom of the Vanir."

"Freedom?" I asked. She seemed to be speaking madness, in riddles of opposites.

"I'm telling you this, Brynhild, because I hoped, of all of them, you'd be the one to understand. I've always liked you best, thought we two had the most in common. You were the only one who dared to speak up against this mission. You were the one who went against orders. You came to my rescue when Helgi would have abducted me and killed Geirðjof."

She had placed her hand on my knee in affection, but I didn't return the touch, so she soon withdrew.

"I'm not going with you," I said in disbelief.

"Of course not. Certainly not now, here. But I thought, just in case you might someday grow tired–"

"How can you say such a thing?"

"Just in case. I wanted you to know it is possible. Like I warned and encouraged you before you set out into the winter night for your two-week trial. There is a way. I want you to know that. Then you won't spend such a long time as I did in turmoil, thinking I might have to walk into a flying spear someday to escape."

"You would have done that?"

"I was so desperate some days, yes. I dreamed of such an escape until I learned–"

"Thora, after all the trials you went through – we both went through – to become Valkyries?"

"It is your successful trial with nature that allows you to enter the sisterhood. It is also your key out – if you should ever want out."

"I don't want–" I quickly amended to, "I don't understand."

"For his warrior maidens, Odin knows he must have superior individuals. But a superior individual also has it within herself to go her own way. I conjured him by the skin of the fox I killed during my trial, by the cuffs I wear here on my arms. By the skin of your bear, by its claws that protect you in the midst of battle, you can also claim your freedom – should you ever want to. Remember how, when you returned from your two-weeks' trial, you had lost the torc? You had only the claws about your neck. Remember that. That is the token."

"What of All-Father's wrath? I am getting the feeling I should run you through right now for a traitor." A constriction in my throat made me think, *She might be better off dead.*

"My trophy skin is proof against his wrath."

"Even the wrath of All-Father?"

"Even the wrath of Odin. You cannot kill me; he cannot kill me. Only the Vanir can come for me and take me back to the bosom of the earth in the natural course of things."

"Surely All-Father can take his vengeance in other ways."

"Surely he can try, and I am ready to endure them."

I saw Thora seeking for the words that might call divine help to her wish; I saw her fail to find them anywhere but within herself. "By touching the fox fur and speaking runes that came to me of my heart, of the part of my heart that always revolted when we had to betray someone, I was able to claim one more bequest. Odin has had to swear that he will never have power over my children. He cannot kill them either."

"You intend to have children?"

"I do. And that was one thing I didn't think I could bear. That was the hardest thing for me as a Valkyrie, to send girls like my own children out into the winter nights and never see most of them again. I've always thought, for myself I don't care. I can look after myself. I endured two weeks alone in winter. I killed a fox with my bare hands, I've ridden and fought with the Valkyries. I can look after myself. But my children–"

"I wouldn't worry about my children."

"Perhaps you wouldn't. I just wanted to tell you that with that bearskin and your own self, you may claim something from Odin that he can't touch, God though he is."

"I don't desire anything from All-Father but what he's already granted me."

"This is good-bye, then."

I squinted into the sun again. "He's very dark, this Frank of yours," was all I could think of to say. The light had changed, and I could see his features better now. They burned against the back of my eyes. "My mother always used to say a child that dark hadn't a very good chance of living," I told my friend. "They get rickets so easily."

"When I was growing up, we said rickets came from dishonor in the kindred. That is why adulteresses were sacrificed, to appease the Gods who sent that disease. Yes, I'm well familiar with those afflicted children, their over-large, square, flat heads, their bowed legs that will not carry them, the barrel chest, the lost hair. And familiar with the hatred folk sometimes bear against the dark ones because of their fear of the disease. But perhaps that is why I like Geirðjof so much," she persisted. "He has fought against such odds with such patience. When

I first became acquainted with him, he hadn't a horse to his name, and now – look how he rides in his earl's trappings!"

"I hope you haven't forgotten he owes you for those trappings."

"And that's another reason. His life is really *our* life, isn't it? Mine and his. This is how it should be."

"But how shall that life fare when no one on the immortal side watches out for you?"

Thora gave me a look – as if she expected me to volunteer. I opened my mouth to call her mad, but the words faltered.

She shrugged. "I am willing to give it a try alone."

Only when I saw the tears streaming down her cheeks did I began to believe her. A Valkyrie does not cry.

"Good-bye, Brynhild. You may as well have my brynie. It'll be out of place where I'm going. And the helmet."

She removed the crest of ravens' feathers and shook out her hair. The hair seemed to turn color as she did so, going from rust to carrot, the color of a living, growing thing. Then she twisted the torc off her neck, not without leaving fierce red marks, but she rubbed the skin of her throat and breathed deeply, as if taking her first breath of fresh air in years.

When I wouldn't touch them, Thora loaded the torc, helmet and brynie in front of me herself. She dismounted then and handed me her horse's reins, clasping my hands and peering into my face as if to infect me with her tears as she did so. I remained immune and silent.

"Take Alsvider, my horse. Beautiful, sacred white that he is, he isn't mine to take away with me. But I'm sure there'll come some hero or a new Valkyrie soon enough to be deserving of the honor. Good-bye, old fellow. Don't forget your Thora. We had some good times together, didn't we?"

Overcome by tears, she hugged the horse's head, then quickly turned and walked toward the Earl of Saxony and the setting sun. I watched until she reached him, took his hand, and swung up into the saddle behind him. They turned and rode off together without a backwards glance, which was just as well. When I looked down at the brynie in my lap, I was amazed and horrified to find it spotted with my own tears.

No one said anything when I caught up to the rest of the Valkyries with Thora's empty mount and accoutrements, and no Thora. Perhaps they'd seen it coming, as I had not. They turned their own heads with the same firmness with which they turned their horses' and rode on.

A warm tingling close to an ache ran throughout my torso. I knew that my time of month had come, coinciding by chance with the deep loss of Thora. I didn't want to ignore my blood this time as we battle-maids usually did. I wanted to go off into the woods and bleed into the sod, alone, and for once be truly myself as I was created. But I did not. I turned Faxi's head to follow the rest.

"We haven't a moment to lose," Valfreya told us two days later when we had crossed the Oder River and entered the land of the Burgundians. "Brynhild, why don't you take care of the Burgundians this time? The rest of us will go and make berserks of the Goths."

"As if the Goths weren't mad enough to begin with," commented Hlokk with her deep voice like the sound of her hammer in her forge. Everybody laughed, shaking off the silent dejection that had been hanging over our ride.

So I stayed behind as the rest rode east into Gothic territory. Hobbling Faxi a good distance from Agnar's hall, I dressed myself in rags and dirtied my face and hands to go among the Burgundians in the guise of a soothsayer as they prepared for the morrow's battle, to dishearten those I could with fortunes of doom and gloom.

chapter 17

WENT FIRST TO THE door of the women's quarters where Agnar's queen welcomed me beneath the low eaves wreathed with sweet pine smoke. To the clap of a maid's carding combs, the queen herself quickly fried up an omelet for me with mushrooms and some of her good sharp cheese melted throughout. Afterwards, she presented me with a bowl of strawberries that, like the mushrooms, had been gathered just that day from the Burgundian woods in their summer mugginess. I had not stopped to think until the food swelled wonderfully in my insides how hungry I was, or how tired of surviving on the dried jerky that was a Valkyrie's riding fare.

Having seen with satisfaction the last of her offerings disappear into my mouth and unable to press more on me, the queen of Burgundy sat at last on a stool next to my straight-backed chair and asked, "Well, aunt, what news have you of the world?"

How could I speak what I'd come to speak with the taste of those tiny strawberry jewels and their rich setting of cream still on my tongue? With the lulling rhythm of carding combs in the background, I watched the dust moats dancing into the cozy room on the shaft of sunset light that came through the open door, and knew what I must do.

I swallowed once or twice to make certain I wouldn't choke, and then said simply, "It grieves me much to inform you, lady, that Odin All-Father has set his one eye against your man."

The queen grabbed my hand for strength as the words struck her. She couldn't have known that I was one of Odin's own. Yet somehow she grasped my very weakness for comfort. Certainly she believed me, even without feigned trance or scrying bowls.

"Come. I'll bring you to my husband," she said.

The men had congregated outside in the gathering darkness where the logs of Burgundy's stockade encircled a rough sort of yard. I stood in the shadows, smelled supper cooking, horse dung, the night beyond. I knew Agnar the King the moment I saw him step out from among his men. I watched his wild fox-colored beard and mane bend down to his wife's mouse-brown hair which she wore caught up in a delicate chaplet of knotwork high on the back of her head. He stood bigger, rougher, more unrestrained than she in every way, yet she remained more persistent, and persistently she brought him to the point where he deigned to come and talk to me.

As they walked toward me, he slung an arm causally about her shoulders. *How unalike they are*, I thought, *and yet they fit perfectly together like the left and right hands clasping, like the albumen and yolk of an egg, like garden peas inside a shell.*

My eyes blinked fiercely at an untoward stinging of tears. The vision of king and queen called the loss of Thora to my mind. Tall, red-haired Thora and her short, swart Frank were another such match. And I thought myself the one to break off so close a twining?

I could hardly bear to form the words I knew must be said to Agnar. Then I wished I had used trance or runes, anything else by which seers could make their words more believable. Or was it only my sex that put him off? Where the queen had believed me at once, perhaps the king needed me in helmet and brynie before he could attach verity to my words.

"Listen to her, husband, I beg of you," said the queen, and she continued to speak on my behalf, stronger in her words than a Valkyrie.

"Thank you, aunt, for your concern," he said to me. "But now, wife, you must leave us. We will dance the dance of war."

"Dance?" she said. "How can you think to dance when tomorrow–"

"Hush! Don't bring more evil on us by saying it. You ask how can we dance? How can we *not* dance? If All-Father will not deign to come and make berserks of us, we must steel ourselves in the best way we know how."

"But against such–?"

"Yes, steel ourselves against Heaven, if need be."

I realized then that he didn't disbelieve me. He had never disbelieved. Simply, as a man, no prophecy could turn him from the course of action upon which he'd already embarked.

He kissed the queen lightly, fondly on her netted hair, and smiled bravely. Then he turned and, in a minute, seemed to have forgotten that anything like a woman existed anywhere in the world. The queen and I remained in the yard to watch. The other women joined us. We might have been no more than the yellow smears of torchlight that starkly lit the logs of the stockade walls against which we pressed.

With a fierce, grand gesture like some solemnizing priest, Agnar suddenly threw his cloak from himself, his cloak that had been his only scrap of clothing until then. He stood stark naked before the night that caught and sharply exaggerated the male hollows of his buttocks. With a yell, he swept up a pair of spears leaning against a nearby tree and began to clap them one against the other in a definite rhythm: slow, quick-quick, slow, quick-quick.

And suddenly, in the sooty smears of torchlight, two close ranks of Burgundian men appeared. All were as naked as their king, and as beautiful in their nakedness as he, all with their hair cut to mimic horse's manes, short in a fringe in front, long and shaggy down the back. Other spears, sword upon sheath, ax upon shield, took up the rhythm, and then fifty pairs of feet. Each man grasped the hand of the man next to the man beside him, locking arms in a weave like the tight mesh of a basket in which one might almost hope to carry water. One man's quick step landed in the exact print his neighbor's slow step had just vacated. Slow, quick-quick. Slow, quick-quick.

And then they began variations, variations in form but never in pulse as Agnar called out the steps' mysterious power names to the night sky. The "slow" became a deep knee bend, the whole line dropping like a single man, the quick-quicks transformed into heavy stamps. The two lines advanced on one another with a fury like opposing armies. Their steps brought them so close, chest hair brushed chest hair. At these close quarters, they feinted, growled at one another, whirled like spokes on a wheel, and bent one line forward, the other back.

Then, in waves that began at one end of the double line and ended at the other, they whipped like a lash passing though rawhide. At some signal beyond my kenning, the lines reeled back to opposite edges of the torchlight. Their speed threatened to catch unaware the little boys following behind their elders in little lines of their own. Always shouts and whistles punched the pace, changing sometimes to roars, bird calls, shrill trills, and deep grunts. To every movement, a wagging of both beards and genitals pronounced "male" as clearly as a wall declares itself stone. Both seemed as solid and painful to run into.

As Agnar led one line, the facing line was led by Giuki, his son. Still youthful, Giuki bore little down on either chin or privates, but in him both maleness and the bond with his father stood as firm as mountains. Even the little boys, copying steps behind their fathers, catching the rhythm on sticks and stones or on pudgy palms – little boys whose bare buds of sex bounced sweetly instead of wagging with unconcealed threat – even these little ones were unashamedly, uncompromisingly, irrevocably male. Already they shared a secret sacred brotherhood. This brotherhood counted among its mysteries the din of battle and the smell of blood in the hunt. But the greatest of all its mysteries, to me, was the crying dependency on openness. Men could trust feelings neither when they passed water nor when coupling released its sexual tension.

We should dance like this, I thought, *my Valkyrie sisters and I. It clearly leads to better warriors and a tighter camaraderie.* At the same time I thought the notion ridiculous. A single one of us standing up in this line would be like a chink in a wall, curving in when it should curve out, a sign of weakness. On our bodies, these movements would seem like only so much clowning. And yet, the mouse queen was just as necessary to Agnar as his shadow. *What are we Valkyries but trying to combine in one body both hands, the active right and the retaining left, both egg white and sweeter yolk? That's what removes us from the sphere of the mundane and sets us up with the divine.* But did I want this power to play at God, separating what clearly – like Agnar and his son, Agnar and his wife – belonged together? It jarred as if one opened a pea pod and found, instead of peas, sweet berries. Or perhaps a slimy slug.

Anybody who looked at our world with anything but visions of fancy could be tempted like Thora to leave it all behind.

Agnar's queen offered me the hospitality of her rooms that night, but I didn't sleep well. My womanhood was uncomfortable. I remembered the loss of my friend Thora. Women in the room about me wept in dread of what the morrow would bring. Their womanhood was easy enough to hide within. The men, already under the battle ban, could not enter the room to comfort them.

When at last I slept, I slept soundly and thoughtlessly. I didn't wake, the spell of the night's dancing lingering like sand in the eyes, until dawn had already set the Burgundian warriors chanting under their uplifted shields. I had still to retrieve my horse and change into helmet and brynie before I could take up my place with my sisters, so I hurried away.

chapter 18

 CLOUD-WEAKENED SUN LIT the battlefield adorned with knee-high grasses and wild flowers. The forces assembled. Coming up behind the Burgundians, I got my first glimpse of Ermenaric, the Gothic King, and a fearsome sight he was, his face scarred, his arms like battle clubs.

In the whitened sky over that man's head, I saw the black bow of a raven in flight. If I hadn't known where to find them, that would have told me where my sisters waited. But of course they waited exactly where they were supposed to be, concealed carefully behind the Goths, waiting to lend aid if they must, to carry off to the joys of Valhalla any Goth who fell. I turned Faxi's head to make my way carefully and unseen to join them.

Surely the Burgundians could hear the echo of All-Father from under their enemies' shields. Surely, when the first spears of offering were thrown, the Burgundians could see the Goths' went further. It flew out of sight into the wood on the Burgundians' flank, and the God accepted the offering.

Yet the Burgundians did not back up. They advanced – as if they had been promised victory instead – onto those dreaded boars' head phalanxes. Those phalanxes that only the favored of Odin may deploy curled back like a boar's lips to reveal the berserks as knife-like tusks.

I skirted the field as closely as I dared, watching the first parries with dread fascination. Although they couldn't see me, I still found it difficult to look straight into a Burgundian face or to meet an eye under horse-mane hair.

I was not watching my way very carefully, for suddenly I had to pull back deeper into the forest at my left-hand side, vexed at myself. A battlemaid should be above such sudden moves. One huge Goth with the bear shirt on seemed larger than nature and quite compensated for the gray in his hair. He had picked young Giuki Agnarsson out of the compact host of Burgundians as a wolf would cut off the weakest from a herd of deer. The young prince was fighting bravely for one tasting his first battle, but he stood no chance against the huge berserk.

The Goth pushed the lad backwards into the tripping undergrowth and poor light of the wood. I watched from between the trees, the cover allowing me closer than usual. Not only was it Giuki's first battle; it would prove his last.

The Burgundians were fated to lose the day. I knew that. I should have ridden on hurriedly to join my sisters and given the lad at least the honor of falling first of the fight's fruit. But I couldn't tear my eyes from the spectacle.

Suddenly his father was there, too, among the trees, having missed his son at his side and deserted the rest of his men to come to the boy's aid. The wood rang and bark flew as tree trunks received the blows meant to bite flesh. Now it was the berserk's turn to edge backwards, but he was nothing if not battle-mad and foaming at the mouth. He was a close match for both father and son.

I could hear the voice of All-Father in my ear, his voice sent by divine power.

> "As daughter, you've donned dispatch.
> I have altered my eye against Agnar,
> And his plots and prayers displease me.
> It is Geirrodsson against whom the day goes,
> Who must fall on the field and feed
> My ravens in his rot, not to be rescued

To Valhalla. A Valkyrie in your venue would see
Her duty and dawdle not to do it.
Take up your spear, Shieldmaid, and let it soar."

I did not take my own spear from its holster on my saddle. I happened to find myself near the spot where the Goths' first spear offering, flying harmlessly over the heads of the Burgundians and into the woods, had sunk itself into the white trunk of a tall, slender birch. That gave a good omen, the birch being emblematic of fertility. Yes, clearly, All-Father had accepted the Goths' offering. I knew no reason why I shouldn't take the spear to myself; it had been offered to my master, after all.

The spear slipped easily out of the wood, bleeding heavy sap at the wound as it found its way into my hand, almost of its own accord. And what a fine weapon! The Goths were justly renowned for their spear-making; no wonder it was their favorite weapon. I couldn't go wrong with such a well-balanced, smooth piece of iron-tipped ash in my hand. I took just a moment to look at the three men fighting and adjust my arm to that distance. Then I let the lance fly. I don't think I'd missed a target at such close range since my first year of training. But that morning I missed.

Or perhaps I didn't miss at all. Perhaps I never meant to hit Agnar. With the instinctive motions of battle, perhaps I'd always meant the berserk to fall. Berserks aren't supposed to be cut down in battle. Indeed, it is supposed to be divinely impossible, which is part of their terror. In any case, fall this one did, caught through the back with the Goth offering spear at about lung level.

Agnar and his son looked up amazed, even a little dazed, wondering from whence their help had come. But I had faded into the woods before they noticed me. The only clue they found was the spear of Gothic make, still quivering in their adversary's back.

Reflexively, like a parry in battle, I pulled my senses back from the monument of what I had done. One part of my mind knew I must leave that place instantly. But the other, the part that gained control, lingered. Not daring to feel on its own, my heart hoped to learn its emotion from common mortals who still knew the skill.

"Son," I heard Agnar say, panting with his exertions, "are you well?"

"Fine, Father."

"Then we must return at once to the battle to aid our kinsmen."

"May we not take a trophy off this berserk, Father? Cut off his head, his scalp? Take the sword?"

Agnar shook his head thoughtfully. "Our hands did not kill him. We must only thank All-Father who, it seems, for all the sayings of old crones, has not abandoned us after all."

That was enough, more than enough. With a soft clink of harness, I turned Faxi and secreted myself deeper in the forest. I began to make my way to my sisters with a singleness of purpose. But then a rasping caw drew my glance upward. Circling overhead between the full crowns of the trees flew a lone black raven, waiting for his feast at battle's end. He had seen it all.

I came upon my sisters in a hollow close behind Gothic lines. Ten raven-wing helmets shading ten brave, dear, beautiful female faces. Ten strong women, spears at the ready. Ten god-white horses. All waiting for the first sign, missing only Thora. And me.

The sun rode at my back, although too weak yet to cast any shadow or to catch the Valkyries' breastplates with bursts of light as they shifted under battle tenseness. Their mounts caught tension from their mistresses and shifted likewise with creaking leather and clomping heavy hooves. The sight could make any heart swell with pride to join them, or with dread if remaining but an onlooker, beholden to these iron wills.

I kicked Faxi's white flanks, though he needed no urging to join his old companions. And my heart did rise 'til it pressed against my throat and constricted my breathing. But I knew I had had to push the rise into being – whether from pride or dread, I couldn't say.

Valfreya acknowledged my arrival with but a glance. She had more important things to worry about. "Where is Hjalm-Gunnar?" she was asking. "Has anybody seen old grey Hjalm-Gunnar in the last few minutes? Where is he that All-Father sent us in particular to guard?"

"Wasn't he among the berserks?" asked Reginleif.

"Berserks are not something you can lose on the battlefield," remarked Raðgriðr.

I cleared my throat. "Is he a grey-haired man?"

"Yes, but very big and powerful all the same," Valfreya replied, looking at me sharply.

"Then I have seen him. Over in those woods – there where Agnar and his son Giuki are just emerging."

"Hlokk," said Valfreya with a sudden panic she could hardly conceal. "Go, scout."

"Yes, sister." Hlokk turned her reins sharply and prepared to ride off at once.

"And here. Here is the horn of life. You may need it."

The battlemaids had but one horn of life, and Valfreya wore it strapped across her brynie at all times. This auroch's horn, yellow with age, contained a powder of simples, the secret of which only All-Father knew. Sprinkled on a fallen man with the appropriate runes, it had the power to raise him to life once more. I had never been entrusted with the horn, nor even seen its magic worked. But my heart raced as I watched my sister ride off into the woods from whence I'd just come. If the berserk should rise–

The horn of life had no success that day. Either Hlokk arrived too late, some part of the rite went awry, or one fallen by a Valkyrie's hand had no hope of rising again at the hand of her sister. In any case, Hlokk returned shortly, grim-faced and ashen. "He's dead," she reported. "He cannot be raised."

"Dead? Dead!" cried Valfreya. "How can that be?"

"We must ride for him, then," offered Hilda, stirring anxiously in the saddle.

"No," said Hlokk. "His wound is in the back."

"In the back?" snapped Valfreya in ever-growing disbelief. "In the back? How can that be? How can a berserk take his wound in the back?"

"I don't know," said Hlokk helplessly, "but that's the truth of it."

"Agnar and his son have practiced base treachery," Thruðr accused.

"Certainly that appears to be the case," said Valfreya, catching my eyes again. "But at this stage of the game, we can do nothing about it." She repeated the saying all of us knew by heart. "'No man can enter Valhalla who has his wound in the back.' For all our master's love, Hjalm-Gunnar has entered the realm of Hel this day."

No answer but silence replied to this somber news.

Perhaps the careless bragging of the young Giuki alerted him, perhaps the man just happened on the body when he went to relieve himself from battle-pressure on his bladder. Whatever the case, shortly thereafter, some Burgundian came out of the woods with a triumphant shout, holding the severed head of Hjalm-Gunnar aloft by its grey hairs.

At the sight of their leader thus fallen, for all his berserkhood, the Goths lost heart and soon began to quit the field in twos and threes. The Burgundians had the honor not to pursue them. Wounding the retreating enemy was not worthy of a man, so the day came to little more than a draw. The Goths would surely return for revenge sooner rather than later – as soon as Ermenaric could replace his old retainer on this western border of his kingdom. But our work in the area was clearly done.

Over our heads, the lone raven led the way back to the Hall of the Slain, underfed, cawing crossly, and eager to tattle blame.

PART IV

SIGNY'S CHANGE

chapter 19

 AWOKE MUCH LATER IN the bed inside the compound, after my last view of Mathesuentha. I lay holding my breath for the next birth pain. It didn't happen. Instead, I felt a strong, healthy kick as the baby turned and made himself comfortable against my rib cage. He wasn't going anywhere, not for three months or more.

Here I was, back in the bed, back where the evil of my dreams knew how to find me. Without Mathesuentha to hold it at bay. I waited, but it never came. Sometimes I heard a rumble of evil. I would cover my ears and try not to listen, but it turned out to be only my husband, rumbling with laughter as he drank from the bleached skull of the chief of the Veneti in the great hall. I heard him, but I never saw him. The evil had me where it wanted, and I had no escape.

Ababa's linen hung on the loom, beckoning, but I didn't move. I felt myself retreating from the world as if shuffling down a long forest tunnel of barren trees. I retreated completely into a silent place where I moved as little as possible, made as little sound as I could, took up as little space, ate as little. I would not weave for this child. And without Mathesuentha, I didn't have to move or talk. I didn't have to live.

I did see a young woman with hair that couldn't decide whether to be brown or dirty blond. Her eyes were of the same mind, and her large feet, usually bare and dirty, moved as if made of lead. Her name was Aslaug, she told me. She had a son just toddling she called Rekitach, and her eyes turned cloudy grey whenever she looked on me. Sometimes when Ermenaric laughed out in the hall, she laughed, too. She slept with him and made no secret of the fact that she took a dim view of the legitimacy a dowry purchased for children – legitimacy and the right to lie in bed all day, while true love and devotion brought only drudgery.

Aslaug didn't cook much. She hated it. She boiled meat of all its juices, and that was the limit of her skill. Sometimes she brought me slabs. I drank mostly. Water when I could get it. Or mead.

"The cow," Aslaug told me, "died of neglect. Not *my* neglect, I'll have you know. I wasn't here. It happened before I came. Most of the chickens, too. I let the rest out to fend for themselves, and the soldier's dogs got them."

Aslaug let the fire go out frequently, then she would come in and scold that I wouldn't lift a finger even to warm myself. Well, the days were definitely getting warmer. Unfortunately, little chance remained that I'd be able to freeze to death for another nine months at least. By then this child...

But I couldn't form the thought.

Sometimes Aslaug's child wandered in by himself and took a lively interest in the weaving. He soon had the whole thing dismantled.

"Boys will be boys," his mother said proudly when she came to fetch him, drawn by his hollering because a loom weight had fallen on his bare toe.

I lost all track of time. Day or night meant nothing to me. For all I knew, winter might have come again, except that this baby still pressed up against my lungs.

Then one day, Aslaug came in, exchanged a dried-out slab of meat for a fresh one and glowered at me. She'd given up trying to hold conversation with me weeks ago, so it quite made me start when she spoke. "Your family's here."

"What!" I sat up in bed. The sudden, unaccustomed movement made me dizzy.

"Huh! She can talk after all. You family's here," she repeated, as if talking to the hard-of-hearing or the dim-witted. "Just thought you'd like to know."

"Where?"

"Downstream a bit. You can see them if you just walk to the first bend."

"Sigmund, my brother. He looks like me. Is he there?"

"I don't know. Probably. There are seven boats of them."

"Seven? Only seven? That's not so many."

"No. Not many at all."

"When can I see them?"

Aslaug smiled cruelly. "Well, tomorrow or the next day at the latest, you may see their heads on spikes around the compound. They've come this far into Gothic territory. They're surrounded."

"Ermenaric, my husband, he invited them as in-laws to feast."

"Did he? And you believed him? You don't know your 'husband' very well, do you? Stupidity must run in the family." Aslaug laughed and shuffled out of the room on her leaden feet.

I rose in a moment, though the room whirled around me and the great lump of a belly set me terribly off balance. I was short of breath already, and my legs felt like warm chicken fat beneath me.

The first thing is to find something to wear, I told myself. But I'd grown so much since I'd worn a dress that nothing fit. Eventually I came across the herringbone of white and brown wool right where Mathesuentha had folded it with her distinctive neatness before beginning on the linen. The tears that thought caused broke up my progress for a while. But she'd made it for me – for this present, monstrous me – whom she had seen and cared for, even at this distance. Knowing this gave me the strength to get up again and try the garment on.

The selvages really needed to be sewn together to make a tube-like sheath. Mathesuentha would have seen that it was done in a thrice. Even with a belt – and where should the belt go, above or below this enormity riding before me which crashed into everything before I judged it should? – I would risk an immodest gap.

Well, I have no time for modesty, I thought, and fastened the dress with my best brooches, one to each shoulder. Since I had no intention of returning to this room – ever – I ransacked my coffers for a few more of my favorite pieces and put them on. But I was already clumsy enough, so I resolved to live the rest of my life without the major portion of my dowry. I had a father and brothers, did I not, who could always plunder more. Oh, but could I reach them in time? Between me and that family now stood only the door to my room ... the door to my room and the hall and the porch and the yard all full of warriors and Aslaug – and Ermenaric.

There is nothing for it, I thought. And thought was not easy, particularly not downright scheming, for I'd forced myself to think as little as possible for three full months and was out of practice. *I must wait until night, until they're asleep.*

Such fidget filled me that I could hardly follow my own good advice. I did, but my energy had to go somewhere. I set to trying to repair the damage Aslaug's son had done to the linen work.

The brat! Every other warp will have to be rehung. Well, what do I care? I certainly will never use this.

It busied my hands, however, and the activity strengthened rather than tired me. I was so angry with the child Rekitach that I felt I could throttle him and his mother and still hike all the way back to Xanten if need be to regain my family.

I had only managed to unravel and rehang two threads when the sound of the door opening behind me gave me a start. I turned and saw that it was the very source of my anger. "What, you wretched imp? Have you come back for more? You come near this loom again, and I'll tan your hide. Just see if I don't."

The lad looked at me – by the Gods, with Ermenaric's eyes – and showed not a flinch of fear. He began to prattle. I suppose Aslaug found the babbling cute. I couldn't understand a word, and the boy grew impatient when I failed to joined his mother either in affection or understanding.

"Go on, be off with you."

He prattled again, with emphasis. His emphasis only stressed the wrong parts of each word. But he did manage to call my attention to the length of soft woad-blue fabric he was wearing tied about himself. What he was playing at in that costume, I couldn't fathom. Something very swaggering and masculine. The femininity of the fabric was lost on him, how the fine threads of the fringe were knotted together in diamond shapes before falling a good two hands in width. Probably the shawl his mother threw over her head when she went out...

I had an idea. I moved closer to him and pitched my voice just about as high and as sweet as it would go. "That's a very pretty – pretty cape are you calling it?" My tone made the back of my neck creep, but I kept it up. "Come here and let Auntie Signy have a look at it. No? No, you won't let me touch it? Oh, please. Please. You'll make me so sad."

He said a very clear and decided, "Mine."

Another idea. I went to one of my chests, dug down until I found a very nice dagger in a hammered sheath. "Here. You see this?"

"Sharp," the scrap said in the midst of a lot of gibberish.

"Yes, it is sharp. Only big boys can have daggers."

"Daddy," and then more I couldn't make out.

"Yes, I'll bet your daddy has one like this." I choked on that word "daddy." "But, look here, I think you're such a fine, great lad, that I will give you this dagger. What do you say?"

Well, I've no idea what he said, but he obviously took to the notion.

"Great. But I'll tell you, I'll only give this lovely dagger up if I can have something in exchange. Something ... something like that lovely cape of yours."

We made the exchange quickly, the dagger thrust incongruously through the bit of cord at his waist, and Aslaug's shawl thrown over my head. "There now. Aren't you the big man with a dagger, though? Just like Daddy. Would you like to go for a little walk with Aunt Signy to show off our fancy clothes?"

I didn't have to ask twice. He took my hand and dragged me towards the door.

What a wonderful little hand he has, I thought in spite of myself. *So small and trusting. It should never have a dagger placed in it. And could this child within me – there, it just kicked again – could it have such a perfectly formed little hand even now? One even smaller than this?*

Well, I had no time to grow tender-hearted. We were now out into the main hall.

Just beside and above the hearth, in the center of the hall, a great wooden rack hung from the ceiling. Carved with intertwining horses' heads, it held the round loaves of bread, which faded into the carving like cartwheels, up off the floor and out of reach of mice. Under this canopy, Aslaug busied herself with big cauldrons and big flanks of meat, her back to us. The child prattled something in her direction, and I wanted to smack him but didn't.

"That's nice, honey," his mother replied without looking up. It occurred to me that perhaps she didn't understand him, either.

We made it across the room to the outside door. The upper and lower halves of the door swung separately. The upper half stood open to bring in air and brilliant afternoon sunshine. I blinked blindly at the light. Spring had come and gone, summer was almost upon us, and I had not known it.

The lower half of the door was latched shut, a latch the boy could not open. Aslaug trusted that latch to keep him close by. The boy pounded with a firm flat hand against the door. As quietly as I could, I threw the latch. The child chirped in triumph. We didn't bother to close the door behind us.

A great number of retainers were practicing in the yard. War hung in the air, treacherous war against my loved ones. The Goths' thrusts and throws compacted a grim diligence. I had that diligence to thank. They did not look below the shawl I pulled closely about my face and over my belly.

At the gate of the stockade, the child began to make incoherent sounds of protest. He wanted to watch the training, or he knew already we had gone too far.

No, brat, I must get past these horsemen putting their mounts through their breakneck paces.

"Come, let's look at the pretty horses," I insisted, and dragged him until he forgot the previous attraction and came of his own free will.

Just past the smokehouse in our broad circle around the horsemen, he squawked again. I'd promised him we could look at horses, hadn't I? He sat down and refused to move. I picked him up and tried to carry him, but that proved impossible. I was already carrying more child than I could, left with no waist to straddle him on, and he kicked furiously.

"Come on. Just a little farther. Just a little farther."

I could no more. My lungs burned and my heart beat so hard, it made my stomach queasy. I set him down and went on alone. I was quite content to see that he sat where he was and squawked. He didn't know enough to wander back up away from the river bank and to the stockade. As long as he didn't wander right under the horses' hooves, the cavalry would not bother with him. The galloping would cover up most of the noise. Men's natural tendency to suppose any crying child none of their duty would also help.

I pressed on, following the river downstream. Anything like haste was of course impossible. But soon enough I'd reached the bend in the river and the small copse of stately poplar, sagging willow, and pine on a sandy dune. Around these trees, over summer meadows, a clear view opened to the ships of Xanten, their sails down, their awnings up. My heart soared as if the firm wind caught it and floated it there among the dragon emblems on the banners.

My steps grew lighter still. Here the meadow would reach to a horse's belly. Life-filled grasses sprang quickly upright again at my passing. Wildflowers sprinkled them liberally – poppies, wild carrot, morning glory, yellow buttercups, yarrow. Bees drifted heavily over it all, as if they, too, were with child. The song of a lark enlivened the meadow, and a cuckoo from the copse vied to outdo it. I realized finally that plenty, beauty, and life could be found in this land. My first seven months here, with the world so dead and hoar-brittle, had not taught me to expect anything like this.

How I wanted to bend and pick a crown of blossoms for myself, now that I could toss Aslaug's shawl off my hair. How often had I given Sigmund pleasure with such a vision of myself in such midsummers past! But that would have to wait for another time. This year I still carried the burden of my kidnapping. I couldn't bend past the middle of my thighs.

"Hullo? Hullo! By the Gods, it's Signy!"

I might have guessed it would be Sigmund who would look up, see, and recognize me first. Sigmund, who could always read my thoughts, whose thoughts in turn I could read.

He reached me in a dozen strides, picked me up and carried me, big lump and all, into the Xantenese camp. "Father! Brothers! It's our Signy!" Then, in an undertone, gentle and almost sad, touching me as if I might break, "We were not told – you're carrying his child."

At that, I could bear it all no longer. I burst into tears and hid my face on Sigmund's chest.

chapter 20

"ATHER, PLEASE, YOU MUST BELIEVE me," I said. "The King of the Goths means to surround and kill you all. Send spies up to the stockade if you doubt me. Simply watch what earnestness is in their weapons play. He ... he is a hard man, Father, a man in whom there is no mercy and nothing whatsoever to trust. By the Gods, by your great protector Odin, Father, don't I know it?"

I felt Sigmund's great strong hands tender upon my hair as he stood behind me. "It is clear we made a grievous mistake when we gave our sister to this monster who is half troll. Who can doubt by looking at her that she has been sorely misused?"

"We should take vengeance," spoke up Siggeir, the most hot-headed of my brothers.

"You must not," I pleaded. "You cannot imagine the numbers of Goths and their allies that surround us now, days in all directions – allies that *he* has. They are on alert. You cannot hope to beat him. Your seven small ships will be crushed like kindling."

"This is woman's talk," said Siggeir.

"A woman who knows her husband," Sigmund challenged, coming to my defense. "What can appease the King of the Goths now, sister?"

"I fear nothing can. He wants your sword, Sigmund."

"I do not part with Balmung without first parting with my life,"

Sigmund said, his hand leaving my hair for Balmung's hilt. "Even for you, sister."

My gaze turned to follow that hand, greedy still for its touch. But I let myself be satisfied with the reflection of my weak self, whole and brave, as seen in my brother. "It only started with Balmung," I assured him. "Now you could present the sword to him on a silken cushion, and he would only brush it aside. Now his thirst for revenge for imagined insults has grown so great, he must have your blood flood this river before he finds satisfaction. The only hope I see, Father, is that you – we, for you must take me with you – we must hoist anchor tonight and head downstream under cover of darkness."

My father, who'd been hearing all this talk with a bemused look on his face, now actually burst out laughing. Had I been so long away from him that he seemed a stranger, or did something of my husband's laugh growl in his?

"Father, it's our only chance."

"Daughter, you are talking of turning tail and fleeing. You're saying this to *me*, Volsung, the beloved of Odin."

"I am saying this to you as my father, as the leader of my brothers, as the joy of my mother waiting at home, and as my only hope."

"I am the beloved of Odin. He gave me wife, children, riches, all. He has never failed me."

"Yes, Father, we have much to thank the One-Eyed for. He is helpful to those he loves. But he is also, from all accounts, very fickle. And I wonder, can even a God help against such overwhelming odds?"

"You are a woman, and in a very womanly condition, so it is easy to see why you might say this. But All-Father never helps those who doubt, even for a moment. I have never balked at any fight he sent me, whatever the odds, and he has never let me down. Hasn't my own son been the receiver of a divine gift at the hands of the Battle Lord just within the last year? A gift, I may add, that has yet to see action. It is a shame to waste Balmung a moment longer. No, I will not fail to meet this Ermenaric of yours head on, and neither shall any man here, if he calls himself a man."

"Please, Father, I beg–"

I had risen to my feet, but I sank back down with a groan. Despair at the feebleness of my words weighted me, but it was more than that. I had managed to ignore the first twinges even as I was crossing the meadow, but now there could be no more ignoring. Hadn't I felt this before, by lamplight at Mathesuentha's hands in the smokehouse? It didn't seem, however, that even then the pains had been quite as forceful.

"Signy, what is it?" asked Sigmund.

"Can't you tell, son?" said my father. "There's a baby to be born – to help refill the places in Ermenaric's host we shall empty for him tomorrow, if he is so inhospitable and foolhardy as to come against us."

The men cheered, that mindless cheer they give when no careful thought could give them any hope of reason. The screams of a woman in travail are similar, that nothing on earth can really succor.

"But, Father, what shall we do for Signy?" asked Sigmund.

"Signy? Why, she should go home to her husband where she belongs."

"No, Father, I can't–" I began.

Sigmund spoke up for me. "She can't go back to him. She isn't well, don't you see? Besides, I will not let her return to that troll of a man."

"Well, we are all men here. She should be able to see that. This is a camp of war. We don't have midwives. We can do nothing for her. I've said it, she's better off in her home where women can attend to her. Come, men. If it's a battle Ermenaric wants, a battle he shall have!"

Another great cheer rose, which I answered with a muffled scream. Surely they heard no echo of Odin behind them.

"Well, I won't let you go back there," Sigmund reassured me. "Balmung here by my side says as well that you don't have to go. I will midwife you if a man can do such a thing, if you trust me."

"More than anyone alive," I gasped at the end of a pain.

"Do you think, if I hold your arm, you can walk to my ship over there?"

The ship rode at the very edge of my sight. Every step jarred up my legs and compressed its pain at my pelvis. But I bit my lip and said, "I think so."

"Let's try it, then. Lean on me. You can make it."

We did make it, stopping three or four times for me to ride out a pang, when because of the pain no room remained in my body for even the thought of putting one foot in front of the other. Sigmund did his best with furs and cushions to make me comfortable on the overlapping planks of the hull. No place on earth was better for me. If worst came to worst, Sigmund could cast off. We could be scudding downstream in a moment. But always the slap of the current on the hull below me and the shift and rock of the ship came first to my senses as each pain faded away. To my pain-racked mind, these sensations recalled those earlier nights on board the Goths' flagship. Fighting with those memories did little to ease me.

All evening, while others sparred and sharpened their weapons, Sigmund sat beside me. All night, while others slept, he gave me sips of water and cooled the sweat of my labor with a damp cloth.

"You should sleep, brother," I said to him I don't know how many times, as often as I could speak.

"How can I, with you suffering so?" Even in the dark, he was particularly gentle in sponging my torn but healed-over earlobe. "I swear in the name of One-Eye and all the Aesir, I shall not sleep again until I've paid that man back all the evil he's done to you."

I knew dawn had come. Pain clenched my eyes shut, but I heard my father raise his voice in a song of praise and of pleading to his god in the old war chant meter.

> "In my dream, the battle goddess
> Seemed to stand beside the hills of warriors.
> Now, as night and day are meeting,
> We, guardians of the spear's path,
> Call on you, Odin, Gallows' Burden.
> Hear our song, echo our song,
> As we head with boldness
> Into the tumult of steel.
> Arrows swim like mackerel in the sky,
> And the flame of battle rushes over men.
> Allow that we do not remain idle,
> That no wizard bind with fear-fetters our limbs.

But bind, rather, those of our foes,
Those keepers of spades and turf,
Unworthy of your affection."

The men echoed his words. Did they hear Odin's voice chant with them that day, a good sign of his favor? Clearly none of them had received the divine gift of being a berserk. Still, none flinched. All upheld perfect trust as my father swore to offer to Odin every sword he won by throwing it into the river, and every foe who begged for quarter by hanging him in the nearest tree.

Such oaths assured me of nothing but that Ermenaric had appeared on the meadow above the river. He did not come alone, and he did not open empty arms as hospitable son-in-law to my father. I heard an unearthly shout like the roar of beasts, and then the clang of metal on metal.

Sometimes I opened my eyes enough to know the angle of the rising sun. It streamed over the gunwale like rancid butter in color and – somehow – smell. That smell settled a cowl of nausea over my pains. Sigmund stayed by me still, though I could tell he paid less and less attention to me, and more and more to what he spied in the greasy morning light through the rigging.

"Signy..." he stammered. "Signy, you were right. Battle is enjoined."

Just coming down from another pang, one ridden without the help of his hand, I couldn't respond. I tried to nod that I understood his distraction, but I didn't know whether he could set my nodding apart from my repeated gasping for breath.

"By the One-Eyed," Sigmund exclaimed, knowing better than to speak Odin's name aloud when a battle was raging, which brought ill-luck. "I had no idea this birthing would take so long. A wounded man is either ready to be buried or able to pass some time in forgetful sleep after such an ordeal as you have had this night, but you women..."

He was gone to the gunwale again, and when he returned, Balmung quivered unsheathed in his hand. He failed to notice another pain building as he raged, "Signy, Signy! I must go to our father's side. The swords are singing so fast and wild! Every hand is needed. I'll be back.

By the Battle-Rager, I'll be back as soon as I can."

Even had I wanted to, I could not have stopped him. Before the pain finished, I heard the distinctive ring of Balmung on shields and my brother's cry, "Courage, Volsungs, courage, to me!" rising above the din of all others. I closed my ears to it and turned full, lonely attention to the tos and fros of the battle raging on the narrow field of my body.

The sun crept to its zenith, then passed it and began to shoot its rays beneath the shield of my awnings directly at me. Thirst parched my throat. Sigmund had returned to me once or twice during this passage of time, each time dirtier and bloodier than before. I couldn't tell if he wore his own blood or another's, but he certainly bore a deep gash on his shin and another on his lower arm.

Now it seemed a very long time since I'd seen him. Could I still hear the rhythmic hammering of Balmung above other noises in the fray? I wasn't sure, above the hammering of my own body against itself. Were these only my screams, or the screams of the dying?

And suddenly he appeared, blocking the sun from my face with his form. I couldn't see with the sun at his back – maybe he meant it that way – but it seemed that the horn plates of his helmet were caved in on one side and that a wound in his neck still curled blood. I tried to reach a hand to stop the wound, but had not the strength to more than scratch at his cuirass with my nails.

"Signy, listen to me. Can you hear me? Things are going badly, sister. Father and our brothers and I have managed to make eight sweeps between the Goths' ranks – like reapers across a field – but there are too many of them, and we have suffered heavy losses. There's hardly a one of our retainers who is not dead or so badly wounded that he cannot fight on. Now I cannot spare even worse news from you, though I would if I could. Six of our brothers were taken prisoner in the last pass. I think if I can but beat my way to where Sieggir is under guard and loose those thongs, the pair of us may yet do some damage."

He swallowed water I craved for myself, bitter on his tongue, and went on. "To what purpose? Ermenaric has allies, more allies. They arrived on the further shore, but are now setting off from there in rafts.

In a moment they'll be upon us, and that'll make the odds fifteen to one. Then it will not matter if I can get to Sieggir or not. Signy, the One-Eyed is blind to us. He has not come today. He will not come, bringing his battlemaids to give my father a hero's greeting. For I must tell you as well, Signy, our father – I don't think he can survive these wounds he's sustained. He will enter Valhalla – or, as there are no battlemaids – Hel's realm, before nightfall. The One-Eyed is not coming, for all our father's prayers."

Worse than all his recitation of our woes was the blank I suddenly noticed on his left hip.

"Sigmund, where is Balmung? Where's your sword?"

"Don't worry about that, sister."

"Have you surrendered the sword, Sigmund?" My voice reached a high pitch of horror.

"Signy, I must take you to Ermenaric."

I made a stronger gesture of protest than I had all day, but a pain overcame me, and I could not give more.

"No, I must. If I surrender you, he will see that you and your child receive the care you need. I am not a midwife. I was a damned fool to let you stay for this, to think... Well, maybe Fate will allow that you have a son who'll grow to take revenge for the death of his grandfather and mother's brothers someday. We were all damned fools."

None too gently, Sigmund scooped me up into his arms. Sweat and warm blood oiled the crush of our bodies. I tried to clasp the familiar scent of his exertions to me, to ignore the way serum reinvigorated the leather of his belt and cuirass, to recall all the smells of the hunt, of gravy in the pot, of death.

And Sigmund clung fiercely, too, so fiercely I wonder the baby wasn't pressed from me. But I understood that the effort of keeping his feet on the gangplank caused this and, after that, on the meadow grass, trampled and slick with gore. He struggled to keep his feet while his own head reeled with loss of blood.

Halfway up the hill he stopped, unable to move further. "Ermenaric!" he shouted. He stopped to pant and then shouted again. "Ermenaric, here's my sister, your wife, about to give birth to your child. Come and get her. I surrender her – and myself."

I looked up the slope into the face of my husband. A cruel smile split his face like a second scar. He flung an arm in orders to a number of retainers. At the end of that arm swung a battleax. The moon-shaped blade of the ax sprayed an arc of blood as it flung. The retainers came forward as Sigmund sank to his knees before them. But he did not fall face forward into his own gore until they had relieved him of me and hoisted me to their shoulders on a cradle made of an overturned shield. Another wave of Ermenaric's ax, and my brother's prone body vanished under a swarm of Goths like offal under flies on a warm summer's day.

"O Lover of Battles, come to me!"

My father's voice. I caught a glimpse of him, backed into one of his ships and taking a stand with his spine to the mast against ten Goths who might have had a berserk's potion.

"Oh, All-Father, do not leave me in Hel–"

But the sky remained an impassive summer glare. No blessed clouds announced the arrival of Odin's maids.

A fierce blade caught my father in the neck and cut him through the armor to the heart. He lies forever at the bottom of the Goth's river, no hero's mound for one the gods lured on and then finally abandoned.

And then the pain overwhelmed me, and I screamed a scream with no end.

chapter 21

"BABA HERE TELLS ME YOU have a boon to ask of me, wife."

My husband glowed with mead and appeared not a little annoyed at having been hauled away from his victory celebration to enter a birthing room. I'd already caused him enough trouble for one day. First, by providing kinsmen who were defeated, true, but whose defeat probably cost more loss of men and arms than their numbers and the booty they surrendered warranted. Then I had appeared in a helpless labor, in indignity on the straw-strewn floor, screaming a constant disruption to the celebration. Dull Aslaug hadn't been with me too long before she had gone to him, telling him it seemed a hopeless case. "Such a foolish, useless thing!" she had muttered. "Can't even birth a baby without making a big nuisance of herself. I have a child to tend to, and these battle-hungry men."

"Ababa. Send for Ababa," I had managed to plead on Aslaug's return.

Ababa, the woman from the nearest croft, I had never met, but since Mathesuentha had first babbled the soothing, brook-like syllables of her name, I had come to think of her as a friend, help in time of trouble. Fortunately, Ababa was not far off. Her husband and elder son had come to pay their fealty dues to Ermenaric and fight in his battle. Ababa had come along to cheer her menfolk on and, afterwards, to seal up their wounds with balsam pitch. These wounds were not very grave, else she might have been as likely to murder as to deliver me. The way things stood, she had nothing against me.

"Indeed, I was hoping we might soon meet," Ababa said as she washed her hands from tending her husband and son and put water on to boil. "Mathesuentha said such nice things about you."

"Mathesuentha ... is dead," I said with as much bitterness as pain and exhaustion allowed.

Ababa astonished me by saying, "Now, you don't know that." How could she say that so easily? Hadn't Mathesuentha been her friend?

"They ... took her ... away," I insisted. "To ... the swamp. A long time ago."

"We can talk about that later. Right now, let's get this baby born."

Ababa watched through one pang, holding my hands, and then made the observation. "This is going to be a bit difficult."

Another two pains, and my tongue rolled again in the taste of the bitter-sweet brew and the rye pancakes. Mathesuentha might have still been alive, but when my eyelids struggled to open, only Ababa leaned over me. In her lap she held a thread of wool knotted down its whole length. At each pang, she cut through one of the knots with her sewing scissors and laid it to the flame of an oil lamp with the distinct burning odor.

"Something inside you holds life back," she announced grimly when the last knot was cut. "You wish, perhaps, to ask a boon of the King, your husband?"

How had she known that? Having had a husband and son wounded that day, one would have expected her heart to lie elsewhere. Perhaps such things lay beyond sides in a war.

"Thank you," I murmured.

So she sent for him. And now, here he stood, drunk and gruff, and demanding to know impatiently what I wanted.

"Speak up, child," Ababa ordered, much as Mathesuentha might have done. "Do you want to die with this baby stuck inside you?"

"My brothers—"

"Yes, I gave your brothers a beating today they'll never recover from, by my good battleax," Ermenaric said. "What of it?"

Ababa gestured to him to be a little less gruff while I suffered the screaming speechlessness of another pang.

"Alive?" I asked when I could.

"As a matter of fact, I have taken all ten of your brothers captive."

"Even Sigmund? Sigmund is not dead?" Life and strength rushed within me. I could feel them center on the pain and, for the first time, I managed it without crying out.

"Yes, they are all still alive. But I intend to hang them all at dawn to Odin, as I have promised the Giver-of-Victory. Very comely acorns they'll make, too."

"Please – no."

"What? You're asking me to go back on an oath to Odin? Odin, to whom your father was so devoted he died with the God's name on his lips."

"Please, don't hang them. Not yet. Keep them ... keep them only in chains ... until I have a chance to see ... to bid them farewell..."

Ermenaric watched through another pain while Ababa wiped my brow.

"It cannot be such a hard thing, my lord," Ababa murmured to him through my pain. "Just a little while, keep them in chains. Just to deliver your wife and win your child."

That man who had seen the death agony hundreds of times on the battlefield weakened at the sight of my pain. "Very well," he said. "They'll stay in chains for a while."

"Swear," I gasped.

"Go ahead, sir. Release her from her misery. Swear."

I screamed. Ermenaric turned away and said, "By Odin, I swear. They shall not be hanged to his name. Not yet."

"Thank you, your majesty."

The moment he left the sight of me, Ermenaric gave a burst of laughter. I heard it from the other side of the door, but I already rode on a pain, and the laughter somehow gave me strength to push against it.

"That's right, Lady Signy! Good girl. We've just birthed the baby's head."

A moment's rest, one last, mighty effort, and the torture ended.

"Well done, Lady Signy. Well done! It's a boy! A beautiful little prince."

I passed thankfully into unconsciousness, worrying as I did so that I never should have put my faith in an oath sworn by the name of the Fickle One.

Ermenaric stayed no longer than to see his son and sprinkle him with water to say he was pleased, the child should live. Had he not been pleased, the child would have been sunk in the water altogether. Ababa had gone home with her menfolk, but she'd stayed a little longer, long enough to see that I didn't refuse the breast to my son.

I didn't, though he was a red, scrawny, ugly thing with a piercing, wearing wail and so like his father, I found it hard to believe no battleax scar yet marred his face. His infantile kicks swaggered about his fat baby genitals. Either that, or he kicked trying to rid himself of the burden of his sex. I didn't feel like this very male body could have much to do with me; certainly it couldn't be the product of my female form.

His father called him Randver after his own father, but I hadn't gone as far as naming yet. I slept as one dead, was wakened to nurse the ugly wailing thing and take some gruel, then slept again. All this I did mindlessly, heartlessly. My only thoughts could be for my brothers.

I put off asking after Sigmund and the others for five days. I knew the moment I saw them, Ermenaric would be released from his oath and could hang them. Still, asking wasn't seeing, was it? And at last the force of my anxiety got the better of me. I asked Aslaug, when she took a breath amid her constant mutterings about bothersome new mothers. "How fare my brothers?" I entreated.

"Your brothers?"

"Yes, how are they?"

"With Hel in her realm, I suppose."

"No, they aren't. They're out in the yard or some place. In chains. My husband promised me, in chains."

Aslaug smiled a thin, cruel smile. "He promised you chains, but he never promised to keep them in the yard. Besides, what is a promise to a wife compared to a promise to a God? The morning after the battle, he had them marched out – in chains, yes – to Grim Wood."

"What is Grim Wood?" My heart pounded at the mere sound of the place.

"A wood not far from here. Endless and very dark and dense and hostile to humankind. In Grim Wood run great packs of wolves and bears and trolls and giants. The Gods know what all is hidden in that place. There your brothers were each chained to a great tree and left to die of thirst – or be eaten by wild things first. Pray for that. It's more merciful."

"But Ermenaric promised!"

"He clearly thought better of that promise. Besides, he kept the letter of his promise, didn't he? He didn't hang them, but kept them in chains, alive, 'til nature ran its course."

"But he promised I could see them." Inside me, a pain wrenched as if I still had a child to birth.

"And so you may, if a trip to Grim Wood and the vision of bundles of gnawed-on bones is to your liking. Now, feed that brat of yours before we all run stark raving mad with his sickly wails."

Whether he was crying or sucking greedily at my breast, I was certain I should go mad from that thing they called my son, to which my fate now seemed bound.

Grim Wood, I could face any Grim Wood. I could welcome the fangs of the beasts there, yes, and gladly. But mounds of bones caught in treacherous chains and my inability to do anything for them or for myself – I doubted I could bear that. Yet, Grim Wood it would be, I decided.

I got up as soon as the child had sucked himself to a fitful sleep and tried to walk around the room a little. Too soon, too soon I tired and had to sit down again. *Too soon to walk to Grim Wood. Too soon to walk out of the stockade – forever. Too soon now, but not long from now. Not long.*

As I sat, I happened to notice that the loom work was all repaired and ready to take a shuttle. Well, that must have been Ababa's doing while she sat and watched my early hours of motherhood. I threw the shuttle back and forth in idleness a couple of times. I remembered what Ababa had said – or hinted at – about Mathesuentha, and shivered. Of course I couldn't believe Mathesuentha was alive. But I was sorry I hadn't had a chance to ask more.

Perhaps, I thought, *I should stop at Ababa's house for a little while on my way to Grim Wood.*

But for now, the thing to do was to eat every bit of this tasteless but nourishing gruel, pass as little of it as I could into that measly infant, and gain strength. Gain strength enough to go and join my brothers in death.

chapter 22

 HE MORNING OF THE FOURTH day after learning of my brothers' fate, I woke up feeling better than I had since I'd come to Gothland. Today was the day. I would wait no longer. Ignoring my wailing son, I began to dress and to consider what, if anything, I might need.

A woman who goes to die should need nothing.

But what was this? A cat sneaked into my room. I'd never seen this one about the stockade before. Such pretty golden fur, almost the color Mathesuentha's hair had been. Now why had I thought of that? Quite a yowler, too. *Look! Look at those teeth when she opens her mouth to yell persistently at me. Look at them! They are crooked just the same way Mathesuentha's had been.*

"Mathesuentha?"

I hardly dared to speak it, it seemed so impossible. *But look how she seems to respond and nod when I speak that name. And purring now and rubbing up against this jug. What is in this jug?* I'd never noticed it before. Perhaps Ababa had left it...

Honey. It was a pot full of new honey, at this time of year!

"You think I should take this pot to Grim Wood with me?"

The cat purred, rubbed the jug, all but spoke the word, 'Yes!'

"Very well. But I'm only going there to die, you know. I suppose if you've come back as a cat, you know everything. And water and some bread and cheese as well? All right, I'll take them. But don't expect me to eat any of it. Good-bye, then, puss. Mathesuentha—"

The cat rubbed greedily at the hand I offered her and purred.

"Take care of that baby, too, if you've a mind to. You're probably better at it than I am. Good-bye."

I had no great trouble walking out of the stockade this time. Ermenaric and most of his men had sailed off many days ago, having a great wide empire to keep in line during these few short months of summer. And Aslaug looked me straight in the eye as I passed with a small smile on her face. She clung protectively to her son but didn't say a word. She was only too glad to see me go.

I learned the general direction of Grim Wood from a man dozing in the guardhouse on sentry duty. Asking everyone else I met after that as well, in spite of their grim faces and dire warnings when I mentioned my aim, I unfailingly reached the edge of the place by noon. Ababa's house stood in the neighborhood, but I decided not to take time to stop there and ask further into her cryptic words about Mathesuentha still being alive. Hadn't I seen Mathesuentha herself in the flesh that morning? Hadn't she given her blessing to my quest?

This last thought gave me the courage to take a deep breath, reshoulder my bundle of honey, bread and cheese, and enter the terrible wood. Almost instantly, darkness as thick as twilight settled there under the netted branches of fir, beech, and oak. The under-growth was thick, too, almost impassable with ferns, slippery moss and, very frequently, patches of unsure mud and boggy puddles. But sweet woodruff also grew, just ending its bloom, an herb with the properties of other worlds. I found it difficult to believe that any other human beings had ever been to this place, even for a brief and skittish stay. A stay no longer than it takes new straw to become fouled on a drizzly day.

And yet they had. These branches were newly bent. And this limb newly hacked off, the sap still dripping like rain. These signs made a path where otherwise I would have found none. *Such a path could be made — well, by men-at-arms leading prisoners in chains.* I could think of nothing else.

And then I saw my goal. The warriors, brave conquerors that they were, had not dared to go so far into the woods themselves. Here they had stopped, here chained their first man. This pile of bones with flesh still clinging had been my brother Sieggir. I recognized the iron armband that had been gnawed around, the tooled buckle of the belt, remains of the grisly meal.

My head reeled. I sat down hard and tried to gain control of my senses. I heard only greedy flies and wasps at their feast until I thought my head would burst.

Eventually I found strength to get up and go on a bit. That must have been Sigurd, that one Sinfjotli, this Sigi, then Sigrun, Sigrgard ... nine mounds of bones mixed with chains I found and wept over, nine brave brothers...

And then, the worst of all, I saw Sigmund. Sigmund, my twin, the dearest...

But Sigmund– From a distance, his body seemed whole. No beast had torn his flesh, though his battle wounds still gaped and he was markedly thinner. Sigmund, slumped over on his chains against a great oak tree, a precious sacrifice to Odin. And yet, it seemed – it was! He breathed!

"Sigmund! Sigmund!" I caught his face in my hands, stroked the sweated, matted beard in disbelief, then shook it. "Sigmund!"

The dear eyes flickered open. The tongue was so thirst-swollen I could hardly understand him, but I knew he spoke my name.

Quickly I gave him water, hardly taking time to think what I should have done had I not obeyed the advice of Mathesuentha the cat to bring some along. Then, as soon as he could, I coaxed a little bread and cheese on him. Presently, he was able to tell his tale.

"They brought us here and chained us up, each one out of sight of the other, but we could still shout to one another, shouting encouragement, giving the Volsungs' battlecry. Sieggir was the first to go. The first night. A great she-wolf, gnawing him to bits and carrying the portions off to her lair."

I gave Sigmund another drink of water, and he continued. "She'd found herself a brave flock to plunder. Easy work. Each night she came back and killed another. Just one a night; clearly none of us was going anywhere. We could hear the screams: 'By the Gods, it's me tonight!' I heard Sigi say. 'She's got me! Sigmund!' And I could do nothing. Nothing!

"The next night I saw her, her eyes like yellow stars, hot with pus. She seemed to stop and grin at me. That night she dragged Sinfjotli's arm away to her cubs, chewed off at the shoulder. I knew it by the ring that caught the moonlight from time to time as it bounced along the ground beneath her belly. Rain fell sometimes during the day, and I could quench my thirst somewhat with that. But I've had nothing at all to eat – is there more of that cheese?"

I gave him cheese, holding it for him like a baby because though I'd undone the leather thongs that held his hands and feet, his limbs were still numb from the effects. Then he continued.

"One a night. So they went. It is my turn tonight. No one is left. But you are here, Signy. You ... you! Bless you. The world has not seen the last of us Volsungs yet. One remains to take revenge against that troll of the Goths."

"Alas, Sigmund. I don't think I can free you. A curse upon that cat."

"What cat? Why talk of cats now?"

"I'll tell you all later. She told me to bring bread, water, cheese and honey, but nothing to undo your chains. I only thought to die here with you. I never thought to find you alive."

"Well, try, Signy. Let's see what you and I can do together."

We tried for over an hour. I managed to unknot the thongs on his hands and feet, but no more.

"You must go back for a file, Signy."

"But it is such a long way, and I'm not as strong as I was, Sigmund, when you and I could chase all morning and hardly feel tired. I thought I only had one way to go today, and now I must go two."

"You must bring a file."

"But I cannot be back here before nightfall, Sigmund, for all my good will. That's what I'm trying to say. I cannot be back before the she-wolf comes for you. It will be better if I stay. Then she may have me instead."

"No, Signy, go. I beseech you. You've freed my hands and feet. That's something. I may be able to fight her off, in spite of these chains, with my hands and feet free to move. But I shall never be freed without a file."

"Very well. I'll do as you say, brother."

"And Signy – you must also bring me Balmung."

"Balmung, your sword? But didn't my husband take that as booty when he conquered you?"

"Did he tell you he did?"

"No. He tells me nothing. But I heard him howling for it."

"Then he has not found it, else there'd be no end of his gloating. I hid it, Signy, don't you see? Lest it fall into his hands, I hid Balmung. Before I came and got you to surrender to him. Balmung is carefully buried, in the sand bar at the edge of the battle meadow. Do you know the place I mean?"

"Yes, I do."

"Five pines stand there. It's buried beneath the soft sand under the second one from the river. It should give you no trouble to find it and dig it up. Go now, Signy. Bring a file and my good sword Balmung. Ermenaric shall yet feel its bite, as I am the only remaining son of Volsung."

I fed my brother as much as he could hold, put the remnants where his hands could reach them, and washed and bound his battle wounds, some of which were festering dangerously. I carefully cleaned off the maggots and striped the wounds with balsam sap and some woad I found growing nearby. Still I was loath to go.

"Go, please, Signy. In you lies our family's only hope."

But what of this honey the cat had had me lug all this way instead of the much more useful file? "Are you sure you don't want any more honey before I go?"

"I've already taken what I want. It's good for quick energy, but of what use to me is energy until I get that file? Signy, the honey is much too sweet to eat more of. It only makes me thirsty. Signy – here, now, what are you doing with that awful stuff?"

"Smearing it on your face, what does it look like?"

"Honey in my beard? Can you think of a more uncomfortable thing?"

"The cat told me to bring the honey. It must be for something. She knew stealing a file from under the blacksmith's nose would be a difficult thing, but a pot of honey..."

"What cat? What nonsense are you talking?"

His hands, even unbound, were not enough to fend me off. How should he manage with a wolf? So I kept spreading until all the pot was gone.

"There, now, see? The wolf will be first attracted to the honey. She will stand up with her paws on your chest, so, to lick it off. Then you must – well, you must do what you can. Perhaps you can grab her tongue between your teeth–"

"My teeth?"

"Whatever you can imagine. Hang on for all you're worth. Do what you can with your hands and feet, but hang on to that wolf's tongue. I'll return as soon as I can with a file. Hang on to that tongue. Try to ignore the flies and wasps 'til nightfall. And hang onto that tongue."

I kissed him lightly on the chin, getting a face full of honey myself, and hurried out of the wood.

"Baby's crying," Aslaug greeted sharply when I returned. "Thought you'd forgotten all about him."

As a matter of fact, I had, but the moment I heard that dry, choking wail, my breasts let down. I couldn't ignore the wet front of my dress, the wetness perhaps dulling the edge of the file I had managed to steal from the blacksmith and hide in my bosom on the way in.

"I'd've seen to him myself," Aslaug grumbled, pursuing me into the room, "but that cat! Wouldn't let me near him. Just look at the scratches I've got on my arms for trying to take a little care. And she had the nerve to attack my little son. Miserable cat. Where did it come from? I've never seen it before."

I shrugged.

"My bets are it's a troll cat. We should kill it."

"No!" I exclaimed.

"You have to kill these things. They rove among the herd from cow to cow, stealing the milk, then go home to the witch who sent them and spit the milk out into her own pail."

"This is not a troll cat."

I found the cat curled up next to the baby. One could almost imagine she'd been nursing him herself – one did sometimes hear of dumb animals doing such things. She got up quickly when I approached, however, arched her back, yawned delicately and kneaded her paws into the marten fur coverlet.

"Well, I never," said Aslaug.

"Hello, there, Mathesuentha." I greeted her before the baby. She purred and rubbed my arm. "Good puss."

"Mathesuentha!" Aslaug snorted. "What sort of name is that for a cat?"

I didn't answer but turned to the baby. When I saw how wet and red in the face he was, how dirty the coverlet beneath him, I couldn't suppress a wave of guilt. I changed him quickly, dropping the wet, unpleasant woolen swaddling to the floor.

"For me to wash, I suppose," said Aslaug, picking it up between the thumb and one finger only. "Aslaug, always left with the dirty work."

The moment she had gone, I could at last unclasp the brooch at one shoulder to drop the bodice down and reveal a breast. I took out the file and hid it under the coverlet first before I succumbed to motherly feelings. As I hushed and fed my son, the cat came up and rubbed my knees.

"You saw that, didn't you, Mathesuentha? Now, you mustn't tell anyone. I have to make the same trip tomorrow and bring Sigmund that file." I proceeded to tell her in a whisper all I'd seen and done that day. "But of course you know all about this. The honey was your idea, wasn't it? I only wish there was time for me to go back tonight. But it's already too dark to see where Balmung might be hidden. I tried to look around a bit before I came in, but it was too dark to tell what I was doing. At first light tomorrow."

I sighed, gaining pleasure from the rhythmic tugs at my breast and leaning back on the bolsters wearily. "Until then, rest. And care for this – this poor creature. One more night."

The cat had licked her way up my arm and was now gently kissing the little boy's face.

"You were a good nursemaid, Mathesuentha. Thanks. But you needn't have been so rough to Aslaug. And her son!"

By Mother Frigga, I swear the cat gave me the idea.

"You think so?" I demanded of her. "You really think she meant to kill Randver the moment I was gone? The monster! How could–? Well, you can't really blame her, can you? You and I tried to do the same thing, and it caused your death instead. Or at least, your transformation. I must confess, I almost hoped this child would be dead when I came back, with all that lies before me. What's that? You think I should take him with me tomorrow? Mathesuentha, I don't think– It'll slow me down, and haste is of the utmost... I was hoping I could leave him to you again. No? I guess you're right. I didn't mean to return tonight, but tomorrow I must really not come back. Once Sigmund is freed of the chains, he and I will live together, away from this hateful place where now the heads of my father's retainers have joined the others, rotting on the stakes. Sigmund will care for me, and I shall care for him. We will raise this one together – as our son. And when he's grown, he may help Sigmund to take revenge against his own father. That will be sweet, won't it?

"Will you come with me to Grim Wood, Mathesuentha? I'm afraid that's where we'll have to live, some place prohibited to every Goth, in order to be safe. No? I don't much relish the idea myself. I do wish you would, but you must do as you think best. I can't think what sort of life a cat would want, but I know you'll be able to take care of yourself, whatever happens. As you have taken such good care of me – of us. Thank you."

And so, at first light, I bundled up the baby, the file, a little more bread and cheese, and left, saying nothing to Aslaug on the way out, although she fixed me with a scowl that seemed to say, "I don't know what you think you're up to, but good riddance."

I went first to the sand bank, second tree from the river. There I suffered the first dampening of my spirits. Someone – or something – had been there before me. The sand was still damp, churned up by digging. I certainly hadn't dug that much in my futile attempts last night. I'd barely turned over a handful, as it had been too dark. And this digging – it looked more like the sort a dog might do, not a person. A dog – or a wolf. Here indeed a canine print pressed the wet soil, and there another. They seemed far too big for any of the warriors' hunting hounds.

I began to dig myself, but felt defeated from the start. Before midmorning, I'd given up. Balmung was not there, at least not to be found by me. I picked the baby up, brushed the sand off him, and fed him. When he had finished, I decided the only thing to do was to bring Sigmund the file as quickly as I could. My brother could come and find his sword tonight – if it could still be found.

Grim Wood was even quieter than I remembered, more filled with dread. My heart pounded, for some reason I couldn't explain, more than it had the first time I entered. Carefully I counted nine trees with chains and mounds of brothers' bones. Here was the tenth, the tall oak – empty chains.

No Sigmund.

I knew this was the tree. Hadn't I sat here at his side all yesterday? Here were the thongs I'd tossed away when I'd freed his hands and feet. Here was the empty honey pot. But no Sigmund.

And, yet, no gnawed bones, either. That gave me courage. I took time to look around the back of the tree and saw how, in some violent struggle, the chains had been ground deeply through the bark to the white flesh, leaving it in splinters. I remembered, too, how thin my brother had grown. Given this extra slack, it might have been possible for him, with hands and feet loosed from their cords, to wriggle the rest of himself free.

"Sigmund! Sigmund!" I called.

Only an echo taunted me, like an empty bowl to a hungry man. I wandered a little further, trying to read more signs of a mighty scuffle, ferns torn up to reveal bare dirt.

The caw of a raven clenched my heart. There, rolled over with fronds of fern, I caught a glimpse of bone and gore. Taking a deep breath, I forced myself to creep closer, frighten off the carrion bird, and get a better look.

Thank the Gods, it's not human. Four paws, the claws torn off. And the head gone, too. Without the head, I could hardly be certain, but it seemed to be a wolf to me. A she-wolf, skinned. Skinned by a human for a trophy. Killed by Sigmund with his bare hands. My heart wouldn't let me believe anything else, but I wished I could be certain. I wished the head still remained so I could study the tongue and see – see if any honey remained on it.

I had to believe Sigmund had triumphed. But if so, where was he? Why wasn't he waiting for me? I couldn't go back to the stockade. The sun already rode closer to the horizon than to its zenith. I didn't dare spend a night alone in these woods. Certainly not with a baby.

And suddenly it was already too late. I heard a heavy tramping behind me. I started to my feet, then crouched as best as I could behind the ferns. The footsteps approached, passed. As Fate would have it, just as they did, the baby began to fuss. I quickly gave him the breast, but we were heard.

The steps came tramping back. Of course, I should have realized that no wild beast hunting prey would be so noisy in the woods. The footsteps were human. A band of warriors from the stockade found me. "By the One-Eyed," said one of the men, "it's Queen Signy."

"Lady, what are you doing here?" asked another. "And with the young prince?"

"Men, take a look at this over here," called a third from some distance. "By the Gods, I don't like what I see."

"A wolf, is it?"

"You may be sure it's a wolf."

The apparent leader of the patrol turned to me. "Lady, you must let us see you home at once. A croft near here was attacked early this morning."

The warriors hastened, one after the other, to tell the tale. "All the family mauled to death."

"This was the family of a man who proved himself braver and stronger than most in the last battle. And his son, too, was just become a man."

"Only the little girl is alive, but – forgive me, lady – badly abused."

"The poor little thing just kept saying over and over, 'A wolf! A wolf! A man-wolf!'"

"All the livestock killed, but not eaten. And there were wolf prints all over the place. We followed them into these woods."

"This is not your average wolf. This corpse here confirms it."

"It is no normal beast we're dealing with, content to stay in his woods and eat squirrels and deer, to creep out only once in a while for a lamb or two. No, this is a beast that craves human flesh."

"And what's more, it can change into a human, too, with all our species' fiendish cunning."

"The ferocity of a wolf, the cunning of a man."

"This is a werewolf, I'm sure of it."

"A werewolf..." I repeated.

I'd been watching the banter bounce back and forth like an inflated sow's bladder, but my statement brought a heavy pause that crushed their tale, as if the ball had burst. I watched the pallor creep into even the firmest warrior's face, but the thrill of it settled in prickles at my shoulders. I could not keep the color from my cheeks. I had to struggle to hold at bay a smile of new hope.

Fortunately, the men did not regard me. Their leader broke the silence first, attempting for calm by stating the facts and not backing down from their irrefutable truth. "This corpse confirms a part of how he's done his black magic. A wizard needs a wolfskin to complete the spell."

"I thought all he had to do is drink water collected in a wolf's paw print," said another.

"That's part of it."

"I'm sure you're right."

"It isn't good to look into these dark secrets too closely. But we can and must get you, Queen Signy, and the child home to safety at once. It is the blessing of the Gods that no harm has come to you."

The warriors were themselves in pretty much of a hurry. I had no choice but to follow them. But when I had only their backs to see me, I let myself indulge totally in a quiet smile.

chapter 23

HEY BROUGHT ABABA'S ORPHANED DAUGHTER to the stockade for us to care for. I guessed she was about ten or twelve years old when she came. Her night of terror had cost the girl her wits. At least, she never spoke a word to anyone afterwards and would start at any sound. Dogs in particular frightened her, dogs barking or, worst of all, howling. But cats scared her, too, and sometimes just a dead fur. She often cried, silently, tearlessly, without cause and could not be consoled. We never could even learn her name, although Aslaug took to calling her Thiudigotho, Thiudi for short, because, she confessed, she'd always wanted a daughter named Thiudigotho. The girl didn't seem to mind; at least she answered to it as well as to anything. So I took to calling her that, too.

Thiudi hadn't her wits about her, but she could fetch water from the river, once shown how to step into the shallows without drowning herself. She could also be set to the most mindless tasks – grinding grain, for example – and sit at them all day without complaint. She'd grind the whole winter store at one sitting and her fingers, too, into a bloody gruel, if we didn't stopped her and gently lead her to something else.

I hadn't intended to ever return to the stockade, but here I was. I hadn't intended to be a mother, either, but that grew on me, too. As the child I bore lived from day to day, I did, too. And as I recovered from

my brothers' deaths and my son's birth, I managed some of the household duties. Carding and spinning I did a lot, as well as the weaving,
which became my particular tasks. I had linen swaddling for Randver
in time for him to get some months' use out of it and spare him the
worst rashes that winter before he was toddling. Then, when he didn't
need swaddling anymore, we used that linen for our moon times
which, what with two, then three women bleeding, was very practical.

I also took an interest in cookery. I took my place under the royal
crown of the bread-canopy, but more to see that our meat was no longer boiled juiceless and flavorless in plain water. I swept the crumbs
up off the table after every meal, as Mathesuentha had done, and kept
them carefully in a basket for breading, puddings and thickening. I
took pleasure in how Mathesuentha's utensils, marked with her magic
runes, conformed so well to my hand. And I experimented with herbs
until I could tell just what was needed: juniper berries for venison,
sage for pork, tarragon for chicken.

Of course, since I'd never taken much of an interest in the leafy
world before, this took some learning and not a few mistakes. I shall
never forget the time I mistook dock for sorrel and made a broth
that purged us all mightily. I did have the best of teachers, however –
Mathesuentha the cat. It began with the hellebore. One day I happened to notice the knot of leaves among the field of herbs and grasses
that had all seemed the same to me, and I remembered the pale violet
flowers Mathesuentha had pointed out beneath the melting snow.

She had wanted the roots, I remembered and, just for her sake,
I decided to dig one up to see if it was interesting. It was, black and
tuberous. The smell of cut root where my wooden spade had nicked it
caught in my throat and reminded me so powerfully of that brew I'd
been made to swallow on two occasions. That smell I matched to one of
the great number of small earthen jars Mathesuentha had left behind
and Aslaug, with a turned-up nose, kept threatening to toss out.

But how to turn the dark root to this grayish powder remained a
mystery until the cat leapt up into my lap, sniffed at the fresh root –
and winked at me. Then she jumped down and, before Aslaug had
time to scold and toss Mathesuentha over the open half of the hall

door, she had leapt onto a shelf of my guardian's old implements. The cat rubbed herself against a saddle-shaped slab of clay. The tool had been pierced with little holes a nail's breadth apart over the whole surface, then fired with the rough refuse of the crumbs from the holes left clinging all to one side. It grated the root quite handily. The pulp I spread on a cheese cloth in the sun, turned from time to time, and, before three days were up, I had grey powder identical in every way to that in the jar.

Mathesuentha the cat led me to many herbs after that. Any cat, of course, will make a beeline for catnip and rub and roll on it. This cat did it for other things. I would go and study what she pointed out on our early morning rambles through the meadow or copse. I would bruise a leaf and smell it. Or she would swat at a dangling head of seeds, and I would bruise them.

Almost invariably, I would be struck with the powerful memory only scent can give of something from my childhood or something from my time with Mathesuentha the woman. And my guide only pointed out the herbs when the essence was of the strongest and best to pick. It would come strongly to my mind, *This seed is good with apples and pork in the fall.* Or, *I know this goes on a lanced boil to draw the poison out. It stings powerfully, but is very helpful.*

Now the meadow, which had held such fearsome memories of the fall of my kinsmen, became my favorite place instead. My family had fertilized the place to new growth with their blood, proving helpful to me and mine even when they were gone.

Sometimes when the cat rolled, I couldn't place the smell. But I would pick the leaves anyway, or dig if she herself had dug about the roots, and complete the task while the puss would recline on a sun-warmed rock and idly twitch her tail. Then I'd take it home and dry it and try to match it to one of the pots on the shelf. If I couldn't match it, I would leave the bunch hanging – annoying Aslaug who, no matter where I hung them, insisted she bumped her head on them and came away smelling like a sick room.

Then, sooner or later, I had only to say, "By Frigga, I wish there were something to ease Randver's teething," or "This cough is likely to choke poor little Thiudi to death," and, as I live, that cat would get up from her curl by the fire and set to batting at the appropriate bundle. And then I'd know.

So it happened that, with three pairs of female hands working at it, we managed to make a life almost as comfortable as I remembered under Mathesuentha's care. Of course, Aslaug and I frequently jostled for position. No doubt that I was queen and she maid. But no doubt existed either about whose bed Ermenaric liked best, on the few nights he deigned to stop with us on his constant wanderings about the land like some wild beast. He often would retire with me and then creep away to her bed afterwards, to take a second pleasure before dawn.

Eventually, the cat taught me how to cure this as well. A small sachet of hops mixed with my menstrual blood and tied with strands of my hair under Aslaug's bed made my husband lose interest in her. I preferred she have nothing to lord over me. And a handful of alehoof in both our broths at a certain time of the month kept either of us from conceiving again, which was the way I wanted it. When Aslaug lost interest in the frequently absent king and took up with a fellow stationed at the stockade, a member of the Rosomonen kindred, I knew this was the way she wanted it as well.

As for the smokehouse, its roof collapsed under the heavy snow of the first winter. Nobody bothered to rebuild it, so I never learned to use its secrets. But what I did manage to learn was enough.

Then there were the wolves. Or wolf, rather. I was convinced only one prowled, only one worth commenting on. Once a month, at the full moon, just as a reminder to me to toss some alehoof in the broth, I could hear him howling to shake the very center of every beam in the compound. Everyone would grow nervous and watchful, and Thiudi would be wretched.

Every so often at these times, we would hear of another attack on another croft. Or a warrior on some mission that kept him out late would not return. Come light, he'd be found with his throat torn out, perhaps brained with his own leg bone.

Warriors on watch would sometimes even catch a glimpse of the beast. "Bigger than any wolf I've ever seen," they'd say. Or, "He walked upright like a man, his eyes, hollow, dark, yet wildly glowing."

The claims continued. "I saw him trying to dig around the posts of the stockade. Our king's spiked heads are taking a mauling. The heads of Volsungs' retainers got it worst. Taken right off the stakes and disappeared. Taken somewhere and buried, as dogs bury bones."

Or, as one man suggested, "Perhaps given a decent burial..."

Another would add that he'd taken several shots at the beast. "It was full moon. By all that's in mid-earth or in Aesgard, I should have made a clean hit. But this morning, when we went out, no blood, no scrap of fur. Nothing. Nothing. He cannot be killed."

I took care to ask and had my suspicions confirmed. Every one of the casualties by this wolf had either taken part in wiping out my family or was related to someone who had. Myself, I began to await the full moon with joyful watchfulness. Not only did my menses come at that time, as if I, too, cycled in response to the wild world out there, but I knew that creature, half wolf, half man, was my brother. My brother taking his vengeance on the Goths.

PART V

BRYNHILD'S SENDING

chapter 24

 ELGI HUNDINGSBANE SETS SAIL FOR Saxony again," All-Father announced to us, his daughters. And how should he have known this except through the wisdom of his carrion birds?

Perhaps seven years had passed since the departure of Thora from Valhalla and the fall of Hjalm-Gunnar the berserk. Nobody mentioned the matter again. Seven years of riding and fighting beside my remaining sisters had passed when All-Father told us this news of Helgi Halfdansson, whose name now morphed to Hundingsbane – because he had indeed been the bane of the late King Hunding.

"To take revenge for the last time, I suppose," commented Skeggjöld.

"Well? I suppose we're to reteach him the same lesson over again?" asked Göll.

"No," All-Father said. "This time Helgi will hold the honor."

"Helgi!" I exclaimed, unable to repress the word, remembering with disbelief the wild Dane with whom I'd struggled in the sea. I had learned fairly well to curb such exclamations, no matter how they expressed my emotions. And plenty of times, the majority of times, I was glad for the trust One-Eye put in me, proud to be his daughter. I had ridden all over the northern world for him, and the times when my soul struggled against what I had to do were months, sometimes years apart. Now I remembered only the struggles.

> "My groin is set against Geirðjof,
> The scion of Saxony's second,"

the God declared.

Set against Geirðjof? I asked myself as I echoed my sisters in declaring, "Odin ordains!" *More likely against Geirðjof's wife, who chose to go her own way instead of following yours.*

Right glad I was that I had curbed my tongue and so avoided the sort of divine wrath I saw in All-Father's eye against Thora. I had not expressed mutiny for all these years, nor had I seen or heard of her in that time. I knew All-Father had given two chests of magically runed gold with which he hoped to lure Geirðjof or Thora or even all Saxony to their doom. When I learned that Thora had helped her adopted people see through the ruse and reject the gift, I had hidden my relief from Valhalla. I had almost succeeded in hiding that relief from myself. But Thora remained, in my heart of hearts, my best friend. None of the other Valkyries had moved in to take her place, and I still thought of her as that.

Formerly I had found the God's thinking to be a wonderful divine riddle, why he would one year favor one man, and the next another. Sometimes I had followed Odin solely to untangle the riddle. Now the reasons for his wrath glared all too plain, totally without dignity, like those of a petulant boy who'd been justly punished, yet rails against the punisher.

We did not need the fire in the center of Valhalla on that warm night, and the hall was suddenly too stifling. I went out into the darkness the moment the morrow's riding orders had been given. A coming storm overcast the night as if with a down comforter. I could see nothing and heard only the distant rolls of the God Thor's great hammer and the talons of the ravens as they shifted in sleep, roosting on the shields of the slain.

I had not been given much to do on this mission. No one said it – nothing could disturb the surface of the battlemaids' divine unity – but I knew I was on trial and would not be left unwatched when there might be a conflict of interest. I certainly wouldn't be left alone with the back of a hero until I had proved myself.

As the Norns spun things out, none of us had much to do at that battle. Once Helgi and eleven of his men had been turned berserk, they became the Maelstrom themselves from which no man or ship could escape. We Valkyries didn't even ride that day. The Danes attained their revenge on the Saxon wierde without a single one of them also attaining Valhalla.

Saxons fell instead, scores of them, nearly to a man in defense of their homeland. Those taken alive dangled now from the wierde's beeches, the only trees in the neighborhood, as a sacrifice to Victory-Bringer. I saw Odin's ravens rejoicing on the body of the dark little Frank where he had fallen, standing on the howe of old King Hunding. Hunding's young son had stood beside him, falling only when his earl lost power to defend him. The whole of the Frank's front was such a mass of wounds that I would not have recognized him but for his stature and his hair, now helmetless, which the birds tore out in tufts, as black as their own plumage. No one came to shoo the birds away, let alone give burial. Soon enough, there would be no telling his bones from any others.

No one came because the Saxons had too much to do that night up on the wierde. The Danes had fired the buildings, starting with the king's hall, once the rooms had been rifled for valuables and the best things hauled down to their boats. Arms and armor off the battlefield went first, of course, then silver tableware and jewelry, silks and furs. Even earthenware and hay rakes found worthy places.

The other battlemaids slept around me as if battle easily won were a sleep potion. But I could not sleep, the night fog rolling in off the sea, bitter with so much burning. And then, from time to time, when the wind was right, I could hear a plague of screaming women and children spreading from one end of the wierde to the other like the linden's red plague. Such are the weird colors the Norns weave in their intricate patterns of Fate on warp stretched from horizon to horizon; none escape.

Presently, I thought the fire must have spread and encircled us. I saw it coming from the east, from the opposite direction as the wierde. No, only the sun struggling to push the fog back out to sea. We would soon be saddling up and riding on. I got up off my bear skin and walked down to the gully to relieve and refresh myself. Nothing could free me of the smell of things burning which should not burn. It clung with the fog like nits to my hair.

The wierde had been deadly still for an hour or so, but suddenly my neck crawled as if with vermin from the sound of another cry. Was yet more to be done? And then I understood that the fog had fooled my ears as well as my eyes, stuffing them as with wool. The thin little wail I heard was much closer at hand than the wierde. I thought to probe the sound, but from elsewhere I heard Valfreya's call for battle-maids to saddle up and ride. So I ignored the little wails and turned to answer her. But then suddenly a figure formed itself out of the fog from another direction, and closer to hand.

"Thora!" I cried. But as the figure grew clearer, I felt less certain of my identification. If it was Thora, she was a woman changed, as much as the grinding of a kernel of wheat changes it to make flour. She wore a blackened and bloodied housewife's apron-dress from which both belt and brooches had been torn. She'd found a bit of thorn to hold up one shoulder, but not the other. The rings had been ripped from her ears, the bracelets from her arms. Both eyes were blackened and her lips swollen. And the way her hips moved, broader than ever, I could tell she was favoring a tender pelvis. None of this seemed to concern her, however.

"Thora!"

We passed close enough that I could speak it, but she did not even blink at me. She slid past me into the gully. I must have made a mis-take. The fog haunted me with cruel visions. But I could not take my eyes from her. I watched as, from a large clump of salt grass near the bottom of the gully, she pulled a covered hamper. Magic runes of pro-tection marked its lid in dried mud. When the woman had removed the hamper's lid, the little mewing cries I'd heard filled the air much clearer. She pulled a baby from the basket and immediately put to her breast, sinking beside the basket as if the first tug of baby mouth were the blow of a grown man's fist.

I tried once more. "Thora?"

She did not move or open her eyes, but murmured, "Hello, Brynhild."

"I'm sorry," I whispered, kneeling in the grass beside her. "Truly, I am. If there had been anything I could have done ... if there's anything I can do now..." Words failed me except for another, "I'm sorry."

Thora sniffed in what might have been a chuckle, save for exhaustion. "It's not like it wasn't expected, is it? It's not like I didn't know what Odin's wrath is capable of."

The infant in her arms stopped between sucks and gave a deep sigh. No doubt it had reached the point where its terror at being abandoned suddenly vanished with the magic of forgetting only babies know. Indeed, that sigh did work a sort of magic between Thora and me as powerful as any I'd ever seen All-Father work. Suddenly, all thought but that child was wiped from both our minds.

"Is it yours?"

"Of course." Thora smiled, a thing one would have thought impossible just a moment before. "Mine and Geirðjof's."

"A boy?"

"Yes."

"What's his name?"

"Hogni."

"You wanted a child."

"Yes, and how long it took us to get him! Seven years. That must have been a curse of Odin as well, but the Vanir came through eventually."

"You went to the Vanir with your prayers?"

"Now I wish I could name him Geirðjof for his father, or at least Gerhard or something else to alliterate. But it's too late. At least Geirðjof got to hold him before–"

"He'll look like his father," I said, touching the dark fuzz on top of the little head.

Valfreya's call rolled out of the fog again.

"Sounds like you'd better go," Thora said.

"You don't forget these things, do you? I mean, your life's so differ- ent ... was so different..."

"Being a Valkyrie never leaves you," she said. "Helgi bragged as much when he – when he claimed his victor's rights."

Valfreya called a third time. I answered her.

"Yes, go answer Odin," Thora said. "Odin is a powerful God." More bitterness than awe burdened her voice. "But remember, when you go, what you see here. Remember the power of my foxskin, your bear claws, the things we have won for ourselves without him. Remember what you see here. Up there on the wierde, there's not a male left alive, not even a child under three, or a girl over that age left a virgin. But look, look what I have saved here, for myself, by myself. He may kill my husband and burn my home, but by the skin of my fox, Odin has no power over my children, even as I made him swear."

Thora looked up at last from the face of her son. Her fears for him had suddenly eased as his for her. I could not meet her glance.

"Brynhild? Are those tears?"

"No," I said firmly. "It is only the wind come to blow the fog away."

I climbed to the top of the gully, gave the Valkyrie cry, and went to join my sisters.

PART VI

SIGNY'S PLAN

chapter 25

"MAMA, MAMA, COME QUICK! YOUR cat's had kittens!"

I looked up from my weaving into the freckled face of my Randver, somehow turned, overnight it seemed, into a seven-year-old.

"Come and see!" he insisted. "Rekitach and me found them when we were playing over by the copse. Rekitach said we should drown them in the river."

"Oh, no!" I cried, dropping the shuttle and losing the row.

"I said no. I told him you'd never stand for it. But you'd better come quick."

I came at once. I had been missing Mathesuentha for a week or so now. My shoulders, especially after days spent hunched over the loom, missed when she wasn't around to knead them in the evening with her clever paws. But of course, being a cat, she had been known to absent herself before. Never had she returned with such effect, however.

I stopped in the hall on my way out only long enough to answer some little animal sounds made by Ababa's witlessness daughter, now grown to seventeen.

"What, Thiudi? Would you come and see the kittens, too? Come on, then. Leave the grinding and come on."

They were the sweetest little things, four of them, blind and helpless little balls of fur, with stiff little twigs of quivering tails. None of them seemed to have the mother's coloring at all. Their dark browns and blacks made me scold her gently for getting herself mixed up with a stray of no pedigree. But Mathesuentha remained just as proud of them as she could be and lay purring in her nest of cattail fluff and straw stuffed in a hollow log. She sprawled so they could nurse, never minding their tumbling all over one another and her.

I threatened Rekitach with his life if he should even mention drowning kittens again. Aslaug's ten-year-old said he wouldn't, but the scratches I saw on his arms told me that only Mathesuentha's nervousness had kept him from it.

"A beastly child," I said to Mathesuentha after he and Randver got bored with kittens and wandered off elsewhere. "You should let me bring your family into the compound for you. Then I can help you care for them. And care for you, too, with dishes of cream."

Mathesuentha didn't seem to take to this idea.

"Well, you do as you think best," I told her, knowing she would do that in any case.

Thiudi and I sat there all afternoon, watching the kittens and wishing Mathesuentha joy. I had suffered enough to earn the name "Queen of the Goths." If I couldn't act like a queen and do as I pleased for an afternoon every once in a while, the title was vain – and so, I thought, was "The King of Goths" as well.

Sweet-tempered Thiudi had overcome her fear of cats a little, if never that of dogs. She had grown into a beauty, too, although always in a quiet, sad sort of way. I had a full-time job trying to keep the warriors from taking advantage of her witlessness. Even Ermenaric had started to take an interest, but my magic quickly nipped that in the bud.

If warriors had to be beaten off, I saw no reason why Mathesuentha and I shouldn't take pleasure in the girl's beauty. So while the kittens slept, I crowned the girl's soft brown hair with daisy chains, strung them also about her waist and neck, and sang to her tales of fair maids and courting princes. Mathesuentha purred and rubbed Thiudi's legs and brought the pretty flush of pleasure to her cheeks.

Then suddenly I realized the sun set earlier these late summer days. We needed to return to the safety of the stockade.

"Are you sure we can't bring your family in with us?" I asked the cat again.

Mathesuentha shook her head definitely, so I bade her a quick fare-well, "Until tomorrow," and called to Thiudi. "Come, lass, we must bring the cows in, and the goats."

We kept the animals tethered out in the meadow all day. Thiudi usually helped me bring them in; the task was easy enough. The animals seemed skittish this evening, however. "Probably just upset at being left so late," I commented. "Their udders are full and uncomfortable."

But then suddenly, as I looked back to encourage one of the goats who threatened to scamper off in the wrong direction, I saw him. Standing on a rock at the edge of the river, in the unreal light of the gloaming, he was like the proud statue of a young god. I knew Sigmund at once.

"Thiudi, do you think you can take the animals back by yourself?" I asked. Thiudi shook her head vehemently, setting the daisy chain lop-sided. She seemed as skittish as the animals, and I couldn't guess where she might leap. She had seen Sigmund as well, or at least sensed him.

"You must try, Thiudi. There is someone ... something I must do."

Great silent tears welled up in her eyes. I looked back to my brother impatiently, desperate lest he should vanish even in that short time. He remained there, standing like a statue. But then, even as I watched, the sun set, and the eerie light that had been playing on the hills of the distant shore melded into the huge round globe of the rising moon. In that moment, as quickly as one might turn carding combs from the smooth wooden side to the side with teeth, I saw my brother transform himself.

It appeared like a ritual, a prayer, how he unfurled the wolf skin from under his arm and fit its furred skull over his own as if trying on a crown. Whole paws dangled still from the ends of the legs so he could imprint moist ground. His enemies would see only the beastly paw prints and ignore the two-footed man's prints that were too much like their own.

He turned toward the moon as one moment it smoothed the planes of a man's body, the next sank into thick grey fur. For a long silence, he remained, soaking up the night's silver power. Then he threw back his head and howled. He had become the werewolf even as I watched. He had allowed me to see his magic. Still, the howl shot prickles up my spine, and my heart urged my feet to match its pace.

"Quick, Thiudi! To the compound!"

But the girl froze with fear. No amount of prodding and pulling on my part could move her and all the other creatures in the same direction at once. I looked over my shoulder again, and what I saw nearly crippled me with fear as well. I knew it was my brother – no one could tell me otherwise – bounding towards us with inhuman speed. The animals bolted in all directions, filling the air with their cries of terror. I chose to save Thiudi. I put my arms around her and tried to get her to run with me. She refused to move, fixated with horror.

The next moment he sprang upon us. He wrenched the girl out of my arms and met my stare. His eyes, sunken and fiery, glared beneath the white fangs of the wolf mask. Yet it was my brother. I still had no doubt.

"Sigmund!" I whispered.

What he said in return sounded like only a snarl. With a toss of his mane, he scooped the petrified Thiudi off her feet and ran with her down to the river.

"Sigmund! Don't! Don't hurt her! Please!"

The girl was past all ability to scream. I think she must have fainted. I found myself tumbling down the slope after them.

Sigmund heard me coming, gave a backwards glance and a bark. Then he lunged into the water, taking Thiudi with him. When the water reached his chest, he began to swim with great, powerful, one-armed strokes, never letting his burden go.

"Sigmund!"

Tied to a stone on the shore, the small dugout the warriors sometimes used to go fishing or to cross to the far shore on patrol lay anchored. Half aware of what I was doing, I loosed it from its mooring and shoved with all my might until it floated free of the pebbly bank. I clambered in and found a pair of oars.

I had no skill at handling such a craft. The current did most of the work, but I managed to keep my brother's figure, like a black scar on the moon-white surface, in view over my shoulder. Burdened by Thiudi, his progress was slow. I even managed to gain on them a bit by the time we reached the opposite side of the Vistula, so far downstream of the stockade that we were out of its sight.

Sigmund paused on the shore, either to wait for me or to rest from his exertions, I couldn't tell which. The moment the boat dragged bottom, however, he set off with Thiudi tossed carelessly over his shoulder, taking the bank and the moon-ghosted fields beyond at a steady lope.

On we went, uphill and down, across fields of knee-high grain, over streams. We skirted the corners of woodlands lit even to the third or fourth rank of trees by the strange silver light of the moon. A hedgehog about his night feeding curled up and rolled away at our coming, the light on his spines making him seem an earth-bound moon. Straight toward that rising sphere we ran until it rode no longer in the east, but behind us.

Sometimes, when I couldn't go further and had to rest, Sigmund seemed to sense this. He would drop his burden, who lay sobbing helplessly at his feet, and sit back on his haunches over her, panting with his tongue out and sharp eyes fixed on me. Every time Thiudi made a move even to raise her head, his great paw patted her into motionlessness again. And the moment I felt strong enough to get to my feet and start moving towards him, he sprang off once more, never letting me close enough except to shout his name. On the other hand, he never let me drop too far behind, either.

At last, the moon set behind us, and the first of the birds began to sing. A lark ascending made all human trials as nothing with the fleeting beauty of its song.

My head reeled with exhaustion. There, in the dark grey light of the first throes of dawn, I saw my brother lope down a slight incline set with willow and bristling larch. He paused just at the edge where the incline met a marsh. From what I could see in the half- dark, the marsh had no end but the horizon. A dark, dark place of cattails and rigid sedges, it masked ground that was no ground at all. From it the smell of the rot of living things rose and hit the back of my nostrils like a well-aimed fist. With the sun, all manner of Hel-spawned insects would rise.

Thiudi or no Thiudi, Sigmund or no Sigmund, I would not follow him in there. Didn't he know it would be death?

Sigmund stood at the edge of the reeds and watched me push aside a needly larch branch to come close enough down the slope to make no mistake about his next move. Then he forced his way into the sedges and, in a moment, vanished into the marsh. I stood at the edge of the dry land for a moment, gasping for breath, sobbing a little and feeling completely betrayed, alone and afraid. As I stood, somewhere at the far edge of the marsh, the sun rose. I couldn't see it, but it touched the tops of the sedges with glowing color.

That was the end, then. My brother was no longer a wolf, but someone I might reason with. Someone I might embrace, if I could but find him.

I still saw where his passing had bent the first few clumps of reeds. The growing light revealed a paw print for me in the damp ground. I ventured to set my foot upon it. The ground gave a little with a soggy sound. My heart beat fiercely, and sweat slipped down my hairline, although the air was by no means over-warm.

I found another print and matched it, then a third. As I lifted my first foot up, the ground sucked hungrily after, and I felt the reeds close behind my back like a curtain. I found two more prints and a broken reed, but no more. The ground was too wet now to hold a print and soaked my feet to the ankles. I would have to give up.

I turned around and at first could see neither prints nor clear ground for the dense growth of reeds. Fortunately, my sense of direction did not fail in such a short space, and I quickly retreated to solid ground again.

I had no choice but to return to the stockade and perhaps bring warriors to this spot in an attempt to rescue Thiudi. I didn't like that idea very much, because that would also be leading them to my brother. But first I had to find my way home. Could I do it?

In any case, I was too tired from the night's chase to make the attempt at the moment. I made a nice bed on slippery but soft willow leaves and, in a moment, fell asleep.

How long I slept, I do not know, but the sun rode high when I wrenched my eyes open, startled by a sudden dark shadow.

Over me loomed not a wolf, but a creature such as I'd never seen before. What sort of animal it could be, I couldn't guess. It stood on two legs, about a head shorter than me, but stocky and powerful. The color of acorns stained its face and hands. The hands seemed human, and one of them carried a very human bow. It appeared more cleverly made than the bows I had seen about the stockade. But these hands dangled at the ends of extraordinarily long arms and brushed the knees of very short and bowed legs. Shaggy brown fur covered the legs as well as the head. No amount of covering, however, could hide the monstrosity of that head. The slight forehead sloped steeply down to beetling brows that shielded a face with most grotesque features. Flattened until almost noseless, and beardless but wrinkled, the high cheekbones pushed the eyes up until, in their squint, they might have been as blind as Mathesuentha's kittens.

Those eyes fixed me with a ferocity like the thin edge of an iron blade. I had assumed this creature to be a dumb beast, but the wit sparkling in those black eyes frightened me speechless. Were there more man-beasts in this world than my brother?

The creature grunted and gestured at me. I shrank back into the willow leaves as best I could, but slipped on them and ended up closer to the shaggy legs instead of further away.

With another grunt, the thing had me by an arm and dragged me to my feet. I couldn't cry out for fear, let alone try to protest or break away. Keeping a firm grip on me, the thing led me down the slope to the precise point where I'd attempted to enter the marsh before, and shoved me in.

The water came up to my ankles – but then it came no higher, though I was herded deeper and deeper into the marsh. My beastly captor, I soon realized, knew some secret submerged path of solid ground. As long as I walked single file the way he herded me, I would not sink. When I strayed one way or the other, a quick jerk of his arm brought me back to safety. He meant me no harm – or no immediate harm. Still, I couldn't feel at ease with the brutishness of his appearance and manner. More than once I called up his gruffness by descending into tears of despair, which made me clumsy, and this was clearly no place for clumsiness.

We walked thus, lashed by sedges and soggy of foot, for what seemed like a God's age but probably lasted less than an hour. Then I felt the ground rise up out of the moss beneath me and grow solid. The next moment, the reeds vanished before me, and I found myself in a clearing. The marsh had not ended. This was but an island in the midst of the wetland which began again no more than a hundred yards ahead of me and continued, for all I knew, to the end of the earth. But here emerged land dry enough and large enough to support, of all things, half a dozen or so huts.

These huts were of curious build, round and raised up off the ground on posts so that any flooding of the marshland would leave them unaffected. Materials close to hand formed the huts. Overlapping reeds fashioned the roofs and mud-daubed windowless walls. So much a part of the place, I could easily imagine the structures had grown there as some natural function of bog gas and mosquitoes. Fish – carp, perch, pike, and bream – hung split and strung on twigs before the huts, drying in the sun. Only the tumble of little naked children about the hut doors betrayed the hand of man to me. And the children were of such a swarthy color – like the acorn creature at my side – that perhaps I did better to call them not children at all but cubs or pups.

The creature pushed me across the clearing then, up three rough steps and into the largest of these huts. My eyes took a moment to adjust to the dimness within, but when they did, I had the shock of my life. I was quite prepared to see any sort of gruesome torture or bestial debauch, portent of what my captor had in store for me. But never in my wildest kenning had I thought to see what then appeared.

There, on rugs and bolsters in one corner of the hut, quietly nursing the very smallest of little brown creatures, if anything plumper and more content than ever, sat none other than Mathesuentha. Mathesuentha the woman.

"Ah, Signy, my dear. It *is* you." And although baby and bare breasts had to be included, she gave me a powerful hug.

"Goodness, child, you're looking awfully pale. Was it Basiq?" she prattled, looking over at the creature who'd brought me to her. "Was he gruff with you? I warned him not to be."

The creature answered to the harsh sounds in the word "Basiq" in such a way that I knew it must be his name. Mathesuentha now let loose a barrage of strange sounds in his direction. The creature barked back a monosyllable or two and then slumped out of the hut, leaving us alone.

"When I heard you might be in the area, I knew I should send someone who spoke your language to run and get you." Mathesuentha turned to me again with a beaming smile. "But, since I am still as you see me, on the birthing bed, I had to send Basiq. Men! What can you do? Gruffness is the only thing they know."

"That's ... a man?" I stammered.

"Of course," she said. "Basiq's my husband."

"Your–?" I couldn't make my lips form the word.

"These seven years. Oh, it wasn't a mead-toast like we're used to, but they have a nice little ceremony where the bride and groom hold hands over a burning torch stuck in the ground, and water is poured over the hands while each repeats in turn some very nice words. 'Through fire and water I come to you. Neither fire nor water shall take me from you.' It's quite nice, really."

"I ... I didn't even think he was human."

"Oh, Signy, you always did have a lively imagination. Of course he's human. And a better man than that Gothic 'hero' of mine ever was. Never got a single mite off that one, but look at this."

She proudly showed off the little brown thing at her breast. I could hardly resist offending her new mother's feelings by revealing how repulsive I found the child. It was a boy, clearly. What looked like a great dark bruise discolored his little bare bottom. He was not quite as foreheadless as the father, but they were working on it. Bandages bound a plank of wood on the still pliable little skull to deform it, and horrific scabs covered the flat little face, a copy of his father's.

"Oh, don't mind the cuts. That's what Basiq's people do to a male child when he is born. It's supposed to make them tough. 'A boy should know pain before he knows the comfort of a mother's breast,' they say. And they like the effect such fearsome visages give the enemy. The scars soon heal. We put this ointment on it. That helps. Of course, it does leave them without much beard as adults, but that doesn't hurt their manhood any."

"And – this?" I gestured toward the plank and bandaging on the forehead.

Mathesuentha stroked it fondly. "A flat head is considered handsome."

"But the brain–?"

"No damage to the brain that I've ever noticed. And none at all to the balls." She laughed. "This is my fourth, you know."

"Four!"

"Yes."

"Just like your kittens."

"Kittens?"

"Nothing."

"There are the two girls," Mathesuentha picked her own out of the litter playing around the front door. "And the oldest, another boy. No, I don't see him right off. His father must have him."

"But Mathesuentha..." I finally formed the nagging thought into words. "I thought you were dead."

"Not anywhere near, Gods shield me! It takes more than a little swamp water to kill old Mathesuentha. But let me offer you something to eat before you perish. Then, when you're comfortable, I'll tell you all. The other women have been very neighborly, as usual. Why don't you look among these pots and see if you can find something to your liking."

Marsh food was unlike anything I knew. For all my good intentions not to get Mathesuentha off her bed again, she did, expertly burping her little one over her left shoulder while she guided me with her right.

"Let's see, this is Herka's cattail root. It's very nice. And this is some roast duck in a gravy. And here is some carp – don't mind the blue of the skin, that only tells you it was alive when Aleta plunged it into vinegar to cook it."

I took a bit of fish and cattail root and found them just as tasty as anything Mathesuentha had ever offered me. I realized how hungry I was and had soon finished both bowls.

"Now where were we?" asked Mathesuentha as she slipped her sleeping son into a bent-reed cradle that hung from the ceiling of the hut.

"You haven't told me how you came to be here."

"Well, you know that. Ermenaric's men brought me here after – well, when they thought I was trying to burn you alive in the smokehouse. That was a failure, wasn't it? You had the baby for all our efforts. But he's a fine, strapping lad now, isn't he? And you're not too sorry he came, are you?"

"No. Not now."

I remembered that she had said she saw no deeds of manhood in Randver, even before he was born. The thought now made my blood run cold. I wondered if she still saw that and meant to ask her presently. But first I had to ask, "But how did you know all this?"

"I've kept an eye on you."

Then I wanted to tell her about the cat, about how truly careful I thought she had been of me. But I felt too foolish.

"There's also your brother."

"Sigmund?"

"He lives with us, yes, all us exiles. You see, I was not the first healing woman – witch, they call us – the Goths brought to this marsh. They've been doing it for generations, ever since they started getting notions of empire-building, and we happened to trip them up. Empire-building is not a healthy pursuit, not for women, not for children. Not even for men, if they'd think about it. We like to prevent it if we can.

"Now, when Ermanaric's men first brought me here," Mathesuentha continued, "I thought I was done for, for sure. Those two brutes tossed me into the muck at the edge of the swamp – they didn't dare go further themselves – and pinned my arms down so I couldn't move. I was lucky they were afraid of the place and didn't take me deeper. The way they pinned me, my nose stayed dry if I held very still, but I couldn't even open my mouth to shout for help without getting a mouthful. The first rainstorm I would have been done for, if I wasn't pickled before then. Fortunately, the Huns keep a close watch on the borders of their territory. Basiq came and let me up the moment Ermenaric's men were out of sight."

"Huns?"

"That's the name of Basiq's people."

"But I thought this was Gothic territory."

"So it is – right up to the edge of the Bog. But no Goth knows the path here, and they avoid it like the plague. Not only is there real danger of sinking to those who don't know the paths, but they also believe it is haunted."

"Haunted?"

"Home to the offspring of dark marsh spirits and Gothic witches – as indeed it is, if you give the Huns the name of evil spirits."

"Tell me more about these Huns."

"Actually, these marsh Huns are not a very good example of the people. Very mixed up with Gothic blood, as you can see. If you take the path out of the marsh in the direction opposite to that which brought you here – to the east – eventually you will come to a great steppe."

"The marsh is not the end of the world, then?"

"Not at all. The steppe is what is endless. I cannot begin to tell you."

"You've been to this steppe?"

"Indeed I have. We go once a year in spring. To visit my husband's relations and to take part in a great gathering of all the clans of the Huns. The Huns are a vast people. And they are a people of the steppe, not of the swamp. They learn to ride before they can walk and are fair demons with their bows. The women and children live in wagons and go wherever their herds must go in order to find pasture."

"Then what are they doing in this marsh?"

"Ah, that is a legend here among us. It is said that one day some Hunnish hunters were stalking a great white stag at the edge of the marsh. It escaped from them onto what they thought was unsolid ground. They pursued it nonetheless, marking the path it led them on with secret Hunnish symbols. The stag – which must have been a gift of their god Hadur, for they never caught it – eventually led them right out of the swamp into Gothic lands.

"'What a fine land is this!' the hunters said to one another. 'What good pasturage this would be for our herds.' They went back with word of this land to their chief, careful to mark the path along all of its length. But when the chief asked omens for such a move, the response was not favorable. 'Some day,' the God said. 'But not yet.'

"So the hunters were set here to watch and keep the path until Hadur should be pleased to sanction the move. While waiting here, they rescued the first of the Gothic witches and were impressed at once by how wise she was. 'These people to the west will be easy to conquer,' they said among themselves. 'See how they weaken their own stock by getting rid of the best women instead of the simple and weak.' Soon enough there were more witches and, when they agreed, as we usually do, for no woman would willingly go back among a people who tried once already to kill her, we were married. So – here we live quite comfortably – and wait."

"The signs are not favorable?"

"Not yet. But they will be."

"And did I hear you right? My brother Sigmund is also here with you?"

"Yes. He came, oh, about a year and a half after I did. He'd been wandering and living on his own until he happened to stumble here one evening, and we took him in."

"Poor Sigmund! May I go to him?"

"I'll have Basiq show you to his hut when he comes back. It's the smallest hut. Maybe you could find it on your own. But sit, Signy. First I must talk to you. About Sigmund."

"Yes?"

"This is not good. This is Ababa's daughter he's brought back with him."

"That's right."

"I recognize her, all grown up. She is too frightened to say a word as yet, but she doesn't seem to me to be a willing bride."

"Bride?"

"That seems to be your brother's plan. He should have a wife, I suppose. He's been grumbling about it for a long time, and we all get tired of having him coming around, begging for food, begging us to mend his clothes, begging ... well, men are helpless, aren't they? Unfortunately, the Huns, like most people, will only take daughters from other people. Their own daughters they give only to their own. These fair-haired races! They know no way of getting brides save by abduction."

"She will never have him," I said. Sigmund was my brother, but I did remember my own abduction. "He killed all her family."

"Ababa, dead?"

"Yes, I'm sorry. A long time ago, not long after you – left. Just after my son was born. Sigmund did it. And raped that girl when she was but a child. It was revenge, you see. Ermenaric killed all my family – nine brothers and my father – and only Sigmund survived. Ababa's son and husband fought against my people in that battle."

"I see. Your brother is a difficult man."

"He has had a difficult life," I protested, suddenly fiercely loyal. I told Mathesuentha of the she-wolf.

"Ah, that explains much. He lives here, but he's never been much a member of the community. Of course, it's hard to belong to a community when you're unmarried, only half of a whole, as it were. But he's never bothered to learn Hunnish – I'm the only one he can talk to, me and one other Gothic witch who hasn't forgotten too much of our tongue. But she hasn't much patience with his wild ways. If he can't talk to the men, he can't go hunting with them or fight with them. All the ways of the steppe to which this is only the barest shadow mean nothing to him. All he can mutter about is revenge and raising up a new little generation of Volsungs to help him in that revenge. And at times he seems ... he seems a little mad. Sometimes he recognizes people, sometimes he does not."

Mathesuentha smiled in that little crooked-tooth smile I remembered so well that meant, although trying to be pleasant, she was also deadly serious. "Signy, what are we going to do about that brother of yours?"

chapter 26

RETURNED TO ERMENARIC'S STOCKADE the next day without Thiudi. Sigmund defended his right to keep her as viciously as a wolf defends its mate. I was too glad to see my brother after all these years, haunted-eyed and restless as he seemed, and too used to thinking of his good as my own to argue. Perhaps, in time, she might come to love him as I did.

Mathesuentha had argued fiercely against this – as best she could without leaving her hut, which was forbidden to her for another fortnight. In the meantime, the rest of us could escape the force of her arguments whenever we wanted to. Out of the hut, her husband saw nothing wrong with the match – it kept Sigmund from eying Hunnish women with his wolfish leer. As for the girl, she was too overwhelmed to do anything in her own behalf. So I left her for the moment and went back to the stockade – although the marsh seemed more like home to me now, even after so short a stay.

"I followed Thiudi as far as I could," I explained. "But I lost her in the marsh."

"That was very brave of you," Aslaug said. "We'd given you both up for dead when we saw the wolf tracks. I am very glad to see you."

She said this with more gush than I had expected from her. But Aslaug had other things on her mind. I'd hardly made myself comfortable and was in the midst of greeting Randver, reassuring him as he fought bravely to keep tears off his freckles, when she announced, "Sarus is going back to his people."

Sarus was her warrior-lover, the man she'd taken up with when it became clear Ermenaric, even on his rare visits, had lost interest. It had made quite a difference in her personality, a definite turn for the better, to have her slept with on a regular basis. Still, Sarus's people were the Rosomonen, and her statement astounded me.

"The Rosomonen are in rebellion against Ermenaric," I said. "At least, they were when I left."

"So they are," Aslaug said. "Sarus has a duty to join them."

"And you?"

"I have a duty to join Sarus. He waits for me even now in a secret place outside the stockade."

"Aslaug..." I took her hand with unaccustomed intimacy. "That's ... that's dangerous."

"Yes," she agreed with a shrug, trying to keep courage by pretending carelessness. "I didn't want to expose Rekitach to this danger, and he is Ermenaric's son, not Sarus's. Only that put off my departure. Now that you've returned ... may I leave him here with you – if you agree – just for a time? I hope the day may come when I can send for him to join us."

I didn't ever really say yes. It seemed too dangerous a thing to do, even to commit to that one word. Aslaug threw her blue shawl over her head and left.

Rekitach's feeling of abandonment was instantaneous. He fought all afternoon and all the next day, a bigger bully than ever to my Randver. Nothing that needed to get done got done, I spent so much time trying to keep them separated. When I went to bring in the livestock, I insisted that Rekitach come with me, just to see that he stayed out of trouble. He was too sulky to be any help rounding up the animals, but at least he kept away from Randver. While I worked the beasts, Aslaug's son kicked at clods and threw rocks towards the river.

My mind completely diverted from this boy's difficulties and the animals when I turned back toward the stockade and saw a group of about twenty horsemen arriving at the gates. My husband, King of the

Goths, rode at their head. And I had planned no more than a cream soup and bread for supper!

"Rekitach! Rekitach! Come quickly!" I called. "Your father–"

I stopped midsentence in horror. The clod I saw leave Rekitach's hand at that moment was not a clod at all. It wriggled helplessly as it flew through the air and vanished in the utter grey of the river. It was one of Mathesuentha's kittens.

Usually my son and I slept together in the big bed in the converted armory. When Ermenaric came to visit, Randver had to sleep out in the hall, sharing a bed with Rekitach. Listening for the sounds of mayhem from that bed was diversion that made my wedded duties less loathsome. But a foul mood haunted Ermenaric. He did not roll over comfortably and go to sleep when he was done. He lay on his back, combing my hair with his fingers, giving it a fierce yank from time to time.

Outside we could hear, covering even the shrieks of the boys, my brother's haunting howls. I had come to like the noise when only Randver slept beside me in the bed, feeling comforted and protected by it. But now, every time the howls rang, it meant a yank on my hair.

"This place has gone to Hel," Ermenaric told me with a yank. "Two hours to get a bit of meat for road-hungry men."

"I'm sorry," I said, "but, as you may have noticed, Aslaug is no longer with us."

"Aslaug? Oh, yes. Your girl. Well, what? Did she die?"

"She ... she ran off."

"Ran off? Ran off? I go to the trouble of giving you a slave, and you let her run off?"

A yank, a cry from Randver, and a howl from Sigmund came all at once.

Ermenaric spat noisily off the edge of the bed. "And now I'm expected to find you another one, I suppose. At a time like this!"

The sight of that kitten sailing through the air and into the river suddenly came to me again. No amount of boxing Rekitach's ears put me at ease with him after that. I couldn't get that image out of my mind. And now he was out there with my smaller son at his mercy.

The wolf howled, and Ermenaric yanked distractedly on my hair, bringing involuntary tears to my eyes. "You know, all last night, my men and I were kept awake by that infernal prowling wolf. Unnatural, it was. We threw brands at it and spears. It would vanish, only to appear on the other side."

"Did you ... did you see this wolf?" I hardly dared to ask, tentatively rubbing my scalp even as Ermenaric wound his fingers tighter in my tresses.

"The moon was full. We saw it quite clearly. Walking like a man and uttering the most fearsome howls."

"Yes, we have seen ... signs of a werewolf around here as well."

"Werewolf. That's what the men said, too, and that if I were haunted, it was a sign." He yanked my hair again. "Foolishness. Womanishness. Now, when the Rosomonen are in rebellion, and I'm haunted, and you've got—"

Another scream came from the boys' bed. I turned to my husband, growling, "Aslaug has run off with your man Sarus. She's joined the Rosomonen." I shoved the words at him as if physically shoving him away from me with them. I couldn't keep from crying out at the yank he gave my hair then.

"Sarus gone to the Rosomonen? And Aslaug with him?"

"Yes," I said, gritting my teeth as his fingers tightened in my hair.

Just then the door to the room opened a crack, at which Randver sniffled pathetically. "Mama?"

Ermenaric was on his feet in a moment and lunging to the door. "What's that brat doing—?"

I rose just as quickly to put my arms around my son and stand between them. "Husband, he's your son, the prince."

"Well, he hasn't a scrap of sense in him."

"Husband, he's been hurt. Aslaug's son is a brute to him."

"Well, he should learn to stand up to him."

I pulled my son closer. Ermenaric swatted my shoulder with the back of his huge hand. It was *me* Ermenaric hit, *me* he was teaching to stand up for myself with his wild blows falling anywhere in the dark. I dodged a halfhearted fist headed for my shoulder again and yowled, "I'm left here with all the work, plus Aslaug's son, while *she* runs off to join the Rosomonen, and *we're* to be punished for it?"

"Yes, she did have a son, didn't she?"

I took a thankful breath, for Ermenaric's hands hung at his sides, signaling the blows had ended.

"*Your* son, too," I reminded him, adding for spite, "although her quickness to follow that Rosomonen does make one wonder."

"Let it never be said that Ermenaric, King of the Goths, does not know how to reward those who betray him. I'll butcher that boy of hers and toss his carcass out to that wolf, that's what I'll do! See if that doesn't give us some peace around here."

And now I saw that my anger had driven me too far. A kitten had died, boys scrapped like puppies, the runt got hurt, and for that, a lonely, abandoned boy should die? For surely he would die. Ermenaric never threatened idly. And the royal Goth's blood in Rekitach's veins was just what my brother sniffed for.

"Men! Alaric, Blood-ax, here!" my husband yelled into the darkened hall highlighted only in blotches by the low-burning fire.

"No, husband, wait!" I cried. "Give the lad until morning."

"I have determined: I will not have treacherous blood under my roof."

"Even if that blood is your own?"

"Especially if it has tainted my own."

Outside, my brother howled.

"Husband, I know where the wolf's lair is. At least – near it."

"You?"

"We have lost many head of livestock to this beast and followed their dainty hooves until ... until we realized we were too late. Let me take the boy to this place tomorrow – tomorrow by the light of day when we need fear nothing supernatural. Please, my lord."

Another howl shivered the timbers of the hall, and my husband relented. "Very well," he said. "Go back to sleep, men."

A few muffled grumbles met his words, and then the light caught not the sleeping figures, only their weapons hung about the walls above them, as if only the weapons lived.

"My lord, I'd better bank the fire, or it will burn out by morning. I'm sorry I'd forgotten this, but usually it was Aslaug's job."

"You shall have another maid. No wife of Ermenaric should have to bank her own fire." This my husband said and went back to bed.

Well, I thought with pride. *I am learning to handle this man at last.*

I banked the fire with Randver clinging to my skirts and whimpering. When that task was done, I went and tucked my son in the bed, threatening Rekitach with the morrow and worse than the morrow if I had any more trouble from him that night. When I returned to my room, the King was asleep. After a brief time spent fretting, I joined him.

chapter 27

Y MID-AFTERNOON THE NEXT day, I had left our armed escort behind and brought Rekitach to the village in the midst of the marsh the rest of the way alone. Notes of a wild, moaning song greeted our arrival. All of the Huns had sawed off half of their long hair roughly with their daggers so the flatness of their skulls became even more marked, and the men had reopened the scars set on their cheeks at infancy.

Aslaug's son clung to my hand as if I'd brought him to the very edge of Hel. It took all my courage to bring him to Mathesuentha, but we gained no comfort there.

"My two-year-old," Mathesuentha told me between her tears. "Last evening she wandered off and was drowned in the marsh. They warned me these things happen, when one is busy with a new one at the breast, but I didn't believe them."

I hugged her and took up some of the burden of her grief. "You mustn't blame yourself, although I know only time will erase the thought."

For my part, I couldn't erase from my own mind the image of the little bundle of brown fur sailing through the evening light to Vistula's waves. *The world of men and of animals is more closely bound than we can know,* I thought. *And to think that young hand I hold in mine had done this.*

I turned with more resolve than ever to what I must do. As soon as I could, after grief had been answered, I sought out my brother's hut.

"Well, sister. I see you had yourself a husband last night," Sigmund snarled wolfishly at me. "A curse that I could never get so close to him. I would not stand before my brother the next afternoon, still unwidowed."

I spoke soothingly as one does to an angry dog. "I have brought you something to help with your revenge."

"*Our* revenge."

"Our revenge," I echoed.

I pushed Rekitach out in front of me. He cringed from the sight of my brother, but my hands sat firmly on his shoulders and would not let him turn away.

"What is it?"

"A boy, Sigmund. His name is Rekitach. You can train him however you please to be your aid against Ermenaric."

"You plot against my father!" The boy squirmed. "I'll tell!"

"It was your father plotted against you," I reminded him in a sharp hiss, then turned to my brother again. "He already has quite a good throwing arm. This way, you can let me have Thiudi back again." I cast an anxious glance to the corner of the hut where the girl huddled motionless. "Any way you look at it, the way things are now, you'll have to wait at least ten years until you can get a son off her who's this big and strong."

Rekitach relaxed somewhat to hear himself so praised. With such compliments, he surely believed we did not mean him the harm he had suspected. My brother pinned me down with his feral eyes, trying to catch me in a trick.

"Sigmund, trust me. I want this revenge every bit as much as you do."

"Very well," he said. "Very well. We shall give this lad a try."

"Good." I left Rekitach and crossed to Thiudi.

"And where do you think you're going?"

"May I not take Thiudi home now?"

"No. No, I keep her until he's proven himself. He must prove himself first. You all stay right where you are 'til I get back."

We did. Presently Sigmund returned with a small sack of what looked like flour on his back. He tossed it at Rekitach's feet. "There," he said. "Now, I'm going out to get some wood and reeds to build up the fire. While I'm gone, I want you, boy, to make up the bread."

"But that's woman's work," Rekitach protested. He must have thought he'd at least be challenged to a wrestling match.

Sigmund glared at him with his wolf's eyes, and the boy fell silent. Sigmund nodded gruffly at the compliance and stalked out.

As soon as I figured he was out of earshot, I stepped up to the bewildered boy and said, "This will be no trouble at all. Some nice pan bread, we'll have it done in a moment. Now, look, first we take a basin – this'll do – and..."

Rekitach was not attending.

"Pay attention," I said. "You may have to do this again after I'm gone. Now, take three good handfuls of that flour – look, I'm not going to do this for you, I'll only talk you through it. Three handfuls of flour – maybe four since your hands are smaller..."

The boy could not take his eyes off the flour sack, but he made no move towards it.

"Rekitach, do you hear me?"

"There's something in there," he said.

"Of course there is. It's flour."

"No. Something alive."

I scoffed, but then I took a closer look. Something indeed lashed up and down just under the surface of the sack like a whip end. Now, I'd had mealy bugs in flour before, but never anything like this.

We remained at a nervous stand-still until Sigmund reentered and dropped his great load of wood by the hearth. "What? No bread?" he asked, grinning. "Have you failed even in such a womanish task, boy?"

"But there's something alive in the sack!" said Rekitach.

My hopes rose at the courage the lad displayed.

Sigmund's grin turned into a chuckle, then a wolfish howl. With a quick lash of his dagger, he cut the sack open and pulled from it a wriggling worm, a serpent. Though covered with flour, its thick brown body with black diamonds on the back and its cat-like eyes betrayed it as a viper. Sigmund tossed the thing at Rekitach. The boy juggled it until it fell to the floor and quickly slithered out the door to its marshy home – but not before it had landed three good bites on Rekitach's neck and arms.

"Sigmund!" I screamed. "Rekitach is Ermenaric's son!"

"Good. I have not misplaced my vengeance. I knew there was not blood in him to stand at my side. Ermenaric's blood? It is a coward's blood."

I went to the boy, writhing and moaning with pain as he was. I helped him into Mathesuentha's hut, but all her magics did no good. By morning, he had died and joined her little kitten in the marsh.

Indeed, the animal world is so closely connected to ours and takes its vengeance on us in ways we cannot fathom.

I visited the marsh frequently until coming winter put the trip out of my reach. My magic together with Mathesuentha's managed to keep Thiudi from the ravages of a pregnancy, but did nothing to ease her situation in other matters.

Then, when spring came again, my brother stopped me one day as I was about to make the trek back through the marsh and home again. "I fear you are right, sister," he said. "My seed is too strong to take hold of this girl."

"She is not very strong," I agreed hopefully. *And she seems all the worse for the winter.*

"How am I to avenge the Volsungs without blood to match their power? By Odin, if only I had a woman like you to grow my seed, then I should know no more disappointment."

Sigmund caught my face roughly in his hands in a way that made me feel the wolfness underneath them and sent half fear, half love down my spine. He let my face go, but I felt the sting of his touch still. I knew from it that our desires were one and the same, and that they burned fiercer than ever desire had burned in mortals before. It included a burning for revenge against the Goths – but something more, something even an outlawed wolf didn't dare name.

"That cannot be, that cannot be," Sigmund whined. "And since it cannot be, I must admit that you were right. I must get a son from elsewhere and raise him up. But none of Ermenaric's cowards, no. I must have your son, Signy."

"Randver?" My stomach grew sick.

"Yes. You must bring him to me to raise. It is common for uncles to foster their nephews, isn't it?"

After Rekitach's fate at Sigmund's hands, I feared mightily for Randver. "What if ... what if I simply raise him until he is a man and then send him to you?"

"That won't do. By then, he'll love his father too much. I need your Volsung blood, Signy."

"But Randver is half Ermenaric's, too."

"What else are we to do? We must try."

"May I take Thiudi back in exchange?"

"Let me see the boy first. Try him and see what stuff he's made of."

Sigmund had caught the back of my neck and was rubbing it with such a passion that I knew I couldn't deny him.

Once back in the safety of the stockade, I tried to deny him for a while. I tried to take all my delight in my son and forget the duties of vengeance. I tried to forget my father and brothers and cling to no other but Ermenaric. To deny my brother would mean to have no other than this King of the Goths. But one return visit from my husband taught me that it couldn't be done. At night, at the full moon, Ermenaric's mood grew unbearable, and Sigmund howled for me to remember him.

The morning Ermenaric left the stockade, I brought Randver to meet his uncle. For the first time I pointed out to my son the heads on the stakes as we passed them, told him of his uncles, piles of bones beneath the trees of Grim Wood, showed him the meadow where they fell while I lay helpless in the throes of his birth. I took him to the shore where his grandfather, beloved of Odin, had been tossed without ceremony into the Vistula. I finally revealed to him all the landmarks that had silently worked on me, forging an implacable character and lust for revenge. I tried to get them to harden his heart as they had done mine. They made me willing to risk even a son to revenge the deeds. But one cannot repair in a morning the silence of years. My fear of the father hampered the son, one more evil I had to lay at Ermenaric's feet.

And while, on the way, I carefully told Randver how to make a quick bread and warned him about the worm in the flour, my words amounted to nothing. While trying bravely to remove the thing himself, he lost courage, called on his father to help him – that name that set the nightmare on me – and was struck.

Mathesuentha had truly seen before his birth that he had no deeds of manhood in him. I myself had tried to kill him before he was born. But these facts could not begin to repay eight years of mothering the best I knew how, lost all at once with two pinpricks of fangs.

I sought solace with Mathesuentha, who also knew what it was to lose a child, whose younger boy was just learning to crawl, and into everything. We sat, my head in her lap, watching her son as she fondly combed the nits from my hair. I remembered that my son had been at just such an age when I learned to forget the burden of him and to love the four-toothed smile whenever he looked up from his mischief.

"How shall I fill this horrible emptiness?" I begged of my friend through tears. "Now I have no prince to help me wield control over my husband and, without that, I will be at his mercy as I was when I was first a bride. I am so empty, here in my womb, bereft of my only son! I suppose I must stop taking the alehoof and fill it again. I suppose I must, but the thought of Ermenaric's blood inside me is too vile. Oh, Mathesuentha, what am I to do?"

Mathesuentha shook her head and blew at the comb she held up to the light for inspection as if it were the most troublesome thing in our lives. "And what, Signy," she asked, "are we to do about this wolf of a brother of yours?"

Then all of a sudden I had a plan. I explained it to Mathesuentha.

She tried me carefully on each point, as if it had really been a plan of her mind in the first place ... testing my resolve as she picked the nits from my head. The more details we uncovered, the firmer I became in decision, the clearer the plot grew, until it seemed reality already.

"So, the next time Ermenaric comes to this part of his kingdom, you must come to me, Mathesuentha. You will not fail me?"

"I will not fail," she promised, embraced me, and sent me on my way out of the marsh.

chapter 28

HE NEW SPRING CROP OF staked heads around
the stockade announced Ermenaric's arrival. Rosomonen
heads they were, Sarus's among them, for the rebellion
had been squashed. Aslaug was among those taken alive, but this was
no sign of mercy. My husband desired to make an offering to his
horse god in a prayer to replace the two sons he had now lost to the
wolf that haunted him. I had made my return to the stockade after
Randver's death so full of grief that all who saw it testified to my
complete innocence and helplessness in the matter. But Ermenaric
decreed it was Aslaug's fate to be tied spread-eagle in the yard and to
be trampled by his favorite horses as a sacrifice to his Gothic god until
nothing remained of her for either display or burial.

And I must sleep with this man tonight? I thought as I listened to my
husband's calls to his mounts and the crack of his whip playing over
the woman's screams almost like the rhythm of lovemaking. He had
ordered me to attend in the yard and, although nothing could force
me to keep my eyes open, I couldn't close my ears.

*Not only sleep with him but hope to get his child? I can't do it.
Mathesuentha, you must come. You mustn't fail me.*

Evening came slowly, delayed by spring's love of light. At its first
sign, however, I told my new slave girl – not a particularly active
thing – that I would bring the livestock in that night. I couldn't bear

another minute under that roof with the sound of horses' hooves still echoing off the stockade's ring of white stripped logs.

The cattle called a greeting to me, but I walked right past them and into the copse. There Mathesuentha, as she had promised, waited for me precisely where Mathesuentha the cat had chosen to birth her kittens.

"You still have resolve for this?" she asked as she watched me unknot my braided belt and unclasp the brooches at my shoulders to wriggle out of my dress.

"Of course I have. Come, give me those Hunnish deerskins of yours before I have to tear them from you."

Mathesuentha laughed at my mock anger and, in no time at all, we had made a complete exchange of costume. I had worn my most loose-fitting dress on purpose, but I saw it still clung a bit tight on her motherly figure. And I felt as if I would drown in the volumes she customarily wore.

Mathesuentha must have been thinking the same thing, for she said, "Perhaps it would be wise to compound the transfer with a bit of magic."

Before I could protest that we hadn't time, she had produced the trappings, so I knew that she had prepared for this all along.

For my face and hands she had a tincture of crushed acorns and comfrey, which stained them a nutty brown. For herself she had an ointment of cowslip and beanflower. "To attract a little of your youth, that's all," she explained with a laugh. Then she had us sit facing each other while she chanted some of her magic shape-changing runes. And when we were done, I must confess I did feel like a different person. Not like Mathesuentha exactly, not quite as jolly and chatty. But certainly every bit as competent and capable of doing everything she could do, and even more, perhaps, in some areas than she.

We got up, embraced quickly, and went off our separate ways. I stayed to watch Mathesuentha untether the livestock and herd them back to the stockade, just as I might have done. She even sang an old song from my childhood that I couldn't imagine any other soul in Gothland might know.

I crossed the copse and came out on the other side around the path wild animals used to come down to the river to drink in the early evening. Warriors had often reported seeing wolf prints in the mud there. I found a comfortable stone to sit on and waited.

The sun set, and a chill settled in, a reminder that winter had not too distantly released us. The silver glow on the eastern horizon announced the rising of the moon. I didn't have too long to wait.

I sat so still that other animals, a rabbit, a fox, came to drink, passing so closely I could have reached out and touched them. Then there were none, as if they scented what was coming and kept to their burrows.

I heard him first, the long, wrenching howl of the lone wolf, almost as if in pain. My heart answered it with a thrill, not fear. A thrill and, yes, a pity at the sorrow I heard in that howl. *It is I*, I thought, *I alone who can answer your howl.*

He appeared at the top of the rising bank somewhat behind me to the west. He approached loping, restless, sniffing the air. His sense of smell found me before moonlight could have picked me out of my shadows. He stopped, a little puzzled perhaps, then growled. I didn't move.

He made a running charge at me on all fours, down the hill, snarling. I watched placidly. Just at my knees, he skidded to a stop, puzzled. He seemed to know me – but he did not. I realized then just how easy it was going to be to give my brother what he wanted.

He got to his feet and scratched the wolfskin as if for once he felt the uncomfortable closeness of it on his shoulders. "Who are you?" he said, almost forgetting to put the bark in his voice.

"You don't need a name to know who I am."

"You're not afraid of me." He spoke a statement more than a question, but a statement full of wonder, of suspended disbelief.

"Not a bit." After a beat, I continued. "Night has come upon me unawares, and I have no place to stay. I wonder, sir, if you'd be good enough..."

He shook his wolf's head as if to free it from a bothersome burr. "It's a long way."

"I don't mind."

The wolf's head tossed in the direction of the river. "Come," he said.

I walked after him until the river rose chest high. Then I caught hold of the fur at his neck and stuck with him as he stemmed the current and brought us quickly to the other side. Sometimes our legs brushed together in the water, the slip of chilled water between them. I was aware of the power of his limbs and almost sang aloud at their closeness.

We reached the bank, and he looked at me quizzically as he shook himself dry. The coldness in his eyes seemed troubled in the moonlight, like water under ice in the first thaw, as if he couldn't quite believe I remained with him. I fought the urge to hurry things up and lead the way, but stood waiting patiently until he took a breath, more human than beastly, and set off at a trot.

About halfway to the marsh, we broke out of a forest shadow and into the white light of an open field. There he noticed I was shivering from the damp and chill. He grunted, then took his wolf skin off and laid it gently around my shoulders. He didn't walk on ahead after that. Although he said nothing, he stayed by my side.

When we arrived at the hut in the marsh, the moon had already set. Thiudi, who had been asleep in the corner she never quit, sat up when we came in. I could tell by her eyes that the shape changing did not fool her simple wits. I tried to give her a sign not to let on. She obediently lay back down, but couldn't keep from watching our doings with all the passion of her little soul.

"Perhaps you're hungry," my brother said.

"Yes, some food would be most hospitable of you."

"I'll be back in a minute."

In a minute, he returned – with a sack of flour. I saw the sack twitch with life in the low firelight.

"Here's flour. Why don't you mix us up some bread while I go get some more wood?"

He seemed almost reluctant to ask me to undertake this test, reluctant to leave me alone with that sack. But I assured him, "Certainly."

The minute my brother left, I picked up a big ax handle standing near the door and beat the sack until it lay lifeless. Then I opened the sack and scooped three handfuls into the basin. Pulverized serpent thoroughly mixed and dampened the flour. "Well, I shan't have need for as much fat, then," I said to myself.

I found a bit of honey and added it with salt and water to the basin, mixing it all to a nice firm ball. I let it sit while I added the last of the hut's wood stores to the fire to make sure the flat hearthstone grew good and hot. Then, having tested it with a wet finger and hearing the satisfying sizzle in reply, I slapped the ball flat on the stone and marked it with the cross slashes that always asked a benediction on the eaters of the loaf.

I was just turning it over, filling the hut with the rich, strangely meaty smell, when Sigmund returned. He stopped and stared in open amazement. "How ... how did you do that?"

"There's nothing to baking bread. I've done it all my life."

"I mean, how–? Wasn't there anything strange about–?"

"Oh, yes. There was a serpent in the bag, if that's what you mean."

"A serpent? Yes?"

"No matter. I slew him."

"And?"

"Well, I'm afraid he's all mixed up with the bread. It couldn't be helped. Looks like it's done now. Won't you have some while it's hot?"

I reached toward him, offering a farl of the bread with my skirt as a hot pad. He caught the hand so violently that the bread tumbled to the ground.

"That's impossible. There's enough poison in such beasts to kill, even after they are dead, even just by touching any part of their flesh."

"I didn't notice. But you've made a mess of that farl, anyway," I said, stooping to pick it up off the floor.

"Only people in my family have a natural immunity to the venom."

"Well, then, my family must as well."

"Yes, it must. A powerful family."

"We always were."

Our eyes met, identical eyes – like in a mirror, knowing, under-standing eyes. I had to look away, the gaze was so overwhelming.

"Won't you try some of the bread?" I asked in distraction. "I'll have this piece that fell on the floor. It doesn't look too bad. You have that on the stone, now before it burns."

Sigmund knocked my hand away from my mouth and held it there at my side. "I won't let you eat it," he said.

"But I'm famished."

"I could eat it."

"Are you such a poor host, you won't let me join you?"

"I have built up my natural tolerance so that I can take the flesh of such serpents into my body as well. But it makes you very sick the first few times you ingest it. I-I don't want to see you sick."

"But such a tolerance must be a good thing to gain."

"No. No, there is something else here to eat. Some cold cattail root, I think and ... and I will fetch you more flour. Don't be sick. Please."

Such yearning honed the end of his voice, I wanted to catch and comfort it. He had not let go of my hand, but the touch was gentle now, almost afraid that if he once let go, I would vanish. He worked the hand up my arm, under the voluminous deerskins to my shoulder as a man gropes in the dark for something he knows he left beside his bed but until now has eluded him.

Sigmund's hand slipped off my shoulder. "Would you ... I mean ... would you care to ... I mean ... there is more to share here than just a hut and board."

My throat could not hold back a little groan of delight as the pressure of his hand on my breast shot down through my belly and even weakened my legs.

Sigmund, this was meant to be, said that groan.

My hand wrapped about his. Its grip, yearning for that strength that had carried me so swiftly over the Vistula, was suddenly broken.

"Girl! Girl! Up!" Sigmund shouted desperately to Thiudi who blinked in the corner. "Go on. You're to sleep in Mathesuentha's hut tonight. Yes, go on. And I'll have Basiq take you back where your people at the stockade can find you tomorrow morning. Go on, off with you."

That night, in my altered shape, I knew love that few in this world can know. Love from a man who knows your every desire before you know it yourself, a man who has been with you since time began and whose body is as familiar to you as your own. I remember the scent of blooming linden on that night. The cool of the air on my face mixed with the scent was almost stifling, as if someone put a pillow over my face and almost but not quite snuffed the life out. Life snuffed out for joy.

After such a night, I returned to the copse and shape-changed back again with Mathesuentha.

"I don't envy you that husband," she said tersely. "He was so drunk with anger over the Rosomonens and the loss of his sons, he paid me little real attention."

"He is always like that," I assured her.

"A more uncaring brute I never met. Perhaps it's because he has so many wives. Or perhaps I'm only used to Basiq – we do have fun! I could have been a hole in a log for all Ermenaric cared."

"Thanks for doing it for me, anyway." I had picked some linden blossom on the journey home, and now I looked over it at Mathesuentha shape-changing.

"No problem. But let's not do it again anytime soon, all right?"

"All right." The cat-like tongues of the linden seed leaves licked my face.

By the next time the moon rose full and the werewolf howled, more longing and loss in his voice than ever, I knew another time would not be necessary.

PART VII

BRYNHILD'S QUEST

chapter 29

S WE, THE DAUGHTERS OF Odin, rode slowly and silently through the forest, I couldn't help but notice the silver-edged leaves. The night's rain spattered from them at the slightest touch. The low-lying clouds dragged themselves through the black-green fir trees like wool through the teeth of carding combs. Here and there they looped about the mountain crags as about loom weights, taut and ready for the shuttle.

Curiously, I had not thought in such images since I was a child, when I expected to become a woman someday and endured having carding combs thrust into my hands any time they were empty. Such mountain and forest terrain had always seemed very masculine to me, bristling like an army on the march. But this country, on this day, seemed all-absorbing, forgiving, patient in a way distinctly feminine.

The smells climbed damp, sour, and moldy, yet grew even as they decayed, almost like the blood which, once a month, I put from me as quickly as possible. These smells in this place would not be shaken off. They all but demanded that we wallow in them as they rose in swirled loops of smoke off the east-facing tree trunks and night-rain-wetted hillocks in the morning sun. And here, ivy wound around the trunks of the trees in such an embrace that its hand-like leaves might have done the sustaining and not the trunks beneath. The ivy under our horses' hooves twisted like yarn on the spindle. I kept feeling that my spear, carried upright in riding formation, might get hopelessly entangled in the weird spinning that went on in this place. Fir branches I could avoid, but this—

The sky had been invisible all morning. Or, rather, in the form of grey woolly clouds, it had come down to meet us. At such close quarters, a wide view to give a sense of direction was impossible. Nonetheless, from tree to tree, the pale green moss still seemed to shy from us. Odin had not altered our course from a generally northeast direction. We were heading towards the Goths again. Of course, with a king like Ermenaric at their head, they always provided action. We would have to go down from these mountains, as we seemed to be doing now, followed by a day across rolling hills, then to the plain where the battle would be fought.

Abruptly, Odin gave the signal to stop. We were all surprised when he ordered,

> "Don't bother with a big bivouac.
> We'll repose a petty pair of hours."

That many hours of daylight remained, no more. The spot in which we found ourselves had a definite north-face slope to it, clear 'til sight vanished in the mist. Free of trees, the meadow offered good grass for the horses.

"Make the most of it, maids," the god said,

> "For we'll ride the rest of the raven-time.
> In the interim, I've interest in an escort.
> A couple – Valfreya, come, and your comrade."

His one steely blue eye fell on me. "Brynhild."

So I remounted as quickly as I'd climbed down. Flanking All-Father, Valfreya and I continued on in the direction we'd been going.

Gradually, the forest began to change, to take on a leafed tree now and then. Acorns nosed pinkish sprouts downward towards the loam made from their own parent leaves. Then, all at once, little four-leaved saplings unlocked themselves from last year's carpet of ash seed. Rough grey trunks of the adult ashes took over from the firs. And up ahead, a long, even row of wrist-wide saplings of five or ten years' growth blocked the way. The pattern of the tree plantings revealed it could only be the hand of man at work, yet it formed so much a part of the surroundings, it seemed divine.

"Attend me here among the ash," All-Father cautioned, his voice hushed as if even he sensed greater powers.

He swung his leg off Sleipnir and tossed the reins to me. With a series of hoarse croaks, he told the pair of ravens on his shoulders to absent themselves. Then, leaning against the saddle, he did something I'd never seen him do before. He took off his boots, marten fur and all, and stuffed them under the saddle bag for safekeeping. His bare feet seemed tender; at least he depended heavily on his staff as he approached the fence.

A grey figure appeared before him, materializing as if by magic through the ash-tree barrier by no doorway that I could see. To this figure All-Father removed his hat – yes, the Masked One performed this homage I'd never seen either – and exchanged a few words beyond our hearing, some of which went along with gestures in our direction. Then he strode back, appearing younger and lighter on his feet coming from the fence than he had going towards it.

"The verdict is, I'm vouchsafed but one," he said, not meeting our eyes. "Valfreya?"

"Yes, All-Father." Valfreya dismounted and likewise removed her boots.

"Brynhild, you'll be behind and bother with the beasts."

"Yes, All-Father."

So All-Father left me alone as he and my companion-in-arms vanished behind the screen. Yet I was not quite alone. The grey figure remained as if a guard. I tethered the horses where they could forage happily, then moved toward the screen a bit, but only because a comfortable stone loomed in that direction. I would have been more content to find the stone in the other direction.

The grey figure likewise found a stone, much more convenient to its needs, as if put there on purpose. The figure took out a spindle and began to spin, for of course, in long grey linen – holy cloth – held up by double shoulder brooches, the figure was female. The close wrap of white linen about the head betrayed indeed a married woman.

I couldn't escape the uneasy feeling, however, that she mirrored, almost mocked my movements. It began with the finding of a seat but continued after that in subtle ways, for all that she was spinning and I, to pass the time, untied my quiver from my saddle and began to eye and feather arrows with thought for the coming battle.

"This must be a Vanir place," I commented, speaking only after the silence had become heavy, made contradictorily more silent still by the racket of birds in the forest canopy and, from somewhere behind the screen, the purl of water. My speech also had to wait for me to reach the conclusion that the figure, being a woman faced by a warrior such as myself, would not speak until spoken to. Besides, I had to speak or become daunted myself.

The white coif tossed a "yea" while her hands tossed the spindle, while I stretched out a new arrow.

"How different from an Aesir place," I said. "The Aesir set their shrines high on hills so they can see everything and everywhere be seen. They expect power and brawn to be their protection, whereas there is no protection here."

The spinner got up, taking her spinning with her, and quickly vanished behind the screen. Then the screen itself seemed to vanish, blending into the surroundings like a single leaf on a great shade tree. Just as quickly, screen and figure reappeared, her spindle having missed not a beat.

"Very well, I can see," I said, laughing softly. "I can see that a good cover and lying low may also be a defense – of a sort."

The spinner smiled. The smile did not come with ease. It had to force its way in cracks left between a massive jaw and equally massive cheek bones, in the small but craggy hollow intervening.

"So what can you tell me about the insides of your shrine? Anything? Or are they all secrets?"

"This is the grove of Yggdrasill," she said, speaking for the first time in a voice uncommonly deep and solid.

My heart thumped against my brynie in spite of myself, and I could not help but be a little ashamed at the patronizing tone I'd let into my voice before I heard this. Yggdrasill, as any child knows who asks how the world is made, is the World Tree, the Great Mother Ash whose branches hold up the sky and whose roots reach down into the realm of Hel, binding the two together. The first human beings were created of splinters of Yggdrasill. And this grove wherein I stood, the magical fence, even the little saplings on which I carelessly trod, might well be descendants of that tree.

"Do you actually keep Yggdrasill within your sanctuary?"

"Certainly. Or she keeps us. It is among my duties every day to rake the pebbles around the base of the tree, dung it with the droppings of the sacred goats, sprinkle the roots with water from the spring Urdar. If we did not do these things, the world would cease to exist." She worked at her spinning with the same sort of earnestness she described, as if it, too, held the fiber of the world together.

"The spring of Urdar is also within your compound?"

"Of course."

"That is the purling water I hear."

"Yes."

"Is the water really white?"

"As white as the film inside an egg."

"And swans?"

"Yes, the sacred birds swim there. Have since the start of time."

"And in the beak of one–?"

"Yes, in the beak of one is a golden ring."

"Which if he drops–?"

"Will signal the end of the world."

"Do you have much of a following?"

"But of course."

"I mean, it's easy for me to see how a man, in the fury and terror of battle, will call on All-Father, promise him all the booty if he'll but strengthen his arm. Important as Yggdrasill may be, holding up the universe seems to have little to do with everyday life."

The boulders of the white-framed face cracked in a chuckle.

"Perhaps not with men as much as it should. But women have battles of their own, you know, and come from all over the world to us here."

"What can you do for them?"

"The Ash is well known for its healing powers. A woman has only to pass her child through its lower branches to see rickety legs made straight or a serious rupture return within the stomach walls."

"Rickets and ruptures are not things that hold the world together."

"More than you realize." Yet another fissure of a smile worked its way between the cliffs of that face again. "But of course much more urges the faithful here. None fail to consult the Norns while here."

"You also play host to the Norns?"

"Their cave is the center of our rite, and we have holy priestesses who can read the fiber of their weaving, the commingled strands of *was, is,* and *will be.*"

Knowing this, I got a chill now, watching the spinner's spindle on its whirling drop. I looked along an arrow shaft, but focused on her work instead of mine. Did she even now spin thread for the Fates to weave? Was this even now someone's life she was preparing, as I was preparing someone's death? No wonder, then, at the earnestness of her work. If she spun amiss, how much easier might it be for Skuld, the destructive Norn, to snap a thread before its time.

I hesitated to speak again, loathe to distract her from her task and thereby become the agent of some great hero's untimely demise, perhaps on the battlefield, just when he was most needed. Snap could go the thread, and snap would go a horse's leg, caught in a rabbit's burrow, throwing the rider down and breaking his neck. This spinning suddenly seemed more important even than how I, a Valkyrie, feathered my arrows. Why, who had not heard of a hero dying in his bed the night before honor could have claimed him in war, suffering so the peevishness of the fateful Norns?

The nimble hands before me seemed confident enough, and I still had so many questions to ask that I incautiously pursued. "But I don't understand."

"What?"

"What All-Father, Lord of the Aesir, has to do here among the Vanir."

Another smile cracked the rocks. "Odin has been known to come to Yggdrasill. Even in my short years here, he has come."

"But why?"

"To consult the Norns, of course."

"He is All-Father and All-Wise."

"Perhaps, but even he is subject to their work."

"Do they know even the day of Ragnarök?"

"Yes, the end of the world is known to them, but this they will never tell Odin. Except perhaps in riddles."

"Riddles are something Odin excels in."

"Perhaps. But he has yet to guess theirs."

"Who can defy Odin?"

"They can, of course. So he comes from time to time and tries to riddle it out of them. So far, they remain mistresses of that great secret and many more besides. He always goes away beaten."

"Now his coming here does begin to make sense."

"Does it?"

"At least, I know what I'd ask."

"Perhaps in this place, inkling, that gift the Norns have bestowed on all women, begins to work more strongly in you."

This I rejected as handily as I put down one arrow and replaced it with another. The logic of my thoughts seemed too compelling. "We go even now to aid the Goths in battle," I said, "which we have done many times before with omen-worthy results. This time, however, the enemy is neither Volsung nor Burgundian, hosts whose strengths are a known factor. An army more demonlike than human besets Ermenaric this time. Huns, folk are calling them, and their strengths are completely unknown to us. Our forest world works up and down, meadows tipped on end and hung from the sky as well as stretching between tree trunks. But these creatures come from land that is flat; their vision is only in two dimensions. Even their language is out of kenning. If they know any Gods, Odin is certainly not one of them. How to deal with such a people is not known."

"And yet the Huns, too, are a branch on Yggdrasill."

"Are they really? Then Odin will indeed learn important wisdom here."

"Perhaps. But perhaps not. Perhaps you should not be discussing such things with me."

I grew defensive at this. "War is a Valkyrie's business," I said. "We think of little else."

"But do you remember the battle in which the Lombards won their name? The goddess Freya supported the Lombards, and Odin hadn't quite made up his mind, although he did tend towards their foes for the simple fact that his wife supported the others. Odin said:

> "I will give victory to those whose voucher I voice
> When Nat and her night mares near
> The golden gates of their gloom-time goal,
> And first the mid-earthlings find the froth
> Of her night drive as dew upon the dales."

"That certainly sounds like All-Father," I admitted.

"He thought that certainly he would remember to name his favorites first thing upon rising. However, Freya taught the Lombards – before they were the Lombards, but called by another name – to dress in women's clothes for the battle according to her Vanir rites. She taught them to stand in their ranks in such a spot that the sun would hit them first in the morning, right outside Odin's window.

"Well, the sun arose, Odin awoke, and his wife turned him at once to face the window. A host in women's dress but waggling long beards was such a strange sight that instead of speaking the name he had thought to, he had to exclaim, 'By Odin whom I love, who are all those Long-Beards?' Freya quickly taught the Lombards to change their name from what it had been to Lombard, Langobardi – the Long Beards. That became their battle cry from that moment on, and so they carried the day."

"Are you a Lombard?" I asked, for she recited this ancient tale as if it were the present. So was past, present, and future knotted together into one fabric here before Yggdrasill.

"In some ways, perhaps." The smile almost yawned into a laugh. Almost, but not quite.

"I wish you wouldn't speak in riddles. But perhaps that is the way of things around here."

"Perhaps."

"So, judging from the fate of the Lombards, what do you think the augury is for battle with the Huns?"

"It is not my calling to read the future."

"Can you speak of it in riddles, then?"

"Well, if I were reading omens from the sky–"

"Yes?"

"That black streak threading from north to south through the lowering sky would concern me."

I followed where her eyes led and found that indeed a streak, somewhat darker than the rest of the mist, led straight to where the battle was to be. "That does indeed seem ominous," I said, needing no oracle to fathom that.

"But is it ominous for Odin? For those he supports? Or is it ominous only for you – and me? Perhaps we are the only ones who see it, so we are the only ones affected."

"Which is it?" I asked, my heart thumping quickly, for my own fate had little concerned me until that moment. Odin's fate must needs be mine, and that must be good, unless–

"I cannot say. I haven't that skill."

"Perhaps it is your own future," I said, certainly doing my best to deflect such a sign from me.

"Now, of my own future I can divulge somewhat."

"Indeed?"

"Well, the Norns attended my mother when I was born," the spinner said. "At least, the latter two, Is and Will Be, Present and Potential. My mother failed to invite Urd, Was, the Past, because she'd always found her an ill-tempered old crone, and she wanted only a blossoming future for me, not a dark, backward-looking, brooding sort of life."

"I cannot blame her. And so?"

"So Verðandi came and promised I would be a great warrior."

"A Valkyrie?"

The spinner ignored this question, but as her tale continued, I didn't stop her for an answer. "Skuld, as patroness of the arts, promised me that I would be a great skald, a poet."

"What more could any mother wish for? Girls are so rarely poets."

"Indeed. But you cannot have the full and waxing moons without the waning. Spring and summer do not come but after winter. Urd came, bidden or no and, full of wrath, she spoke her fortune for me."

"Which was?"

"Warrior beyond any hero I might be, skald beyond any skald. But these blessings would last only as long as the taper burned there by my mother's bedside. Now a wail of mourning went up, for the candle had been trimmed when first my mother had gone down on the floor to labor, and even now sputtered in the last pool of its existence."

"Then you should have died before seeing the end of your first day."

"So I should have."

"So much for Urd's prophecies."

"Not at all. For while all the room wailed in either fear of the future or dread of the past, Verðandi, present action, jumped to her feet and blew the candle out. 'There,' she cried to the room plunged in sudden darkness. 'It may make the warrior fiber of my gift not nearly as strong, but it shall assuredly make it longer.'"

Both mine and the spinner's eyes watched a long, thin drop of the spindle before she continued. "'Keep the candle safe,' Verðandi instructed my mother, handing it to her when the wax had cooled. 'Never burn it, and hand it to your child when he is grown, that he may likewise keep it and light it only when he is full tired of life and of living.'"

Now the spinning stopped for a moment as the figure pulled from her dress a little stump of wax, grown smooth and dirty with age, which just barely had the form of candle still about it, being now wider than it was tall. "You see," she said, "I have it still to this day."

"You haven't grown tired of life, then?"

"Not in these hundred years."

"A hundred years." I smiled, humoring her in the impossible, for there was much in the tale that stretched belief. Yet the little lump of wax, cradled so carefully in the smooth, white, though uncommonly large, square hand, held attention like a lodestone. "Clearly the warrior thread of your life did not amount to much."

"True. But perhaps more so than had I died then, while still in my cradle."

"And so you sit and spin," I said, proudly swinging my full quiver to my back.

"I have devoted my life to the blessed Vanir; that is true."

"I, for one, should have found such a life tedious unto death long before now."

"The fabric of our lives is different, then, like the wrong side and the right side of a tablet weave."

"I certainly don't consider *my* life the wrong side."

"Nor do I. Wrong side is perhaps not a very good term. If you cut away all the threads from the side you wear on the inside, the fabric would instantly fall apart. Both sides are necessary for the fabric to exist."

"This is all very interesting," I declared, rising to stand tall. "But your story contains too much of an old wives' tale to be believed."

"Does it?"

"Of course. When you gave the middle Norn's words of promise, you slipped."

"Did I?"

"You said 'he,' referring to yourself. If the story is true, then it must have been told of someone else."

Something wriggled through that smile I could not resist. I knelt beside the grey covered knees again, drawn with a lure I could not explain. Some might even have been tempted to call it love, although I would have spat the idea from me as poison, had I been presented with it at the time.

As she spoke, her jaws moved like a grindstone: "You know, of course – or perhaps you don't."

"Know what?"

"Know that to come into the presence of the Vanir, one must be a woman."

"Not all women. You don't let me in."

"Perhaps someday you will enter. Now? No. By your dress and hardware, it is clear you turn your back on womanhood, on all the ways of the Vanir. To come into the presence of the Vanir, one must be a woman, as you are. But to fight with the Aesir, you must don the clothes of a man."

The thought crossed my mind how easy it would be to force my way in, past such a guard, although she was tall, broad-shouldered, with powerful hands. For all that, they did nothing but spin. "Another tale," I said dismissively.

"To come into the presence of the Vanir, one must be a woman," the figure reaffirmed.

"I saw with my own eyes All-Father enter the shrine."

"Ah, but you haven't seen how he had become female on the other side. How he is obliged to put on a grey linen dress such as mine here before he ever approaches the Norns."

"All-Father? But the thought is impossible."

"It is nonetheless true. The ash, you may know, is one of the few trees – holly is another – where each tree is definitely either male or female. In spring, the blossoms on one tree are all either male or female. They litter our forest floor here, little knots of black-red, washed down with the rains when they are spent. In the fall, it is on the female that the oar-shaped seed-keys hang in their rattling bunches like the keys at the waist of a housewife."

And now I suppose the sun must have set, for suddenly the light changed and, peering closely at the face before me, intent as ever on its spinning, I could see a strange and different shadow there. Like the shadow of bristling pines on a granite crag.

"What is your name?" I asked, a chill running down my back beneath the quiver, a chill the arrows remained useless to guard me from.

"Rüdeger," the spinner replied.

And that was the first inkling I had that I spoke with no married woman at all, but a man.

chapter 30

 OTHLAND IN EARLY SUMMER WAS a fine place to ride. The grain in the first fields was turning golden for the harvest. Its sharp, sweet, dusty smell filled the air. Poppies and feverfew sprinkled every field richly, pleasant little surprises for the eye like bog berries and nutmeats in a creamy custard. I took pleasure in being there in the warm, dry sun which served the earth like a fire. I took pleasure in being able to help Ermenaric, this man whose realm extended farther than I had even ridden. I would help his peasantry finish warring quickly and return to their haymaking while the good weather held.

Helping Ermenaric rout these short dark creatures called Huns presented no emotional ill. They hardly seemed people, really, rising out of the eastern marsh as they did like bad spirits. So short and dark, with wild faces and no human speech, they made Franks and Romans seem commonplace. Killing them caused less grief than hunting. At least when one shoots a deer, a twinge of sorrow comes at having struck down something of beauty. With these Huns, I did the world, not just my belly, a service. I was proud then to be a Valkyrie, and felt no qualms about obeying Odin's orders instantly and with honor.

Surprising to say, the Goths called heavily for our help. Ermenaric, with all his vast empire to rely on, was not outnumbered, but it seemed like it. These troll-Huns rode like clouds of wind on their stout little ponies. Like the wind, they came at us with unearthly shrieks. They kept fighting and riding when stuck with as many bolts as a hedgehog. They seemed to be berserk, the whole race of them.

As many of his allies as could reach him in short notice aided Ermenaric, including young Burgundian Guidi whose father Agnar had eventually been overrun by his old foes and died of a broken heart. Even with such help, Ermeneric was hard pressed. Odin's ravens were slow to understand the ways of these Huns. We Valkyries had to join the King of the Goths early and fight late.

The Huns knew no sacrifice of spears to Odin to begin a fray, no fear of battle runes in its midst, nor did the entry of the battlemaids make them freeze with awe. Only by sheer weight did we eventually drive off those little brown hornets we couldn't kill. By then, Ermenaric himself had been grievously wounded under his right arm.

All-Father's major objective had been accomplished, certainly – to cause the death of Sigmund Volsungsson, who rode at the head of the Huns as if berserk. Sigmund swung the angry sword Gram, nearly dragging his long legs on either side of his Hunnish pony that seemed to be the largest their herds had to offer. I wouldn't have believed it could be him if I hadn't recognized the face under that wild wolfskin myself.

"I thought he was dead," I yelled to Valfreya over the din of the charge when I saw him. "I thought only his sister was supposed to be left alive, and that the race of Volsungs died out in her life of bondage."

"So did we all," Valfreya yelled back. "The planting of that sword and the wrath of Ermenaric should have done it long ago. Somehow Sigmund managed to avoid Fate and cheat All-Father. Now our master will take his revenge."

Take revenge All-Father did, and in person. For, when several passes of his warmaids failed to accomplish the needed results, All-Father entered the fray against the swirling, screeching Huns himself.

"Sigmund Volsungsson!" We all heard the voice of the God like thunder over the maelstrom. And Sigmund turned from finishing off his sixth Goth of the morning to face his maker.

Sigmund, like us, stood tall and blond. By rights, he should have bowed down the minute he recognized his father's God. But this man was different from the one who had first pulled Gram from the Branstock oak in his father's house that night long ago. Could swinging a divine sword change a man so? He didn't pale for an instant, but charged with Gram held aloft as if Odin were a mere mortal he could hack and cleave like all the rest.

All-Father raised his divine spear over his head to catch the blow. In his hands, the simple ashwood took hold of the divine iron and snapped it in two like no more than a brittle reed. That blade, which had never even suffered dullness before, dropped useless from Sigmund's hand. But Sigmund himself hardly faltered. With a wolfish snarl and his bare hands, he went for All-Father's throat.

Every maid took instant aim, but had Odin not been more than mortal, we would have been too late. As it passed, All-Father swung his spear down to his side and, faster than the eye could see, had planted the butt in the ground. The point caught Sigmund under the belt, and so did this last of Volsung's sons die, with a loud, long howl that gripped the bowels and wrenched them.

After that, Odin retired from the field. His maids fought on, however, beside the Goths and Veneti and Burgundians in their boars' head phalanxes, until the Huns galloped off faster than we could follow. They entered a marsh where we had no desire to pursue them.

Valfreya called "regroup." We left the Gothic warriors to their business of booty-taking and gathered round her behind a copse, out of human view.

"One of us should go and see how King Ermenaric is doing," our leader told us. "Perhaps we must still send him into a howe for eternity. I didn't like the looks of that wound."

The rest of my sisters were worn from the day. I was sure it would catch up with me as well, sooner or later, but at the moment, energy filled me rather than fatigue. I felt as if a heavy cloud had been lifted from a seat just above the rim of my helmet. This noisome cloud kept nudging me that this life which meant everything to me and to which I could imagine no other, was somehow evil, for all its God-sanction. Now that doubt had vanished, washed clean with the sweat of battle, and a trip to visit a brave hero seemed to be just the thing to celebrate. "I'll be glad to go visit the king," I said.

"Good. Thank you, Brynhild," said Valfreya, seeming doubly glad that I had shown myself still a faithful battlemaid. She dipped her head to remove the life horn from across her chest and handed it to me. Thus, with the life-giving powder, I rode off towards Ermenaric's stockade.

My horse stabled in the yard, guards showed me into the hall. Here the victorious warriors were eating, drinking, and tending their wounds on the encircling benches. They remained very quiet about it, not a good sign. Clearly they feared for their leader's life. Fevered moaning led me to the little room off the hall where Ermenaric lay. His face sagged bloodless and white, save for where an old scar careened across it. He did not look well, and over the Gothic smell of rancid butter lorded the smell of death.

"Where is she? Where is she? Where's that bitch, my wife?" came the burden of the king's feverish torment.

Definite signs of a woman filled the room. A piece of brown and white herringbone filling the top third of a loom. On a chest lay combs, a looking glass, pots of herbs, and simples. But an old man, not a woman, tended his wounded lord.

"Where is she, damn her?"

"My lord, rest easy," the old man answered with mounting vexation. "I'll never get this blood stanched if you don't. As I've already told you, no one in this compound knows where your lady wife is."

"Lady wife!" the king sputtered with contempt.

"But at least a dozen have been sent to look for her. Rest easy. If she's to be found, we will find her."

"Those monster Huns. They have her."

"My lord, the Huns were routed. Your men carried the day – with the help of Traveler God and his maidens," he added with a quick nod in my direction. "The Huns have taken not a scrap of grass to curry their demon horses withal. They have certainly not taken your wife."

"But they had her. Before this day ever dawned, they had her under their spell. That child–" And now, for all the old man's efforts,

Ermenaric pulled himself by his nurse's arm to sit up and would not let go. "That child she carries isn't mine."

"It is the fever that makes you say so, lord. It is the pain. Rest and let me work on you. I will make such fancies vanish, if the One-Eyed is willing." The old man looked with unconcealed hope towards the horn strapped to my chest.

"That bastard isn't mine, I tell you."

"There are ten men out in the hall – ten faithful men – who will swear on their lives that your virtuous wife did not spend a single night out of this compound save once or twice long ago last year when she was concerned about the idiot girl. Too long ago, in any case, to have made you a cuckold, lord. Certainly not a cuckold to any troll-like Hun."

The word "cuckold" truly set the king to madness. "I have seen it. I have had a *seiðr* read and saw this day as plain as if it were past instead of future. 'You will receive a wound under the arm,' it said, 'a wound by an unborn child, and it will kill you.'" And the King of the Goths picked up his sword as if to fight off the vision.

The old nurse tried to disarm his patient, but the flailing sword backed him off. "My lord–" the old man whimpered helplessly.

"That child is not mine. It was read in the *seiðr*, by the will of the almighty Vanir. By some evil spell – I know not how – that child is a Volsung and will yet be the death of me. It is written by the Norns, knotted in their tapestry, and no man can pluck it out."

Ermenaric rose on his feet now, struggling against what neither the nurse nor I could see. In one dreadful lunge, he sliced the herringbone on the loom from top to bottom. But this action could not alter Fate and gave him no peace.

"That child!" he screamed. "That child has escaped me!"

And then, before either I or the old warrior could stop him, he had propped the sword against the folds of the coverlet on the bed and, with the last of his strength, ran it easily through his own unprotected heart.

"Alas!" cried the old man.

"Alas, indeed," I echoed him. "For I am here with Odin's Horn of

Life to revive him. But it is well-known I cannot use it on one who has taken his own life."

So I saw that the Valkyries' business in Gothland was done. I left the Goths to bury their king in a flat grave, no eternal howe. And, as the Goths themselves believe in offering the dead, even a king, no weapon or food or treasure to aid on his journey to Hel, one could guess that in a flat grave, his memory would not last long. Perhaps not even so long as those of his enemies whose heads he himself lifted up and ensconced on the stakes about his stockade.

I gave Faxi an easy rein to let him pick his own difficult way over the battlefield in the dark. Suddenly, he shied as if at a ghost, and I saw it, too. A figure rose from among the dead as one come to life. A wolf might be expected, come to feed on the God-provided plenty. But this figure did not slink off, growling, as we approached; this was human.

Other Gods, of course, could raise the dead, but I doubted my master would be pleased at this breach of his territory. I patted Faxi on his neck to reassure him and urged him a little closer to probe.

The figure had made its way to the top of a hillock. I could see it clearly in silhouette against the star-filled sky. I quickly drew an arrow from my bow and set the notch to my bow string. Just before I let fly, the figure turned, and I realized no felled warrior rose, about to undertake a haunting, but a woman. This called for closer scrutiny before I caused her death. I swung down off Faxi quietly and whispered to him to stay. Then I crept up on the figure, picking my way gingerly around the dead men and beasts and stepping on slippery things I knew I would rather not see.

She was not aware of my presence as a beast would have been, but she did suddenly become aware of something on the ground at her feet. She gave a little cry, half of triumph, half of dismay, and bent to retrieve it. Whatever it was caught the starlight and reflected it, blinding in my eyes for a second. Then it vanished inside the bodice of her dress.

This find was the woman's leave to go. She suddenly began to flee the battlefield as from Hel herself. I increased my pace as well and, in a moment, had caught her around her waist. That waist seemed a little stouter than the tall willowy figure would have warranted. It suddenly occurred to me, although I couldn't see her face, who this woman must be. "You are Signy Volsungsdaughter, Ermenaric's queen."

"Yes, yes, I am," she stammered, trying not to choke on fear. I could feel the racing of her heart beneath my arm.

"You know your husband is dead."

"Is he?" Relief washed through that voice.

"He died calling for you," I said. The King still deserved to be treated as a hero by those who loved him. I didn't have to tell her all the details.

"I'm not going back there."

"That is a brave thing to tell me," I said, impressed by the Volsung spirit that must first have attracted All-Father to this girl's ancestors. I eased my grasp on her a bit; that's how impressed I was. "You don't even know who I am."

"I can tell you are a woman, for all your feathers and metal. That is enough. I trust you will understand."

"What is there to understand? You want to go friendless into the world when the child you carry may grow up to inherit the throne of the Goths?"

"There are already too many claimants to that throne, princes already come to their manhood who would run my child through the moment he was born – if, unhappily, he should be a boy."

"I see."

"Please, let me go."

"Perhaps – perhaps I should take you some little way, then. On my horse."

"In the interest of preserving the fallen hero's seed?" she tested me.

"Ermenaric's seed."

"Yes," she said, perhaps too firmly.

"You are tired and ill, and it is late. Where did you imagine you'd go?"

"I ... I don't know." I caught her looking over my shoulder in the direction of the marsh where the Huns had vanished, and she mumbled, "Anywhere but there." She buried her face in her hands. "I have no friends." Tears clogged her throat as more and more she gave herself over to me. "No family, no friends. No one left in all the world."

"Then come, take a seat on my Faxi. I will lead you to some safe haven until the Gothic succession wars are over. Then perhaps you may bring your prince back in safety."

I thought at first I should go and warn Valfreya of my plans, perhaps ask her suggestions for a place to take the young queen. But something in me rose up against taking orders again that night, and I did not. I decided of my own inkling to head south. Valhalla was southwest, so I would not ride too far out of my way in any case. It occurred to me that the young woman might find sanctuary in the shrine of Yggdrasill, safety with the enemy, as it were. As it happened, however, I couldn't find the mythic place again.

Before dawn, we had entered a forest. Pines sprung high, but many rocks and the bands of evergreens spreading the rocks apart looked like stretch marks on the breasts of a woman many times a mother. Thinking these good cover from any who might be pursuing us, I suggested we should rest a while. Signy, who had almost fallen off the horse several times from weariness, readily agreed.

We slept on my bear skin under a great chestnut tree until the sun rose high. Then a shadow passing over my face awakened me with a start – the shadow of a raven's wings. He flapped to a perch in the leafy branches over my head, knocking some of the year's first nuts to the ground around me. There he sat watching and, now and again, scolding. I wished I'd learned the raven tongue. It certainly made me ill at ease, and I watched anxiously until Signy awoke, too, probably from the force of my stare.

"You ... you're a Valkyrie," she said, seeing my costume for the first time in daylight.

"Yes," I said, not at all flattered by the terror in her voice unmatched even when I'd first caught her among the dead on the battlefield. "I serve All-Father."

"You and your master have betrayed me and all my family. What evil do you plan for me now?"

"No evil, I assure—"

"Why should you want to help me?"

I glanced up at the raven whose scolding seemed to be giving the answer. But I couldn't make it out. "You are the last of the Volsungs," I said. "The male line is dead. Odin is done with you."

"A curse on those who caused that downfall."

Again, that spirit. Although a woman alone, she did not fear to curse All-Father to a Valkyrie's face. "Why should I not help you, you who carries Ermenaric's child. Ermenaric died a hero, and in All-Father's favor." I did not believe all the King had said in his final mad ravings.

"Come," I continued. "I have a little jerky here. Eat it, drink from the stream yonder, and refresh yourself. We must be on our way. I must return to my companions soon."

In silence, she did as I told her. As she walked back up from the stream, however, new will steeled her. I felt my heart reach out to what I saw. Perhaps something of Thora's motherhood worked in her. In any case, I felt glad to be doing what I was doing, making amends somehow.

With these feelings, I suffered unexpected hurt when she refused my hand up on the horse. "No," she said. "I cannot accept your kindness any longer. You are in some way to blame, you and your sisters, for my family's demise."

I struggled with the pain of that blow and wanted to tell her a Valkyrie could serve as sister to any woman in the world, but that didn't fit the realm of belief. Instead I said, "All-Father is worthy of love as well as fear."

"Not from me," she said.

The blasphemy stung. "That makes me all the more determined to do right by you."

"Please, warriormaid, leave me here, to my Fate."

"What sort of Fate can you, a woman alone, have in these woods?"

"The Fate that is woven for me, I suppose."

"It was Fate that led me to you on the battlefield."

"Then I must tell you – you labor under a false notion. The child is not Ermenaric's."

"I see."

"There are other times to get a child besides nighttime. And other means."

"Then they were true, the rumors I heard."

"I don't know what rumors you heard, but it is not his child."

"Whose is it?"

"That doesn't matter, does it? Suffice it to say, he died before my husband. And I loved him. I loved him more than my life."

This confession, rather than throwing me off, made me more determined than ever to see her safe. Here stood a woman who had known in her heart what she wanted. I would not have chosen as she had done, but it was her choice. She knew it, trusted it, and that trust made her undaunted. She had not been afraid to gain it, even at the risk of going against one of the greatest kings in the world. Even at the risk of going against a God.

"Come on. Get up on Faxi. I will leave you at the first likely house we come to. But I will not leave you here in the woods all alone."

"Take the 'likely' out. The first house, likely or not. That will be my Fate."

"Very well," I replied. "It cannot be long."

She mounted the horse.

It unnerved me a little to see that the raven took wing as soon as we set off and continued to follow us in slow, sweeping circles. Sometimes I would rejoice and think that we had lost him, but always he reappeared just above a treetop, just ahead of us or just behind. I grew so concerned with watching him, and with his watching us, that I almost missed the thin curl of smoke we came upon near evening. It rose out of a hollow already in darkness and up-sweeping mist.

Signy saw it first. "There," she said. "That hearth is my Fate."

"Very well," I said and began to urge Faxi carefully down the steep sides of the hollow and into nighttime.

A very small hut emitted the smoke. And it did so without a proper smoke hole, merely through the cracks in the roof and walls. It was a low, round hut. One would hardly think it had room inside for a hearth, let alone living space around it. With a rough-hewn wooden face and a sod roof, it sat back in the side of the hollow as if it had grown there naturally.

To the left of the hut stood a secondary structure, and a proper smoke stack topped this one. Although at the moment it remained breathless, this spoke aloud that the caring hand of man had not completely abandoned the place. The smooth clay stack, also set into the embankment, led down to the mouth of a blast furnace. Beside it, under a lean-to shed, loomed a forge and anvil. To one side waited a handcart full of blocks of charcoal.

The entire settlement, I saw, had been devised to take advantage of neither light nor pleasant prospect, water nor fertile fields, nor to escape from dampness. It existed solely to capture the prevailing winds and force their power through a furnace at the face of stubborn metal.

"I fear, Signy," I said, "we have come to the home of a Celt."

"What is to fear? This is my Fate."

"Some people call the Celts dwarves," I explained further to make certain she understood, but that still didn't seem to daunt her. "They are, as a race, small and dark and speak their own language full of deep magic. They were the more ancient settlers here throughout much of the north land, and we, by the will of All-Father, have slowly driven them off the best fields and farms, sent them west and north and onto the tender mercies of the Romans."

"They will sympathize with me, then. I, too, have been driven off from among other folk. See, the Celts have not been totally driven off, and neither shall I be. They have this foothold. It shall be mine, too. It is a good omen."

"Yes, here and there an isolated settlement survives, and will certainly survive until Ragnarök if our people show any wisdom at all.

For, though we surpass them easily in ferocity and brawn, we will never match their cunning at the forge."

"My family had a sword made by Celtic hands," mused Signy, touching her bosom thoughtfully as she did so.

"Ah, yes."

"Balmung." She said it like a prayer to her own body. Perhaps pregnant women are more sensitive of their bodies, wherein they hold the future, than are those of us who had never borne.

"Is that what you call it?"

"What other name can it have?"

"All-Father named it Gram."

"Anger?" Her voice quavered.

"I've held that sword in my hands," I told her. "A miraculous blade, yes. But you should know All-Father gave it to your family to destroy you."

"So it seems."

"That's not the least of the Celts' magics," I continued. "In many ways, the dwarves are more cunning than the Gods. When the trickster Loki cut off all the beautiful Goddess Sif's hair, it was they who made her a wig of gold spun so fine she could comb it. They built the Gods' ship Skiðblaðnir, so large and sturdy that it can sail any ocean, yet at the same time, Freyr is able to fold it up and keep it in his pocket. They forged the Thunderer's hammer that nothing on earth can resist, not mighty oak, not mountain giant. And, it is said, when the world was being made, the ancestors of today's dwarves – or Celts – forged hoards of precious metals and hid them under the giant's bones in the mountains. Only they know where these treasures are hidden. Their wealth is thus unlimited, although they deceive with a show of poverty."

All my attempts to impress Signy with the unnatural potential of the house upon whose charity she'd determined to throw herself did nothing to dissuade her. "Perhaps such a Celt is just the craftsman I need to repair my broken life," she said.

When I wouldn't lead the horse down to the door for her, she slipped off and walked down by herself.

Without a moment's waiting, she knocked on the door. I was down in the hollow, standing beside her and working my feet in a puddle of water that probably never drained, when she knocked unanswered for the third time.

"Nobody's here," I said.

"Then I shall just let myself in and wait for their return."

Before she could turn the latch, a gravelly voice thick with accent rumbled the walls of the hut from the inside. "Go 'way."

That he spoke our tongue told me that we had been seen, probably through a crack in the wall of which there were many, and that he didn't like what he saw.

Signy persisted. "Please, sir. I am a woman alone, with child."

"I see another with you," growled the voice.

"But she is a Valkyrie. She means to abandon me here in the woods–"

"I won't abandon you," I hissed.

"And after I've been driven out by Ermenaric and–"

"You are opposed to Ermenaric?" Interest sparked behind the door.

"He killed my father and my ten brothers."

The door opened a crack, not enough for me to see into the darkness, but enough for the hut's tenant to get a better view out. And what Signy, who stood in front, chose to show him was that hidden by the bodice of her dress.

Well, I'd always thought the Celts a greedy people, but never particularly lustful. The light that sparked in the little man's eyes proved me wrong. Her breast might have been not soft female flesh but flint off which one could strike fire. He instantly welcomed us in.

The dwarf's name was Alberich, a particularly dark and unfavored creature. Besides being even shorter than is common among his race, he was cursed with a hunchback, twisted legs, and a particularly gruff personality to go along with them.

I had to stoop to enter his hut and couldn't even stand upright once within. The small space's corners disappeared in heavy smoke. The dwarf offered us no chair – he had no room for more than his own three-legged stool. The entire place made me feel like a root, and the rooty smell of turnips roasting added to the feeling. They might be soft and sweet inside, but at the moment, the turnips were blackened and indistinguishable from the coals in the hearth amongst which they lay.

"I'm a passable cook," Signy was telling him, "and particularly good with herbs and simples. I can clean while you work, and my weaving – you'll see – if we can find room for a loom–"

I couldn't imagine how a tall woman like Signy could make a place for herself there, let alone for a loom, let alone for a child. But neither she nor her host seemed too worried about that.

"Well, I'll be off then," I announced.

"Yes," replied the host with no attempt at graciousness. "I have no love for the Aesir. The less I have to do with that man, Odin, the better I like it."

"He's not a man, he's a God," I said stoutly.

"That's your opinion," the dwarf said, and closed our conversation.

I felt an urge to embrace Signy before I left, but she seemed to shy from the metal on my brynie. The aspect of womanhood she had embraced with all her soul, I could never hold in my arms, not even for just a minute.

chapter 31

OME MORNING LIGHT, I COULD see no hovering raven. Nor was I shadowed all the next three days until I returned to Valhalla. The cloud just above my helmet brim had also gone, and I enjoyed a very pleasant ride on my own through the forests which, in late summer, would never again seem so generous. I had a life and a purpose any could envy. I was good at what I did – and, best of all, I had to bare my bosom to no man, least of all a crawling dark dwarf, to have my will. No, a Valkyrie's brynie encased my bosom and, by Odin, it would stay there.

The rest of the battlemaids had already returned from Gothland when I arrived. I tossed my reins to one of the girls in training and entered the hall to join them.

A dead silence greeted my entry. The heat of the day required no fire, but this meant the only light we had, thick with motes in the stiff, breathless air, trickled in through the chinks in the walls and the smoke hole. The shields and arms on the walls caught no glint on their blades and bosses. Compared to their usual life, they seemed like eyes closed in a mortal sickness.

On such a day, my sisters should be out with the girls on the training field, or picnicking together by the cool of the stream. I couldn't think of that stream without remembering how it had saved my life two winter weeks long ago. And this led me back to the thought that this was my home; I couldn't imagine another. I rejoiced to be back, but not to be indoors.

And yet, here all the Valkyries sat on their benches at the far end, grimly mute, as if they expected a siege. And here I stood before them. Yet I wasn't with them. None of them rose or spoke to bring me into their company.

I lifted the Horn of Life over my head and handed it back to Valfreya. She reclaimed it without thanks but jealously. Then she spoke, in a voice as flat as an empty sack of flour, "All-Father wants to see you, Brynhild."

"Very well," I said with a deep breath. "Where am I to go?"

"You'll find him in Jutland where the land ends at the edge of the Great North Sea."

I turned and went at once. I retraced my steps out of Valhalla and to the stables. No word of parting followed me, but I knew it was farewell forever. All of us did.

In a minute I had Faxi resaddled. I rode out of the compound's great double gates. The young girls at their training watched me go, envy in their eyes, envy for my horse, my black wing helmet, my proud carriage in the saddle, my strong spear arm and keen archer's eye. They clearly didn't know yet, would never be told. Better to leave them in ignorance, hoping, straining towards a goal. They were too young yet to be cast adrift.

"What's your hurry?" I asked myself as more than once I caught myself urging Faxi onwards. "You hasten to obey Odin this time, now when it makes no difference. A month, a year from now he will still be waiting for you there in Jutland. You can put it off forever if you like, but there is no other purpose for you until you meet him there."

So I didn't dawdle. But I didn't hurry, either. I decided to go half a day out of my way, to break the Valkyries' enchantment which must have been tenuous in me in any case, and spend a night with Thora in Saxony.

I came first to old King Hunding's howe when the setting sun hid behind the bank of a storm approaching off the grey and simmering sea. In the east, night already reigned. The memories with which the place flooded my mind rushed in like waves upon the flat shore, one coming faster than the other could get out of its way. I remembered finding the body of the dark Frank there, fallen beside his king. Perhaps young Hundingsson had come to the howe during the battle to try and raise his father with magic runes, and the devoted Frank had followed him there. Hunding Syriksson had not opened the howe and saved the day; Odin's curse had more power than any raising runes.

Then I remembered a deeper time than that, back to the funeral that had immortalized Hunding and his men and carried them to the eternal Hall of the Slain. I remembered how his wife had willingly joined him on his journey and how Thora had told me she'd done it not for the blessings of eternity but for the here-and-now blessing – or curse – of love. I wondered what Thora thought now, now that her love was raven's meat, and she still lived. I would soon be able to ask her.

But for the moment I couldn't break the spell of the howe at twilight with the coming storm whipping the sea grass flat to the sandy soil. Power indeed lurked here, power of an eternal nature. I could almost feel a living presence, as if the mound of dead earth could open up at any moment and release its heroic occupants into the world of men to influence it once more. This was the power of All-Father I felt. What a fool I'd been to think that I, a mere mortal and a female besides, could hope to thwart that power for any lone cause that might move me. I should have gone through fire if need be, as Hunding's wife had done, in order to remain a part of my master.

Perhaps, perhaps the old Wise One had simply called me to him to chastise me. Perhaps, if I were penitent enough, he would take me back into the ranks of his nuns. So I scratched the rune for "need" into the mist-softened side of the howe and determined to try.

As I formed the angular marks, more suited to carving on wood than scratching in soft dirt, I heard a low moan. The howe itself seemed alive, some great belly rising out of the earth. Had my scratching caused some hurt? Or perhaps Hunding or one of his men was indeed about to rise or warn me off as if he thought I meant to rob them.

The moan came again, more distinctly this time, and distinctly from around the other side of the howe. If this sign came from All-

Father, I certainly wanted to learn of it. I stepped cautiously around the other side of the howe to see.

This side of the howe indeed yawned open, the smell of grave mold strong on the sea-storm air. And beside it sat, or squatted rather, a living figure. Assuming the figure to have knowledge of divine communication, I gave the low chirp of a Valkyrie greeting.

"Hello?" the voice of that dark figure asked. "Brynhild, is that you?"

It was no spirit at all, but Thora.

"By All-Father, Thora, what have you been doing? Digging into a sacred howe?"

She didn't deny it. "The Danes destroyed all our stores last fall. We've been close to starvation all winter, living on fish and seaweed. All winter, the sight of that big earthen pot full of parched grain we left for the heroes haunted me. How I wanted that grain for me, for my starving son! I've come out once or twice before to see if it couldn't be dug out by a single woman and a broken spade, so I had something of a start already, you see. Today I just decided it might be tried again. It's no use."

"You mean to rob a howe?" I asked in disbelief.

"What else are the treasures in a howe for, if not to preserve the hero's offspring in days to come? I didn't want the swords or daggers anyway, the things Hunding would miss the most. I only wanted the grain."

A sudden shortening of her breath which worked its way up to another moan cut off any further excuse.

"What is it, Thora? Have you hurt yourself?"

"No–" she managed to say, but no more.

"Thora?" I reached out to put a comforting arm about her waist but found my way blocked by a great hard, round lump of flesh. Then Thora turned from me and my care. The new angle enabled me to see that the lump formed part of her. Thora was far gone with child.

"And it's time," she said as soon as her breathing steadied again.

"By Odin, you came out here to dig in that condition?"

"We are hungry," she said, without apology. "Besides, I didn't know this morning that it would come today, did I?"

"Surely there were warnings."

"Yes, there were warnings, beginning about mid-afternoon. But I was first too hungry to heed them and then too tired. And then I thought, surely it would be best to bear the child here, alone, in secret. It would be best never to darken the wierde with another mouth to feed. I can bear it here, and then, in a little, when my strength returns, I can stuff it here in this hole in Hunding's howe, cover it up, and go quietly home."

I couldn't hide my shock. "You would kill your own child? You, Thora, to whom it was worth leaving the sisterhood to get them?"

"This is not my child," she said between clenched teeth.

"Not your child? Thora, you are feverish."

"This is Helgi's brat, may Hel devour him, raped upon me when he burned any food I could feed it and all the food for my little son. To Hel with Helgi, I say, and to Hel with this little bastard."

Her curses were strangled by another moan that grew into a scream.

"Come," I said. "Let me bring you home to the wierde."

"No, Brynhild–" she protested, but she was too weak to put me off more vigorously. I soon got her up on Faxi and led him gently to the settlement.

Once on the wierde, however, I began to feel I'd made a mistake to force her here against her will. Helgi had burned every structure on the settlement and left no menfolk alive to rebuild them. The women and girls not killed or carried off as slaves to Denmark had spent the bitter winter in the burned-out shells of their homes, in the best lean-tos they could fashion of burnt beams and lumps of sod. As many as could, I suppose, emigrated away to distant relatives elsewhere, but many had no place else to go other than this man-made hill near the sea where they'd spent all their lives. I don't know how they survived. Indeed, a number of shallow, flat, unmarked graves being attacked by starving dogs told me that mere survival had not been the lot of many.

Among the survivors was Hogni, Thora's young, dark son just learning to pull himself up to stand on legs already growing rickety. Mostly he preferred to sit, however, sit and wail until somebody picked him up. Then he didn't always stop wailing, but at least the pitch dropped.

You never saw a more pathetic, sunken-eyed little waif. And to such demands I had returned Thora!

A dozen more competent hands than mine, however, saw her into the largest of the huts, one where I could not join them. I could only feel clumsy and useless, less than human, while my friend endured what seemed to be a harder trial than any man in any battle ever faced.

"She wanted to get rid of it," said one dull-haired woman, her cheeks sunken with famine. This woman had been set to try to keep the children away and quiet while woman's work was done. A Valkyrie counted among the children, I guess.

"We tried everything we knew," this woman continued, "but what worked easily for the rest of us did not work for her. Thora says All-Father promised she should never have a child die an unseasonable death and, rather than a blessing, this is turning to a curse."

Fortunately, the birth did not take long. Soon enough they invited me into the larger hut, but by then the storm had come into shore on the waves. How scant the shelter was! I had to avoid sitting in a puddle to be near my friend. Other women held a blanket sagging with rain over her head. Little Hogni was brought in at the same time, and she bared her breast for him. The newborn, a hale enough daughter, my friend would have nothing to do with.

"Will you give her a name?" I asked.

"Yrsa, perhaps," Thora said with a bitter half-smile.

The other women joined in a rather harsh chuckle.

"Yrsa?" I echoed. "I've never heard of it."

"It's a Roman name, but one they give to dogs. Geirðjof had a hunting bitch named that. It means she-bear."

I thought this unspeakably cruel, but I said nothing. The little thing was wailing in the puddle where the midwife had set her with hardly a rag to cover her.

"Take her away, Ingrid," Thora said. "In this rain. You know what you must do."

Ingrid got up quietly to do so.

"Here, let me do it," I said. "It is the least I can do for you, Thora."

"Very well. Thank you, Brynhild." Those thanks were truly given, the first thing I'd heard from my friend free of pain or bitterness since I'd found her.

I picked up the infant with no skill. Her little head kept flopping this way and that, and nobody bothered to help me master the art. When I tried to get more of the rag about her, Ingrid came and, rather than helping, took the rag clean away, saying they had desperate need of such around the wierde. At length I got the naked baby secured in my arms. When I did, the little pink mouth began trying to work on the iron of my brynie. I was ashamed.

Thora seemed to be sleeping with her finally comforted son at her true breast, so I bent to leave. Then she opened her eyes and recalled me. "Brynie," she said.

"Yes."

"You are on your way to Odin?"

"Yes."

"To be dismissed?"

"Perhaps. Yes – perhaps. I ... I do not know. I hope not."

"But you did disobey."

"Yes."

"Three times?"

"It depends what you choose to count."

"Depend on it. He will count them all."

"I felt I had to."

"I know. Well, good luck. Come here again on your way into real life if you'd care to. Saxony is a great opening into real life. The real life of a woman."

"I will if I can," I promised.

"He cannot kill you."

"No."

"So don't be afraid."

"But I see you, Thora, and–"

"Not a pretty sight, is it? Well, maybe I wanted too much."

"That cannot be. I will come if I can. I will come and help you."

Thora nodded thanks. "Cling to your bear skin, Brynie. And the claws. Make him fight for each one of the claws."

I lifted the string of claws free of the torc around my neck and touched them hopefully. "Thora, I will."

"Those things are yourself, things he cannot take from you."

"Yes, Thora."

"Good-bye."

"Good-bye."

I rode almost blind through a wild night. I put the little one in my pack, after I'd emptied it of what food I had to leave with the hungry Saxon women. By the sound of the crashing surf alone, I steered my course towards my Fate. The infant, though human, offered no company. I spoke to Faxi instead, giving him his head. He replied with nickers of encouragement and avowed faithfulness. I had no other friend in the world, but couldn't ask for better at this time.

The infant slept a good part of the time, but by the chill of dawn her lusty cries could not be ignored any longer, nor put off for the more sensible banter of a warhorse. Warrior's heart though I had, I simply couldn't set her out on this soggy ground to die.

Fatefully, just at that moment I heard the lowing of cows. A small herd grazed on a low cliff above the strand. I turned inland and rode towards them. They seemed thriving enough, with several new calves skipping under their mothers' udders.

"Good morning," I called to the woman who appeared out of a solid long house backed against the cliff face to shield against the wind. "I wonder if you couldn't spare a bit of milk from your beasts to feed a poor motherless infant I have here."

My battle gear caused a stir. These people had never seen a Valkyrie before, although they'd heard of us well enough. But even more thrill rose than that. The woman, I learned, had lost her own six-month-old daughter to a fever not four days before.

"Could I be a mother to the poor waif?" she pleaded, tears of disbelief clouding her eyes.

"Of course," I said. "And welcome."

"Oh, All-Father, how I prayed to you for my child! And now I see, you *are* a faithful hearer of prayers.

"What should she be called?" asked the new mother, taking the little thing expertly out of my pack and into her arms. "A child coming by such miraculous means must have an equally divine name to go with her."

"Her name is Yrsa," I announced.

"Yrsa?" the woman repeated, looking doubtful, hoping she had it right.

"Yes. It means a she-bear."

"A brave name indeed," cooed the mother, "for a brave little sweetheart."

And so I left them, already consumed in one another. On this woman's tongue, it did seem a divine name after all. Such animal names do not have the bad connotations among us that they do among the Romans. And the bear was my totem, which I would depend on for my future in the next day or two, whenever Odin and I found each other. I couldn't help but think it should please him that I had helped him keep his word by sparing Thora's child.

chapter 32

FOUND ALL-FATHER SITTING stark still on the bare rock at the edge of the land. The place was absolutely devoid of humankind, a place where the breakers fought together like stallions with foaming manes. The sea roared up like Ragnarök, the end of the world, and spewed up spray five times the height of my head in anger at its given bounds. The rock of the wild seashore it crashed against lay broken like crockery from a giants' hearthside brawl. Among this, drifts of gulls waddled, surveying the damage, shaking their heads with stern but neighborly disapproval.

I knew better than to disturb my master when he was entranced like this. The glaze over his one eye told me his body sat here, but Odin himself wandered elsewhere. Then I saw where. On a dagger-shaped black rock amidst the surf below, a pair of bull walruses engaged in combat. My master infested the body of one of those monsters. He had changed his shape in order to do battle with another sorcerer or perhaps another God. So I carefully spread out my bear skin next to him and sat down on it to watch.

I saw now that some of what I had considered the roar of the waves before was really the bellow of these beasts as they went at one another. They seemed such clumsy things, like great, rasping, overgrown slugs. But their clumsiness was an illusion. Their forms perfectly matched the task at hand, the supreme embodiment of warlike maleness. Each tusk curved as long as my arm. They bore down upon one another with these weapons like men who had learned the skill of working a dagger in each hand. One of them – the one I decided must be All-Father – had already made bloody ribbons of the great red-brown shoulder of his opponent. Their sheer weight alone was brutalizing, and the noises coming from beneath their all-too human whiskers sounded like nothing so much as the vilest of curses.

The battle raged for a good span of time until at last the other beast broke a tusk and knew he'd been bested. Off into the sea he slunk, leaving behind only the broken tusk and a swirl of pink foam. The victor bellowed in triumph once or twice, then lumbered off to join his wives at the far end of his rock. I noticed twelve cows made up the herd, very like their lord in appearance as if they were trying to copy his very being. Only they were smaller and tuskless, and for all the respect, he used them almost as brutally as he had the pretender.

A faint smile began to play between All-Father's moustache and beard as his other body enjoyed these spoils, and he seemed in no hurry to take on human form again. The glaze remained in his eye, but I noticed his hands had begun to take on human business. From somewhere, a broken walrus tusk had appeared in his left hand. He carved runes on it with the dagger in his right.

"So."

I jumped at his first word. I hadn't been expecting it.

He continued. "So, now you embark to do battle with Abaser."

"No, my lord. I am your faithful handmaiden."

"Surrender your sword.
Have off your helmet.
Unbuckle your brynie."

I did so with instant obedience and laid them out on the stone beside me. "My faithful handmaid?"

"Yes, lord."

"So you say.
And yet you traipse a trio of treasons."

Dare you deny that, so-called daughter?"

"Only twice, my lord."

"Don't discount
The occasion when your comrade
Had help out of Halfdansson's hands,
Off the jade of the jagged juggernaut."

"You are all-knowing, All-Father." I bowed my head, for the magic of his words, although in the confusion of riddle, had the power to conjure in my mind a vivid picture of how I'd saved Thora from Helgi's ship. I could almost feel the foam about my legs once more.

"So. What's to be done with you, Brynhild?"

"I hope, lord, you will give me another chance to prove–"

"Another chance?" He shut me off with such rage that magic verse was not even required. "No. No fourth chance."

He jumped to his feet in a moment, striding away from me, his dark grey cloak indistinguishable from the lowering sky. He flung the broken tusk into the sea. My attention thus distracted, magician that he was, he whirled around to whack my horse across its faithful, strong, supporting back with the flat of his sword. Beneath the sharp blow, Faxi's back broke. Then, even as the animal crumpled scream-ing, the God plunged the dagger into the stallion's jugular. Blood shot out like the stone from its sling. I screamed involuntarily, but quickly smothered it with my hands. Poor, patiently waiting Faxi. He never knew what hit him.

With the skill of one who had put those horse sinews together, Odin began to hack them apart.

"Here," he said, tossing a newly-skinned shank to me. "Eat."

The bloody flesh, without the easing white of any fat, came shock-ingly warm to my hands after the brisk sea air. My fingers stuck to it and then to each other.

"Eat," Odin repeated. "Sup of the sundering sacrifice."

I put the shank to my teeth, but found it too sticky, too warm, like trying to eat sun-warmed honey by the cupful. My throat rebelled.

Odin had taken the other shank for himself and tore off great mouthfuls like a man famished after a successful battle. He set the shank down, chewed and butchered, gulped, then took the shank up for another great bite. Soon his beard and moustache turned the virile color all Saxons longed for, the color of a great bull walrus.

"Eat!" Through the sea air, he waved the flesh against which I had set my heels for a gallop within the past hour, as if he meant to set the bone as a goad to me.

I ate the raw warm meat flavored with salt spray and my tears. Once I had eaten, no sealant could arise for the severance.

Odin spread a major part of the sacrifice wide upon the rocks, then called his messengers to join with the gulls and puffins in accepting and witnessing the sacrifice. Faxi's great gentle head, however, along with the front cannons and hooves, he set to one side. Then the God took his staff and thrust it into the crevice between two rocks, propping it with smaller stones until it stood upright so solidly that the strongest gale was not likely to bring it down. Onto the point of the staff he thrust the cannons down by bits of their skin until they stood firm against the ground supported by the staff and the hooves. Then followed Faxi's head with a sickening crunch of flesh and bone until my horse stood looking dolefully across Jutland, indeed all of Europe, at about the same height as he had in life.

Then Odin took up his dagger again and began to carve runes upon the staff, chanting them aloud as he carved.

> "Guardian spirits of the land, lose
> Your ways until you have driven the wound–Valkyrie
> Everlastingly from the land."

He rubbed his bloody hands over the nicks to stain them so the spell would last forever.

All at once anger flooded me, partly at Odin, partly at myself for having let it come this far while I did nothing but sit weeping over Faxi's dear leg bone. I tossed the shank from me, far out into the sea, and stood up, wrapping my bear skin about me. "You may kill my horse, but you can't kill me, you one-eyed beggar," I shouted at him over the thunder of the waves.

Odin turned from his task and fixed on me the baleful eye that I had seen turned on many a seasoned warrior until that warrior stumbled and fell for fear. I planted my feet firmly and stood my ground. He advanced threateningly toward me and, with one bloody hand, wrenched the torc from my neck. What had gone on with difficulty when I was a skinny girl came off even harder now, now when Odin had no care to be gentle. For a moment I thought indeed he would succeed in strangling me. But even the Gods have natural limits.

He tossed the torc off into the waves after Faxi's shank. "Yes," he growled,

> "But the visor of a Valkyrie you vacate.
> Let's learn how you loiter life now."

My hand went involuntarily to my throat to massage my bruised windpipe to keep it working in spite of him. My neck felt so naked and exposed without the torc. Yet I still wore the necklace of bear claws. The bear's sinew had held for all the God's violence. I fingered them, holding the first claw as I told him, "There's many a soldier of fortune who goes throughout the world until he finds a chieftain willing to give him a place on the benches in his hall..." My tongue took an attempt at the power of runes as I tried to envision this future for myself.

> "...If that soldier will but put his spear
> And his shield in that lord's service.
> Who is such a fool as to take on one
> I, Fire-Eye, have refused?"

"I shall not descend to the level of other women."

> "There is nowhere for a woman in this world without Valhalla,
> Save 'twixt some man's sheets and in his shadow."

"By ... by the sea and these rocks and this second claw, I shall not!" I didn't know what to take my oaths by, now that Odin was out. But in that second claw, I knew I'd found the right thing.

"There is nowhere. Watch and wonder.
And what kind of man can you claim,
without dowry, without kin, the Gods withdrawn?"

"I am not like Thora. I want no man. I have my fighting skills."
Third claw.

"Yes, you own your aiming and Odin's ointment.
Still you should know this, swaggering slut,
Once you mislay your maidenhead, my magic
Will abandon you in the identical instant.
You may retain your training, but not the thews.
Behold the battlemaid's bane."

"Then I shall fight off all comers for my maidenhead. By this fourth
claw, I swear it."

"Someday Fate will send someone,
A fellow you cannot fight off or fend against.
You won't have wish or will to war with him."

"Then I will die." Fifth claw. They were half gone already.

"Daughter, you cannot die before your due time.
That, too, is a curse, as you may come to ken."

I grasped all five remaining claws and clung to them until I nearly
choked myself a second time. "Then by all five of these claws at once,
I conjure you, All-Father, that I shall not succumb to any man but the
greatest of this age – of any age. Only he may overcome me, because
if I am his, then I know no other can defeat me and I can live in peace
into my old age. He must be a hero so great – so great that never in his
life has he known fear. He must pass through linden-plague and por-
poise-roof for me, undaunted. Only to such a spouse will I surrender
my battle main and my maidenhood."

Odin worked his tongue thoughtfully at the beginnings of God-
runing in my speech. He worked it throughout his mouth, raising the
beard here and there like bristles on a hedgehog as he did so. Then he

rubbed that beard from the outside with his hand, now dusty with drying blood.

"The natural plane knows no such man," he admitted, as one who could surely make such sweeping statements. "Knows no such man – *now*," he added.

> "All are attached to an area.
> They favor family or friend or farm and this force's fear.
> If not for individual ends,
> Then for the threat to these things."

I rocked back on my heels, relaxing. By my bear claws, I had won. Odin had admitted no such man existed to be my downfall.

"The natural plane knows no such man – *now*," he repeated.

> "But one can come. I can create
> Just such a gentleman. In a generation."

"In a generation? Then he is of no concern to me. A mere infant? He will be too late to be anything to me."

"Barb yourself with your brynie, Brynhild."

Reflexively, triumphantly, I did so. But as I fastened the leather thongs at the side, I felt a sharp prick.

Odin smiled. "You palpate the prick presently?"

Too late I realized that the word barb can have more than one meaning, and that I had been fooled by the God's riddle into taking only the meaning "to arm oneself." I quickly tried to undo the laces to get the pricking out.

> "It's vain and valueless, vixen.
> You can't demur. Life-dew is drawn,
> And poison pumps your pulse."

"You cannot kill me," I insisted, "not even with poison."

> "Not slay you, no. It is sleep thorn.
> You'll simply sleep."

"Sleep?" I asked, clutching again at my claws, but it was too late.

The virtue was gone from them. And I was, already, having to battle to keep awake.

> "You'll simply sleep – oh, until the sun
> Sees today's sons are sires.
> Long enough for Lore-Master to lure
> This longed-for lover from the loam to loosen
> All you have or hope to have,
> To the harassment of Helway's hounds.
> Well then? We shall see who wins the war."

Odin began to chant more runes. Not much of the lullaby wove through them, but they served just as well for me. Still, I fought off sleep and stood my ground until, looking out to sea in an attempt to refresh my face with spray, I saw the approach of a long boat. Twenty pairs of oars rose and dipped, rose and dipped in a spellbinding rhythm, the rhythm of a heartbeat at sleep.

"This boat," came Odin's voice from a place far away, like in a dream,

> "will bear you to a bower
> No mortal man may know.
> Nor may any mortal attain it –
> 'Til that Traveler-tuned man
> Shall make the margin into mist,
> Unchain you from this charm only when I choose.
> 'To pass through sea...' I think those were your thoughts.
> By my own battle spear, this shall be done.
> Then he shall wake you and wind you in your Weird..."

That was the last thing I heard. My eyes opened for a second after that as I felt myself lifted up. Then I caught a glimpse of sky, grey, swirling clouds the color of Odin's all-smothering cloak. Framed against the sky I saw a face I didn't know. This man was no hero but possessed a wind-beaten sailor's face as he carried me down the rocks to the waiting boat.

I knew he was a sailor, and a skilled one who had spent most of his life on the whale's road, for in his left ear he wore a golden ring. Sailors know they may drown any day where no one can ever find them and prepare their burial. On the long, floating way down through Aegir's cold, icy realm, they will doubtless be separated from their sea chests, their chests that hold all they own of this world. They will be separated from their chests in spite of the fact that they use them to sit on when they row and will hardly allow themselves to be taken out of sight of the things while they live. If they drown so – Aegir forbid and accept the sacrifice that it does not happen – they will have no coin to pay for passage to the realm of Hel. So they fasten the fare to their persons permanently, so as not to lose it as they fall endlessly down through the cold and grey. They fastened it to them in the form of a gold ring through their left ear.

And what shall I use for my fare? I thought confusedly. But that was the last thing I thought for a long, long time.

Watch for Book 2, coming soon!

SUGGESTED FURTHER READING

This is a historical novel based on the saga which comes in several medieval versions: the Old Norse *Poetic Edda*, *The Volsunga Saga*, and *The Nibelungenlied*. All are available in affordable Penguin translations.

The verses in Chapter 4 are quoted from *Gods and Myths of Northern Europe* by H. R. Ellis Davidson, and those in Chapter 16 are from "The Lay of Grimnir" in The *Elder Edda* translated by Paul B. Taylor and W. H. Auden. Permission has been written for. All other verses are either in public domain or written by me.

The answer to the question, "Isn't there an opera where the fat lady sings?" is ... yes, there are four very long ones by Richard Wagner. The interested reader might watch the operas *Das Rheingold*, *Die Walküre*, *Siegfried*, and *Götterdämmerung*.

The thirteenth-century *Danish History* by Saxo Grammaticus provided the quote at the beginning of this book and served as a source for many details.

On bogs and the bodies found in them:
- *Through Nature to Eternity* by W. A. B. van der Sanden
- *The Bog Man and the Archaeology of People* by Don Brothwell

On other aspects of Norse life and religion:
- *The Religion of the Northmen* by Rudolph Keyser
- *Myth and Religion of the North* by Gabriel Turville-Petre

- *Norse Mythology: A Guide to the Gods, Heroes, Rituals and Beliefs* by John Lindow
- *The Lost Beliefs of Northern Europe* by Hilda Roderick and Ellis Davidson
- *The Well of Remembrance* by Ralph Metzner
- *A History of Old Norse Poetry and Poetics* by Margaret Clunies Ross
- *The Skalds* by Lee Milton Hollander

And for the Huns:
- *The Huns* by E. A. Thompson

about the author

Ann Chamberlin believes that the purpose of storytelling – as of all true art as well as all true religion – is to support positions in exact opposition to the views prevailing in a culture's powerhouses, whatever those views happen to be. Nowhere is this more crucial than in the retelling of history. As Milan Kundera tells us, people in the powerhouses are not so interested in who will control the future as in who controls the airbrushes in the labs where the past's photos are retouched.

Born and raised in Salt Lake City, Ann Chamberlin also spent big blocks of time as a child in Europe where her father was visiting professor of mathematics. After flitting from school to school and major to major including theater, history, and English, she finally majored in Archaeology of the Middle East at the University of Utah. She spent a summer in Israel excavating the biblical city of Be'er Sheva, traveling throughout the Holy Land and living in the old city of Jerusalem for a month. She reads Hebrew, Arabic, Egyptian hieroglyphs, and ancient Akkadian, as well as French and German. She has traveled across all of North Africa, Turkey, Syria, and Jordan. She has two sons and twelve chickens, and lives in an old farm house on nearly two acres near Salt Lake City.

Ann is the author of fourteen historical novels, several of them named best foreign historical of the year by *Romantic Times.* She is the author most recently of a memoir of her Yorkshire grandmother published by the University of Utah Press.

She is the author of many plays which have been produced across the country from Seattle to New York. To find out more about Ann and her books, please visit her web site at http://www.annchamberlin.com